To Jenn:

THE NOTHING

A Book of the Between

Kerry Schafer

wishing you all good dreams

Kerry S

THE NOTHING

Cover art by Derek Murphy
Interior design by Laura Kreitzer

This is a work of fiction. All of the characters, names, incidents, organizations, and dialogue in this novel are either the products of the author's imagination or are used fictitiously.

Kerry Schafer's books may be ordered through booksellers.

Because of the dynamic nature of the internet, any web addresses or links contained in this book may have changed since publication and may no longer be valid. The views expressed in this work are solely those of the author and do not necessarily reflect the views of the publisher, and the publisher hereby disclaims any responsibility for them.

Library of Congress Control Number
2015904108

ISBN: 978-0-9861202-0-6 (sc)
978-0-9861202-1-3 (digital)

For David, who kept the dream alive

Acknowledgments

Words are insufficient to express my gratitude to all of the people who helped this book come to be. My Viking tops the list, as always, followed closely by my informal writer support group - Susan Spann, Heather Webb, Jennifer Spiller, Laura Kreitzer and Alexandra Hughes.

I can't say enough good things about Derek Murphy, who began as my cover designer and ended up as my marketing, Kickstarter, and website guru. Thanks again to my amazing editing team, Vikki Ciaffone and Richard Shealy. I feel truly fortunate to have found my way to both of you. Also to Alex Hughes and Laura Kreitzer, who stepped up at the last minute to take care of formatting the manuscript for publication – bless you both.

So many people helped out with the Kickstarter project. My thanks to Jeff Seymour, Jamie Wyman Reddy, and Harry Connolly for tips and advice on creating the project. The Kickstarter video was an event that never would have happened without an overwhelming amount of assistance. Much love to my son, Ryan Schafer, who cobbled together a great video out of the fragments I sent him. To the lovely people who appeared in the video – Ara Grigorian, Jennifer Spiller, Susan Spann, and Chris Petersen – all of you deserve a special circle in writer heaven.

Last, but not least, thank you to all of the people who are financial backers for the Kickstarter. These wonderful folks are, in no particular order: Jennifer Tatroe, Frau Wyrt Wicce, Vicki Brown, Kristin Centorcelli, Susan Spann, Kari Lynn Dell, Erin Kent, Joe Conley, Sue London, Derek Murphy, Alexandra Taylor, Inge Atkinson, Stefan Friesen, Zachariah B. Ward, Sally Janin, Marcia Wilson, Skye Christakos, Silver James, Kevin Brucks, Corinne O'Flynne, Linda Grimes, Teresa Horne, Jim Barrows, Gabrielle Connors, Jessica Meade, Aletia Meyers, Rachel Sasseen, Leslie Brost, Stephen Merlino, Adriana Cloud, Sunnie Andrews, Sarah Wheaton, Liv Stecker Weston, Gaylyn Faulk, Ara Grigorian, Holly Hunt, Noortje de Graaff, Bill Cameron, Jamie Wyman, Jaymi Elford, Courtney Schafer, Kristina L. Martin, Arne Radtke, Coralee Hanson, Chris Pitchford, Margaret Plover Martinez, Ann Youmans, Katherine Webber, Michael R. Underwood, Heather Bragg, Silver Hart, Beth Sanderson, Pam LeFavour Bordelon, Krista Long, Chelle Olson, Melissa Hayden, Aimie Runyan, Kellie Rice, Audra Gutierrez-Ritari, Warren Friesen, Natalia Sylvester, Candra Campbell, Dana Kaye, Alexandra Hughes, Janelle Lowe, Xen Sanders, Caleb, Rhonda Rogers, Jean Ann Robertson, Kristine Krantz, Avi Sirlin, Steph Bochenek, Mia Marshall, Janet Smith Brodie, Mary Brosseuk, Trudy Morgan-Cole, Sandra Blackwell, Diana Paz, and Jennifer Spiller.

Other books by Kerry Schafer

Between
Wakeworld

The Dream Runner
The Dream Thief
The Dream Wars

One

Sooner or later, the Between would try to kill them.

The fact that it appeared peaceful at the moment only made Vivian more uneasy. Any moment now, they could be attacked by poisonous butterflies or stabbed in the eyes by rabid hummingbirds. Maybe the fragrance of the flowers was toxic, or the ancient oak behind her might crack open and swallow her whole.

They needed rest, though, and she leaned back against the gnarled trunk, her travel-weary legs stretched out before her. Zee lay in the grass with his head in her lap, eyes closed, while her hands smoothed his forehead and combed through the tangles in his long dark hair.

He lay perfectly still but was not asleep. Vivian's wandering fingers registered the tension in the line of his jaw, the knotted muscle at the base of the skull. His right hand, open and seemingly relaxed, just grazed the edge of his sword hilt. It was both disturbing and comforting to know he could be on his feet in a heartbeat, sword drawn and ready.

"You think he'll be okay?" she asked, curling a lock of dark hair around her fingers.

"Weston, you mean?" Zee's eyes opened and looked up into hers, light-filled agate etched in umber. Her own face reflected back to her from his pupils, tiny and upside-down. She swallowed, her heart thudding erratically under the directness of his gaze. A warm hand on hers, tracing her fingers and up over wrist and forearm, did nothing to calm either heart or breath.

"It felt wrong to leave him alone. What if he never wakes up? He's got nobody."

The hand had reached her shoulder, lingering on the place where neck and collarbone met.

"So soft," Zee murmured. "Sometimes, when the light hits this place just right, the scales shine as if they're real, but when I touch it, it's only skin.... Weston is an incredibly tough old bastard. True definition of survivor. He'll be all right. Safer back in Wakeworld than here, although he may not thank you for making that decision for him."

The fingers began moving again, tracing the line of Vivian's collarbone. It was hard to get her breath. "Safer if he's really healed. We only have Callyn's word on that."

Zee's fingers paused in their exploration. "You don't trust her."

"Do you?"

She followed his gaze along the grassy path to where it bent around a corner into a grove of trees. Callyn, the Giant, impatient with her companions' need for rest, had gone ahead to scout things out and get a line on the best way to navigate the unstable world of the Between.

"Insofar as our paths lie together, I do. She wants to stop Aidan. And her concern for Weston seemed genuine enough. I can't see any ulterior motive for her putting herself in exile in order to help us."

"That doesn't mean there isn't one."

Zee's eyes moved back to Vivian's; his fingers continued their journey. She held her breath, all of her, body and soul, waiting for the inevitable moment. She kept her eyes open and held his gaze, not allowing herself the escape of closed lids as his touch faltered on the edge of the healing knife wound just above her breast.

His eyes darkened and closed. A long, shuddering breath escaped him. "Does it hurt?"

"Only a little."

This was true, as far as it went, but not the whole truth. There was very little pain at the site of the dragon-stone wound, but a constant uneasy discomfort gnawed at her, as if the injury were to her soul more than her body.

"I almost killed you. If my aim had been more true…"

"You have to let this go," she said, her hand covering his. "I was a dragon. If it had been any other, you'd be damning yourself because you missed."

He stiffened and drew back his hand, sitting up and pulling away from her. "I hate this whole 'born to be a dragon slayer' business. Killing without provocation, without need. It just… I can't trust my instincts. Can't trust myself. What if I hurt you again?"

"Since I'm not going to be turning into a dragon again, I think you can trust your instincts just fine."

Her effort to lighten the mood fell heavy as a stone. The moment of intimacy had passed and he was all warrior again, shields up and ready for danger. "Where's Poe?"

"Behind you. He's been staring at the dream door over there for the last hour."

There had been at least a dozen doors along the way since they'd left the plains and the Black Gates behind. None had been of any interest to the little penguin, and his ongoing vigil in front of this one was becoming unnerving.

Zee stood and stretched, eyes moving all around, glancing at the sun, which hung directly overhead. "What time do you think it is?"

Vivian shrugged. "Time means nothing here. The sun hasn't budged. We need to get moving."

"Or make camp."

"Could." But her eyes went again to Poe. The restless feeling intensified, manifesting in a need to get moving and keep moving. "Help me up."

Zee reached down, and she marveled all over again that his hands could be so strong and yet so gentle. She shook her head. "Other hand. I really wish you wouldn't use that right arm until it heals."

By the time she'd had a chance to treat the jagged laceration that ran the length of his right bicep, shoulder to elbow, it was too late for stitches. All she could do was keep it clean and try to keep him from using it long enough to let it heal.

His lips quirked in a smile, pulled crooked by the scars on his cheek. The right hand remained outstretched. "As if you're heavy enough to do it any harm."

"I'm a doctor; you should listen to me." But she let him pull her to her feet, groaning a little despite her best intentions. Her bones ached with exhaustion. She felt bruised and battered from head to toe, her muscles sore with the constant tension of waiting for the Between to attack. Both of them needed time to rest and heal, but they'd pushed hard the last couple of days, driven by a sense of urgency.

"Look out!" Zee put his arms around her and pulled her out of the way as a small dragon, about the size of a draft horse, careened down out of the sky and crashed into the branches of the tree where she had been taking shelter. Wings hampered by branches, flailing with all four feet and snorting smoke all the way, the creature bounced and slid down to the ground, leaves swirling around him in a small storm.

"If a dragon is ever going to kill me it, will probably be this one," Zee said. "By total accident. Can't you tell him to stay on the ground?"

"He doesn't listen very well. If I had a way to mend that broken wing he could fly better."

The little dragon butted his head against Zee's broad chest, and Zee scratched the skin around his horns. One wing folded properly along his back; the other, skewed and bent, hung at an awkward angle. It didn't seem to be causing pain, at least. A burbling sound, almost like a purr only much louder, vibrated in the creature's throat. Puffs of steam escaped his nostrils and Zee leaped back. "Easy, there, Godzilla. You're going to roast me."

Vivian stifled a laugh. The little dragon adored Zee, following him around with a puppy-like devotion to which Zee responded with off-handed gruffness and a touch of bewilderment. He'd come up with the name Godzilla, grumbling that having a pet dragon could not end well and they would all likely be trampled and spiked in their sleep.

Vivian's amusement faded as her eyes went back to the penguin. Poe's fascination with the door worried her. Just an ordinary dream door, so far as she could see. Unpainted wood, weathered to a pale silver by sun and wind, half obscured by vines. But Poe had an uncanny sense of things, and his scrutiny meant the door needed investigation.

Just as she took a step toward it, Poe hissed, turning around with such speed, he tangled his feet, impeding a mad waddle in her direction. Before she could react, a twist of pain knifed through her vitals. She doubled over, gasping, both arms wrapped around her belly. Her vision darkened at the edges, her knees went weak, and she would have fallen if Zee's strong arms hadn't caught her.

"Easy," he said, lowering her to the ground. "Head between your knees."

She tried to tell him that something was wrong behind that door, but the words wouldn't come. Her vision kept checking in and out, giving her glimpses of grass and earth between her knees. Then even that gave way to flashes of dark layered on dark, and with each one a sense of loss, of something gone missing from the worlds.

"Vivian." Zee gave her shoulders a little shake. A blast of hot wind struck her, gritty with dust. Poe pressed up against her, shivering. She was shivering too, head to toe, but the pain in her belly eased and she managed to get her eyes open, surprised to see that the sky was still blue, the sun still shining. But the Between, as far as her eyes could see, was now nothing but rocks and sand.

"What happened?" Zee demanded.

"The door, the Dream World just…" Vivian broke off, staring. Nothing was left of the door but splinters. Through it she could see what looked like blackest night. She could feel it reaching for her.

Zee shook her again. "Just what?"

"Went black." Words were far away. Her tongue felt clumsy and thick. But what she had sensed was beyond her ability to describe. The world behind the ruined door was gone, leaving a hole in the balance of things.

And then the wind struck with a high-pitched howling. It was thick with sand, carrying tumbleweeds and dead branches. Vivian's face burned and stung, scoured by the tiny wind-driven particles. It was hard to breathe and she bent her head down and pressed it into her knees, waiting for the wind to die away. It didn't.

"We need to move." Zee spoke directly into her ear. "Find shelter." A moment later, she felt him tying something around her nose and mouth, blocking out the sand so that she could breathe. She managed to get a look at him to see that he had a T-shirt tied around his own face, and then took the hand he held out to her and staggered to her feet.

Keeping her head bent, eyes toward the ground, she shouted, "Which way?"

Visibility was limited to a few feet in any direction.

Wind buffeted her body and ate away at her exposed skin. Something soft and heavy thudded against her legs and she peered down to see Poe, windblown, unable to stand his ground. She picked him up and clung to him as the wind tried to snatch him away.

"Can you walk?" Callyn's solid bulk appeared out of the murk.

Vivian nodded, clutching Poe more tightly to her chest. Zee was right beside her and she could make out the shape of the dragon just beyond him.

"Come, then."

The Giant turned and strode away, vanishing almost at once into the swirling sand. Vivian tried to follow, bent over, hands clutching the penguin. The wind pushed her back. She couldn't see, couldn't keep her eyes open.

And then Callyn was back. "Sorry. Try again." This time, she moved slowly ahead, acting as a windbreak. Vivian could manage to stay upright and stumble forward, shielded a little from wind and the scouring sand. She risked a glance over her shoulder to see Zee behind her, steadying himself on Godzilla's shoulder. All right, then. They could manage. All she had to do was focus on taking one step at a time and finding the way to shelter.

One slow step after another. The wind an empty howl, the blowing sand a torment. An ordeal surely sufficient to keep mind and body fully occupied, and yet there was just enough space left for her to worry about what it all meant.

The total obliteration of the Dreamworld had been sudden, the consequences swift and alarming. Vivian was certain that the shift in the Between was a direct result. In her mind she'd had a vague understanding that the dream-spheres Aidan had destroyed in the Cave of Dreams meant the deaths of Dreamworlds. But knowing something theoretically was very different from a physical experience of the thing. A whole world had been wiped out of existence. Anybody in it—whether denizens of Dreamworld or dreamers in Wakeworld—had been wiped out along with it.

Her mind reeled at the significance of that and she stumbled. Would have fallen if Zee's hands hadn't steadied her from behind. Callyn stopped and turned back, the three of them forming a huddle with their heads at the center.

"We can't keep this up too much longer," Zee shouted. "Any suggestions?"

Vivian shook her head. Entering a Dreamworld would have been her only offering, and that was now more dangerous than continuing through the Between.

"There used to be an intersection up ahead," Callyn shouted. "Keep going. Hopefully, it's still stable there."

Vivian saved her breath, nodding acquiescence, and they set off again, plodding forward one slow step at a time, the wind and sand trying to devour them as if it were a living thing.

Two

Weston's last memory was of burning.

Eyes closed, he could still see the black dragon towering over him, feel the crushing weight of a talon pinning him to the ground. Beneath him, gravel and stone. A sharp spike piercing the wall of his chest and the poison burning its way into his blood, spreading through his body, heating him to the point of incineration.

A dragon spiking meant certain death, and he was as certain as he'd ever been of anything that he had died. He was equally certain that hell wasn't a room full of shelves upon shelves of books. As for heaven, his sins and failures weighed too heavily upon him to make heaven seem possible.

He sat in a comfortable armchair with his feet propped up on a coffee table next to a half-played game of chess. A glass of water and a bottle of ibuprofen sat beside the chess board. Two empty armchairs faced him on the other side of the table. His head pounded with the too-rapid rhythm of his heart and his entire body felt bruised and sore.

If he wasn't dead, then where was he? What was he doing here?

The room was very dark, lit only by a streetlamp that shone through two large plate glass windows. Outside, snow drifted down in large fluffy flakes that heaped and drifted on the sidewalk and an empty street. There were painted words on the window, meant to be read from the outside, and it took a minute to turn them around and decipher their meaning:

A to Zee Books.

Which explained a great deal, though not everything. He'd been here before. The store belonged to Vivian's lover, Zee, and if Vivian had found a way to save Weston's miserable existence, it made sense that she would bring him here.

He rubbed his aching head and then touched the place between collarbone and ribs where the dragon claw had spiked him. His fingers found a sore place, scabbed over but healing. That at least was real, then, but he also wanted to believe the dragon had been masquerading as his long-lost little sister and then had shifted to Vivian's body, and had claimed to be pregnant with Zee's child.

None of that could be right. He stretched out his muscles, one at a time, feeling like he'd been stampeded by a herd of buffalo. Hell, he thought, moving his feet from the table to the floor and testing them there to see if they would be likely to hold his weight, he'd been in the Between. Maybe everything had happened. Or nothing. Maybe he'd been dreaming for years, a modern Rip Van Winkle, dozing in a bookstore chair. It was a relief to find that although there were a twig and a dried leaf in his beard, there was no hundred years' growth.

Nothing moved outside, except for the ever-falling snow. Irrational fear crawled cold over his skin. Maybe all the humans were dead and gone. Plague, or rapture, or some creature escaped from the Between. He calmed himself with logic. The darkness outside meant an hour somewhere between midnight and dawn. Likely the people were all just home in their beds, a good place to be on a snowy night like this one.

A rustling above his head startled him and he looked up to see only shadows and the twisting shapes of some of Zee's hanging sculptures.

The sound came again.

Weston picked up a book sitting on the coffee table in front of him, weighing its use as a weapon. It was a solid, oversized hardcover, perfect for his purposes. Keeping his breathing shallow and light, he waited. When the fluttering came again, he flung the book up into the darkness. It struck something metallic with a jangle before crashing down to the floor.

Something whooshed over his head and he ducked, both arms up in self-defense.

Again the thing came at him, but this time, he only swatted at it with his hand.

"Goddamn bird. If I woke up in hell, you'd still be with me. Where are the rest of them?"

The raven landed on the table in front of him, stirring the pages of the books with its wings, knocking over chess pieces lined up for a game, sending a loose paper skittering up and onto the floor. Weston bent to retrieve it. When he lifted it to the light, he caught the shape of his own name and got up to carry the paper into a clearer light.

It read:

Weston, I brought you home, as promised. You've more than fulfilled your end of the bargain. Aidan's gone into the Forever but we're shut out. Long story, but I'm off to ask the Sorcieri for help. Be well.

Vivian

Well hell.

She'd gone off without him, then, dumped him off like a bad penny. The raven fluttered up onto his shoulder and poked an inquisitive beak into his beard, but he didn't bother to shoo it away. When he'd made the bargain with

Vivian—to help her get back into the Between—he'd fully intended to finish up the suicide attempt she'd interrupted.

Somewhere along the strange journey, he'd stopped wanting to die. When this had happened, he wasn't clear exactly. Maybe all of the brushes with death had cleared it out of him, that or the dragon poison. He also had no desire to go back to his old life, leading hunting parties into Dreamworld in search of trophies they would never have found in the usual locales. He'd become accustomed to companionship and a common goal.

He didn't question the decision to drop him off here. Obviously, he'd been unconscious, since he couldn't remember a damned thing, and would have been a dead weight and a danger to drag along. Still. To his own great surprise, he discovered a strong desire to be part of whatever came next.

Wakeworld had nothing for him. He had no ties to any living being, apart from the infernal raven. Unless he went back to his guided tours, he had no way of making a livelihood, and he had no idea of where else to find work in the modern world.

Which left him with only one recourse.

Making a door was an easy thing now, but he needed to take some thought as to where it should open. He had now idea how to get to the Sorcieri, and Vivian and Zee would be well on their way. No point going back to the place he last remembered; it would be empty.

Hopefully. That dragon abomination could still be hanging about. That was unlikely, though, and it wasn't like he had anything better to do. There had been Giants in plenty down on the plain in front of the Black Gates. The note Grace had left for him in her empty coffin had said she was hanging out with the Giants. So, maybe he could go there. It should be easy enough to follow their tracks.

Closing his eyes, he conjured an image of his last

view before losing consciousness. A vast plain spread out across a valley floor, studded with Giants in formation. Dragons darkening the sky high above a snowcapped mountain. The Black Gates, monstrous and looming even from a distance.

When he opened his eyes, the door hung neatly in the center of a shelf of books. It was of rough, unfinished wood, built of planks split by hand, and barred with a band of iron. It opened easily to his touch, and he paused for a moment, looking out into a place familiar but changed.

Same flat plain, empty now of both Giants and dragons. Same wind keening over it, raising eddies and swirls of dust. But something had changed; something felt wrong. In the depths of his bones, at a cellular level, he felt it. An unsteadiness, as though what had once been solid and real was now about as substantial as mist. He felt that if he set foot through the door, the whole thing might disintegrate and take him with it.

A banging behind him made him jump nearly out of his skin. He spun around in the midst of an adrenaline surge to see a man on the other side of the glass door, thudding with a fist. It took a minute to also see the car, parked right up in front of the store windows, and that the man was in uniform and had a familiar face.

Brett Flynne, deputy.

Weston didn't have much love for lawmen, in fact, he'd spent an extraordinarily long life avoiding them. He took a step through the doorway. He could smell the dust on the wind, overlaid with the hot stone scent of dragon and something else he couldn't define. Even from this distance, the Black Gates emitted a vibration he could feel throughout his body, part summons and part warning. After years of refusal, for the first time, he truly felt the allure of the Between.

Another step. Before he pulled the door closed

behind him, he looked back over his shoulder.

Men have died for such hesitations.

The deputy stood with both hands flat against the glass. His face was caught in an expression between fear and loss, the eyes desperate with hope. His lips moved in the shape of a single word.

"Please."

Weston stretched one hand out into the Between, letting the sun shine through his fingers and throw a dark shadow on the ground. Again he felt the echo of wrongness course through him. With a sigh. he closed the dream door and went to let Deputy Flynne in out of the cold.

A flurry of snow, the sharp, cold smell of the north, made Weston shiver as he stood with the door open, waiting.

"Where's Vivian?" Flynne asked, not bothering with formalities. A heavy dusting of white already covered his shoulders.

"Traveling."

"You mean she's gone through that door."

"Well, not that one in particular. Why?"

"Can you take me to her? You can open the doors like she can."

Weston shivered in a wind so searching it seemed to be a thing alive and suggested, "Why don't you come in and talk about it?"

Flynne did so, shaking snow out of his hair, and strode directly over to the door still hanging in the middle of the book store. "Take me to Vivian. I need to talk to her."

"Wait up a minute. The Between is a pretty big place. It's not like we just walk through that door and there she is."

"There's got to be some way to reach her. Don't you have some sort of—I don't know—magic communication device or something?" Flynne looked haggard, and Weston bit his tongue on a sarcastic response.

"Maybe I can help you."

Keen eyes looked him up and down, obviously doubtful of his ability to do much of anything. Weston granted that this was fair, given that his appearance had never been in the well-groomed category and recent events had left him worse for wear. Besides, he'd spent his whole life resisting his calling of Dreamshifter, which meant he had a fair bit of knowledge but very little practical ability.

"You're sure we can't—"

"I'm sure."

"So, where were you heading, then?"

"Nowhere that you want to go. Look—I'll be honest. I know where she was headed, but that doesn't help much since I haven't a clue how to get there. Unless you're prepared to venture out for a year and a day, and maybe never come back, I wouldn't advise the attempt."

Flynne stared him down with an implacable expression. When the silence became pressing, Weston raised his hands in a gesture half surrender, half futility. "Think of it like this. Every dream ever dreamed—well, not every dream, maybe, but every different type of dream, is connected to a different world, just as real and complex as this one. And each one is set into yet another world, the space we call the Between, that winds in and out among them as a connector. She could be anywhere. If we figure out which world she's in, even then we have to find her."

The deputy paced the length of the store, stopping in front of the dream door and rapping on it sharply with his baton. "Seems solid."

"It is."

"So, what I saw last time we were here, when Vivian was...shifting. Is she..."

Weston didn't answer, just waited, and after a long

silence, it was the deputy who admitted defeat. "I guess you'll have to do. Something is happening that I don't understand."

"Can you tell me what?"

"I'd rather let you draw your own conclusions."

Weston had a premonition that whatever he did here was going to have echoes rolling on down through eternity. On the other hand, maybe it was time he paid a little something back to society. He shrugged. "All right."

The deputy's eyes narrowed as the raven fluttered onto Weston's shoulder.

"That thing coming with you?"

"Unfortunately."

Serious misgivings hit him the instant the car door slammed shut and he found himself buckled into the back seat of the patrol car. No inside handles, everything locked. Smooth plastic, no upholstery, easy clean, and nothing anybody could hurt themselves with. At least he wasn't wearing handcuffs. And he could make a door from pretty much anywhere if he needed to, even jail. Besides, it was unlikely he'd be prosecuted on a charge of crimes committed eighty years long gone, so he sat quietly, watching the town go by.

The patrol car pulled into the parking lot of Krebston Memorial Hospital, bypassing empty parking spaces in favor of the ambulance bay, just outside the emergency room doors. An ambulance had just pulled in, and the crew lifted a stretcher out of the back and rolled it through the automatic doors, moving fast, faces intent.

Weston's hip cramped as he squeezed himself out of the car, his lower back wrenched by a muscle spasm. He caught himself thinking wistfully that a nice retirement home might be a good idea, sitting warm and safe in front of a TV and letting people serve him meals…

The raven landed on his head, clutching at his hair

and spreading its wings for balance. Retirement homes didn't allow for ravens, he was pretty sure. Hospitals frowned on them as well.

"You can't bring that bird," Flynne said as the doors opened for them.

"Tell him that." Weston shoved at the bird with one hand. "Get off."

Claws dug into his scalp and the bird squawked reproachfully.

"Roxie will have my hide," Flynne muttered, stalking off through the automatic doors.

Weston hung back, reluctant to enter. In all of his hundred and some years, he'd never set foot in a hospital. Besides the dragon spiking, he himself had never been injured or sick beyond something minor like a cold. His family had all been dead long before modern hospitals sprouted up, and he didn't have any friends. The doctor had come out to the house a time or two in his childhood, and he had vague memories of a black bag and bitter medicines. So, although he knew what this was, in a general sort of a way, he came to a halt just inside the doors to assess the situation.

An unfamiliar smell, sweetish but sharp, stung his nostrils. The fluorescent lights overhead were too bright. The linoleum under his feet was scuffed and stained. Somebody not too far away groaned, a sound of misery and pain. Weston stood right at the boundary of outside and in, cold air and snow flowing in around him.

A small woman, blonde hair making a fluffy halo around a small, narrow face, pounced on the deputy at once.

"Did you find Vivian?"

"Afraid not. This is Weston. He can do whatever she does. Except for the medical part…" Flynne scrubbed a hand through his hair, his voice trailing away.

The nurse put both hands on her hips and looked Weston over from top to toe, not missing the raven perched on his head. "I don't believe this. We need her. Do *you* know where she is?" Weston had faced blades less dangerous than the expression in her pale blue eyes.

"I have a general idea. But I can't get to her right now."

"Look, Roxie—" Flynne began.

She flung both hands up in disgust. "Don't even talk to me. If you think you can help, come this way. Otherwise, don't even bother to waste my time."

Weston opened his mouth to say that he didn't see how he could be of any possible use in a hospital, caught the expression on Flynne's face, and thought better of it. "If there's aught I can do to help, ma'am, I'll be glad to do so."

"Fine. But that bird has to go out. If the health department sees him here, we're toast on a stick."

The raven stretched his wings and then flew up to perch on the top of the exit sign, where he took to preening his feathers.

"You have a way to get him out, make yourself free with it," Weston said.

"But he's your bird."

"And that's where you'd be mistaken."

She stood surveying him for long enough to make a rivulet of sweat find its way down the center of his back. The raven croaked down at her and she spun on her heel and turned her back. "I don't have the time for this."

Small as she was, she moved at a speed that made Weston stretch his legs to keep up. "Five more of them tonight. Four last night. Spokane won't take them anymore, said they have enough of their own. Nobody has a cure, anyway. Nothing but supportive care. So, we've just been sending them all upstairs. They're not even being treated. Just watched."

Halfway down the wide hallway, she stopped and slid open a glass door. "Bringing nonmedical personnel in here is such a total HIPAA violation. I'm gonna lose my job and probably go to jail." She led the way into a curtained room beyond. "But what else am I going to do?"

Behind a screening curtain was a square room with a counter, a sink, and a bunch of machinery Weston didn't know the point and purpose of. A small girl knelt on the floor in front of a chair, using it as a table for paper and crayons. She glanced up briefly when they came in, then went back to her project without a pause. On a narrow bed in the middle of the room lay a big man, tall and heavyset. Tattoos sleeved both arms from wrist to shoulder, where they vanished beneath the sleeves of a blue gown. His eyes were closed, his jaw slack, his chest rising and falling as though he were asleep. A thin plastic tube traveled from a bag on a hook through a ticking machine and into the skin of the arm.

"Shit," Flynne said.

"I told you." The nurse checked the tubes and screens.

The deputy approached the bed. He placed his hand on the man's shoulder and shook it. "Max! Hey. Wake up!"

Not so much as a flicker of the eyelids from the man on the bed. The deputy moved to the foot of the bed. Squeezed a bare toe, smacked the bottoms of the feet. "Max."

"He won't wake up," the little girl said, not looking up from her drawing. "The Nothing got him."

"Lyssa called 911," Roxie said, her forehead creasing as she looked at the little girl. "She was drawing when the ambulance got to the house, hasn't stopped since she got there."

For the first time, Weston noticed the stack of papers on the floor beside the little girl. She was using a black crayon, its brightly colored mates tumbled in a neglected pile. Oblivious to the three pairs of watching eyes, she turned the crayon on its side and scrubbed it across the paper, obliterating her drawing, but not before Weston caught a glimpse of something that chilled his blood.

"Well, hot shot," the nurse's voice lashed at him from behind, "are you going to do something?"

"I'm not a doctor."

"What good are you, then? Brett Flynne, why did you bring him here?" The anger in her voice was undercut by grief, and Weston felt a distant sadness that he couldn't help her, but all of his focus was on the child.

Silently cursing the stiffness in his knees, he knelt on the floor beside her. "Can I see?"

She shrugged, then glanced up at him from under her tangle of curls with a pair of knowing blue-green eyes, unsettling in a face that had yet to shed all of its baby fat. Lifting her hands, she let him see the page. Whatever had once been in the drawing was wiped out by the black scribbling.

"The Nothing," she explained helpfully. "It eats up everything."

"I see." He ducked as something large whistled over his head and then crashed down onto the chair, widespread wings just managing to keep it from skidding right across the slick surface and onto the floor.

The raven regained its balance and smoothed its feathers. Tilting its head sideways, it fixed the little girl with a bright black gaze.

"Hello," she said solemnly. No grabbing, no sudden moves. She didn't even register any surprise.

"Hey," Roxie barked. "I'm over here. Max is over here. I need you to figure out what's wrong with him."

"I keep telling them," the little girl said, reaching for a fresh sheet of paper. "It's the Nothing."

One of the papers she'd already filled with drawings fluttered to the floor, and he bent to retrieve it.

"What's going on," Roxie said, "is an epidemic. People go to sleep at night and don't wake up. Perfectly healthy people. Everything tests out normal with blood work and CT scans and MRIs. So, we were thinking maybe….there was that weird thing with Flynne, here, where he was freezing to death for no reason and Vivian knew something about that…"

The flood of words registered, but Weston couldn't take his eyes from the picture he held. "Did she ever meet Vivian?"

"What?" Roxie's white face registered confusion. "She who?"

"This child."

"Lyssa," the little girl said.

"I don't know. What does that have to do with anything?"

But it was still the child Weston spoke to. "Lyssa. Where did you see this?"

He held a near-perfect drawing of Vivian's pendant—a penguin caught in a dream web.

"It's in all the dreams. With the Nothing."

"She's been drawing those pictures for a week," Roxie said. "Max was worried about her. Made an appointment with a counselor."

"Because she was drawing pictures?"

"Because she papered her room with pictures of that penguin thing. She'd started putting them in his room, too. He kept taking them down, he said, but she'd put them back."

"Tell me about the pendant," Weston said, touching the child's shoulder.

"He wouldn't listen," she said, her hand moving over the page. "What do I know? I'm just a kid."

It had been a long time since Weston had dealt with a child. He remembered Grace saying something similar, her small, freckled face set in lines of defiance. "Just because I'm a kid doesn't mean I don't know anything."

""I think you know plenty," he said now. "What's the pendant for?"

"It stops the Nothing. But I don't have one, so I thought maybe if I drew enough of them…" Her lip trembled. "It didn't work."

"Maybe it did. You're still here."

The raven hopped onto the paper and pecked experimentally at the crayon. Lyssa touched his head lightly with one finger, and the bird closed its eyes and rubbed against her hand.

"The infernal creature likes you." Weston kept his voice calm, but the way she'd said "the Nothing" brought goose bumps up on his skin. "What is this Nothing? Can you tell me?"

She turned full on him then, eyes judging. "You should know already. Vivian would know. Probably you're not as smart as she is."

"Lyssa!" Roxie reprimanded.

Weston ignored her. "You're right. I'm not as smart as she is. You'll have to tell me."

The little girl sighed exaggeratedly, then sifted through the pile of papers and picked out a drawing. As she turned to show him, a sharp alarm went off beside the sleeping man.

"Shit," Roxie hissed. "Max!" There was a note of panic in her voice. "He's gone flatline. Flynne, get me some help in here!"

Amidst the blaring and beeping of alarms, the nurse climbed up onto the exam table and started CPR.

Well-organized chaos followed. Medical professionals scrambled into the room, one of them pushing a cart on wheels. Flynne grabbed Weston's arm. "You're in the way. Bring the little one, would you?"

Only too happy to comply, Weston picked up Lyssa. She still clutched the paper in one chubby fist, the crayon in the other. "My drawings!" she wailed, struggling in his grasp.

"I've got them, I've got them." He stooped and grabbed the stack, abandoning the crayons to their fate. The raven fluttered to his shoulder. For just an instant, he used his dream senses to reach out toward the man at the center of the storm of activity. He met a black hole of emptiness that nearly sucked him in. Reeling, he clutched child and papers more tightly and fled the room.

"You can wait here," someone said, leading him down the hall and into a small sitting room. He settled into an armchair, the little girl still in his arms. She buried her face in his chest, sobbing, and he put a hand on the back of her head.

"Shhh, little one. The doctors will fix him."

"Doctors don't know about the Nothing." She pulled away a little, looking up into his face. "Can't you stop it?"

"I might be able to help." Not soon enough to help her father, though. A sick certainty had come over him, a realization of what exactly was going on. He needed to get to Vivian, make sure she'd grasped what the dying dream-spheres would mean to people in Wakeworld. A series of uncontrollable shivers shook him as he remembered the spheres gone dark in the cave, how many had been still dying.

"Curse you, Aidan," he muttered under his breath.

Lyssa, tear-stained and frightened as she was, looked up at him again, curiosity stopping her tears. "Who's Aidan?"

"An evil dragon queen," he answered without stopping to think.

She nodded solemnly, as if this came as no surprise. "And Vivian will have to fight her."

God. He was so out of his depth with this child. Despite his limited experience with kids, he was pretty sure she was something other than the norm. But she seemed distracted for the moment, and his heart threatened to burst at the thought of witnessing her being told her father was dead.

So, he shifted her to a more comfortable position on his lap, tucking her head under his chin. "Vivian or maybe Zee. He's the dragon slayer."

"Does he carry a sword?"

"Indeed. Just like a knight in a storybook. He's very brave. He'll help her with the Nothing. And so will Poe."

The compact body had begun to loosen and relax against him, the child's breathing slowing and softening. Her voice sounded dreamy. "Who's Poe?"

"He's a penguin. Sort of like the raven. He helps her, too."

"What's the raven's name?"

"He doesn't have one."

She stirred at that, twisting around to look up into his face. "Why not?"

"Because." When he was young and bent on refusing the role of Dreamshifter, he'd hoped the bird would go away. He thought of it as Stupid Bird, or Hey You, or, in later years, the Raven.

"I'm going to call him Bob." Lyssa burrowed her head a little deeper into Weston's shoulder. She seemed to be asleep, and he sat perfectly still, hardly breathing lest he disturb her, a whole swirl of unfamiliar emotions tightening his chest. The little girl was so fragile, the warm weight of her against him a trust of which he felt completely unworthy. Memories threatened to swamp him. Grace's face, set in hard lines and spattered with blood. Jenn, floating lifeless in the stream. Vivian with the dragonstone knife plunged into her breast.

Over and over, he had failed to protect those in his charge, and a dark dread combined with the rush of warmth. His eyes caught those of Bob the Raven, perched on a chair across from him, and a sense of unreality stole over him.

It seemed a long time that he sat there, keeping vigil over the sleeping child. Long enough for muscles to stiffen and a cramp to start in his lower back.

When the door opened, it was Flynne, and one look at his face told Weston everything.

"What happens to the child?"

"CPS. Although they've got their hands full and I don't know where they're going to put her. They'll find her somewhere to sleep tonight, and then we'll see."

Weston looked down at the armful of child and thought about Grace. Her whole family murdered in front of her eyes with the exception of the older brother, who not only failed but abandoned her. Dragged away from everything she'd known to strangers in an orphanage.

"Surely she must have some relatives somewhere?"

"Yeah. Mother's an addict and lost her rights. But maybe there are grandparents or something. Look—thanks for your help with this. Like it or not, CPS is the only option for now. I'll give them a call, see how soon they can get somebody in here."

A burst of static on his radio and dispatch came on. "Control to three nine seven, do you read?"

"This is three nine seven."

The woman's voice sounded shaken and on the verge of tears. Flynne heard it too, dropping the usual formality for small-town friendly. "What is it, Dell?"

"My neighbor, James Gregors. They just found him. Like the others."

"Did you call the ambulance?"

"They're all out on other calls."

Flynne took two steps toward the door, stopped, turned back.

"I'll watch her," Weston said.

"It might be awhile."

"You're needed. She's as safe with me as she'll be anywhere."

"I'll call CPS on the way out. Can you—"

"I'll wait."

Weston held his breath, careful to meet the deputy's eyes with a level gaze. After a long minute, Flynne nodded and was gone.

The room fell silent, no sound except his own breathing and that of the child. Her eyes moved beneath the closed lids, her breath grew more rapid.

"Only a dream, Lyssa," he whispered, "only a dream."

Her whole body jerked once and her eyes flew open, wide with terror. Bolting upright, she flung both arms around his neck and clung there, sobbing. Awkwardly, he patted her back and made what he hoped were soothing noises.

"You were dreaming," he said at last.

"It was the Nothing," she said, snuffling into his shoulder, wet now with tears. "It was coming for me. I ran and ran but it was faster."

"What is this Nothing?"

"Dark."

"Sweetheart..."

"Daddy's dead, isn't he?"

He'd thought it would be bad to watch as someone else delivered the news. This was worse, watching her face, hearing his own voice deliver the blow. "Yes. How did you know?"

"The Nothing got him. I saw it."

Somebody has to do something.

But what? For the moment, his path was clear. Shelter the child and offer her what little comfort and safety he could until somebody came to take her away. And then he'd try to find Vivian.

As it turned out, the waiting wasn't long. The door opened again, this time for a young woman, maybe twenty-five, thirty if he stretched his guess. She looked tired, eyes bleary. She wore a long coat, dusted on the shoulders with snow, black hair cut severely short doing nothing to soften a face that was all sharp angles.

"Hey there. I'm with CPS. I've got a home willing to take her for tonight, at least. We'll see in the morning."

Lyssa's arms went around Weston's neck and squeezed so tight, he could hardly breathe. "No. I want to stay with Weston."

"You can't, honey," the woman said. Her voice was matter-of-fact but not unkind. "I'm sorry about your daddy. But you're going to have to come with me now."

"No."

Lyssa's legs were in on the action now, clamped around Weston's waist.

"Hey," he whispered in her ear, smoothing her back with one hand. "It will be okay. It's just for tonight."

Her entire body thrummed beneath his touch, legs and arms locked in a grip of iron. "The Nothing will get me."

"I hate this part," the social worker said.

Weston hated it, too. Especially since Lyssa had a point. "Can I see your ID?" he asked, suddenly realizing that any random stranger could walk in claiming to be from CPS. If this woman wasn't who she said she was, then he wasn't going to have to let this small person be forcibly wrenched away from him and dragged away screaming.

A flash of annoyance crossed the woman's face, but she opened her coat to show him her badge. It looked perfectly official, bearing the Child Protective Services logo, a photo of the social worker, and her name, Rose Evans.

"Satisfied?" she said. "Let's get this over with."

It didn't seem possible, but Lyssa tightened her grip.

"Give me a couple of minutes to talk to her, will you?"

"Look, I know this is hard, but in my experience, it's best to just get it over with. You can't reason with a kid this age, not when she's scared like this. She'll be better once she's settled." The social worker reached out and tugged at Lyssa's shoulders.

"Don't let her take me away," the child wailed.

The raven hopped onto her head and stretched his wings before shaking out all of his feathers and settling into a waiting stance. This pushed Rose back a step, where she stood, eyeing both bird and Weston with a look fast moving to unfriendly.

"If I have to, I'll call for a police assist."

"That won't be necessary. Give me five minutes. I'll bring her out to the car. Where are you parked?"

"I'll wait outside the door," she said, her face saying outright that she thought he was lying and had thoughts of absconding with the child.

Which meant she'd read him accurately.

As the door closed, Lyssa's grip eased and she pushed back to look up into his face. "Why can't you take me home? You'd let me put my pictures up, right?"

"I can't."

"How come?"

"For starters, I don't have a home to take you to."

No vehicle, either, to make a quick getaway and run for a motel.

He smoothed the tangled curls away from her face, flushed and hot and wet with tears. "I need to go look for Vivian and I can't take you with me."

"How come?"

"Too dangerous." Truth, he knew, completely besides the fact that the social worker would call the cops. At the same time, leaving her unprotected from dying Dreamworlds was equally dangerous. He couldn't take her; he couldn't leave her. And the clock was ticking. He was pretty sure Rose was on the other side of that door, literally counting off the seconds.

"It's just for tonight," he said lamely, seeing in her eyes that she recognized this for a lie. "Tell you what." He reached for the leather thong around his neck and lifted it over his head, holding it out to the child. "See this pendant? It's like Vivian's, only it has the raven."

Lyssa took it from him, fingers exploring the intricate dreamweb with the figure of a raven flying at its center.

"You can wear it as my promise that I'll come back for you. And to keep you safe from the Nothing. Okay?"

He slipped it over her head. She continued to hold onto the pendant, and after a long interval where he feared his last shot had missed the mark, she nodded.

"Now let's clean you up a little." He mopped her face with his shirt and smoothed back her hair. "Ready? Let's go find you a place to sleep."

"Can Bob come?"

"I'll bring him to visit."

"Promise?"

"I promise." And looking into her eyes, he swore to himself that for once in his life, his word was going to count for something.

Three

The city grew up out of the land so naturally that Jared had been staring directly at it for several hours before he registered what he was looking at. Even when he realized that the geometric shapes were spires and towers and a massive city wall, he was inclined to think it mirage or a fever-born hallucination. This thought was given substance by a fountain of light at the center, so bright it dizzied him, and he covered his eyes.

All the long day, he'd alternated between burning up and shaking so violently with chills that he nearly fell off the horse Kraal had procured for him. His injured leg didn't hurt anymore, all sensation fading into an ominous numbness. The other leg, unaccustomed to riding horseback, ached fiercely. He hated the horse and the ongoing clopping of hooves. He hated the Giant. He hated his own decaying flesh so fiercely that he wanted to grab a knife and cut the infection out himself.

Kraal made a clicking noise with his tongue, catching the horse by the reins and easing it to a halt.

"I'm going to blindfold you now, little man."

Jared pushed greasy tangles of hair out of his eyes. He swayed in the saddle, weak and dizzy. "No," he said, both hands twisting into the coarse brown mane. "I need to see."

"You get much closer to the Fountain of Light this time of day, and you'll never see again. Fight me if you will, but I'll win in the end."

No point fighting, not against an opponent of Kraal's size and strength. But he barely suppressed a whimper when a length of cloth blotted out his sight. The big hands, surprisingly nimble, tied a knot tightly in place.

"Don't be tempted to sneak a look, now. Not if you value your sight."

Jared nodded. He had no reason to believe Kraal would lie to him, and already at this distance, the light had been dazzling. Still, riding blind was a new form of torture. Unable to see what lay ahead, he remained in a constant state of tension, muscles braced, hands clenched in the horse's dusty mane. Even so, when the horse began a sudden descent, he jolted forward, unable to properly brace himself. His right leg was useless, so there was no way to clench tighter with his thighs, although the muscles in his left leg tried anyway. He was sliding forward, up onto the neck, losing his grip on the mane.

And then a big hand grasped his shirt in the back, half lifted him, and set him back in place. As if he were five years old. He was too miserable to be angry at the indignity, too busy trying to hold on and to keep from vomiting all over himself.

How long this went on, he couldn't tell. It felt like an eternity, time slowly unwinding for the sole purpose of his torment. Despite himself he must have dozed, missing the moment when the horse came to a stop, rousing with a sharp instant of panic to find himself in the dark.

His hands flew toward his eyes, only to find the strip of cloth and the onrush of memories. A voice was speaking. Had to be a Giant voice, deep and grinding, but it was not Kraal's.

"You would bring a stranger into the city? One who

looks like a heap of garden rubble?"

"He has a message for the Queen."

An inquiring sound followed. Heavy footsteps approached the horse and circled around it. Jared held his breath but discovered he was not afraid. His pain and misery had reached the point where death would be welcome. Just so long as it was quick. One sound whack to the head from a Giant fist ought to take care of it.

"He stinks. You can't take him to see Her like this."

"Let us in. I'll see that he's cleaned up and healed."

"Your word is not sufficient as bond. What price will you pay?" The other voice had turned formal.

"I offer my blood as bond of fealty for myself and the stranger."

A moment ticked by. Jared began to drift again, but then the horse was moving. He didn't even try to keep track of the turns taken. Voices reached his ears from a distance. He was burning up again and wanted only to lie down and be allowed to die in peace. Every time he began to sag off to the side of the horse, Kraal's big hand caught him and straightened him, sometimes shaking him a little.

After what seemed to Jared like hours, the horse stopped again. He felt a hand fumbling with the knot of his blindfold, and then he was blinking in a light that felt far too bright but was really moving into evening.

The city was nowhere to be seen. He and Kraal were alone in a grassy space enclosed by a high wall. At the center gleamed a small pond. Kraal forestalled any questions.

"You, little man, are going to have a bath."

Jared stared dully at the pond. A bathtub would have been welcome, a place to lie down and soak away the dirt, to let the heat ease his muscles. Although he wasn't sure what the effect of hot water would be on his leg, and he was pretty sure hot water wasn't good for a fever. But neither was sudden immersion in a cold pond. In any case, he was too weak to swim.

Kraal lifted him down from the horse and then held him on his feet as his knees gave way.

"None too early," the Giant said, letting Jared sink slowly down into the grass. "No, don't lie down. Drink this."

A flask appeared at his mouth. The first sip was bitter and he tried to turn away, but Kraal held his head in the iron grip of one hand and poured the bitter liquid down his throat with the other. Jared swallowed to keep from choking. A delicious coolness spread from his throat and stomach out into his limbs. His head cleared. Kraal released him and stepped back a little.

"That will hold for a few minutes. Now, clothes off."

Jared shook his head. He was not going to strip. Enough of his dignity had been compromised already and he felt well enough to care again.

Kraal didn't ask twice. He simply bent down and tore the front of Jared's tunic, stripping it off of his body. As the big hands reached toward his breeches, he scooted backward in the grass.

"All right, all right. Give me a second."

He tried to get to his feet, but the bad leg wouldn't work and whatever miracle medicine he'd been given hadn't restored his strength enough to let him overcome its dead weight. So, he wiggled out of the breeches by lifting first one hip and then the other. It felt almost good to get his healthy leg out of the itchy wool and into fresh air. The wounded leg was another story.

At sight of it, he gasped in dismay, choking on the overpowering stench emanating from the wound. His stomach heaved and he gagged. Flesh was literally rotting away from the bone. What was left of the skin on his lower leg was mottled green and black, with livid red streaks running up into the thigh. A blister the size of his hand swelled above the knee, filled to near bursting with a dark green fluid. The dull ivory gleam of bone made his head spin, but Kraal was dragging him to his feet.

"Don't look," the Giant said. "It will be better soon."

It seemed that walking under his own steam, rather than being dragged or carried, was the last bit of humanity left to him, and he stumbled and staggered toward the pool, Kraal ever right beside him. When he reached the edge of the pond, he wished again that he'd stayed in Surmise. Maybe this pool was a cure for Giants, but he was pretty sure it would be the end of him.

The water was very deep but clear all the way to a bottom lined with flat, black stone. The sides were smooth and steep. Once in, there was no way out without help. He looked at Kraal and then at the water. It all came down to trust, and he wasn't at all confident that the Giant would pull him out before he drowned.

As if that wasn't bad enough, the pond teemed with flat-bodied silver fish, all equipped with sharp little white teeth. They swam together in a tight school, darting this way, then that. They looked a lot like piranhas, in fact, and Jared took a cautious step away from the steep edge.

"In with you," Kraal said. "You asked for the cure of the Giants. I can't take you to the Queen rotting away like carrion."

Jared had been managing to hold his nausea at bay, but the rotting leg and the circling fish were too much for him. Leaning forward, he vomited a thin, bitter stream into the pool. A flash of silver and the fish were on it, cleaning the water so fast, he only had time to blink before they were back to their regular pattern.

"Get in," Kraal ordered.

Jared shook his head, mute, stumbling backward.

He met resistance. A big hand pressed against the flat of his back, shoving him forward and off balance. Arms windmilling madly, he fought the momentum that drove him toward the pool. And then his feet were no longer on earth, his flapping arms doing nothing to hold him back.

The icy water immobilized his limbs at first contact and made him gasp. He went under. Water filled his nose and burned in the back of his throat. Panic kicked his body into action and he churned his way back to the surface, gagging and spluttering. He wouldn't be able to stay afloat long, not with the cold water already leaching the strength from his muscles. Vertical walls rose several feet above his head, smooth and slick with moisture.

"Get me out!" he shouted up at Kraal, but the Giant stood calmly watching and made no move to intervene. The fish closed in, swimming in tight circles, their slick sides brushing Jared's skin, tails flicking. A tugging sensation on his leg drew his eyes down to see silver scales and flashes of sharp white teeth as they darted in and away, tearing off loose flesh and then retreating, only to be replaced by their fellows. Blood swirled into the water, red first, then pink.

"Kraal, please get me out of here. I'll do anything you want, I swear..."

Blood increased the frenzy of the fish. Jared splashed and struggled, kicking at them with his good leg, shooing with his hands, but they were quicksilver and he could no more catch and hold them than he could hold the water. His flesh had begun to shiver and jerk with cold and terror, teeth chattering.

Kraal's booming laughter came down to him from above. "Relax, little man. They are wound cleaners. They only eat the dead flesh. Your cock and balls are safe enough."

It was true that they touched no other part of his flesh with their teeth. And what they did was painless. He felt the pressure, little tugs and pushes, but that was all. As he calmed and was able to pay more attention, he realized they were doing more than eating, circling the leg, over and over again, brushing against it with their bodies, almost like a purring cat looking for attention.

"You might have told me," he was able to gasp after a moment. "That they wouldn't hurt me."

"You have so little trust. I told you they were for healing. If I had wanted to kill you, I could have found easier ways than carrying you all the way here. Looks like they're done—let's get you out of there before you freeze to death and their efforts are wasted."

The Giant knelt at the pool's edge and reached down a hand. Jared glanced at the fish. They swam around the outer edge of the pool in perfect synchrony, as if he no longer existed. Reaching up both hands, he clung to Kraal's while the Giant lifted him effortlessly up onto dry land.

A gigantic towel descended around his shoulders, falling all the way to his feet like a robe.

"Hand towel for a Giant," Kraal said with his grating laugh. "How does the leg feel?"

Jared tested it, surprised to find it felt more or less normal. A little loss of sensation. No pain. He looked down with some trepidation, expecting to find the flesh stripped to the bone. What he saw made him bend down to look more closely.

All of the sloughing dead flesh was gone. He could see far too much bone for comfort, but healthy muscle was also visible. Wherever he lacked intact and healthy flesh or skin, a clear, thick layer of what looked like gel filled the empty space. When he touched it, the surface was firm but flexible.

His gaze flicked back to the pool and the circling fish. "Where do they come from?"

"One of the Dreamworlds. Nystan, the great hunter, was once badly burned while battling a dragon. Seeing a pond, he threw himself into the water, hoping it would soothe his burning. When the fish surrounded him, his heart filled with fear and dread that his glorious life of conquest would be ended in such an ignominious way. He discovered the same thing you have. When he returned to the kingdom with the tale, his burns coated with invisible skin, those wiser led a party to catch and transplant the fish here for our use."

"It's incredible," Jared said. He walked a few steps, testing the leg. If he concentrated, he could walk with very little limp, although the absence of muscle was apparent. He wouldn't be running races or anything, but this was infinitely better than an amputation, and covered by a pair of pants, the deformity would be unnoticeable.

A giddy rush of emotion washed through him as the specter of deformity and pity faded. He'd conjured up a vision of himself sitting in the parking lot outside the local Walmart with a hand-lettered sign, begging for handouts. But when he managed to get back to his own place, surely he could go back to the life Vivian and Zee had dragged him away from.

Then he caught sight of Kraal's face and his hopeful thoughts scattered like leaves in the wind. He had no way back, and he now owed a debt to a Giant. He had no doubt that Kraal could snap his back like a matchstick, one-handed and without breaking a sweat, if he tried to break faith.

Fear filled belly and throat with acid, and he had to swallow twice before he found his voice. "Now what?" he asked.

"Now we find you clothes and shelter. And then we take you to the Queen."

Four

Vivian staggered, slowing her pace a little to try to catch her breath, nearly impossible despite the shirt tied over nose and mouth to keep out the sand. Her face and arms, exposed to the scouring sand, felt like they'd been flayed. Poe, clasped tightly in her arms, was no longer moving and she worried the sand had been too much for him.

Callyn's broad back, her only landmark, faded out of sight and Vivian pushed herself to walk faster. Zee walked somewhere beside her, moving in and out of her peripheral vision, depending on the vagaries of the wind. She hoped the little dragon was still following, but she couldn't see him at all. As long as they all held together and kept moving in one direction, there was hope of walking out of this part of the Between.

A lot of ifs. She tried not to think about the possibility that Callyn was leading them about in circles. Heart thudding with fear of losing him, Vivian looked around for Zee. He was there, just behind her left shoulder, head bent, face shielded to the eyes by the flimsy barrier of a shirt. She cringed at the thought of what this sandblasting would do to the unhealed gash on his arm, the scars on his face. Nothing to be done now, though. Not until they were safe.

If there was any safety to be had. Horrible to die

here, like this, lost and at the mercy of the wind. As if some malign fate had just been waiting for that thought, the wind shifted direction. Braced against its force and then struck from the other side, she toppled, hitting the ground. Poe slipped from her grasp and she lost him. The wind rolled her a time or two before backing off. She lay where it dropped her, holding the T-shirt over her mouth and nose and trying to catch her breath while looking around for the others.

Scrabbling near her for Poe, she thought she touched feathers, but the next instant, there was only dust. The only thing she could see was the brown air.

"Zee!" She tried to scream, but choked on the dust caked in her throat. When she tried again, she couldn't hear her own voice over the shrieking of the wind.

Down here on the ground, the dust was even thicker. Her breath caught in her throat. When she tried to get up, her legs wouldn't support her and the wind shoved her down flat on her belly. Wild voices moaned and wailed all around her, wordless, like spirits of the damned.

Again she groped around for Poe, stretching her arms as far as they could reach, dragging herself forward on her elbows. The fingers of her right hand brushed something soft. Straining until it felt like her shoulder would separate from its socket, she managed to get a handful of feathers. With all of her remaining strength, she pulled against the resistance, felt it give and come closer. The wind fought her but she clenched her teeth and tugged again. And again, until she had the little penguin safely snugged against her breast.

He wasn't moving. His feathers felt like grit and dust. She couldn't see, and her strength was failing. Forcing herself to focus, she reached out with her mind for a door. As dangerous as the Dreamworlds were just now, if she stayed here she was going to die. If she could make it through a door, there was at least a chance of survival.

It was hard to concentrate. Every breath was a struggle requiring her attention. But she thought she felt the tug of a dream door not far off. Clutching Poe with one arm, she tried to scramble upright. And again she failed, the blood draining from her head and leaving her dizzy and half unconscious.

When she could move again, she stayed flat on the ground, crawling until her legs refused even that and she found herself inching forward, wormlike. Even with the shirt tied around her face, down low like this, there seemed more dirt than air. Only her will kept her moving, until even that was no longer enough.

She drifted in and out of awareness. And then came completely clear, just long enough to realize that she wasn't moving anymore. Just lying there with her cheek pillowed in the dirt, head turned away from the wind. This position allowed for her to get some air, and she gulped it in. Deep breaths set her coughing, though, her body turning itself half inside out to get rid of irritants in her air passages.

Unable to drag herself forward any farther, she stretched out her free hand, pushed with her toes. Miracle of miracles, her fingers brushed against something solid. Wriggling forward, she pressed her whole hand against wood. A door. She could feel the energy running through it and her heart convulsed in a beat of hope.

"Open," she gasped with the last of her strength.

The door sprang ajar. Through eyelids scrunched up almost closed, she glimpsed grass and blue sky. So close, and still so far away. Her fingers twitched, but her arm refused to move any farther. Digging her toes into the dirt behind her, she managed to lever herself forward a couple of inches. So close to the door was she that she could feel the warmth of sunlight through the blowing dirt.

Another push with her toes. And then she was through to the waist, her legs still out in the dust storm, her cheek pillowed in grass. Sand blew in around her through the open door, but she wasn't about to close it and shut Zee and Callyn out of a place of refuge.

Tears streamed from her eyes, obscuring her vision. Sand clogged her nose and mouth and throat, setting her to spasmodic coughing and gagging. Still, she managed to crawl away from the door and into blissful quiet.

Sunlight shone down warm and gentle. The grass was soft and cool. When the coughing eased a little, Vivian sat up and pulled Poe into her lap. He lay limp and still, but he was breathing. Vivian cleared the sand from his beak and smoothed his feathers. She tried to look around for water, but her eyes kept tearing up and she couldn't see.

Which made her question the vision that came through the door a moment later.

It looked like a moving sandcastle more than anything else. One of those fantastic sculptures made during festivals. A man, arms twined around the extended neck of a dragon, and behind that a Giant, supporting the man from behind, one hand on the dragon's back. And then the man dropped to hands and knees, coughing. The dragon shook itself and sand swirled up and around like a snow globe before settling down into the grass.

"Zee!" Vivian cried, running toward him as fast as her unsteady legs would take her.

He tilted his head up at sound of her voice, the tears from his watering eyes creating channels through the dirt caked onto his face. It would be a while before he could speak, she knew, having just been through the same process.

His two companions had fared better. Godzilla seemed unbothered by the dust, other than a dulling of his scales. He'd wandered off, sniffing at things, investigating.

Probably looking for food, Vivian thought with a little shudder. Remembering her own kills as a dragon repulsed her now. Callyn dusted off her clothing with her big hands, considerately stepping well away from the humans so the resulting small dust storm wouldn't affect them again. The Giant looked more like a stone sculpture than ever.

"I hardly dared hope you'd find the door," Vivian croaked.

"The dragon found it," Callyn said. "Neither of the two of us could see, and Zee was fading. You'll want to look to his wounds. The dirt will have been driven into them."

Vivian was already on her knees beside him, investigating. The laceration on his side, even though it was protected by a shirt and somewhat sheltered from the wind, was covered with a fine layer of dust. As for the wide-open wound on his arm, it was packed full of dirt. The healing scars on his face had been abraded until they bled, making a darkly red mud on his cheek.

"We need water," she said. "This has got to be cleaned before it starts to fester."

"I'll be fine," Zee gasped before another fit of coughing took him. "We can't stay here."

"We can't go out there, either."

The door stood open, and all that was visible through it was murky brown.

"There is no water in this world," Callyn said, turning in a slow circle. "At least not close by. Only grass and one lone tree."

At the words, the thrum of familiarity ran through Vivian like a plucked cord and she remembered. She stood, and looked across the wide field to where a single oak tree spread its branches wide. A swing hung from one long, low branch.

"I know this world," she whispered. It was the first

Dreamworld she'd ever visited, when she found a box of dreamspheres in her grandfather's cabin. He'd rescued her, talked to her, given her the penguin pendant.

And he was currently waiting in a purgatory just for Dreamshifters, waiting for her to save him and the others. She sighed. Zee was right. Even if it was safe to stay here, they couldn't linger. There was too much at risk. But neither could they go back out into the Between, not so long as the dust storm raged. Looking wistfully into the distance at the swing which had given her such great pleasure on a long-ago afternoon, she turned back to her companions.

"It's dangerous to stay here. But we can't survive traveling through that again for a bit. We all need to rest. I'd say we set up right close to the door. If something starts going wrong with the Dreamworld, hopefully either Poe or I will have warning and we'll have time to get out."

"If not?" Zee rasped, making his eyes worse by trying to wipe his face with his sand-coated hands.

"Then that's the end of it," she answered. "There's nothing else to be done."

"I don't like it." Callyn stood at the open dream door, looking out. "Don't you have some way to take us directly from one world to another?"

Vivian slid down flat into the cool grass, feeling the blissful stretch and release of tense muscles at rest. Every crack and crevice of her skin itched from the sand. Her face burned as if from hours unprotected in full sunlight.

"From one world into another? Not that I know, not without a dreamsphere."

"And from the Between?"

Vivian sighed and opened her eyes, peering up at the Giant through a distorting film of tears. "I might be able to do it from the Between. Where did you want to go?"

"Home."

"You said they'd kill you." Giving up on the idea of rest, she pushed herself back up to sitting and peered up at the Giant.

"They will."

"You're not making sense," Vivian said.

Zee started to say something, coughed again. He fumbled at his waist for the canteen that hung there and began to wipe it down in the grass. "If they're going to kill you, I don't hold much hope for our safety."

"My life will stand for yours."

Vivian's skin crawled with something more than sand. "What are you saying?"

"The Between is too unstable for much travel. I'm not confident I can get you to the Sorcieri. The Queen has maps and knows the secret doors. You could travel more quickly and safely."

"Let me get this straight. We go to your kingdom and the Queen has you killed but helps us?" Zee said. "Why doesn't she kill us, too?" He opened the canteen and passed it to Vivian. She took one long, blissful swallow and passed it back.

"The laws are very clear. A bond of my life for yours will be honored."

"And then she's under some sort of obligation to help us?" Vivian scrubbed her hands in the grass, trying to remove the grit, watching Zee take what looked like little more than a sip of the precious water before putting the lid back on.

"She is only under bond not to harm you."

"So, she might be no help at all."

Poe stirred, stretching his neck, but his eyes didn't open. Vivian stroked his dusty feathers and looked up at Zee. He nodded once and opened the canteen, pouring a little water onto the sand-crusted beak. Poe's eyes opened and he shivered all of his feathers, upright in an instant.

He looked both indignant and embarrassed, and immediately began preening, as if he had no other concern in the world.

Vivian felt a surge of relief, directly followed by the weight of responsibility and decision. They were all still alive, but that was touch-and-go. There was no question about what was going to happen to Zee if she didn't get those wounds cleaned. Poe needed a lot of water.

She started to run her fingers through her hair by force of habit, and stopped. It was stiff with dirt, knotted beyond repair. "There's still a chance of getting to the Sorcieri without taking you to a sure and certain death?" she asked Callyn.

The Giant nodded, the movement sending a little runnel of sand cascading off the top of her head. "A chance. But we can't stay here."

"Agreed." A restless itch inside her body that had nothing to do with her irritated skin made her twitch. She got to her feet, watching as Poe stopped preening and lifted his head. Godzilla, running away from them across the grass, stopped so short, his legs tangled. A low hissing sound escaped him as he spread his wings and launched himself in lopsided flight back toward the door.

"Run!" Vivian shouted, grabbing Zee's hand and tugging.

"What is it?" He had planted his feet, was reaching for his sword.

"Now, Zee!"

This was not the time to stand and fight. She could only trust that he would follow her as she launched herself into motion, scooping up Poe as she ran. The dragon careened over her head, alighting just in front of the door. She could feel the vibrating thud of Callyn's footsteps. But where was Zee?

Turning to look was nearly her undoing.

At the edges of the horizon, the world was ending. Not just changing or crumbling into dust and ruin, but truly ending. Physics said that what she saw was not possible, that matter might change form but not be completely annihilated. But the darkness dissolving field and grass and sky was a nothingness so vast and profound, it trapped her mind like a fly in amber.

Her feet slowed and stopped, watching with a sick fascination. The world of grass and sky was smaller now, surrounded by the abyss. The oak tree vanished as she watched, crown first, then the trunk and leaves, the swing, the grass and dirt and roots.

Zee's hand caught hers and dragged her out of inertia and back into motion. Once she was moving forward again, her vision constricted down to tight little clips. Godzilla landed in front of the gate. Callyn thudded past, bent forward at the waist, arms swinging. Poe began to slip from her grasp and she was unable to catch him, her other hand caught in Zee's iron grip.

All the time, her feet had to keep moving, to keep from toppling over as Zee towed her ever faster forward to stay ahead of the coming void. She managed to get a hand under Poe and hoist him back upward. The light dimmed as the sky above them was consumed. Zee increased his speed.

Vivian's heart thudded. Her chest burned with every breath. They were close, though. Godzilla slithered through and faded into storm. Callyn bent double to fit, blocking out the Between as she squeezed herself through a doorway far too tight for her frame. So close now, she could smell the dust. Wind reached in through the door and dust puffed up out of the grass with every step. Then Zee planted his feet and shoved her through ahead of him, just as the Between heaved and shivered and turned itself inside out.

Five

They were through the door but far from safe.

The blowing sand was no longer the greatest threat. The void where a world had once been wanted to be filled. Sand and wind and any loose matter changed course, no longer whirling about in a random wind but flowing straight through the open doorway and into the nothingness on the other side.

Vivian staggered away, clinging to Zee's hand, throwing her weight forward to break the suction. Still it dragged her back, her unmoving feet digging a trench in the sand beneath her feet. Zee came with her. Poe began to slip out of her tenuous grasp. Inch by inch, she felt the sliding feathers. He struggled and wriggled, which only made it harder to hold him, and then he was gone, snatched by the wind.

"Poe!" she screamed, but her voice, too, was lost in the vacuum, sucked away into nothing.

Her feet were yanked out from beneath her. She clung to Zee as to an anchor, while the great vacuum inexorably sucked her in. Her hand slipped. Zee tightened his grip but he wasn't going to be able to hold her. Again the vacuum stole her voice as she screamed. Her hand slipped away and she was free flying toward the dark.

Instead, she bumped up against something solid and

stuck there. Zee banged up against her an instant later with an elbow to her solar plexus that stole the last of her breath. Still the suction continued, squeezing her between Zee and whatever was blocking the door. The object was large, solid, but with some give to it. It was also alive, shifting position to block the opening more completely.

Callyn's voice came to her ear as if from a distance. "I can't hold much longer. You'll have to close it."

Right. She was the Dreamshifter. But closing this door, with that cosmic vacuum on the other side, was a thing she didn't know how to do. Closing a dream door was usually easy—reach for the knob, give a little push, let it latch into place. But this? She wasn't sure if the door even still existed.

The bulwark that was Callyn lurched an inch to the left, giving way to the relentless suction. Zee shifted his position a little, flattening his body to ease the pressure of his shoulder against her rib cage. There was no sand in the air anymore, but there seemed to really be no air, all of it sucked away. It didn't help that her face was smothered somewhere in Callyn's midriff. An effort to move, to at least turn her head, proved futile. She was pinned between two immovable bodies.

"Close." She mouthed the words, lacking the breath to speak. Nothing happened.

She tried to build a door in her mind, to picture the opening closed and sealed. But the darkness stole the image from her before it was fairly begun.

Her body was desperate for air, heart bursting, lungs burning. She didn't have much time before she and Zee and Callyn all joined the vast and growing nothing beyond. A deep darkness filled her at thought of Poe already lost. Rage followed, directed at Aidan, at Jehenna, at all of those who had orchestrated the worlds to bring her to this moment. If she died here, there would be nobody left to exact revenge or to make things right.

She had to stay alive and conscious long enough to close the door.

Oxygen had become an overriding mandate, but her ribs couldn't expand to draw in another breath. Already her brain wasn't working properly, thought processes fading. She was being stripped down to the bone. First, rational thought. Then instinct. Fear. Love. Anger. All sucked away into the dark. A pure consciousness remained, dispassionate and untouched by pain or struggle, observing from far away as a power stirred and shook itself free.

It had always been there, lying within, dormant. She feared it and what it could do beyond all other things. Once or twice it had wriggled free, had manifested as the Voice, but there was so much more to it than that.

Unlike the dragon fire, which had always felt alien, this power was as familiar as her own face in the mirror. It connected to every breath, every heartbeat, was aware of every thought that passed through her brain, every physical sensation, every emotion that had ever stirred her heart.

Watching from that faraway place, she saw it gather all of the threads of her being. The spark that was Vivian, the Dreamshifter, the dragon, depleted though it was, binding them all into one thing.

And then it spoke with her voice, even though her lips and tongue did not move.

"Seal the door." The words rang out above the sucking sound made by the destroyed world.

She watched the door slam shut and the Between go still.

The wind stopped. For a blink of time, three unconscious bodies hung motionless in the air before crumpling downward in slow motion. Before they had time to hit the earth, the Between stretched out of shape and turned inside out. Rocks lifted gently from the surface of the earth and hovered. Leaves drifted gently upward.

A small penguin floated off the ground and into the air. He spread his wings for balance, flapped them once, and discovered he could fly, skimming forward on wings never made for flight. Even Callyn, unconscious but breathing, drifted upward, looking like some stone monolith levitated by magic.

Vivian's consciousness seemed the only thing descending, heavier than air, heavier than all things around her. It met her body, meshed and fused. A moment of darkness, and then she came awake in a body that felt curiously light. Air was a luxury and a delight; for a long moment, she did nothing more than drink it in.

That was how long it took for responsibility and a touch of panic to kick back in. Poe was all right; she'd seen him. Callyn, too.

"Zee!" she called, trying to get to her feet and succeeding only in propelling herself up into the air, where she drifted, helpless as an unmanned blimp.

"Don't move!" Zee shouted from somewhere off to her left. "Don't do anything that will push you up higher into the air."

She craned her neck to follow the sound of his voice and found him fifteen feet above the earth, clinging to the branch of a tree. The dragon stood below, peering up with a dazed and bewildered expression.

"What is this?" Panic edged Callyn's voice.

Vivian choked back hysterical laughter. Her inner landscape felt as altered as the world around her, all of her emotions turned upside down with laughter rising to the surface. Beneath it, though, the anger burned like a steady flame. And that suppressed part of herself was there, too, quiet at the moment but watchful. Waiting.

This sobered her more than anything.

"Seems like every time a world dies, the Between

radically changes. Last time, the winds. This time, gravity." Making little hand and foot motions, as if she were steering herself through water, she worked her way over and down to inspect what she had done to the door.

Not a door as such, not anymore. Sealing the breach in the wall was a luminous weaving of color and texture that shifted beneath her eyes, defying her attempts to define and quantify what it was.

Zee worked his way down to her side. He reached out a hand to touch the weaving, but she gripped his wrist and held him back.

"What is it?" His voice was soft with wonder.

"I'm not sure."

The patterns eluded her, ever shifting into something other just as she thought she had begun to understand. Zee looked at her then, his eyes a question. His long hair was wild and full of dirt and sticks. The half-healed scars on his cheek were crusted with fresh blood. Dirt embedded every line, every pore. He looked wild and fey, as dangerous as the weaving of the door.

"Who did this? I was out. Thought we were done for."

"I did." Even as she said the words, she wondered if they were true. This was a magic she didn't know how to work, an act she could never replicate. The part of her that had done it waited within, quiescent, a power outside her understanding and her control.

Callyn ploughed her way over, as awkward as a rudderless ship. "Grass and stone," she said, making a warding gesture in the air. "I have heard tell of such things."

"What is it?" Vivian asked. She was a little frightened by what she had done.

"You don't know?" The Giant's face, usually impassive, creased in surprise. Again, she made the gesture, then said, slowly, "It's the sort of magic woven by the Sorcieri.

You were right not to touch it."

"You still haven't said what it is." Zee's voice was harsh. "If you know something, fill us all in."

"I can't say for sure; I have only heard tell of such things. Rumors and hints. A word in a book here, another there. A temporal weaving, perhaps. Of this time with another, of this space with another. There is no knowing where such a web could take you."

Vivian shivered. "So, maybe it's not just the destruction of the world that's to blame for zero gravity."

"This is possible, yes. Such magic must have deep consequences."

Zee's hand closed around Vivian's, warm and reassuring, despite everything. "We need to move on before something worse happens. Which way?"

"That is a problem," the Giant said. "Both which way to go and how to travel."

The suspension of gravity was not the only obstacle. There was no path now in the direction they had been going. All that had once been green and growing, and then dust in the wind, was now buried under snow. A glacier towered upward into a deep blue sky. Sunlight shone on ice, highlighting shades of blue and green in patterns that suggested an ancient city of spires and towers.

"I'm not sure how to get to my own world from here," Callyn said, "let alone to the Sorcieri."

If any of it still exists.

The words drifted, unspoken, in the air between them. If one world could be wiped out as this one had been, there was no reason why any world should be safe.

"We have to assume that other parts of the Between are still stable. That your world is still there, Callyn, waiting for us."

The Giant gestured at the shimmering door. "That was to the left. North, and the Kingdom of the Giants, should be that way, I think." She gestured toward the looming glacier.

"You're sure?"

"I'm sure of nothing."

The only paths led off at right angles, straight as an arrow as far as the eye could see through a field of pure white snow. Blue sky above, sun blazing down and turning the snow crystals to diamond so that it was too bright to look at for long. Paths were irrelevant, in any case. None of them were going to be walking.

Vivian's eyes watered from staring into the blaze. Already the dragon was flying upward toward the top of the glacier, his flight path jagged and irregular because of the damaged wing. Poe stayed closer to earth, practicing his moves, flying in a small figure eight, and then a larger one, looping upward and drifting down.

"We go over," Vivian said, her gaze following the lines of the glacier, up, up, against the hard sky.

"And if gravity comes back while we're in the process?" Zee drifted up beside her, his head also tipped back, surveying the obstacle ahead. She had thought of that already. Of the sudden, helpless crash to the earth far below. How many nights had she jerked awake out of just such a dream? But this wasn't Dreamworld; this was the Between. And if she didn't stop it, there would be no more Dreamworlds to fall out of.

"Do we have another option?"

"We go back to the Black Gates, take another path. The way is longer, but perhaps not so perilous."

"Do we have time for that?"

"No. But I don't like this."

"We have to do something," Zee said. "Go back or go forward. If we stay here, we freeze to death."

This was truth. As they discussed things, the snow field had extended beneath them. Vivian was shivering already, her feet and her cheeks gone numb. She'd seen victims of the cold when she'd worked the ER, the blackened skin on noses and toes, the surgery to remove the dead flesh. And beyond the fear of disfigurement, of course, the looming threat of death.

She searched inside herself for any sign of her dragon nature. If she could shift, here and now, it would be an easy thing to carry the others not only up and over, but all the way to their destination. But only a tiny spark responded to her inquiry. The dragon part of her was very nearly dead, and certainly not strong enough to support a shift or to stay alive if she managed it.

"We go over," she said. "Quickly, before the rules change again. I think every time a world dies, it's going to throw off the balance. Do you know how far to the next door, Callyn?"

"A half day's journey, perhaps. Beyond the glacier. Unless the height of the thing is part of the distance as things have warped, and then we're likely to find the door at the very top."

That was a whole lot of might. Making plans in the Between was always a crapshoot, though. Any movement was better than slowly freezing to death.

"Let's go." Making sweeping movements with her arms, she drew herself upward into the sky.

Six

Jared had plenty of opportunity to practice using his altered leg.

Kraal kept a pace that was steady for a Giant, which meant a jog for a human. Jared tried to take in his surroundings, which surpassed anything his imagination could have conjured up. Stone mansions that were true wonders of engineering and art. Paved roads fashioned of cobblestones cut from ruby, sapphire, emerald. Everywhere he looked, he found brilliant color and some new use for stone.

When at last they stopped, though, it was in front of a small cottage with a thatched roof and flat stone porch. Nothing extravagant or noteworthy, and Jared felt a welling of disappointment.

A woman answered Kraal's knock. She was small of stature and rail-thin. She was also ancient, with a face so creased with wrinkles, there was no smooth skin to be seen. Only the eyes were young, bright blue and searching. She wore a simple blue gown and her gray hair hung long and unbraided down the center of her back.

Kraal bent a knee to her, and for a flash of an instant, Jared thought he'd been mistaken and she must be somebody of importance. He attempted an awkward bow.

"Can you make him presentable?" Kraal asked.

Jared bit back a retort as the woman tilted her head and surveyed him. He knew he must look a mess, and it would be best for him to not say anything to aggravate his Giant rescuer.

"That depends on where you plan to take him," the old woman said at last. "I don't like the looks of him, Kraal. Treachery written all over. You should drown him."

"I'm a healer, Traveler." The syllables of her name came out harsh and guttural in his hard-inflected speech.

She snorted. "Don't try that line on me. I've seen what you healers do if a child is born distorted or twisted. Some things can't be healed."

"He is under my protection. I have healed his leg. And now he must be presented to Her Excellence. I ask that you do this thing for me."

"I am old and wiser than you might think. You should listen."

The Giant took her frail old hand in his and pressed the back of it to his forehead. "I do listen, but your words come late. There are great things afoot, and we will have a use for this one, I think."

"What is this, then?" The old woman took his enormous hand in both of hers and turned it, displaying a bloody gash in the wrist. Her eyes looked up to his.

Kraal shrugged. "They didn't like the looks of him at the gate, either."

"Oh, Kraal. And you've made yourself bond for one such as this?"

"It was needful." With that, the Giant rose to his full height and clamped a hand around Jared's shoulder. It might have been meant as a friendly gesture, but it nearly crushed the bone, and it was all he could do to keep from crying out or flinching.

"You do as she says, little man. I will be back for you when the sun passes Third Hill."

"I guess you'd better come in," the old woman said, after Kraal turned a corner and disappeared from sight.

He entered a small, low-ceilinged kitchen furnished with a wooden table and two chairs. Something simmered over a wood stove in a large black pot that made him think, without wanting to—*cauldron, witch.* A narrow, dark hallway led out of the kitchen and ended in a closed door. It had several doors on either side as well, and he revised his original estimation of the size of the dwelling.

The old woman gave him another of those sharp, knowing looks, as though she could read his mind and disapproved. Her nose wrinkled, and she sniffed at him tentatively. "Well, at least you've been bathed, but you'll still need a shave and a haircut. And clothes. What good is a bath if you're putting dirty rags back on after? And where does he think I'm to come by clothes for you at a moment's notice? We haven't many human guests."

Jared clenched his jaw tightly over his anger. He was used to deference and respect, or at least the veneer of it. Even the criminal element he represented called him "sir," knowing that a good bit of their future depended on his goodwill. "Sorry to trouble you," he said.

She laughed. "No, you're not. We'll get on better if you don't try to lie to me."

"All right, then. I'm not sorry. It's not my fault that Kraal brought me to you. I haven't asked you to do a single thing, and you talk about me like I'm some noxious poison you've been charged with the disposal of."

"Accurate except for the disposal part, perhaps."

She walked down the hallway, disappearing through a door on the right. A few moments later, she reappeared, pushing a wheeled wooden cart. On it were a basin, a straightedge razor, some soap, and a clean white towel. Jared took one look and retreated toward the door. Nobody who looked at him like that was getting a straightedge anywhere near him.

"Sit down. I'm not going to hurt you."

"How do I know that?"

"You are under Kraal's protection. If you are harmed, Kraal will be harmed, and he is important to me. For similar reasons, your appearance is important and I'm going to shave you. Sit."

To his own surprise, he sat. She was a force of nature and he wasn't about to cross her. She poured water into the basin from a clay pitcher, whisked up the soap in a small bowl, and shaved his face and throat, one terrifying stroke after another. She also trimmed his hair.

And then she opened a drawer in the side of the little cart and brought out an armload of clothing, which she laid out on the table beside him.

Jared picked up a pair of what he supposed would have to be called breeches, made out of what was obviously homespun yarn roughly sewn together, and a harsh brown shirt that looked for all the world like a nightshirt. Peasants, he supposed, would wear clothing like this. If they were called peasants in this world. Whatever they were called, he wasn't one. Kraal had brought him here because he was of value.

"I'm not wearing that."

"Because what you're wearing is infinitely better," the woman said with evident scorn.

Jared looked down at his bloodstained pants, the right leg torn away to reveal his new, clear gel appendage. The tunic was ripped open down the front.

"But—I'm meeting the Queen. Is there nothing else?"

"If you think clothes will impress her, you know naught of the Queen of Giants. You'd best dress quickly—the sun has nearly passed Third Hill."

"Whatever that means."

"Come. You've got a lot to learn in a very short time."

He got up and followed her down the hallway. When she opened the door, he covered his eyes with his arm, so bright was the light, but after a moment, he looked again and, squinting, was able to see.

A large, square of vacant space stretched out between the house and those neighboring, paved with flat, gold-colored stones laid expertly together in an intricate pattern. Like a city square, he thought, which ought to have a fountain at the center, with a few shade trees and park benches and pigeons. Where there should have been a fountain or sculpture, instead there was a half circle of perfectly symmetrical standing stones, twenty feet tall, all rounded at the top. They were too perfect to have been formed by nature but didn't look like they'd been made by hands, either. Each was a different color, and he realized as he looked more closely that they were gemstones of a size and clarity unimagined.

Emerald, sapphire, ruby.

At the point that would have been the center of a complete circle, a clear crystal pillar stretched upward, catching a few of the sun's rays in faceted angles and reflecting the light skyward in a visible beam.

But the sunlight shone now directly on the ruby stone, the third, on it and through it so that the whole thing glowed and cast red beams across the square.

"When the sun has a clear path," the old woman said, "and lights up the Time Stone, Kraal will come for you. You must be in the Queen's audience hall and ready to present your petition before it moves on to Fourth Hill."

"And if I don't choose to see the Queen?" The stones were too much. Too much light, too much color, an intensity of sensation that made his nerves scream for relief. When the sun lit up that central pillar—what was that, diamond? It was going to be blinding.

The woman laughed, or he thought it was a laugh, a dry rustling sound. “You are a child, with the ways of a child, and if you continue with such foolishness, you will be a dead child. Kraal has no death wish. If you aren’t ready or if you try to resist, he will pick you up and carry you there naked. They take agreements seriously here. Now, will you get dressed or no?”

Her wrinkled face was void of expression, and he knew he’d get less mercy from her than from the Giants. “What’s your bargain with them?” he demanded.

“You would like to know that, I am sure.” Without another word, she turned and went back into the cottage, and after a moment, he followed, his emotions a turmoil. He wished he’d never come here, but then, he hadn’t had much choice. Vivian had dragged him out of his own comfortable life and into nightmare beyond his imagining. She blamed him for things done in dreams, for being that other man in Surmise, the Chancellor.

A twist of longing for that alter ego surprised him. The Chancellor had power and privilege. He wore jewels and satin and took what he wanted. People feared him and treated him with respect. Now he, Jared, was going to appear in court as an impoverished mendicant. At least he had both legs, and for this, he owed Kraal.

Still, gratitude was a long way from his thoughts as he dressed in the scratchy wool breeches and the rough handwoven shirt. The old woman looked him over and nodded, just as two things happened at once.

Kraal’s shadow blocked out the light from the door, and the whole hut lit up as if the stone itself were filled with small suns. Shards of light pierced Jared’s eyes and he cried out, covering them with his hands, but there was no mercy, no relief.

Somebody pried his hands away and put some dark

glasses over his eyes, and then he could breathe, could look up without feeling he was about to die from an abundance of light. The old woman, too, wore dark lenses, but Kraal wasn't even squinting.

If he went outside—*when* he went outside, because Kraal was already towing him mercilessly in that direction—the crystal pillar would be unbearable.

"We find it beautiful and marvelous, but I understand it is difficult for a human to tolerate the sun on stone, even with the glasses. Just close your eyes, and I will lead you."

Jared complied out of necessity, even as internally he churned with bitterness and shame that he must come into the presence of the Queen in this way. His leg, although functional and painless, was also nerveless and felt heavy and awkward, so that he limped no matter how hard he tried to maintain an even gait.

Kraal had his hand, forcing him to reach up as though he were a very small child, a toddler, holding on to an adult's hand to support and guide its wobbling steps. As they passed the Time Stone, even with his eyes closed and the dark glasses in place, the light burned through his eyeballs and into his brain with a cold, sharp fire that turned his stomach and made his knees go weak. For a minute, he thought he would further humiliate himself by vomiting all over the shabby clothes, but he managed to swallow it back and carry on.

Little by little, the light faded from excruciating to bearable to uncomfortable and merely harsh. Color began to tint it, so it was no longer pure white but infused with blue, and Jared knew the sun was moving toward Fourth Hill. He was too out of breath to ask questions or express his fear, but just then, they came to a halt.

Opening his eyes, he saw that they stood on a black slab of stone so highly polished, he could see his own reflection. And deep, deep in the stone, as though it were a lake, shone the twinkling light of stars. He felt dizzy and disoriented, as if he had fallen in and been left to drown, but the anchor of Kraal's hand steadied him.

Across the expanse of the marble sea stood a palace, the breadth and height of which were dizzying. It, too, was made of stone, not gemstones this time but a golden granite with flecks of something like mica that caught the afternoon light and reflected it back.

Two female Giants stood before closed doors. They wore flowing gowns of purest white that did little to conceal perfectly sculpted breasts and hips. Long hair, red as flame, curled over their shoulders in shining tendrils.

The Giantess on the right clasped a stone jar. The one on the left held a knife with a blade as long as Jared's arm, honed to a razor sharpness but rusty and stained. As beautiful as were their bodies, perfect as any sculptor could hope to chisel from purest marble, their faces looked like the work of a child. Flat-featured, with only a crack for a mouth, noses askew, cheekbones jutting and uneven. The eyes, though, were a beautiful sapphire blue.

"Kraal," said the Giant to the right. "What do you here?"

"I come for an audience with Her Eminence."

"And your little friend?"

Jared caught a hunger in the voice, the low purr of a cat confident of a dinner.

"Under my protection."

"And what will you give as pledge, that you should bring one such as this before the Queen?"

"I pledge my life."

"And in token of this pledge?"

The words were formal and formulaic, with the ring of old custom, and Jared began to relax. Of course the guards looked imposing; it was their job to guard these doors, to monitor the traffic of all who would meet with the Queen. But in the end, it all came down to ritual and formula. Kraal knew what he was about.

The guard held out her knife and Kraal took it from her. “As proof of my bond and my pledge,” he said, and then, with one sudden stroke, cut off his own right ear. Blood gushed, pouring in a red tide down the side of his head, staining his neck and shoulder.

Kraal bowed and returned the knife to its keeper, and Jared realized, his heart battering his ribs with sudden terror, that the blade was not rusty but bloodstained, that this was not the first such use it had seen.

The other Giant held out the stone jar, and into it Kraal dropped the severed ear.

“I accept your bond. What price will your friend pay?”

“He is under my protection. My life stands for his.”

“Your pledge has been heard and accepted.”

“Let it be so.”

A child stepped forward from where she had been hidden behind a pillar, dressed like a Victorian doll in frills and lace, with a fur cape pinned at her breast by a giant emerald. Her hair fell in perfect raven ringlets framing a square, roughly hewn face. In her right hand she carried a golden triangle, in her left a baton of the same lustrous metal. Stationing herself between the two guards, she struck the triangle once, twice, and then a third time.

As the sound pealed out, the doors swung open.

Kraal let go of Jared’s hand and strode forward. Jared, confused and disoriented, stayed rooted to the ground, watching his host move away, until the child nudged him. “Go.”

His feet began moving almost of their own accord and he stepped across the threshold into a light-filled room so splendid, he could barely take it in. No windows that he could see, and yet everything was permeated with a golden glow, as if the light came from the stone itself.

Beneath his feet was a marble floor beyond imagining, inlaid with colored stone that formed images of Giants and dragons and other winged creatures, and doors of every imaginable size and shape. Flowers grew without any beds of soil that he could see, in fanciful arrangements that highlighted certain elements of the paving. Large trees graced the vast expanse, their trunks emerging from the floor with no visible space around them, and again no sign of earth.

No time to look, though, because he was busy holding himself straight and walking as evenly as possible. A clear path, red stone like a carpet, led down the center of the room, bounded on each side by a low hedge of red flowers. A throng of Giants stood in ranks on either side, staring down at him out of expressionless faces.

His knees wobbled, sweat crawled down his back in cold insect trails, but he kept moving, at first following Kraal's back as his only landmark.

And then he saw.

A throne marked the end of the red stone path. It was impossible to tell of what it was originally constructed, it was so heaped with flowers. At first, Jared wondered whether they had been piled there or had grown on their own, and then it ceased to matter.

On the throne, amid the flowers, sat the most beautiful being he had ever seen. She wore a short tunic of blinding white, cut low to reveal the perfect swell of her breasts. Her legs, her arms, they were as though sculpted of perfect ivory by a hand too skilled to be human. And her face—

All of the Giants Jared had seen so far had rough-hewn, often distorted features, while hers had been shaped with the same symmetry as her body. Golden hair, twined with red roses, cascaded down over her shoulders. Her eyes were dark sapphire, with stars behind them. Kraal fell to one knee and Jared followed his example and then bowed lower still, resting his forehead on grass unbelievably lush and smooth.

"You are back so soon," the Queen said. "The schools of the healers in Surmise were not to your liking?"

Her voice finished Jared completely. It was the sound of crystal on the wind, he thought, light and musical and perfectly tuned, as if wind blew through the branches of a tree hung with crystal wind chimes.

In contrast, Kraal's voice was coarse and hard, a thing barely to be tolerated in the presence of such perfect beauty. "The schools were fine, Your Majesty. I have brought you information which seemed of greater import than my training as a healer."

"It looks as though you have brought me more than information." Her eyes, her focus, all turned to Jared now, and he found he could barely breathe beneath the ecstasy of her attention. He was aware of every beat of his heart, of the blood traveling through his veins, of the vulnerability of his flesh.

"I have pledged my life for his," Kraal responded. "He has information. I have not brought him as a plaything." There was an edge to the Giant's voice that Jared wanted to reprimand. Surely it was not right to speak to the Queen in this way.

"Stand up, stranger. Tell me your name and your errand."

Jared's knees felt like jelly, but so strong was his desire to obey her slightest wish, he would have tried to fly if she had asked. He got to his feet and braced his legs, grateful all at once for the stiffness of the wounded leg.

"Now, then. Come closer. I wish to look at you.

Jared approached the throne, giddy with the hammering of his heart and an overpowering fragrance of flowers.

The Queen leaned forward, as if to see better. "I have never seen eyes of such a shade of green. They are indeed lovely."

Blood rushed to his face, and for the first time in his life, Jared found himself tongue-tied. No woman had ever reduced him to such a state of confusion; no opponent in the courtroom had ever rendered him speechless. He didn't know what to do, what to say to this.

Her voice sank to a low caress. He could feel it move across his skin, stirring his body into arousal. "If I asked for your eyes, or your heart, would you give them to me?"

"Anything," he replied, one hand over his heart. "Whatever you ask of me, it is yours."

He felt as much as saw her smile. "Tell me why Kraal has brought you to me, if it is not, as he says, as a plaything."

Each word rang pure and perfect inside his head, so that it was difficult to string them all together into sense.

"I—it's about the Dreamshifter, I suppose. And the Warrior." His lips felt numb and it was difficult to form them into the necessary shapes, which made him stutter and flush with shame. He must look like a total imbecile, groveling here in his cast-off clothes, stammering over the easiest words.

The Queen's clear brow darkened in a frown and the whole room seemed to dim. "This is already known. I'm certain Kraal didn't bring me a half-wit, no matter how beautiful. Tell me something new or he dies for his insolence."

Not an idle threat. In case the exchange outside the palace doors hadn't made that clear, two towering guards moved into position on either side of Kraal, each carrying a brutally spiked club.

Jared's brain lurched like a slow-moving beast,

seeking a path to follow in this morass of love and politics. He needed time to think, a clue as to what she might want from him. Kraal had never indicated what, among all the things they had spoken of, he thought would be of such interest to the Queen of the Giants.

"She—they—were seeking a stone key. The warrior was attacked by gray-skinned men. Well, not men, exactly—"

"Again, this I know already. Tell me a new thing. Speak with care, for I am not inclined to patience."

Heart hammering, mouth dry, Jared prepared himself for one last attempt. Falling back on years of habit, he stood to his full height, adopting his lawyer's voice and patterns of speech. "Perhaps if her Majesty would care to tell me what is known, I would be more able to tell what is not."

Silence filled the chamber at his words, a silence so deep, it had a soul of its own.

At last, the Queen inclined her head slightly, as if in respect. "I had taken you for a coward, but you speak sense. We know that the Dreamshifter found the key and opened the gates for Aidan, who led all the dragons of the Between back into the Forever."

This was more than Jared knew. He and Kraal were in serious trouble. They'd been too slow getting here, and the thing Kraal had hoped to prevent had already come to pass. The Queen saw this. Her lips curved up slightly.

"Perhaps you had thought to tell me that the Dreamshifter had found the key, or that it had been taken from her." She shifted her gaze to Kraal, and Jared felt like he could take a deep breath for the first time since they'd entered the audience chamber. "Is this why you brought him to me?"

"I brought him to you because he has a bond with the Dreamshifter."

"Is this true?" Again the queen shifted forward in her throne, her eyes boring into and through him.

Jared's throat was so dry and tight, he wasn't sure he could get words out. "Before this—mission—we were betrothed."

"I see. So, you would be of value to her, and therefore of great value to me."

At that, Jared felt a twisted and bitter laughter within. His value to Vivian was less than the life of an insect. She had stomped on his heart, gone off with that muscle-bound cretin, Zee. With an effort, he cut off these thoughts lest they show in his face. He'd always been good at adapting, at aiming his speech patterns at the particular jury or judge.

"We are bonded, life to life," he said, looking directly into her eyes.

A moment.

And then she nodded and gestured at the guards. They stepped back from Kraal. Jared sucked in a breath, and then another, feeling his clenched muscles relax a little.

"You offered me a generous bond. I accept."

Even as the import of these words struck home, she stretched out her hand toward his face, all five fingers spread wide, and made a slight twisting motion.

"No," he said, shaking his head in denial. "It was a token bond, a figure of speech; I didn't—"

He broke off at the sensation of suction on his eyeballs, as though an invisible vacuum cleaner was pressed to the sockets.

"No," he said again, tripping as he stepped backward, then scrabbling away from her on his hands and knees in the grass. Distance only increased the pressure and he pressed both hands over his face, trying to ease it.

"A bond is never a token," the beautiful voice said.

Excruciating pain struck his eye sockets and from there into his brain. He heard the scream tear out of his own throat as the agony sharpened to an incandescent peak. There was a flash of white light, and then darkness.

A gush of warmth flooded his cheeks and he knew that it was blood, not tears. He could hear his own voice, whimpering like a child, but it was outside of him and separate, not a thing he could control. He collapsed to lie face down in the grass.

From a distance, he heard the Queen's voice. "Take these and have them set for me."

His heart would be next. She would draw it still beating from his body, but then he would at least be dead. Not blind and disfigured and set to begging in the Between. Not living with this pain, with the knowledge that the horrible mewling sound was emerging from his own throat.

"A gift for a gift," the Queen said. "I will give you new eyes when the physicians are done with you. Kraal, take him."

"Take my heart," he spat out, in a voice broken and twisted and not at all like his own. "Take it now and end me."

"Perhaps another day." She spoke as calmly as if they were discussing a financial arrangement. "I own it already, since you have bonded it to me. But I am content to let you keep it yet a while. Kraal."

Tree-trunk arms wrapped around him, scooped him up. The motion sent daggers straight into his brain and he gasped, unable even to cry out.

"Be easy," Kraal's voice said, and something cool and soothing flowed into his eye sockets. The pain eased almost instantly, although the queasiness persisted. He didn't have the strength to fight, and he let the Giant carry him out, too much in shock to worry about all of the staring eyes, the ignominy of being carried like a child.

She took my eyes. She actually took my eyes. He couldn't make sense of a world in which a thing like that could happen. His perception of reality had always been made up of facts. Eyes could be removed, yes, by sharp objects. Not by a spoken word and the twist of a hand. More than anything, he wanted to go home, although now there was nothing for him there. What life would he have as a blind, disfigured attorney? No more reading law books, no looking soulfully into the eyes of female jurists or seducing the judge.

He knew when they left the palace. There was a change in the air, the fragrance of the gardens. But no light. His face was wet again, and when he put his hands up to touch it, he realized that he was crying, could feel the tears making streaks through the drying blood.

Seven

Vivian had dreamed of flying as a child. Some of the dreams had been gentle, just an easy lifting above the earth. Others had been wild and out of control, where she flew higher and higher with no way to land. And she had flown as a dragon, all wings and power and the arrogant knowledge that she ruled the skies.

Working her way up over a mountain peak in zero gravity didn't feel like flying at all. There was no sense of freedom in it, for one thing, and very little by way of control. The air was thin and icy. Her body was wracked with shivers, but that was a good thing. If hypothermia set in, the shivering would stop, her brain grow sluggish. That was one worry. Her other fear was the sudden return of gravity. She balanced her approach between speed and keeping her altitude low enough that she might survive a fall.

Poe and the dragon led the way, the penguin moving as though he were swimming, body streamlined, flippers tucked, paddling with his feet. After some experimentation, Vivian followed his lead, folding her arms across her chest and tucking her numb hands into her armpits. It was much faster to use her feet, kicking along like a scuba diver. Zee kept to her side. Behind them, slow and ponderous, came Callyn, muttering all the way.

As they ascended, the air grew colder and thinner. Vivian's breath came hard, her heartbeat rapid and fluttering. She and Zee shared a glance, not wasting valuable breath. Both of them knew the risk. If the air grew too thin, they would have to turn back after all. There was a risk of losing consciousness and floating upward, dying in a cold blue sky because gravity would not pull them back when they stopped moving.

Poe and the dragon had flown on ahead and had already reached the summit. Much as she tried to focus on this goal, Vivian's gaze kept dipping to the snow-packed trail so far below, and her stomach lurched. She closed her eyes to shake off the dizziness, and when she opened them again, she fixed them on the shining tip of the glacier and the blue sky above it. Breath came with increasing difficulty, and at first she thought the black specks in the sky were due to oxygen deprivation. They danced in front of her eyes and she blinked to try to clear her vision. The specks remained, becoming larger, separating into three distinct spots, drawing closer.

Dragons, she thought at first. But the shape was all wrong. The creatures were more compact, their flight pattern lithe and agile.

"Trouble," Callyn warned.

Zee drew his sword.

Giant and Warrior drew in close to Vivian on either side, weapons at the ready.

Above, three creatures flew in formation, circling their gathered prey. Vivian felt a moment of awe along with a surge of fascinated fear. They had raptor heads, with curved beaks and amber eyes, and a wingspan as wide as Callyn was tall. Their bodies were muscular and feline, covered in a smooth, tawny fur, but the legs all ended in sharp talons rather than paws.

Griffyns, straight out of myth.

One of the creatures dove, talons outstretched, coming in for a killing strike. It screeched as it came, a shrill, terrifying sound. Callyn swung her spiked club upward, but the action pushed her backward through the air. Both club and talons missed and the griffyn screamed outrage, circling up and out of reach before turning and diving once again.

Callyn, still upside down, flailed her arms and legs, trying to get in position to take another swing. Zee had his sword in one hand, a knife in the other. "Get clear!" he shouted, and Vivian edged off to the side to be well out of the way.

With a concerted scream, all of the griffyns dove at once.

Zee spread his arms wide and tried to spin, but the creatures had wings and he did not. They easily evaded the stroke, parting at the last moment to go in separate directions. One dove at Callyn, and this time, the talons found their mark, tearing into the soft flesh of her belly, a split second before the club connected with the griffyn's skull.

Callyn screamed as the creature's wings jerked reflexively in a death spasm, the locked talons tearing into her entrails. Blood from both bird and Giant hung in the air in great red gouts, the two of them joined together in death.

A shadow came between Vivian and the sun. Wind from Giant wings buffeted her about, and she tried to evade. She was no match for a winged creature, though, and braced herself for the death blow, curling protectively around her belly. Instead, talons snagged the back of her shirt, wide wings beat the air above her head, and with a little jolt, she felt herself lifted up, up into the sky.

"Vivian!" Zee cried, struggling vainly to reach her.

Kicking and twisting in the creature's grip, Vivian tried to get free. Her shirt refused to tear, and the resistance between her body and the griffyn pulled the fabric too tight at the sleeves to let her wiggle out of it.

Zee was far below her now, just a small, brightly colored toy, another griffyn circling just out of his reach. She tried to grasp the latent power of the Sorcieri, to use the Voice of Command, but her lips wouldn't move.

She was too cold to feel the wind, too stiff to fight. Even as her brain searched for the medical condition—hypothermia—her body surrendered and she drifted into sleep.

Eight

A thousand years Aidan had planned and schemed for exactly this moment: herself, triumphant, leading a flight of dragons through the Black Gates and into the Forever. All of the childhood tales her mother had told, she had taken as gospel. The golden river. The gemstones big enough for a dragon to perch on. Lush green grass, trees, plentiful deer.

When the Black Gates slammed irrevocably behind her, she'd laughed. Better and better. Nobody could follow, and what could she want with any of the outside worlds? She'd doomed them all when she'd killed the Guardian with dragonstone and spilled her poisoned blood over the Dreamworlds she was bound to protect.

But the growing realization that everything was wrong very nearly made her wings falter. Below, the land lay parched and barren, so dry that the soil was nothing but a network of cracks. The dragon wings raised a dust that came near to obscuring the landscape but still allowed her keen eyes to see what was not there. No grass, no trees, no boulder-sized gems.

Most importantly, no prey and very little water.

The bed of what must have once been the golden river was a long, winding scar cut into the bleak landscape. Here and there, the sun illuminated a liquid glint, but this turned out to be nothing but mud. At intervals on the dry banks lay the twisted tangle of bones. Some were deer and other small animals, dead in their search for water. Others were dragon skeletons, enough of them to inspire unrest in her dragon fleet. Aidan felt the discontent, the fear, all amplified in her own breast.

All of them had been raised on tales of the Forever. Aidan alone knew for certain that they were more than stories. She had them directly from her mother, Allel, who had actually been here before the Rebellion. Before the Giants and the Sorcieri had conspired to lock the Gates and separate the two factions. Back then, the river had brimmed with molten gold. There were more deer than the dragons could eat. Precious stones everywhere. Green grass. The City of Dragons was real, built beside the Pool of the Forever.

Aidan's only problem with the ruins of the Forever was the hardship it created. An ugly world was fine. But she didn't like to be hungry or thirsty, and it would be more difficult to keep her followers on course. Already her wings ached. Her hollow belly rumbled and cramped, the blood craving growing into a fierce drive surpassed only by thirst. She was well aware of the baby growing inside her, sucking at her resources, stealing them for his own use.

She allowed him. She needed her warrior son to be born healthy and strong. And for this, as well as quelling the rising worry from the other dragons, she needed to find water and food.

The land spread out below as far as she could see, an endless stretch of desert carved by dry riverbeds, pitted with dead lakes. But off to the east, her sharp eyes caught a glimmer of reflected light within the hollow of a cone-shaped mountain, probably an extinct volcano. Lakes formed in those craters. Perhaps there was some water left in this accursed land after all.

Shifting course, she made a pass low over the crater's mouth. Not much remained of what had once been a full lake; little more than a pond surrounded by mud.

Thirst drove her.

Sending a command to the other dragons, she circled in and landed. Warm mud squished up around her feet, sucking as if it too were hungry and wanted to pull her down and devour her. The other dragons descended in ranks, arraying themselves according to age and prowess. The wind from their wings shattered the mirror surface of the pool.

Aidan cared only that the water was cool and laced with minerals and sulphur drawn from the belly of the earth. She buried her muzzle and sucked in a long draught, letting the cool tang slake her thirst and even abate her hunger. She took her time about it, even though rumbles of discontent emanated from the waiting dragons, arrayed several circles deep around the water. There would be rebellion if she denied them permission to drink for too long, but she needed also to assert her primacy. Timing was everything. She took one more drink, holding back the press of their desire with the strength of her own will, before she gave the order.

Tier one, you may drink, she sent, feeling the tension ease as the first ranks stepped forward. A young dragon in the back, thirsty, angry, shoved his way forward.

Resume your place.

I have a right to drink. He was young and insolent. Tempers flared all around him and Aidan waited until he had reached the water and the intolerance of the waiting dragons was at its peak.

Kill him.

Five large dragons fell on the young one, tearing out his throat and belly. It took only a moment and he offered no more resistance than a cry of alarm and a frantic, useless beating of his wings.

Asserting leadership, Aidan walked to the body, dragons shifting out of her way to clear a path, and claimed the contents of the belly, dripping with black blood and sulphur. Holding back her own hunger, primed rather than satisfied, she gave the command.

You who obeyed my command, the kill is yours. Eat.

Turning away, she ordered the dragons at the pool to step back, gave permission for the next ranks to step forward. A buzz of reaction flowed through the flight, but they acknowledged her right and justice.

Only one mind stood out in resistance, not even trying to screen his own thoughts. He was a male and larger than she, a red dragon, dusted with gold on his back and sides. He could easily have forced his way into the first tier, but he stood back, not out of fear or subservience, but because he chose.

Was that necessary? He was very young and no real threat.

It was not a direct challenge and he kept his thoughts only for her, closing out the others. Still. It would be easy for one malcontent to diffuse unrest among the others.

You presume. I will not tolerate this.

You would not find me quite so easy to kill.

Anger flooded her, and with it, a sliver of fear. There was something about him that the other dragons lacked. It wasn't just appearance, although she had to acknowledge that he was beautiful. He ran deeper than the other dragons of the Between. He seemed older. The others would hesitate to attack him, and even if they did, a dangerous aura hung about him that implied he would not go down easily. If she ordered his death and dragons died in the attempt, there would be doubts about her leadership.

When she killed the upstart, it must be swift and

decisive and she must do it herself. If she had still possessed her dragonstone, she might have shifted into human form and taken him that way. But she had given it to the Warrior in hopes it would entice him to help her. A mistake, a loss. At least he was shut away behind the gates and could not use it against her. So, she must bide her time and wait for the right moment.

You underestimate me, she sent out to him then. *Do not test my patience too far.*

If you don't want a rebellion, take thought before you slaughter the young and the weak.

It wasn't a direct threat, but the danger ran deep enough to chill even Aidan's fiery blood. Where had this one come from? The long years of exile from the Forever had made the dragons of the Between ignorant and feral. They responded blindly to her leadership, expressing no ideas of their own beyond the demands of food and water. This male was different, with an intelligence and subtlety that matched her own. Had he really come through the gates with them from the Between? She couldn't remember if she had seen him, but then, she had lacked the time to observe, to know them or their names.

Identify yourself, she sent to him now.

I am who I am. Teheren will suffice.

You are strong, Teheren of the dragons. I have need for one like you. Here and now, I name you Lieutenant. Gather the ranks; it is time we move on.

She felt the hesitation as he considered her words. His thoughts, however, he kept well to himself, shedding not even a small emotional vibration as a clue. As her unease grew to the point where she knew she'd made a grave error, he lowered his head in deference.

As you will.

Aidan watched him go. Listened to his commands and the immediate response of the other dragons. He had their respect and their admiration, and she didn't trust him. Let him help her now and be of use. She would know the right moment for his death.

Nine

Weston was missing both his pickup and his shotgun. Last time he'd seen the truck, it was parked near his favorite campsite, way up north in the middle of the forest. A lot had happened since then, including a forest fire, and he was pretty sure he wouldn't be seeing the old Ford again. As for his shotgun, that had been a casualty of the dragon damn near killing him.

He'd spent the last two days holed up in A TO ZEE, pacing, thinking, and sitting for long, mindless stretches in front of Zee's TV. He had a bed, a shower, water, and a stash of canned and dried food in the cupboards. Enough to get by on while he healed up and figured what he was going to do.

Go after Vivian.

That was the obvious thing. It was the course of action he'd already decided on before Flynne had stopped him and dragged him off to the hospital. But now he couldn't make up his mind to do it.

The raven was getting increasingly restless and obnoxious. Time was, it would sit still for a long stretch of time, long enough to make putting a newspaper under the chosen perch worthwhile. Last night and this morning, the creature wouldn't stay still for a minute. It interrupted Weston's already-restless sleep, sitting on his chest and pecking at chin and cheeks. It fluttered around the living quarters, chair to counter, counter to doorframe, doorframe to bed. If Weston ventured downstairs into the store, it flew the length of the big room repeatedly, the whirring of wings a constant noise.

Bob. Now every time he looked at the damned bird, he thought about Lyssa. Not that he needed much reminding. About fifty times a day, he'd fumble for the pendant that wasn't there, and then he would wonder how she was doing, if she was eating, if the foster people were good to her.

Whether the Nothing had caught up to her yet.

That morning, he'd put in a call to Flynne. The deputy was busy, he'd been told by the young voice on the other end. Weston called back three times before Flynne called back, sounding tired and stretched. Lyssa was all right. Not sleeping well. Not eating well, either. Things weren't going well at all. Ten new cases in Krebston, and all of those afflicted earlier had died.

As the dark grew outside the windows on the second evening, he switched on the TV to distract himself. It was tuned to a news channel. The anchor's forehead was creased with anxiety. Makeup couldn't totally disguise the bags under his eyes. His gaze darted away from the camera once, as though startled from behind.

"There have been one hundred more sleep deaths in Spokane since yesterday morning," he was saying. "Authorities decline to give an opinion on the cause. Here's Jim Simons, on site at Sacred Heart Hospital. Jim?"

Weston stared at the screen while the reporter interviewed a doctor. No, there was no known cause or cure. No virus or bacteria had been isolated. Was it contagious? That was difficult to say, but it couldn't be ruled out. People should not come to the hospital now unless they were gravely ill. There were no beds, and no staff to care for them.

The camera shifted to scenes from downtown Spokane. Grocery stores with empty shelves. Looting in the streets. Other cities then, across the country. Seattle, Chicago, New York. Then Europe. The death counts were rising. People were rioting. In the US, the President had deployed the National Guard to help keep order. Problem was, the troops were dying just as fast as everybody else.

"Shit." Weston dropped the remains of his pizza pocket back onto his plate. "Well, that does it, then."

Flynne had given him a cell phone number to keep him from bothering the secretary, already threatening to quit under the weight of alarm calls coming in. Now he picked up on the first ring.

"I want to see the kid," Weston said.

"I can't give you the address—"

"Yes, you can."

"There are rules for foster care." There was doubt in the deputy's voice.

"I think we've moved beyond the usual rules. Let me see her. She's got to be terrified." Weston moved around the store and the upstairs apartment as he talked, turning off lights and closing doors.

"Are you sure there's nothing you can do about this—outbreak or whatever it is?" Flynne asked.

"Tell people to put dream catchers up."

"Be serious."

"I am, actually. It might make a difference. They won't listen to you, but you could tell them. How do I get to this address? Don't forget I'm walking."

Downstairs, Weston took a long look around, then went out the back door, letting it lock behind him. He didn't plan on coming back.

Krebston was a small town and it wasn't much of a walk to the address Flynne had given him. The streets were empty. No lights on in the downtown, but the houses were lit up with lights in nearly every window. Apparently, Lyssa wasn't the only child afraid to sleep.

He started out at a walk, the raven flitting ahead from tree to tree. It croaked once, then flew on ahead. Probably a waste of time getting the address from Flynne. The infernal bird most likely knew the way. Even as he walked, he heard a scream from a house across the street. A dark shadow raced across the room, highlighted behind the drawn drapes.

Weston picked up his pace and then broke into a run.

He'd let the child go, knowing what this was. Yeah, he'd given her the pendant, but he had no real reason to believe it would actually protect her. The memory of her trust, the way she'd clung to him against the detaching hands, made him run faster. Jenn had died because he was too slow. Grace had died because he was too slow.

Not this time. He reached the intersection of Pine and Lincoln and turned right. There, it would be the big house on the right, third from the corner. Lights blazed in all the windows. The raven waited on the metal railing at the top of the three steps that led to the front porch.

Weston rang the doorbell, then, not content to wait, pounded on the door with a fist.

A dog barked. Little yappy thing. A ceramic angel stood in the corner. One of its hands was missing. A hand-painted sign above the door read, "As for me and my house, we will serve the Lord."

He knocked again. The barking erupted into a frenzy.

"Quiet!" a woman's voice ordered. The dog carried on without diminishing its volume at all. Footsteps now. The door opened, revealing a middle-aged woman, softly curved, wearing stretch jeans and a sweat shirt. Her face looked weary but she smiled.

"Weston?"

He nodded, too out of breath to speak.

"I'm Andrea. Brett said you'd be coming. Lyssa is waiting for you. Come on in."

Weston would have preferred infinitely to have the child come out, but he knew this wasn't reasonable. So, he wiped his feet on the doormat and stepped inside.

It was cluttered in a comfortable sort of way that narrowly avoided chaos. A living room was visible to the right. Two boys sat on a sofa, playing some sort of video game, so engrossed in trying to kill robots on screen that they didn't even turn around.

The woman led him away from the living room, down a short hallway. He caught a glimpse of a kitchen, where two teenage girls and a boy sat at the table with schoolbooks open. They were talking, not working, and drinking something out of mugs. A picture hung on the wall of a pale-faced, blue-robed Jesus with children in his lap.

"All of them are scared," his guide said. "Lyssa's the only one who has lost somebody in her own family, but they all know somebody who knows somebody. None of the kids wants to sleep."

"Dream catchers," Weston said.

"Pardon?"

"Put dream catchers in their rooms. Tell them it will stop whatever it is from coming in."

Her pleasant smile disappeared. "I think bedtime prayers are a much better idea, don't you?"

"I don't see that the two things are mutually exclusive." Weston knew there was no point in talking further but had to try. "Double up. Lots and lots of prayers and the dream catchers."

Andrea stopped and turned to face him, blocking a bedroom door with her body. "I'd thank you not to fill her head full of heathen nonsense. There will be no dream catchers in this house. Understood?"

Weston nodded. He understood all right. Far too well. Which didn't mean for an instant that he was making any promises.

She pursed her lips, ams folded across her chest, thinking. But at last she turned, opened a door for him, and stepped aside. Before he could get more than a general impression of a child's bedroom, a small body hurled itself at him so hard, he nearly toppled. Arms wrapped around his legs and squeezed.

"You came back!" Lyssa said, not letting go.

"I said I would." He bent down and picked her up.

She transferred her stranglehold to his neck. "I thought the Nothing might get you."

"You still have the pendant?"

Lyssa shook her head, no, and he eased her away from him a little so he could see her face. "Mrs. Aylford took it. She said this was better." With one hand, she pulled on a chain around her neck to show him a small silver cross.

"Hellfire and damnation!"

Lyssa's lower lip quivered, her eyes flooded with tears. "Don't be mad."

"Sweetheart, I'm not mad at you. Not in all the worlds." Weston tried to compose his face to hide a rush of anger and fear. Funny how the world went around. All the years he'd spent trying to get rid of that damned pendant, and now when he needed it, this well-meaning, totally misguided idiot of a woman had taken it. And that was the positive spin. He wasn't likely to forget that the apparently frail old woman who had stolen Vivian's Dreamshifter pendant had turned out to be Aidan.

"Lyssa, this is important. Do you know what she did with it?"

"Maybe she threw it away."

"Damn it." He paced the room, still holding the little girl, trying to think of a plan. He couldn't leave her here, that was certain. And the Between was dangerous, the Dreamworlds unthinkable. Venturing off without the pendant just made it worse. But he didn't see that there was an alternative.

Sure, he could call Flynne and insist that the child be moved. Ask for help getting back the pendant. Flynne would probably listen. But it wouldn't happen fast or easily, not with the way things were going.

A thudding came at the window. Lyssa squeaked and buried her face in his chest. Weston spun around, adrenaline pumping, only to see a big black bird on the window ledge. Crossing the room, he opened the window and the raven stepped in, the pendant dangling in his beak.

"Bob!" Lyssa squealed. She struggled to get down from Weston's arms and ran to stroke the raven's feathers.

Weston grabbed the pendant and nearly dropped it, his fingers encountering a disgusting coating of grease and what he hoped was egg white. "I guess you're good for something after all," he said to the bird grudgingly as he wiped goo onto his pant leg before hanging the pendant back around the little girl's neck. A moment of hesitation, and he left the cross alone. God would have no objection to the pendant, and the child could use all the protection she could get.

"There. Now, you trust me, yes?"

She nodded. Her eyes were disconcerting, luminous and deep. Weston tried to smile, failed, and went on.

"All right, then. I'm going to take you somewhere where you'll be safe from the Nothing, okay?"

"Your house?"

"No, not exactly. I'm not supposed to take you, though, so we have to be very quiet and secret, all right?"

She nodded, pressing the back of her hand to her lips

as if to keep the words in.

"We're going to play a little game," he said. "Come over here." He sat down on the bed, and she came to sit beside him, Bob the raven riding on her shoulder.

"What kind of game?"

"We're going to make a door."

Her eyes went to the door of the room. "There already is a door."

"A different kind of door."

"Don't you need a hammer and nails?"

"We're going to use magic. What do you think will be on the other side?"

She giggled. "Fairies."

"No, no, no, no. Fairies are tricky and sly and they pinch you and steal your hair ribbons."

"I don't have any hair ribbons."

"Your shoelaces, then. Or your teeth. Think of something gentle or something that will protect you. Okay?"

"Okay, how about..."

"Shhhh." He laid a finger over her lips. "Just think about it, nice and clear, while I make the door. And then we'll see. That's your job, to be quiet and to think."

He set her down, making sure to hold onto her hand, and closed his eyes. Let her be busy thinking about fairies or whatever; it wouldn't make any difference. What was in his mind was a different story, because whatever he was thinking about was precisely what they were likely to run into in the Between. So, no thoughts of the Nothing, or of fairies, or any of the other million and one creatures he did not want to encounter.

In fact, he didn't want critters at all.

So, he focused instead on peaceful and safe. A pool of clear water for drinking. A few small (and harmless) creatures for a food source. Maybe there could be a shotgun waiting for him in the Between, along with a pack containing all of his camping equipment. He ran through it in his mind: matches, cooking utensils, knife, power bars, canteen, tent, sleeping bag—make that two sleeping bags. His mind focused now on the Between, he created a door.

Lyssa's little gasp let him know he'd succeeded, although he would have known anyway; he could feel its shape and solidity before he even looked.

It looked at first exactly like the door he'd made in A to Zee, roughhewn wood, unpainted. A door that fit the memories of his frontier childhood. Only, this one also had a small cat door at the bottom.

Weston frowned. The doors of a Dreamshifter all looked the same, his father had said. Weston had only made a precious few in his lifetime, and they'd all been uniform. Useful. Strong.

Maybe the old man was wrong.

Lyssa looked unimpressed and excited both. "It isn't very pretty."

"Nope. But we don't need pretty." He looked at her again. "Lyssa, do you have a kitty at home?"

"Two."

He looked from her to the door, half expecting a kitten to stick its head through. Nothing happened, though. The door looked like any ordinary door.

"You ready?"

She nodded but reached up and took his hand. When he opened the door, she squealed with glee while he stood glowering at what he'd somehow manifested. There was his pool of water, all right. Trees for shelter. All of the other supplies he'd specified, including the shotgun.

Each and every one of them hanging out of reach on the back of a very large elephant. The creature had tusks, the ends of which had been dipped in gold. It was draped in fringes of gold and purple and equipped with a little riding platform on its back. Very high up.

Lyssa clapped her hands, then whispered, loudly, "I love elephants."

"You did this?"

"You said think of something gentle that would protect me."

She took advantage of his unsettled state to slip her hand from his and scamper toward the towering beast.

"Wait!" Weston ran after her. "You don't know if it's friendly." She eluded his outstretched hands and wrapped her arms around the massive front leg of the elephant. It flapped its ears, exploring her face with its trunk. She giggled and squealed.

"It tickles."

"Lyssa," Weston said, making his voice as firm and authoritative as he could. "You must come here. Now."

The elephant turned its head, just enough to focus one eye on Weston. And then the trunk came his way, wrapping around his waist and picking him up off the ground even as he kicked and struggled.

"Put him down," Lyssa commanded, then softened her voice. "Please. He's grouchy, but he's my friend."

A moment of hesitation, and then the elephant did exactly as she said, setting Weston gently back onto his feet and releasing him. A strong desire to drop to his knees and kiss the ground lasted for about ten seconds, driven out of him by a distant bleating sound. The sound came again, closer, accompanied by a tinkling bell.

A flock of sheep, he thought. Harmless. Possibly useful. But then he took a second look and his heart dropped into his boots. The critters were sheep-sized and woolly. That part was all right. But their legs ended in clawed feet, not hooves. Their lips were drawn back over teeth that were never meant for eating grass. Their ears were pricked forward, tongues lolling out. Wolf ears, he had time to think. Wolf tongues, wolf teeth.

The flock broke into a trot, and then a gallop, headed directly for the door still open into Wakeworld. There wasn't time to get through and close it behind him. He couldn't let those creatures loose on a house full of kids. Slamming the door, he scooped up Lyssa in one arm, picking up a stick in the other.

Something tapped his shoulder. Gray, flexible. A trunk. Well, the elephant seemed friendly and smart. Definitely a better option than ravening sheep.

"Up you go," he said, boosting Lyssa up as high as he could. She scrambled the rest of the way.

"Get out of here," Weston shouted at the elephant.

Instead, it bent one leg and came down lower to the ground, presenting its trunk as a step stool. The sheep flung themselves against the closed door in a cacophony of thuds, baaing, and ringing of bells. Not a second to waste. Weston stepped up onto the elephant's trunk and was lifted off the ground until he could vault upward onto its head. He was backward, but that was okay; he just had to keep his balance as the creature started moving.

The leader of the flock flung itself upward at the elephant's shoulder, only to be flung backward with a blow of the trunk. Its bell tinkled as it flew through the air, where it struck a tree and slid, crumpled and unmoving, to the ground. The bell went silent.

Smarter than the average sheep, the rest drew back, forming a circle. There were too many and they wouldn't be held off long. The elephant was big and had a weapon, but it couldn't fight off so many predators.

Weston scrambled for the gun.

"What's wrong with the sheeps?" Lyssa asked, clinging to one of the elephant's ears.

"Everything. Hang on and lie down flat, okay?"

He should have specified the type of gun and amount of ammunition. It was an old Winchester repeater. Fully loaded, that meant fifteen rounds. Which might be enough, provided he didn't miss a shot. Taking aim at one of the sheep, he pulled the trigger, hoping the sound wasn't going to turn their elephant transport skittish.

A hit.

The sheep went down with a hole drilled right through its skull, kicked its legs once, and didn't move again. As if it had merely been waiting for him to get situated, the elephant went on the offensive. Moving forward, swinging its trunk, it sent two of the sheep flying, one right, one left.

Weston picked off another from behind.

Real sheep would have scattered and fled by now. These regrouped. They also learned quickly. Avoiding the front of the elephant where the trunk was, they moved in from behind. One leaped at a rear leg, gashing the thick skin with its claws, climbing upward as if it were a tree trunk.

It was too close to take good aim, too far to bash it over the head. Weston pointed the gun in the general direction, hoping he didn't get the elephant by mistake, and fired. The sheep dropped off and lay twitching on the grass.

Apparently, no great harm was done to the elephant, which broke into an earthshaking gallop.

"Hang on!" Weston shouted to Lyssa. He was still sitting backward with nothing to hang on to. All he could do was balance on the broad back, clinging to the flimsy cloth that served as a saddle, try to keep his teeth from jarring together, and hope that Lyssa was able to keep herself on behind him. If he tried to turn around at this pace, he was going to be a goner.

The good news was that the sheep pack had given up the chase, at least for the moment, and were busy nosing about the fallen. Just before the elephant rounded a corner, the last thing he saw was one of the surviving sheep tearing into a dead one and lifting a dripping muzzle into the air.

Ten

"Vivian!" Zee shouted, flailing pointlessly to try to get close to the griffyn that held her.

She was alive and unhurt, struggling to break free. Zee had to reach her, had to help her, but there was nothing he could do. The remaining griffyn came at him and he fended it off with the sword, but barely. It shrieked at him and went for the defenseless Giant.

Callyn floated in the air not far off, eyes glazed, arms and legs spread out and motionless, the claws of the dead griffyn still buried in her belly. The blood had stopped spurting ,and Zee understood that it was too late to help her. The griffyn tore off a chunk of flesh with its beak. Zee lunged with his sword, but he was clumsy and ineffective, while the creature was in its element. Staying easily out of range, it darted in again.

He knew that the Giant was dead, that protecting her body was pointless, but he wouldn't allow her to be so violated without trying. He lunged again, and this time, the griffyn flew off, carrying a chunk of flesh in its talons.

Zee stared after it until his eyes watered. He had to go after her.

"Godzilla!" he shouted, just as something bumped up against him from behind. "There you are. We're going after her." He caught hold of one of the dragon's wings and pulled himself onto his back. "Where's Poe?"

He spotted the penguin, flying as fast as he could with his stubby flippers, and snagged him out of the air as Godzilla flew past. Even in zero gravity, the dragon's flight path was an insane zigzag that kept Zee's stomach lurching from one side to the other. At least they were moving forward, faster than he could have gone on his own. And maybe the dragon could actually see farther than he could and would be able to find their now-vanished target. He hoped so, because he had no idea where to search.

What did he know about giffyns? Not a thing aside from the useless fact that they were mythological creatures. Obviously, they were predators and dangerous, but there had been an intelligence there that seemed to make them something more. Would they have an aerie like an eagle, or a den like a lion? Did he start looking high or low? Since one of them had carried Vivian off, did that mean they'd keep her alive awhile so as to have fresh meat later, or had they just been avoiding a battle?

The air grew warmer as they flew, the ice and snow below them replaced by trees and thick green vegetation. A thin blue line of river cut through it all. Zee's eyes were in constant motion, looking for signs of the griffyns in the trees and on the land. He saw two deerlike animals walk out of a grove. A flock of grazing sheep. His heart lurched at a shadow overhead, but it was only an eagle.

Then gravity kicked back in. Zee's heart thudded wildly. The air itself seemed to press in on him from all sides. And the dragon dropped like a stone, Zee's fingers scrabbling uselessly on the slippery scales as he felt Godzilla fall away beneath him. Poe slipped from his grasp. They were free-falling, the earth rising rapidly to meet them.

Godzilla flapped valiantly with his good wing, swinging upward in a wild spiral. Zee hit the dragon's back with a force that dazed him. Poe landed off to the side and both of them careened over the scales. Zee managed to get hold of the penguin's flipper with one hand, using the other for balance.

No matter how hard the dragon tried, a crash landing was inevitable. Zee braced himself for impact, clutching Poe with one arm. He'd seen Godzilla crash before. If he wanted to survive, he needed to get well clear to avoid being crushed or spiked by accident. Just before touchdown, he flung himself sideways and into the air, rolling as he went. He landed on his bad shoulder, but the ground was soft and grass-covered and he bounced only once and rolled to a stop without any other injury.

For a minute, he lay still, letting the shock and pain drain away, catching his breath. Godzilla, at a fortunate distance, rolled over and pushed himself back up onto his feet. Poe shook himself and began preening his feathers. No danger to be seen, although Zee didn't for a minute believe there wasn't any. This was the Between. Something was sure to be lurking.

He got to his feet and reached for his sword with his right hand, stopped as the pain shot through him, and used his left. A look at the wound was not encouraging. It was still packed with dirt and had begun to fester. Red, hot, and oozing. Not good. Much as he wanted to stay in denial, he forced himself to look at the facts.

Any hope of reaching Vivian quickly was gone. Chances were good that she was already dead. If she were still alive, and if he could find her, he was going to have to fight to rescue her. For that, he needed to be as healthy as possible. So, much as the lost time galled him, he strode over to the river and began the painful process of cleaning his wounds.

Vivian woke to pain. Somebody was jabbing her hands and feet with tiny, burning pins and needles. It hurt. There was a tightness around her armpits, a sensation of flying. Her eyes flew open, remembering.

She still hung from the talons of the griffyn, only gravity had kicked in and the weight of her body was back, swaying with each beat of the giant wings. The air was warm, though, and the pain in her hands and feet was due to returning circulation. Below, the snow and ice had given way to a green canopy that looked like rainforest. They were descending, and when she saw where they were headed, she began to struggle, blindly and pointlessly. If the fabric that held her tore now, she would plummet to a certain death.

Which, she thought, might be preferable to the aerie for which they were headed. The nest was roughly constructed of branches and dried grass, lined with fur. Something glittered gold, but her entire focus was on the hungry beaks opening below. Babies.

They screeched in unison. Vivian stopped struggling and held perfectly still, not even daring to breathe. She willed the griffyn to keep flying, but the creature swooped low, opened its talons, and dropped her right into the nest. The instant she landed, she rolled into a ball, clasping her knees and hiding her face in an effort to protect eyes and vitals.

If ever she'd regretted not being able to shift into a dragon, it was then, right that minute. She grabbed for the penguin pendant and found it hanging heavy on her breast. Damn. That meant she was still in the Between and unable to shift anything. She had no weapons.

Holding the pendant in one hand, she tried to summon the Voice of Command.

"Don't eat me." The words came out high and squeaky and not commanding at all. She heard the babies approaching, knew those sharp beaks would tear into her flesh at any moment. Again she reached for the Voice, finding the strength within her, and this time knew she'd tapped into it before any words emerged.

"You will not eat me. You will carry me down to the ground and let me go."

Nothing happened. The mother griffyn continued to watch her. The babies edged forward. The sound of wings above drew her eyes. The other griffyn passed over the nest, something red and wet clutched in its talons. The babies increased their squawking, beaks open like a bunch of baby robins. When the meat dropped into the nest, they were on it so fast, Vivian didn't get a good look at it and was grateful. She had a sick certainty that she knew exactly where it came from.

The griffyn that had carried Vivian sat, catlike, on the far side of the nest, tail curved around her haunches, the tip twitching, green eyes intent and focused. Vivian scooted backward until she bumped up against the edge of the nest. She could see now that something was wrong with the baby griffyns. One of them had the eagle beak, but it also had whiskers and the round ears of a lion. Where its head and neck should have been feathered, it was covered instead with tufts of fur. Another had the eagle head part down okay, with the lion body, but only a small clump of feathers on either side where the wings ought to be. One of them, ribs protruding, lay perfectly still with its eyes half open, too weak to join the others in their feeding frenzy. Its thin sides barely moved with its shallow, rapid breath.

The mother griffyn approached the sick baby with feline grace, nudging it with her beak. The little creature's body flopped away from her without response. Again she nudged it, this time moving the baby toward Vivian. It looked like a lion cub, no sign of eagle about it at all, with the exception of a small sprouting of feathers where a cat would have whiskers. The eyes were closed. The head lolled from the neck with no muscle resistance at all; the eyes didn't open.

With a mournful sound more like a lonely cat than a great eagle or a lion, the mother griffyn nudged the baby again, this time all the way up into Vivian's lap. The little creature weighed no more than a kitten. Keeping her eyes on the mother's, Vivian tentatively ran her fingers over the soft fur. Something was wanted of her. There was an intelligence in the green eyes watching her that went beyond animal.

Still, when the griffyn opened her eagle beak and spoke, she didn't quite believe her ears.

"Mistress of the Doors, your magic Voice will not help you here."

Expectations and beliefs swirled and shifted in Vivian's brain. No reason why a mythological creature shouldn't be able to talk, and yet she hadn't seen it coming. Fear that the Voice hadn't worked combined with hope that a creature that could talk might be persuaded to let her go of its own free will.

Again the creature spoke. "The Between has gone wrong. You must set things right."

Wonder and anger competed for supremacy. Anger won.

"You killed my companion. Why should I help?"

Feathers lifted on the back of the griffyn's head. Her tail lashed side to side. "We do as we must. The babies were hungry."

"I saw deer down there. Sheep."

A growl pulsed in the griffyn's throat. "The land is ours. We do as we will."

"That seems to be working out well for you. What's wrong with the little ones? Is that normal?" Vivian gestured to the babies, done feasting now and watching her with eyes too intent for her liking.

The griffyn lowered her proud head. "Things

changed. The Between is not what it was. You must fix it."

"That's what I was trying to do. You interfered. You killed my guide. Now I will never gain entrance to the City of the Giants."

Green eyes narrowed and the griffyn clacked her beak. "You must not go there."

"Now you're giving advice? I need their secrets."

"Never there. The Queen will kill you or keep you captive. She will not share her secrets. It is to the Sorcieri you must go."

"I don't know how to get there. Callyn was going to intercede for us with the Giant Queen. And now you've gone and killed her!"

"We will carry you to the Sorcieri."

Vivian stared at the creature, dumbfounded. *Be careful, Vivian. All things have a price.* "In exchange for what?"

"You will heal the sick one."

And there it was. The catch. The little griffyn was barely alive. If it died—well, she only needed to look at the sharp beak and the powerful claws to know what would happen. Any chance was better than no chance at all.

"It is more dead than alive," she said. "This is no easy bargain you set for me."

The green eyes narrowed. "What do you ask?"

"You will also carry my living companion. He goes with me."

"The one with the bright sword? The Warrior? You ask too much."

Vivian shrugged. "As do you."

The griffyn drew back a little, sitting on her haunches and thinking. "Very well."

"All right, then. Let's go." No time to be wasted. Vivian stood up, holding the baby in one arm, and settled herself astride the griffyn's back. She buried her free hand in the feathers of the neck.

"Do we have a bargain, then?" the griffyn asked, turning to look at her. "Will you keep your end true?"

"I will."

The great wings unfurled and lifted, and in a moment, they were airborne. Another griffyn joined them, its beak and claws still stained with Callyn's blood. Vivian wanted to close her eyes but kept them open, looking for Zee, hoping against hope that the Between hadn't already killed him.

The river was warm. It was also thick with mud and debris and had an unpleasant greasy feel. Zee would have preferred crystal clear and icy cold. This water was only marginally cleaner than the dirt already in his wounds, and he hoped he wasn't making things worse by submerging himself in it. He also hoped there was nothing in the unseen depths that would attack him. Just in case, he kept the sword with him, telling himself he'd dry it thoroughly as soon as he got out, and the threat of rust was less than the threat of a water snake or crocodile with some sort of supernatural intelligence.

So far, though, nothing had attacked. The sky above was blue and clear with a few puffy, innocent clouds. The air felt tropical, warm and heavy with moisture. The unfamiliar trees were jungle-thick and wound around with vines, forming an impenetrable green front on both sides of the river. There should have been noise, Zee thought. Frogs, insects, birds. But all around him nothing moved. No wind stirred the trees. Even the river ran silently.

Godzilla rested on the riverbank, his good wing neatly folded, the broken one trailing. Poe, not bothered by the dirtiness of the water, was taking a bath of his own. His movements and Zee's splashing in the water created the only sound. Taking a good long look around to make sure nothing threatening was visible, Zee ducked his head under the surface, scrubbing at his face and hair in an attempt to clean away the ground-in dirt. He surfaced, clearing the water from his eyes.

A shadow passed over him, cast by something big and moving fast. Looking up, he saw griffyns. Two of them, descending directly toward him. Cursing, sword in hand, he splashed toward shore, more than ready to fight. Hopefully, they'd underestimate him based on the last encounter. That would make it easier to kill them. If he hadn't had his head under water, he might have seen which direction they came from.

The creatures landed but didn't attack, just stared at him out of golden predator eyes. They clacked their beaks and ruffled their feathers. One stretched, catlike, the tip of its tail twitching. Godzilla backed away, snorting smoke. Zee gripped his sword, standing just at the edge of the water and staring them down.

Maybe they would hate water, catlike, and he could use that to his advantage. All his instincts urged him to attack, to kill, but he waited, letting the griffyns make the first move. A small splashing behind him and Poe appeared on the river bank, waddling straight toward the griffyns on full steam.

"Poe!" he shouted. "Get back here."

The little penguin ignored him. One of the griffyns stretched out its beak with a cry like a hunting hawk. Damn the penguin. Zee started after him, ready for battle.

A familiar voice stopped him.

"Leave the bird alone; he's with me."

"Vivian." He couldn't see her; she was screened by one of the griffyns, but he would have known her voice anywhere. Poe had sensed her without her having to utter a word and was running now, neck outstretched.

He skidded to a halt when he got close, barely catching himself from tumbling beak over tail, hissing. The instant Vivian emerged from around the griffyn, Zee understood why. In her arms she carried a bundle of tawny fur. A long, feline tail draped over her arm.

"Zee, wait. They're not going to hurt us."

He stopped in his tracks, a little more graceful than the penguin, but not by much. She looked all right, not under duress. Had the creatures hypnotized her? Closer up, he could see that what she carried looked like a lion cub. As for the griffyns, their beaks and claws were all too sharp, and he'd seen them kill Callyn. They stood where they were, alert and watchful but making no move to attack while Vivian carried her burden down to the edge of the river.

She crouched by the water's edge and began dribbling water into the mouth of what looked like a lion cub. He joined her. Close up, he could see an odd burst of feathers sprouting on either side of the cub's jaws where whiskers ought to be. It was thin to the point of starvation and barely breathed.

Vivian caught his gaze but didn't speak, trying to tell him something with her eyes alone. "The griffyns are carrying us to the Sorcieri," she said in a voice that revealed nothing of her opinion. "The little one is surety."

He tried to keep his face as unexpressive as hers, even as dismay ran through him. The Sorcieri bit he understood, much as he didn't like it. No point going to the Giants without Callyn to intercede. And he had no trouble believing that the griffyns were intelligent enough that Vivian had had found some way to communicate with them. But the cub was barely hanging on. Knowing Vivian, it was more than just a bargaining chip to get them where they needed to go. She was personally invested in its healing; he could see it. And if it died, the griffyns would seek revenge.

"It looks like it's starving. Can't it eat?"

"Apparently, griffyns don't make milk."

"Well, hell." He stood a minute, looking from the woman he loved to the dying griffyn cub to the watchful creatures. He did not want to leave Vivian alone with them, but he also knew he couldn't protect her against two of them at once if the baby died.

"I'll be back. Don't go anywhere, okay?" He wanted to kiss her but wasn't sure how the present company would react, so he gave her a smile and hoped his eyes would say everything he was holding in.

"Where are you going?" she asked. Her face was a mask of dirt, eyes irritated and red. He wanted to pick her up and carry her into the river, washing it all away with his own hands. And then he wanted to kiss her deeply and relieve her of her clothing.

One quick touch of his hand to her shoulder was all he allowed himself, and then he was off, calling back over his shoulder, "Off to fetch some milk. Wait for me."

"Always," he thought he heard her say, but the sound of his sword slicing through vines swallowed the word.

Eleven

The mirror embedded in the dead tree just north of the seven mud pits was Kalina's favorite. The tree itself had been dead for long past a thousand years. Its bark was as smooth and glossy as stone, and she could detect no magic that had made it that way. But the mirror was special. Of all of the mirrors on the island, it was the most alive.

Running her hand across the glass, Kalina could sense the fingerprint of the maker. Jehenna, the cursed, last of the female Sorcieri. Kalina was not permitted to speak the name, and the Master would beat her severely if he knew that she looked into it, let alone touched it. Still, she could not leave it alone.

The other mirrors had been made by the Master, and the man who had been Master before him, and so on, back two thousand years. They, too, revealed things but were empty much of the time of all but the occasional creature sighting. Kalina didn't care much for griffyns and slime toads or the other creatures. Giants were interesting, but they never lingered close to the mirrors for long. She loved the dragons, but they had all left the Between.

As for the forbidden mirror of Jehenna, it was as close as Kalina could get to the mythical Kingdom of Surmise. She'd discovered Surmise in the secret books that the Master did not know she read, since he didn't know she could read at all. So much power, to be able to weave Dreamworlds into the Between. Kalina, who had never been off of the Island, was fascinated. What was Surmise like now that Jehenna had died? Had it altered, or did her power still bind it together?

The Master knew the answers, she was sure, but he never spoke of the place. Kalina suspected there was a collection of mirrors hidden away somewhere that reflected Surmise. Jehenna would have crafted them, she was certain, but she had never been able to find them. This mirror was as close as she could get. It showed the intersection of a heavily traveled path through the Between and the borders of Surmise.

Today, it was full of life. Human, dwarf, Giant. All sorts of creatures, all crossing into Surmise. Some of them were carrying bundles of possessions, or children. This was no wandering trek through the mazes, and they definitely did not have the look of revelry, as if there was a feast on the other end. All of them looked worried, and they moved with purpose.

Kalina put her hand to the mirror to adjust the focus and then snatched it back as the mirror went dark. In the distance, with a gurgle and a thump that shook the earth beneath her feet, the seven mud pits erupted, heaving boiling globules of mud high into the air. Small spatters stung her face and scalp and she bent double, shielding herself with her arms. The pits settled back to their usual slow, sticky boil, but when she turned back to the mirror, its surface was smooth, black, and unresponsive.

Kalina's heart beat fast but not with fear. The change had begun with the opening of the Black Gates and Aidan's entrance into the Forever with all of the dragons of the Between behind her. Of these things the Master spoke. But of the coming danger he said nothing. If he was aware, he kept it to himself.

She had been waiting, though. Waiting for the change that would take her away from here into a wider world. What it was or who would bring it, she didn't know, only that it was coming. She raced to the next mirror, hoping it would show her more. This one, embedded in the stone sweep of an old lava flow, reflected only empty sky. The one beyond was dark and unresponsive, and the last was fractured across its entire surface with a network of hairline cracks.

There was no point going back to the castle; the Master would tell her nothing and her brother was too stuck on following all the rules. Maybe the dreamflowers would talk to her. Not running now—the trees didn't like sudden movement—she followed the familiar path to the grove. The trees towered over her, a silent, watchful presence. They never said anything, didn't judge or offer opinions on her behavior or shortcomings, or the fact that she was a girl. On a good day, when there was not much to be done, she could linger her for hours, lying on the soft grass between the broad trunks, breathing in the smell of the dreamflowers and letting them carry her mind from one world into another in an ever-changing stream of consciousness.

Not today.

There was a darkness among the trees that made her glance up to be sure the sun was still shining. It was there, bright and round, with no obscuring clouds. An unfamiliar smell lay beneath the heavy fragrance of the dreamflowers, dusty and bitter. Wrinkling her nose in distaste, she looked around for its source. What she saw frightened her for the first time.

The vine to her right held six flowers in all, and five of them were dead. Not only dead but black and slimy. Small white worms crawled over the surface, sharing space with ants. In all of her sixteen years, Kalina had seen maybe two or three dead flowers, and never all at once.

The dead flowers had no stories left to tell. The other seemed normal enough, even though it shared a vine. She bent her face to it, breathing in, and caught a vision of a world that was all flowers, fields and fields of them. Over and through the floral scent she caught a whiff again of that bitter smell.

And watched in horror as the flowers just—went out.

A black shadow at the horizon, thin at first, but growing, expanding, moving toward her and consuming everything before it. The whole dream went black, leaving an emptiness in her brain where once there had been words and thoughts and other images.

She floundered there, unable to move or form a thought, trapped in emptiness; only a tiny spark of consciousness, the part that was purely Sorcieri, let her know that she should do something, take some action, before she, too, became nothing. But it was not strong enough to allow her to move or act, and she hung, suspended, waiting for what was coming.

Vivian waited by the river, dribbling water into the baby griffyn's mouth at intervals and watching, always, the place where he had vanished into the jungle. This was Zee, she kept reminding herself. He could take care of himself, could fight off anything that attacked him.

Unless the destruction of the Dreamworlds stretched into the Between. A million and one things could happen. She hated for him to go off on his own like that. She also wasn't happy about her own situation.

The griffyns weren't into small talk. They lay down in the grass, apparently resting, but this didn't deceive her. Their tails twitched and their sharp eyes didn't miss a thing. Poe stayed close to Vivian's side, but Godzilla crouched down in the grass between the griffyns and Vivian, restless and watchful. She didn't really think he'd be much protection if the baby died, and the little creature seemed to her to grow weaker by the minute.

She would have liked to take a bath, even in the muddy river water, but dared relax her guard only enough to rinse the dirt off of her face. It seemed like forever that she waited for Zee to come back, long enough to imagine a wide variety of painful deaths for him.

He came back, though, more or less unscathed, with a sheep slung across his shoulders. A second glance told her that maybe it wasn't a sheep after all. It had sheep ears, and wool, and the general shape was right. But its muzzle was bound shut with a length of vine and the feet, also tied, ended not in hooves but in sharp claws. The thing stared at Vivian out of a wicked eye.

Zee bent over and let the sheep slide to the ground at her feet, where it struggled to free itself. There was fresh blood on his face, his own, from a deep scratch across his forehead and the backs of his hands were torn and bloody.

"It's got milk," he said. "Bring the baby over here. I'll hold the monster down."

She just stared at him. "It's too weak to nurse, even under good conditions."

"You'll have to squirt milk into its mouth."

Vivian looked from him to the sheep thing. He grinned, that pure clear flash of joy that was purely Zee's, his agate eyes filled with light and a little something more. "Only in the Between," he said, laughing. "Fought off a whole pack of 'em. Getting this one alive took some doing."

"Um, Zee? I've never milked anything before."

"Easy. Just squeeze and pull. Or else you hold this

beast and I'll do it." He flung a leg over the creature's back and sat on it. Instantly it darted its head at him as if to bite, making a totally unsheeplike growling noise. Its legs thrashed in a frenzied attempt to scratch at him with its claws.

"That's quite all right. I'll let you manage that part." Vivian carried over the little cub and set it inside the bound legs, next to the udder. Under Zee's direction, she grasped a teat with her thumb and forefinger. It felt hot and swollen, with very little give. When she squeezed and pulled, nothing happened.

"Try again."

She did so, and this time a stream of milk squirted out and hit the limp cub in the nose. It sneezed. She squirted again, and this time a pink tongue came out and licked experimentally.

"Here." Zee tore a strip from the bottom of his flannel shirt and held it out to her. "Soak it, then squeeze into the cub's mouth. Easier for the little one."

Soaking the rag was easier than expected. And when she squeezed milk into the cub's mouth, it swallowed. Encouraged, she repeated the process again and again, until the little creature's belly was rounded and full. It yawned, stretched, and curled up in a ball with its tail around its nose and went to sleep. A real sleep.

"I'll be damned," Zee said. His hand settled onto her shoulder and stayed there, and she leaned her cheek against it, finding herself wishing once again for what she couldn't have. Time to just be with Zee. They could stay here in this warm grassy place by the river. Feed the sheep thing whatever it ate so it would produce more milk. Nurse the griffyn back to health.

With a regretful sigh she stood, with the cub in her arms, and turned toward the griffyns. "I have done what I can for now. It is time for you to fulfill your end of the bargain."

The mother griffyn padded over, lithe and sinuous as a lion, crest raised on the fierce eagle head. Vivian felt Zee tense; knew without looking that his hand had gone to the sword hilt. One false move and everything would blow up into bloodshed from which none of them would emerge unscathed.

She held her breath.

The griffyn bent its head to inspect the sleeping cub. A long moment passed.

"I will carry you. My mate will carry the Warrior. Time presses." The other griffyn came forward and both lay down in the grass, offering their backs.

Zee gestured at the sheep thing. "I can't just leave it to die," he said. "Are you hungry?"

The two griffyns exchanged a glance. "It would be food for the young. But time does not permit."

"Very well. If you will permit." Zee stepped away from the waiting griffyns, drew his sword, and sliced off the sheep's head with one clean blow. "Perhaps you will eat it when you return."

No answer from the griffyns, but neither did they attack, and Vivian drew a breath of relief mixed with regret. She knew the monster couldn't be released or it would attack, but it seemed twisted and wrong to use its milk and then kill it. No time to linger; no time for regrets.

"Poe," she called. "Let's go."

The penguin stayed a distance, looking warily at the griffyns. Godzilla huffed, snorting out twin jets of dark blue smoke. Zee went after Poe, scooping him up. "Come on, your chariot awaits."

The penguin struggled briefly, his feathers all puffed up, still hissing. The dragon lay down flat on the ground, chin on his forelegs, looking wilted.

"What's wrong with them?"

"Poe doesn't like predators. And your dragon is just jealous." She couldn't help the laughter, even as she pressed one hand over her mouth. The realization that the baby dragon had imprinted on the slayer was such a delicious irony.

"You're kidding, right?"

"He brought you here. Now you're choosing another ride."

"Seriously?" He looked from her to the waiting griffyn to the dragon, who managed to look even more mournful. "Surely he'd be better off not carrying the weight, what with that wing and all."

"Tell him that."

"You're kidding, right?"

She shook her head. "You know dragons. Give him a formal speech. Show him some respect. Last thing we need is a sulky dragon."

"Yeah, I know dragons, but I haven't spent much time talking to them. Oh, hell." He stalked over to Godzilla, hesitated, and then made a deep bow. "O noble sky lord, I am ever grateful for your service. For this time, I must cast my lot with the griffyns, but I owe you a favor in exchange."

Godzilla contemplated him for a long moment and then nodded and got to his feet, ready for flight. Vivian quelled a little tremor of unease at the promise he had made. Dragons did not forget such things, and she had no doubt Godzilla would exact some favor in the future. She stifled the misgiving and buried one hand in the griffyn's feathers, holding on to the cub with the other.

Zee settled himself onto the back of his griffyn, holding onto Poe. The penguin looked decidedly unhappy, but didn't put up any more of a fight. The griffyn ruffled and then smoothed the feathers on its head and neck, stretched its wings, and launched into the air. Vivian's griffyn followed. Behind them came the dragon, veering about in an erratic zigzag flight and narrowly avoiding a collision with the trees.

Twelve

Jared slept fitfully, falling into one nightmare after another, each time waking just long enough to remember that he was blind now and scarred before drifting back into sleep. The dreams were vivid and technicolor in a way his dreams had never been, as if making up for what he would no longer see by daylight.

It was impossible to tell the time. No passage of light, no clock, no ability to look outside and judge from the passing of the stars or the shifting of the moon, not even the ability to see dawn begin to lighten the dark.

It would always be dark.

In the last of his dreams, he stood in the garden where he had once killed a penguin with his sword and tried to rape the woman who rejected him. *No, not me. Somebody else wearing my skin and hair and speaking with my voice.* A man known in Surmise as the Chancellor, clothed in satin and jewels, enjoying the roses and the splash of the fountain and the way the sun made rainbows of the drops of water cast up into the air.

But then it all began to crumble at one edge, as though it were only a picture turning to dust. A tree developed a web of cracks and fell away, leaving nothing behind. No sky, no grass, no stars, as though a pair of scissors had cut through and simply removed it. A rose bush went next, the emptiness advancing and devouring all things before it. As it reached the fountain and the drops of water fell into nothing, he woke, heart pounding, drenched in sweat.

For a moment, he thought he had wakened into the dream itself, because of the darkness, but he could feel the bed beneath him, his hands tightening and twisting in the coverlet, and in a moment, he sensed the old woman at his side.

"Only a dream," she said.

He didn't know how to tell her that the dream was real.

The weight of her compressing the edge of the mattress let him know she was settling in. "Tell me. I know a thing or two about dreams."

A cool cloth settled over his sightless eyes. They didn't hurt, but the sensation was welcome.

"Are you a Dreamshifter?"

"No, never that."

He hesitated, not wanting to hear any homespun psychology about how he dreamed of what he had lost. And then he told her.

When he was done, she said not a word. He knew she was still there because he could hear her breathing, could smell a faint spicy fragrance that was not perfume, more a mixture of baked goods and gardens and flowers.

"What do I call you?" he asked, after a long silence.

"You may call me Grace, although it feels strange to be called so after all these years. It is past first light. Are you hungry?"

Jared shook his head. His stomach felt heavy and dull, and he doubted he would ever truly be hungry again. But she brought him a hot steaming cup which was almost, but not quite, like coffee.

"It's the closest thing to coffee I could manage," she said, and he heard her sip a cup of her own. "Times like this, I wish I was a Dreamshifter."

Jared remembered watching Vivian shift the killer chickens—the ones with teeth that wouldn't stay dead—into ordinary fowl. Changing the swords the gray men carried into nothing but sticks. And a small hope burned in his heart that if he could find her, she might do more than turn a bitter beverage into coffee. An instant later, the hope went out, because there was no reason why she should do anything other than kill him if she were to see him again. He had done nothing but harm her.

With the next breath, he dropped the cup of coffee and drove the heels of both hands into his eyes as a flash of light strobed deeply into his brain. Even with his eyes closed, shapes and colors moved and shifted. He shook his head, blinked, but the shifting patterns had nothing to do with anything around him.

"What is it?" Grace asked. There was a note of fear in her voice.

Jared couldn't speak. Gradually, as though somebody were twirling the dials on a pair of binoculars, the world came into focus. But it wasn't the room where he was sitting that he saw, and when he turned his head from left to right or tried to look down at his own hands, his own body, the picture didn't change.

What he saw was a large and luxurious chamber. Plants he didn't recognize flourished, growing up directly out of the floor and spreading, ivy-like, over walls and floor. A high bed with silken sheets of a dusty rose, other furnishings all shaped out of stone and then smoothed and polished to a high, reflective gloss. The scene shifted perspective rapidly, as if he had bent over suddenly to the right, even though his body remained planted where he had left it, his hands braced on either side of him.

"What?" Grace demanded again.

"Pictures. A room. Grand..."

"She's using your eyes."

"What?"

"You gave her the gift of your eyes. It's not taken figuratively around here. So, she took them and is making use of them."

"But how?"

"Magic. Much of it is lost, but when it comes to growing things, or shaping stone, or the healing of the body, they can do things beyond your dreams."

"But this isn't healing."

"No, it is an abomination, a twist on healing. Which doesn't change the fact that she's done it."

Again the room shifted, far too rapidly, and he put one hand over his mouth and swallowed hard against the resulting nausea.

"Are you going to be sick again? Here—take the bucket. Try to hit it."

"Everything is moving. Seasick. No anchor."

"Maybe this can be useful. What do you see?"

"Just a bedroom. Wait. Moving. Through a door and into a—I suppose an office sort of space. A long table and there are people there. Five of them seated at the table, each with a book. Standing at the end of the table is—I guess—a guard, he's armed and stands like a guard. Whoa—"

He put his head in his hands and swallowed hard, trying to ease the response to a sudden swoop of his vision that shifted his perspective to a place at the surface level of the table.

Again, he heard his own voice whimpering and despised his own cowardice. Zee would never whimper.

Footsteps moved off across the room. When he turned his head in that direction, nothing changed about his view, which was now mercifully static. A stone table. Five chairs. Five large books, five pairs of hands.

"Can you see any of the books?"

He shook his head. "No. They are all closed, the spines are turned away from me. It's not like I can shift my vision."

"Keep watching."

"As if I have a choice." He took the drink she put in his hand and swallowed without stopping to sniff or question. It burned, and he took another swallow, already feeling the heat begin to travel through nerves and muscles and release some of the tension.

The thought of his eyes being carried and used by somebody else made him want to scream and beat his head against a wall.

Only then, hands pressed against his eyeballs, did he realize something. There were eyeballs, of a sort. Not soft and giving, and completely without sensation. Touching one with the tip of an index finger, he felt it, smooth and hard. Glass, maybe. People had glass eyes. Something eased a little in him, that he might not be as much of a spectacle as he'd feared.

He raised his face to Grace. "What are they?"

"Just drink," she said.

"Tell me. Glass eyes, right? What color?"

"Green," she said carefully. Something in her voice told him that although the color matched the eyes that had once been his, there was more.

"Just drink," she said again. "And go back to sleep."

He took another long swallow of what must be a very potent brew. Already his head was spinning, and he lay back on the pillows. Just before he fell asleep, he thought he heard her say, "Sleep well. Be careful not to dream."

When he woke again, he was alone.

Surely Grace was just in the next room, or possibly

asleep. He listened, holding his own breath to listen, but heard nothing. No sound of somebody sleeping, or the turning of the page of a book, or the creaking of a chair.

Panic tore at him like a wild thing.

"Grace!" He shouted into the empty house. "Grace!"

Silence answered him.

It was a small cottage. If she were present, she would have heard him. Which meant he was alone in a strange world. How to find food or water, how to even find a place to empty his bladder— all of these things became urgent problems he didn't know how to solve.

Thrashing and floundering about on the bed, heart so loud now that he couldn't hear anything else, he managed to sit up, hopelessly tangled in sheets and blankets. The harder he thrashed, the tighter they bound him, and the more he panicked.

Too late, he felt the emptiness below him, nothing and nowhere to gain purchase or support, and he slid right off the mattress onto the floor. It wasn't a big drop and it didn't hurt him, really, was just enough of a crash to restore some level of sanity.

Slowing his breathing, he unwound himself from the encumbering bedding and then got carefully to his feet, stretching his hands out in front of him. Moving with slow, shuffling steps, he just kept going, hands out in front of his face, until he encountered a wall.

A wall was good. He could follow a wall to a door, and from there to the outside. Surely somebody would help him.

Or the Giants would just watch him die, little by little. Bloodthirsty race of beings, considering that they called themselves healers. He had to do something, though. Had to take some action. He needed a drink; he needed a bathroom. Sooner or later, he needed something to eat.

She'd come back, he told himself. Out to the market

or to run an errand. People did things. They didn't just sit around by blind people's bedsides all day. And blind people did things.

Hand on the wall, moving carefully so he didn't smack his shins on something low, he moved forward.

Without warning, the pictures came on again in his head.

Disoriented and queasy, he staggered and almost fell, just barely catching himself on the wall.

A wall that, according to his vision, did not exist. Crystal clear, he saw the Queen's throne room. Empty now of courtiers. Only five Giants standing in a half circle. Their heads were bowed, eyes downcast, and Jared was pretty sure they were looking at the Queen.

If he moved according to what he could see, there was empty space before him, no wall, the Giants, and then a long red pathway leading to outside doors. His brain fragmented at the discrepancy as his other senses reported the rough wooden wall his hands were braced against, the homespun carpet under his bare feet, the absence of any living being.

The conflicting signals to his brain were threatening his sanity. He found himself incapable of movement. He couldn't take another step when his eyes said one thing and the rest of his body another. At last he managed to slide down the wall onto the floor, where he took to rocking, back and forth, comforting himself with the sensation.

When the door opened and heavy footsteps shook the floor he was unable to stop, until a flat voice said, "Come. You're wanted."

Kraal.

"Go away." Outrage over the Giant's betrayal pushed back the panic and confusion.

"Unless you want her to have your heart out too, you'd best come now."

"You called yourself a healer!" Jared hadn't meant to shout, but he couldn't help himself. "You're a butcher. The lot of you. She can have my heart, and welcome. I can't live like this."

Kraal made a sound that might have been laughter. "You think having your heart out will let you die?"

"That's the usual way of things."

"And having your eyes out usually makes you blind."

Jared's whole body went cold with horror. There was no end to this nightmare. He could only imagine what she might do, the mechanical monstrosity she could make him into to come and go at her bidding.

Before he had more time to think, strong hands picked him up and carried him, not like a child in arms this time, but like some dirty object, held far away from the body. He was set down on what felt like grass, even though what he still saw was cool marble, and the half circle of Giants.

A splash of cold water over his head jolted him, made him draw a breath. More water, and then rough scrubbing of his face and hands.

"The clothes are beyond repair," Kraal said. "Where is Grace?"

"Don't know."

Despair made him stubborn and obstinate, and he volunteered no information. Kraal's hands clenched around his shoulders and tightened, digging into his muscles with an intense pain that made him throw back his head.

"All right, all right. I woke up. She was gone."

He felt the thud of footsteps moving away from him, a little silence, and then Kraal returned. "She's gone, all right. Come. Now."

Not desiring to feel any more pain, he gathered the remnants of his pride and lurched up onto his feet, swaying and dripping.

"I'm all wet. There must be clothes somewhere."

"No time." Kraal took his hand and Jared stumbled to keep up.

He kept reminding himself as he walked that what he saw was irrelevant, had nothing to do with what was really around him or where he put his feet. Still, he stumbled over an uneven place when his brain told him it should be smooth, began to fall and then felt the jolt in his shoulder as Kraal jerked him back upright.

There was no slow-paced movement this time; he had to trot, every step into the unknown, to keep on his feet at all. It seemed forever, and then there was an expanse of smoothness, the exchange with the guards, verbal only this time, and they were through the doors and into the throne room.

If anything, this made Jared's disorientation worse. He could see the part of the hall where he was now walking, but it wasn't where his vision was focused. And then they reached the circle of Giants, who stepped aside to make room for them. He heard the Queen's voice with a dangerous crystalline edge, "Where is the woman?"

Jared scarcely heard her, staring now at himself, and at Kraal beside him, but from all the wrong angles. He saw a man in bloody, wrinkled, sopping wet clothes. Disordered hair. Pale, unshaven face. And where the eyes should be gleamed two green stones, blank, without pupils. It gave the face an alien expression, like the carved Indian god he'd seen once with the gemstones for eyes. It couldn't be him, not really. He reached a hand up to touch his face, to run it over the rough stubble on his chin, and watched the hand of the man who seemed to be standing in front of him do the same. He blinked, and lids closed briefly over the stone eyes.

"She is gone, O Majesty. Gone in the night."

Dragging his attention away from his own appearance, taking advantage of a moment of sight, however skewed, and took in the appearance of the Giants. Their misshapen faces, usually stoic and expressionless, all carried an impression of shock. Kraal's was the worst.

"And the dreamsphere?" the queen demanded.

Silence reigned as the others all held their breath.

"Taken it with her. I did not take time for a thorough search, but the little box in which she keeps it is gone."

A sigh, like a gust of wind in trees, passed from Giant to Giant.

"She must be stopped. Must be found," one of them said.

"Perhaps the envoy should search for her rather than proceeding to the Sorcieri," said another. Kraal remained silent, his eyes watchful.

"Fools, the lot of you. She will be well beyond our reach already." The Queen clapped her hands together sharply. "Guards—gather a search party. Send them out in all directions. If the woman is found, she is not to be harmed, understood? Bring her back safely to me along with the box she carries. Do not, on pain of a long torture and a delayed death, tell any being beyond this room that there is a dreamsphere in that box. Understood?"

There was a sound of what might have been heels clicking together, and the backs of two Giants came into view, skirting the half circle at the base of the throne and marching side by side and in unison toward the doors.

"Now," the Queen said. "Our visit to the Sorcieri takes on a whole new urgency. You will leave before the sun passes Second Hill. I will now tolerate questions without reprisal."

A moment of silence.

A female Giant with jutting breasts and a scar running down the side of her face that looked like a seam in a granite cliff, inclined her head and said, "I do not understand why we are taking this human. He will slow us. He is damaged and does not seem overly bright."

"My name is Jared." He saw the lips move of the man that must be himself, heard his own voice in his own ears, and still didn't believe he'd actually said it.

The Queen, rather than pulling his heart out of his chest, responded with surprising warmth. "Even so. His name is Jared. You will treat him with respect. Not one of the rest of you has offered your eyes to me as bond. While it is not required that I tell you my reasons, I will indulge you this time. First, we assume that the Dreamshifter will go to the Sorcieri to try to gain entrance. Jared—you are betrothed to the Dreamshifter, yes?"

Not a time to quibble, Jared thought. He was pleased to see that his expression did not reflect the dismay he felt or reveal that he was lying. No eyes to give him away. "Yes, Majesty."

"So you are important to her. Valuable."

"A hostage, then," another of the Giants said.

"Hostage is a rude word to take with you on such a diplomatic mission. Let's call him a motivator."

Jared kept his face impassive, even as a small hope beat under his ribs. He knew full well that he had no special value for Vivian. If anything, she despised him. And where Vivian went, Zee went, and Zee would have killed him long before if it weren't for some ridiculous code of honor. But what he knew of Vivian was that she would try to save him, no matter how much she loathed him.

And if Zee killed him, well, that would be a mercy. At least he'd be out of this godforsaken kingdom of the bloodthirsty Giants.

"Is the benefit sufficient to the cost? I say we can still use him as a bargaining stone even if he is not with us." The female Giant again. Bitches apparently came in all sizes and shapes.

"Would you make promises you do not intend to keep?" Kraal now. "What happened to word as bond?"

"Bonds do not apply to the Sorcieri," another Giant said. "They have consistently broken theirs or twisted it like a serpent so that it seems to mean one thing and then another."

"Silence." The queen's word sliced into them all. "Would you argue with me? Would you put your wisdom before mine?"

Not a word. Not a breath. The faces of the Giants were frozen into unreadable expressions.

"Now. You will go to your homes and gather what you need for this journey. The human will go with you, and you will conduct him safely there and back. If you fail, your lives will be forfeit. I will send a scroll in the hands of Kurian. Kraal has already placed the human under his bond."

The female Giant stepped forward and a scroll appeared in her hand.

"Bear it safely. Present it only to the Lord of the Sorcieri. Now go, all of you. Out of my sight."

Watching himself and the throne room, Jared got his body turned around and began to walk without guidance from Kraal. *Like a video game. Use the joystick to move the avatar through the room.* It was a challenge, but his brain was beginning to make the connections that enabled him to see himself as outside of his own body, an image to be directed and moved around a screen.

A small triumph, to walk from her sight unaided, but it ended the moment the doors slammed shut behind him. A dark loss twisted him as he lost sight of himself, seeing nothing now but an empty throne room. He stood there, trying to make a picture for himself of the wide black marble with its embedded stars and superimpose it over the throne room, but he failed.

Kraal's hand descended on his shoulder, steering him forward, away from the palace and off on a mission the purpose of which he didn't begin to understand.

Thirteen

All day they flew, only stopping once for a break. Not so much so the griffyns could rest their wings, Vivian suspected, but because they were worried about the cub. They alighted on the banks of a river, where they all had long, cooling drinks. Poe dove directly into the water, and the dragon followed, splashing around in the shallows.

Vivian dribbled some water into the cub's mouth. He swallowed, then opened his eyes and mewed for food. Vivian didn't want to take the time to find milk again, but this time the male griffyn did the hunting, returning with a fat doe in his claws. The poor creature broke a leg when he dropped her and had four long, bloody gouges in her back.

It was too late to undo the damage, and one look at the watching griffyns dissuaded Vivian from objecting too vigorously. She took time to splint the broken bone to minimize the unlucky doe's suffering. This time, Zee did the milking, sending streams of milk directly into the open mouth of the hungry baby, which had struggled to sit up.

Godzilla finished off the deer, sharing out his meal with the griffyns. And then they flew, for what seemed forever, the mazes of the Between laid out beneath them in an ever-shifting kaleidoscope of color. At intervals, a sudden updraft or downdraft sucked at them, and whole sections of the Between altered in the blink of an eye.

Vivian was exhausted. The cub kept slipping from her arms as she nodded and drifted into a moment of sleep. Her lips were dry and cracked, her skin tender and burned from the constant wind. Her legs had begun to cramp. Just when she was about to call out that they were going to have to take a rest, they reached the edge of a vast body of water. It might have been either lake or sea; she couldn't tell.

A long, low-lying island lay not far ahead. Plumes of smoke billowed upward, turning the setting sun to an ominous red. One hill marked the very center of the island, and the lurid light reflected off the sharp towers and pinnacles of a castle.

"Is it under attack?" Zee called to her, leaning forward to see better.

"I don't think so."

Despite what her eyes told her, she felt that all was as it should be down below, including the rivers of lava that spewed out of gaping holes in the earth. A few more wingbeats and the sky before them lit up with a wonder that made her gasp aloud.

Like a laser show, if those colored beams of light could curve and dance at will, if they came in colors that human eyes had never seen. The play of light formed a canopy above the island, luminous, translucent, so beautiful that tears wet her cheeks. All fatigue and fear vanished. New energy flowed through her veins. Her heart beat with exultation and excitement.

From a distant place, she felt the griffyn's wings check, the forward motion falter.

"What the hell?" Zee said.

The griffyns circled aimlessly.

"What's the matter?" Vivian cried. All she wanted was to fly into that place of light and color, to the island that lay below.

"What do you mean, what's the matter?" Zee replied.

"Why are we flying in circles? We need to get to the island."

His griffyn was flying next to hers and she could see the look on his face. "Precisely the problem," he said, watching her. "In case you hadn't noticed, the island has vanished."

"It hasn't. It's right there where it always has been."

"I can't see it. And it would appear that neither can the griffyns."

Vivian let this sink in. "Can you see the lights?"

"Apart from the sunset and the stars, you mean?"

"No, I mean the light show, the way it dances..."

"No." He said it shortly. "Vivian, I don't like the feel of this place."

"It's crawling with magic," she said. Not unpleasantly, though. She could feel it playing over her skin, inviting her in.

She made herself stop and consider the possibility that she was the one under illusion, that something was sucking her in to a doom she couldn't even picture. But what other option did they have? They'd come looking for the Sorcieri, and all of her instincts screamed that they'd found them.

Leaning forward, she tapped the griffyn on the shoulder. "It's still down there, where it always was. They've just put a screening spell on it."

The feathered head with its dangerous beak turned to look at her, the amber eye questioning. "We sense the land below, but our vision is blocked by a spell."

"I'll direct you. The others can follow."

But then the dragon took it all out of their hands. With a call of what Vivian recognized as joy, he set out headlong toward the island, as straight as his broken wing would allow, descending all the while and making that sound of ecstasy.

"Come on," Vivian pleaded. "Just follow Godzilla."

The dragon reached the lights and Vivian caught her breath, her one fear that the enchantment would incapacitate anything that touched it, or act as a force field.

Godzilla flew on through, unscathed.

The sun sank lower over the sea. Soon it would be dark. Vivian did not want to be traipsing over that unstable land mass in the dark. The griffyns circled one more time and then dove. As they reached the lights, Vivian gasped in pleasure and astonishment, feeling their touch play on her skin as a sensual pleasure. Only a moment, though, and then they were through and descending, following the dragon, who was headed for a small grove of trees.

"Whoa," Zee said behind her.

"You can see it?"

"I couldn't. And then I could. What are we getting into here, Vivian?"

"The Sorcieri." Her words came out in wonder. "Magic, Zee."

"Jehenna was one of them."

This was not a question, and it jolted Vivian straight out of euphoria and directly back into reality. Jehenna was responsible for Surmise, but not in its current form. She'd seduced Vivian's grandfather to learn the ways of the Dreamshifters, had used their secrets to weave a web of a place that was neither Dreamworld nor Wakeworld. And she had subjugated both people and dragons into captivity and cruelty. She'd killed Zee's double and had very nearly managed to kill Vivian and get herself into the Forever.

If the Sorcieri were anything like Jehenna, then they were in for a world of trouble.

Magic.

Zee could feel it crawling over his skin, invisible and

irritating, poking at his eyeballs, sending out questioning little tendrils into his brain. With an effort, he could shut them out of his thoughts, or at least he thought he could, but it required constant effort. If his concentration slipped, if a battle broke out, then he wouldn't be able to keep this up.

Or if he slept. Or got too tired.

Maybe nothing bad would happen if the magic got into his brain. Maybe the Pope was Muslim. Completely aside from the question of mind control, magic made him useless. He remembered Jehenna using that Voice on him, the way his body had been forced to obey her commands even while his mind struggled to break free. And the dragonstone had seemed to have a will of its own, and look how that turned out.

No, he didn't like this place at all. The sooner they'd completed their business and could move on, the happier he would be. As soon as the griffyn he was riding touched down in a grove of trees, he slid off the furry back and tested the ground. It seemed solid enough, but he didn't trust it, didn't trust anything that hadn't been visible one minute, and was the next.

Vivian's lips were parted, her cheeks and eyes glowing, as she looked around at something he was unable to see. Happiness was a wonderful thing, but not if it came by magic. He was at her side before she dismounted, taking the weight of the baby griffyn in his arms, reaching up to help her down.

But she just sat, as if unaware of his presence, her expression rapt. Zee tried to follow her gaze, directed upward, but saw only an expanse of cloudless sky, moving toward night, and two bright points of light. Stars. Dark was coming and they were still far from the castle in a wild landscape.

"Vivian, come on. We need to get moving."

“Light. Light on light on light. Can’t you see it, Zee?”

“All I see is darkness coming. We’ve got to get to the castle, Vivian. There’s a lava flow between us and there. Looks like Yellowstone Park. One misstep—”

“It will be all right.” She shook herself, as though waking from dream, and brought her eyes down to meet his. Her brow creased as she caught his expression, and one hand reached out to smooth the line of his jaw. “It’s only magic, Zee.”

“That’s what worries me. Let’s go.”

She nodded, her face almost normal, and slid down, stretching stiff muscles. The mother griffyn blocked their path. Zee, on full alert, stepped between the creature and Vivian.

“Warrior, you do not trust us.”

Statement of fact. It wasn’t a question and he didn’t bother with any other response than to put his hand to his sword hilt. He didn’t trust one feather or strand of fur, not with Callyn’s blood still staining their beaks and claws.

“It is understood,” the griffyn said, with what looked almost like a bow. “You will serve her at the cost of your life?”

“At the cost of everything.”

“This is well. Beware the Sorcieri. Their magic turns and twists in upon itself. We mistrust this place and would be gone.” The eagle eyes shifted their gaze to Vivian, who stepped around Zee to stand beside him, the griffyn cub sleeping in her arms. “Our bargain is done. We will leave you here.”

“And the little one?”

“You have our trust.” And with that, both griffyns unfurled their wings and rose, flying upward toward the two bright stars in the darkening sky.

Zee wrapped his hand around Vivian’s and they set

off toward the castle on the hill, Poe at their heels, the dragon trailing behind.

"That way, I think." He gestured toward a grove of trees, thinking anything green and growing was likely to be safer than the steaming ground. The trees looked ancient, with trunks bigger around than the wrap of Zee's arms. Smooth silver bark gleamed in the shadow light. Green grass carpeted the spaces between them, wide enough for the dragon to move between them with ease. No undergrowth, no fallen leaves or branches or even sticks.

Some sort of vine with large, goblet-shaped flowers wrapped around a number of the trunks, giving off a sweet, lazy fragrance that made him think of drowsy summer afternoons of his childhood, with the buzzing of bees and the sweet heaviness of limbs and...

Poe butted his knees. He realized he was standing still, eyes closed, swaying gently. Shaking himself awake, he looked at Vivian, beside him. Her eyes were closed, her face peaceful. Zee squeezed her hand, called her name. "Vivian."

"Dreamflowers." She murmured the words without opening her eyes, her voice dreamy and dazed. He put his hands on her shoulders and shook her.

"Vivian!"

Her eyes flew open, a spark of alarm in their depths. "Better keep moving."

Zee felt better, having seen that touch of fear. She'd seemed enchanted and enthralled since before they had touched down, and it worried him. But she only took three steps before she stopped in her tracks beside a tree where several of the flowers on a vine were black and shriveled. A quiver ran through her, like a plucked string.

"What is it?"

"Dead Dreamworlds. Even here, Zee. We have to hurry."

He had no objection to hurrying, although the castle on the hill was not reassuring. The thing looked like it had grown straight up out of the rock, all angles and sharp points. Distracted, eyes on their goal rather than on the path, he very nearly stumbled over the body of a young woman.

She lay on her back, a cloud of night-dark hair fanned out around her. Her face was beautiful, pale ivory skin, a bone structure that he instantly wanted to paint, along with the perfect bow of her lip, the way her hair rippled back from her forehead, even the shape of the small, fine-fingered hand that lay outflung, lightly cupped as though to catch the starlight. A stone amulet, pure black, lay on her breast, attached to a silver chain.

Vivian, with a soft exclamation, sank down onto her knees at once, setting aside the griffyn cub. Zee, knowing her, waited for the usual doctor things. Checking for a pulse, listening for breath. But she did none of this. Her hands passed over the girl's face and breast, not touching, hovering, as though tracing something Zee could not see.

When she finally put one hand down and curled her fingers around the amulet, he wanted to shout a warning. *No. Don't touch that.*

"Wake up," she said, softly, clutching the stone in one hand, touching the center of the girl's forehead with the other. "Come back."

A breath moved the girl's chest then, not a sharp gasp but just an easy, regular breath. Her eyes opened, dark, deep eyes, taking in first Vivian's face and then Zee's.

"You've come," she said. If she'd been pale before, she was positively white now.

"Can you walk?" Vivian asked.

Putting a hand to the stone, the girl slowly sat up, a soft wonder crossing her face as she took in Poe, the dragon, and the griffyn cub. It mewed at her, and she reached out and stroked its head. "How did you get here?"

"The griffyns carried us."

"I must take you to the Master," she said, rising gracefully to her feet.

Although the words were spoken in a softly modulated voice, to Zee they sounded like a threat. "If he lives in the castle, we're already headed that way of our own free will."

Her wide eyes looked him over again, seemingly innocent and direct. Zee didn't need magic to know that she was anything but. He was worried that Vivian would fall for the ruse, but he needn't have.

"Who are you?" she demanded, and her words were sharp-edged. "What is your place here?"

"It is custom for you to speak first. I require your names to report to the Master." The girl's tone and posture were courteous and formal, a direct contrast to Vivian's rudeness.

"We will keep our names to ourselves. You know what? We've got important business with the Master. Enough of this. Take us to him."

"Not until you identify yourselves."

"You first." Vivian's voice was adamant.

The Sorcieri girl smiled. "Very well. I am the Master's daughter."

"And I am the Dreamshifter. This is the Warrior."

Zee let Vivian take the lead. Clearly, she could sense what he could not. A long silence fell, but then the girl inclined her head in a gesture of respect.

"Follow me."

As if she hadn't been lying apparently lifeless only moments before, the girl took off through the grove at a run. Zee scooped up the griffyn cub; Vivian grabbed Poe. Outside the grove, he wanted to slow down, to check each footstep before moving forward, but Vivian was ahead of him and it was all he could do to follow.

Geysers erupted in the distance. A lava flow ran across the surface of the earth not more than twenty feet from their path. He could feel the heat on his skin, was aware of a low-level quaking through the soles of his shoes. The path skirted around seven boiling mud pits, each making a sucking and bubbling noise, occasionally shooting a bubble upward, where it exploded into tiny mud drops.

Just beyond the mud pits stood a tree taller than anything Zee had ever seen, big enough around that seven men would never encompass that trunk with their arms outstretched. No leaves, only sharp, asymmetrical branches and bark that had cracked and split deep. It was so old that the wood had turned to stone, and embedded in the trunk was a flat, smooth surface, pitch black.

The girl stopped in front of it. "Jehenna's mirror," she said. "Until earlier today, it showed the intersection of a path of the Between with Surmise. And then it just went black."

Vivian sucked in a breath of dismay. Zee wanted to reach out to her but held back, knowing she dare not show any weakness in front of this girl who was much more than she let on. But his heart ached, both for Vivian and the worlds everywhere. If a mirror reflecting the entrance to Surmise had gone black, then Surmise itself might be gone, along with Vivian's mother and Prince Landon and all of the people in the kingdom.

He stepped up beside her under pretense of getting a better look at the mirror, pressing his arm against her shoulder. She leaned into him, just enough so he alone could feel it.

"You said it was near to Surmise," Zee said. "What does that mean?"

"Truly, I do not know. The Master will know. I will

take you to him."

"And if we don't wish to go to the Master?"

"Then I will go to the castle alone and tell him of you. He will send a search party. If you survive until he comes, then they will bind you with a spell and bring you forcibly."

"And if we choose to leave?" Vivian asked.

"You will leave only with permission."

It was a moot point, anyway, and not worth the arguing. One way or another, they were going to see the Master.

Fourteen

If anybody ever, for the rest of his life, expressed a wish to ride an elephant, Weston vowed he would shoot the idiot then and there. He felt a bit like he was in a rudderless boat on a choppy sea. A tall boat. One with no anchor. He tried talking to the elephant, asking her to stop for a minute, but she ignored him and kept right on walking. Bob alternately flew ahead or perched between her ears, like a hood ornament.

At least Weston had managed to get himself turned around to face forward, whereupon Lyssa leaned back against him, closed her eyes, and drifted directly off to sleep. He put a protective arm around her and made himself as comfortable as possible.

Which was not comfortable at all.

His legs were stretched too far apart, and as the time went by, his skin began to chafe from the constant side-to-side motion. Muscles in his thighs and lower back went into spasm. If he'd been more trusting, he might have curled his legs up and crossed them, instead of trying to ride a creature as wide as several horses astride. But it was a long way down and he was afraid he'd fall off and the elephant would carry Lyssa far away from him.

He was tired, though. As dark descended and they continued to move on, his eyelids drifted shut and jerked open and drifted shut again. This was no good. So, he took the rope from his backpack and bound both himself and the child to the harness on the elephant's back. In this manner he was able to adjust himself to a more comfortable position and to doze off and on.

He dreamed, in a disjointed, rambling sort of way, always waking to a sense of increasing uneasiness, thinking his dream had been important but unable to remember it. Finally, he woke to light, of a sort, filtering into his eyes, and a cessation of motion.

The Between had shifted to forest, deep, lush, old growth that made the cedar rainforest of the Pacific Northwest look like a well-tended garden. Vines wrapped around trees so tall and thick, they filtered out most of the light. There was only one way forward, a winding path far too narrow for the beast they rode.

He'd spent precious little time in the Between, and yet this place felt familiar. He examined the trees, the sky, the path, but saw nothing meaningful. Even so, his gut told him they were close to Surmise.

"Stand still, would you?" he asked of the elephant, as though she wasn't doing precisely that. Taking advantage of the opportunity, he untied himself and the yawning little girl and navigated the tricky task of getting them both down onto the ground, thinking about Surmise all the while.

An anomaly, his father had said. A thing that ought not to be, by rights, created by a sorceress named Jehenna who had done what none of the Sorcieri before her had managed to do—learn the secrets of the Dreamshifters. With that knowledge, and after also enslaving a dragon, she was able to craft a space that was neither Dreamworld nor Between. Here, elements of both could exist. Humans who found their way into Surmise through the Dreamworld were not trapped, precisely, but a double was created, a second self with its own thoughts and memories and behaviors.

The result could be a lifetime of reoccurring dreams, an ongoing feeling of déjà vu, with the dreamer always sensing there was something beyond their rational understanding but not realizing they had another self in an alternate reality.

Surmise, under Jehenna's rule, had been a dangerous place. Mind control. Dragons in captivity, fed by slaves and the children of slaves. All of this changed by a combination of forces involving Vivian, her dead grandfather, and Zee. Or so Vivian had said. Whatever it was, with the Dreamworlds dying left and right and the instability of the Between, it was going to be the safest place he could take Lyssa.

Traveling with a child provided complications. Lyssa woke crying for her daddy. Once he'd managed to soothe her, she was hungry, she was thirsty, she needed to pee. What did he know about any of this? One thing at a time, he managed to get her squared away. This meant another good-bye.

"We can't take the elephant with us, Lyssa."

"She has to come!" A sheen of tears in her eyes gave him warning and tightened his stomach in a knot.

"Look, child. We are going that way. Ella is not going to fit between those trees."

"Then we don't go that way."

"We have to go that way. It's the only way to go."

"I don't want to." She stomped a little foot, face crumpling.

The elephant stroked her hair with its trunk, for all the world like a caressing hand, and the child turned and wrapped her arms around a front leg, clinging and sobbing.

Weston felt like a monster. Maybe Lyssa was right. There was no guarantee that this path led to Surmise.

Nothing but the feeling in his gut that they needed to go that way, and that they were running out of time. Years of wilderness living, of guiding hunters on expeditions in search of dangerous trophies, had taught him to trust his gut.

"Ella has to go home to her family," he said, after a long minute filled with tears and sniffles. "She very nicely gave us a ride, and she loves you, but she doesn't want to go to Surmise. Do you?" he said to the elephant, trying to look up into its eye.

The elephant, he swore, gave him a condescending look. Bob flew down onto Lyssa's shoulder and buried his beak in her hair.

Weston threw his hands up and found himself lecturing both elephant and bird. "Look—you both know I'm right. She's not safe here. Things could shift at any minute. If you want to try to blaze a path through those trees, Ella, you just feel free. Or maybe you know another way to get to Surmise. Maybe you could help a little."

The elephant snorted, ruffled the little girl's hair, and then gave her a push toward the path with her trunk.

"Hey!" Lyssa said. "Cut it out."

This time, the elephant gave her a gentle swat on the bottom.

"Ow!" Lyssa covered her bottom with her hands, scooting along the path without realizing what she was doing. The raven *kronk*ed twice and fluttered up into a tree, then flew to another farther along and *kronk*ed again. The uneasiness that had been growing in Weston's breast burst into full-fledged knowing.

Too late. The ground began to tremble beneath his feet. He grabbed Lyssa, abandoning gentleness, and started running. She kicked and screamed and fought him, her flailing fists surprisingly effective. The shaking of the path beneath him increased, and he ran for it, flinging her up over his shoulder to leave one arm free for balance.

All along, he'd felt the threat building, just hadn't understood what it was. Still didn't for sure, just had an undeniable driving belief that if he didn't run fast enough, they were going to be cut off from Surmise.

The path beneath him felt like Silly Putty, his feet sinking into what looked like solid ground and sticking, slowing him down, holding him back. He heard the elephant behind him trumpeting, the child screaming, "Ella, no!" But he didn't stop, even when the level path ahead of him curved up into a hill.

He scrambled up it, using his one free hand to grab hold of branches and roots to help pull himself upward.

Lyssa had stopped fighting him and he shifted her again so she rested on one hip with her arms around his neck, squeezing so tight he could hardly breathe. His heart felt like it was going to burst, every breath burning in and out of his lungs. There was a stitch in his side, and his legs were cramping. He was too old for this. Probably going to have a heart attack or something, but then, miracle of miracles, he'd reached the top of the hill and there was a clear path downward, not too steep, and at the bottom he saw an opening in the trees, and a broad, paved road, and a glimpse of a castle.

There was also a dream door, open, and through it a darkness he could never have imagined. This was Lyssa's Nothing. He knew it. And they had to get past it in order to reach safety. Down the hill he ran, as if all the hounds of hell were on his heels. He felt the sun go out, the sudden silence as the noise of every insect, every bird, every breath of wind was suddenly cut off.

A few more steps, he told himself. Just a few more.

And then his ankle turned as he stepped in a depression. Momentum and Lyssa's unbalanced weight pulled him forward and he was unable to catch himself. He was falling toward the open door and it was sucking him in. As he tumbled forward, he got his hands on the child and flung her away from him and toward solid ground.

He felt the shift as he passed through the dream door, but where he should have struck the earth with a jolt to knees and shoulders and hands, there was only emptiness. His eyes flew open to a darkness so vast, it made midnight on one of his beloved mountains seem bright.

So many near misses, and death had caught up to him now.

His brain softened, grew foggy around the edges as even sensation faded away. The last word that stayed with him was a name.

Lyssa.

And then that, too, was gone and there was nothing.

The unraveling of the worlds tore at Isobel's heart and teased the edges of her fragile sanity. She was not quite a Dreamshifter but should have been. Jehenna had stolen that birthright from her, along with every hope or chance for a normal life. She had just enough awareness of the unseen worlds to feel the wrongness without any ability to define the problem or engage in a solution. In Wakeworld, she had been broken and twisted, in and out of mental hospitals. She'd lost track of the number of times she had tried to stop the constant fracturing of time and place by shedding her own blood.

Surmise was the only place she was whole, and now Surmise itself was under threat. If it unraveled, then there was nothing left for her but madness or death. As for Landon, who was more to her than her own life could ever be, he was tied to Surmise in an even deeper way. He'd been born in a Dreamworld, one that Jehenna had woven into the fabric of Surmise.

He was older than he appeared, as was Isobel. Long

hours in the Dreamworlds slowed their aging, and the recent demands on Surmise had required much more time out of their refuge. Isobel could feel her bones growing more fragile. Each morning, the lines in her face were deeper and there was more gray in her hair. She tracked the same process in Landon, yet the loss of eternal youth seemed a small thing in comparison to all that was wrong in the Between.

Refugees had begun to trickle in about a week before, with whispered stories of Dreamworlds gone dark, of the Between turned upside down. They came in every size, shape, and age imaginable, anything that had ever been dreamed by one person or many over the course of time. Surmise drew them with the promise that it was something more, a place not subject to the devastation falling elsewhere. So far, this had proven to be true.

Refuge, Landon made it clear, would be granted to all, but there had to be rules. Some of the wanderers did not play well with others. Saving the worlds was one thing; allowing their denizens to eat, maim, crush, or destroy those from other worlds would not be allowed. While he worried about martial law and housing refugees in a way that was least likely to result in bloodshed and disaster, Isobel was left to her own devices.

In an official capacity, she had taken it on herself to oversee food and clothing, to make sure the sick and wounded received medical care. Mostly, that meant putting good and efficient people in place to manage these things. Overseeing them was little more than a formality.

On the day everything changed, she had gone to sit in the garden by the fountain, letting her fingers dabble in the pool, listening to the endless murmur of the falling water and letting it soothe her into a state half awake, half dreaming. This was Landon's world and was of her own creation. Dreamed into being by a lonely teenage girl with the latent power of a Dreamshifter, bound into the web that made up Surmise by Jehenna's machinations. Aside from Landon's arms, this was Isobel's favorite place, and she often took refuge here to think or dream. No peace today, though, not with the ongoing lines of disharmony from the Dreamworlds.

So much danger and darkness. Vivian was out there somewhere, trying to save the worlds, while Isobel sat and did nothing. This gnawed at her, along with the constant knowledge that she had not been a good mother, whether it was her own fault or not. The daughter of a crazy woman, in and out of the hospital, always playing with sharp objects—it couldn't have been easy. And now Vivian was the Dreamshifter, faced with the task of sorting out this mess.

Isobel's unease on this day had reached a barely tolerable intensity, even here by the fountain. She needed to know what was happening. There was a way. It was dangerous, and she hadn't allowed herself to pursue it since she'd found herself safe in Surmise. But it was her only access to magic. Closing her eyes, she let herself drift in the old way, her mind running along the fracture lines. That's where the danger lay, side by side with possibility.

A darkness wound through everything. A bitter scent underlay the perfume of roses. A slight disharmony marred the sound of falling water. She could very nearly feel it swirling beneath her feet like a river made of emptiness rather than water.

The danger was closer than they'd thought.

She must tell Landon. When she opened her eyes, it was to the horror of knowing that what she felt was real. A wall of blackness approached from the far side of the garden, rolling toward her.

Her feet refused to move. She stood staring at what was coming, making no move to save herself. Helpless, as she had always been, and nobody there to protect her. It came to her that she need not always be a damsel in distress. She had no power, no magic to close doors or move among the worlds, but she had feet and a voice.

She was running before she knew she'd made a choice. Past the fountain, along the path through the rosebushes, through the weaving she could faintly feel that bound that Dreamworld into Surmise. There she stopped and turned. If the boundary didn't hold, there was no point in running, and she wanted to stare her death in the face before it took her.

Green grass beneath her feet. Six inches in front of her toes, nothing. If she reached her hand out, she would touch it, but her whole being shuddered away from the thought. Turning her back, she walked, with dignity and purpose, away from the nightmare and into the crowded streets surrounding the castle. The sight of her running and frightened would only invoke panic.

She knew she needed to find Landon and tell him, but first she would assess the damage. There were other worlds woven into Surmise. What of those? So, she kept herself to a sedate walk, as if out for exercise, past the castle, out into the field.

A moment, she hesitated. If the field was part of a Dreamworld, just as the garden had been, it could be wiped out at any time. One foot on the grass, she felt for tremors and that sense of wrongness, for the whisper of a crossed dream barrier on her skin. It all seemed solid enough, integral to Surmise, and she proceeded across it.

About halfway across the field, when she judged herself far enough away from onlookers, she lifted her skirts and ran. On the far side, there was a main thoroughfare into Surmise that had been stable for longer than most of the paths of the Between. Five Dreamworld doors opened onto it, just outside the borders of Surmise. Fear pumping adrenaline and driving her forward, she half flew across the grass. And stopped with a cold understanding that for once, the actual danger was greater than her fear.

At the edge of the meadow, where there should have been a wide thoroughfare, there was only a wide, black emptiness. Her mind reeled away from it, from all the resonances of the darkness that had sucked at her soul during the years she had been insane. So many times she had tried to kill herself before it came for her at last, and now here it was, caught up with her. Not a mirage or a hallucination but real.

And hungry.

It wanted more. Sucking at the walls of Surmise, waiting.

It called to the darkness walled up within her, offering a complete and final end to every heartache, every worry, every broken dream or unfulfilled desire. Give them up, lay them down.

Unbecome.

Landon. Vivian. Duty to Surmise.

She ran over the litany in her head, but all of her loves seemed paler now, leached of color and warmth by what waited. Slowly, she took another step, so focused on the dark that she startled and leaped aside when a voice spoke from nearly underfoot.

"The Nothing wants you."

Isobel looked down into the face of a child, tear-stained and grubby but calm. Wide blue-green eyes, a tangle of chestnut curls. A big black raven perched on her shoulder, and the look he gave Isobel was both inquisition and warning.

"What are you doing here?" Isobel asked. "Where are your parents?"

"The Nothing took everybody," the child said. "Even Ella."

Keeping an eye on the raven, which clicked its beak at her and ruffled its feathers, Isobel knelt down in the grass. She'd never been a very maternal woman. One of her regrets was that she had been unable to give the sort of easy, automatic love to her daughter that she had seen from other women. The unthinking caress, the hug. This child must be in shock, must need comfort, but instinctively she realized that caresses would be unwelcome, and that snatching her up and carrying her away from the danger would be the wrong action.

"Who is Ella?"

The child's curls tumbled into her eyes. Isobel wanted to smooth them, to wash away the tear stains. An unexpected warmth made her chest tighten.

"Ella gave us a ride. And then the Nothing took her. And Weston."

"And who is Weston?"

"He brought me here."

The child's right hand clutched something on a chain around her neck, so tightly that her knuckles were white.

"From where?" Isobel asked, carefully.

"The police. I was frightened of the Nothing. He made a door. He said we would be safe here, but he lied."

Isobel glanced behind the child and shivered. "Not a lie, I think. Here, you are safe. He was not quite fast enough. Can you show me what you have there?"

The child's eyes searched hers, not quite trusting. "You're a stranger."

Gods. She was not equipped for this. "Not precisely," she said after a moment. "My name is Isobel. My father was a Dreamshifter and I am a princess. Who are you?"

A long hesitation. "Lyssa," the child said, finally. "Do you know the lady?"

"What lady, child?"

"The lady with the pendant. Like this but with a

penguin." Opening her fist, the child revealed a pendant shaped like a raven in a dream web. Isobel put her hand to her heart, feeling it lurch and flutter.

"Vivian," she murmured. "Where is she, Lyssa? Tell me what you know."

The little girl shrugged. "I saw her in all the dreams before the Nothing came. Weston said she was going to fix it."

"And did Weston say where she was?"

Lyssa shook her head. "He told the policeman that she was in the Between somewhere, and he didn't know how to find her."

"And then he brought you here? Where's your mother?"

The child clamped her lips tight shut and shook her head, but her eyes brimmed with tears and her chin began to quiver.

Isobel glanced up at the empty black vacuum so very near and held out her hand. "Will you come with me?"

"I'm not supposed to go with strangers."

"I'm not a stranger. I'm Isobel, remember? Wasn't Weston a stranger?"

Emphatic shake of the head *no*. "The policeman said I should talk to him."

"Well, and if I tell you I'm Vivian's mother, and that I know all about her pendant, does that make it different?"

"How do I know you're telling the truth?"

A good question. Isobel found a sharp stick and used it to help her gouge a circle of grass down to black earth. She drew a quick dream web and then the shape of a penguin. "My father gave it to her when she was still a little girl, just about your age."

"What did she do?"

"She tried to hide it from me."

"But you saw it?"

"I saw it." Saw it, and ignored it, and was wildly jealous of it. She'd never talked to her daughter about what it was she carried, or what it might mean, or told her any of the dark secrets that might have saved her so much heartache, might even have prevented this current disaster.

"I wasn't a very good mother, I think. Now, will you come away with me, before that blackness sucks us in?"

The child continued to look up at her, assessing, judging, and Isobel had begun to think she was going to have to pick her up and drag her away screaming and kicking when the raven stretched its wings, poked its beak into the child's hair, then fluttered over to Isobel's shoulder. She felt the claws tighten, smelled a faint dusty smell of feathers.

Lyssa got up and held out her hand. "I guess. If Bob thinks you're okay."

"Bob is the raven?"

The little girl nodded. The raven *kronk*ed in affirmation. Well, there were stranger things. Isobel took the extended hand and clasped it in her own. She couldn't remember ever walking so with Vivian, the small hand warm and confiding in hers. So many chances missed. So many mistakes.

Fifteen

At the door to the castle, the Sorcieri girl turned to wait for them. Her long hair was a wild dark cloud, her eyes bright, cheeks flushed. She had an ethereal quality, like starlight or quicksilver, that made Vivian feel common and heavy. She caught herself watching Zee's face to see how he reacted, all the while berating herself internally for the pettiness of jealousy.

Zee remained impassive, his eyes watchful.

"Give us your name," he said. His voice was flat and final.

Vivian caught her breath, recognizing the tone and knowing it meant trouble. She was about to try to tell him what names meant here in this place, the power they bestowed, and then took another look at his face and realized he was fully aware of that.

"You don't need my name to do whatever you will," he said. "I have no power to harm you. But you hold great power over us and we have no reason to trust you."

"Perhaps you have no power," the girl said, looking up at him from under long lashes. "But she does. If I whisper my name to you, do you promise to hold it secret?"

Vivian held her breath. So much depended on this moment. Nothing this girl did was by accident.

"Can't make that promise," Zee said. "We have no

secrets between us."

"Very well. And I will not answer for the consequences of your choice. Forget not that I offered to tell you." She turned and murmured a word in a language Vivian didn't understand. The heavy doors, carved from solid slabs of oak and bound with iron, swung silently inward.

Solemn now, with a curtsy worthy of a Disney princess, the girl intoned, "I bid you welcome to Sorcerer's Stone."

Carrying the griffyn cub, she slipped through the open doors and vanished, leaving them looking into the castle, hesitant to enter despite the invitation. Sorcerer's Stone was dark, dank, and seemingly empty of all but spiders and swallows. A few wooden torches smoked and sputtered in holders along the wall, illuminating stone walls slick with green slime. Puddles of greasy water covered the floor and it stank of decay.

Illusion. Vivian could sense it but was unable to see through it to what was really waiting for them. The edges of the spell flickered at the edges of her consciousness, just out of the reach of thought. There was a hiss of steel on leather as Zee drew his sword. She heard it as if from a distance. Saw him step across the threshold, Poe right on his heels. *Don't*, she wanted to say. *Danger.* But she would have to step away from the spell weaving to find access to speech, and she was so close.

Godzilla hesitated in the doorway, snuffling in the air and snorting smoke out of his nostrils. He took a step forward and the weaving tightened. Vivian could feel it as pain in her head, as if with each step the dragon took invisible strings yanked at her brain.

Danger.

"Godzilla, wait!"

Too late. A length of vine detached itself from the

door and reared up like a snake. The dragon flapped its wings and scrambled to accelerate, feet sliding on the damp, slippery stone. The vine snapped upward at the trailing wing, embedding a spike into the flesh. Godzilla flapped his good wing and skidded forward, dragging the vine with him.

Vivian, head pounding now in earnest, took a step toward the door. Another length of vine reared up, weaving back and forth like a cobra. It wanted to keep her out; that much she understood. Something hardened in her will. Fear vanished. The pain eased. It was as if a knot somewhere within her, always tied tight, suddenly eased.

She pointed a finger at the writhing vine and commanded, "You will let me pass."

The thing stopped, vibrating but holding its position.

Without taking any care to skirt it, Vivian walked past, head held high. "Release the dragon," she ordered, and the vine fell away.

Godzilla scrambled and slid forward to butt up against Zee, very nearly knocking him over. Vivian followed more slowly, a quiet glow of anger lending force to her will. The vines had been triggered by a premade spell, magic that called to magic. But there was a power behind the illusion, and it was waiting for her to declare herself.

"I've come to speak with the Master!" she called out, surprised by the level of command in her voice. "I know this room is not empty. Drop the spell. We have traveled far to meet with you, and our business is urgent."

Silence, but it was a listening silence.

"Were it not for me, your daughter would lie dead down in the grove. Does she hold so little value to you that you cannot even extend the courtesy to hear me?"

A ripple of thought passed through the silence, beyond her ability to read. And then, like a sunrise, came the light, one slow ray at a time, tinged with pink and gold.

No more spiders and slime. They stood in a high-vaulted room with an impossibly large chandelier overhead bearing at least a thousand candles, each shining through a crystal prism. As the light grew, the room turned to rainbows, playing over a floor inlaid with intricate designs that tricked the eye, seeming to create patterns that vanished and spun.

Vivian tore her eyes away. Zee stood staring down, lips parted, eyes moving as if following the lines, mesmerized.

"Hey."

He didn't move, didn't respond. She tried again, louder. "Zee. Close your eyes."

Still, he didn't move.

"Nicely done, Master," she said, looking up, searching through the moving rainbow world for the mind that was controlling all of this. Still not real. "Now, enough of games. Show yourself."

With a burst of alarm, she realized she'd let the Voice of Command slip into her words. Excellent. Nothing like threatening a man who was powerful enough to crush her like a bug without lifting a finger.

The rainbow light swirled around her, laying itself out in a path across the floor. Nudging Zee one last time to see if she could shift him yielded no results. "You coming?" she said to Poe and the dragon.

Poe hopped over to her, bright-eyed and unruffled, and she wondered whether the magic affected him at all. Godzilla looked anxious and unhappy. He nudged up against Zee. A faint burst of static came through the dragon channel from her inner dragon, so terribly weak but still alive. Anxiety, loyalty, an offer of protection.

"Fine. Take care of him," she said aloud, and set off to follow the path laid out for her.

Light swirled and shifted at her feet, moving across

the hall and into a narrow passageway. For a moment, Vivian hesitated, looking back at Zee, who stood as she had left him, oblivious. He was going to be furious that she'd gone off on her own, but there was little he could do to help her here, and nothing she could do for him until she managed this confrontation. Godzilla might offer him some slight shielding from the magic, possibly even protection.

For now, the best she could do was to go on.

Taking a deep breath, she followed the light. The passage was so narrow, she could brush the walls with the fingers of both hands if she lifted them only slightly, low enough that Zee would have to crouch. Godzilla would never fit. Which meant she was fully on her own, with no help.

Except for Poe, who hopped along in front of her. He had saved her a time or two, she reminded herself. And he definitely saw things to which she was blind.

The passageway itself could easily be just another illusion, but she didn't think so. It felt familiar, one of the labyrinths she'd walked in so many nights of dreams before she came into her own as Dreamshifter. In fact, she might have mistaken it for one of the winding paths of the Between if she wasn't fully certain that she was on the Sorcerer's Island.

And then the light went out, leaving her in pitch darkness.

Not the first time. The dungeons of Castle Surmise had been completely dark. That journey seemed so long in the past, so far away, as if she'd been years younger. Only a matter of weeks, in reality. And so much had changed since then. Jehenna was from this place, she reminded herself. Would have grown up here, although the idea of the sorceress as a child stretched her imagination to the limit. Patterns would likely be repeated.

She wasn't frightened, she realized. Her hands were steady, her heartbeat only a little fast. And a rusty, little-used part of her brain itched in an almost physical way, as if it wanted to be stretched and made use of. The fingers of her right hand tingled in sympathy. If she could connect the itch with the tingle, what would happen?

Caution dictated that it was best not to know, but curiosity and a physical need, as compelling as a sneeze or a cough, drove her to make the test. There was a sensation of something joining, completing, and then the fingers of her right hand began to glow with a soft blue light.

Testing, she tried to undo what had been done, to turn off the light. It only glowed brighter. Perfect. Practicing magic without any sort of instruction was bound to lead to trouble. At the same time, a joyful little buzz filled her chest, a sense of something done that had needed to be done, of completeness.

With the aid of the light, she could see passages branching off from the one she followed. She ignored them all, still walking more by what she could feel than by what she could see. There was an overarching power behind everything here. The minute she'd set foot in the castle, she had sensed it, but it had taken a while to fully get a sense of where it stemmed from. Taking one slow step after another, using her glowing fingertips to be sure there was not some great chasm underfoot, keeping one hand pressed against the wall for balance, she worked her way forward until she came to a dead end.

Her eyes told her it was a solid wall made of stones mortared together, blocking the entire passage from floor to ceiling. Her growing magical sense told her it wasn't real. When she pressed her palm against the cold stone, she felt a vibration like that of the Black Gates, but on a lesser scale. If she pushed against it with her illuminated hand, it gave a little.

Opening that part of her brain that still felt new and stiff, she laid both hands against the wall and said one word.

"Open."

The word rang out with a volume exceeding any effort of her voice. Echoes bounced off the stone, gathering in strength instead of diminishing. The stone beneath her touch quivered, vibrated, disparate elements tearing away from each other with a cracking, rending sound. The wall crumbled into rubble at her feet, then vanished, leaving her in the center of a room that matched the castle's rough exterior.

No attempt to make it beautiful. Stone walls with no polish or ornamentation rose to a high ceiling. Narrow slits let in a sullen light from outside, revealing a sky red with either sunset or fire. At one end of the room, steps led up to a raised dais on which stood a throne built of wood, intricately carved and polished to a high gloss. Seven men stood behind the throne, all beardless and young. Their faces were identical, and all seven pairs of eyes watched her without expression.

On the throne sat a man wearing robes of gold and scarlet. A silver crown set with black stones circled his head. Hair and beard the color of ripe wheat, eyes blue as a summer sky. In his hand he held a scepter.

"So, you have found me," he said, his voice milder than expected. "What would you have?"

"An apology, for starters." She had been frightened, lost, coerced into using power that made her right hand glow as though lit from within. Here, where there was more light, the skin looked translucent and allowed her to see bones, ligaments, tendons. She tore her eyes away and took a few steps toward the throne, anger burning high and hot.

"I came in peace, seeking your help. I rescued your

daughter, who was very nearly dead when I found her. Yet I have been assaulted at your very gates. My comrade is under a spell. Not very hospitable of you and yours."

He raised both hands upward in a helpless gesture that conflicted with his words. "This is a castle of sorcery. Many of the spells are woven into its very framework, and it is hardly our fault if uninvited guests become trapped. We do not apologize for what we are."

"Release him."

"I'm afraid that's not possible. The interesting question is what to do about you, who have so boldly crashed through my doors without invitation. What are you, I wonder?" He leaped lightly from his seat so that he stood above her at the top of the steps, looking down.

One hand ran along the smooth surface of his scepter, and then back again. The air felt charged with menace. Black shadows flickered in and out of Vivian's peripheral vision, and the air hummed with power. Flames flickered around her fingertips but caused no pain.

"I am the Dreamshifter," she said. "Come to warn you that the dreamspheres are dying one by one and taking Dreamworlds and dreamers with them."

"True," he said, descending the steps. "And yet not the truth."

Too young. Too handsome. Too affable. Beneath the pleasant exterior was something so deep and complex, her mind spun away when she touched it, but malice and power were clearly part of the combination.

Vivian held her ground and lifted her chin. "Perhaps you should tell me what you see in me, and we can dispense with the games."

"Now, what fun would that be? Suppose you tell me from whence you have the huntress eyes? I think they were not part of your birth."

"Dragon blood will find its way," she said, not sure

where the words came from. She felt them hit home, a small shift in the invisible web that wove through the room.

"There is a dragon in my anteroom," he said, moving slowly around her and looking her over, as though she were a sculpture at a museum. The eyes that traveled her body, head to toe, not missing one hair or tiny mole, she felt certain, were coolly appraising. "As for you, you are no dragon. And yet..."

He ended with a long stare into her eyes.

She held the gaze, taking the opportunity to look deep into his, which rewarded her with such a jumble of faces and forms and emotions, she couldn't begin to catalogue them or guess what they meant.

"The blood has been squandered," he said at last, a dangerous edge sharpening his voice. "So much power. Wasted for such paltry reasons. Do not try to tell me that dragon blood has allowed you past my defenses. It is a lie."

He cupped his hand beneath her chin and turned it up, squeezing his fingers into the skin, pressing into the bone of her jaw hard enough to make her gasp with pain.

"What are you?"

"Can you not read it for yourself?"

"Speak!" he cried, and the whole room buzzed with the Voice of Command. Light flashed into shadow and back again. The pressure of his fingers ached against her jaw. But the command slid over her like water, and she shifted her shoulders to shed the last of it. "I will not be compelled," she said. "If I speak what I am to you, let it be understood that I speak of my own free will. You will first reveal yourself to me. Your true form, Master, and not this shadow puppet."

The silence that followed was louder than any explosion or scream, full of portent. His hand shifted to her throat, resting on the vulnerable soft flesh in what might have been a caress had it not been for the rage darkening his blue eyes. He smiled, a wide, open-mouthed smile full of teeth. The skin at the corners of his mouth split and peeled back over his cheeks, his face coming undone to reveal a grinning skull.

Vivian didn't flinch, didn't blink, kept her eyes on his, burning now like flame in the bony sockets. With a sound halfway between sigh and sob, his whole form folded in on itself, leaving an unexpected pile of soft gray feathers at her feet.

When she looked up, the room had changed once more.

Not a throne room, or a dungeon, this was more like a well-used study. Two large books lay open on a long table of highly polished wood, next to a bottle of wine and eight glasses. Shelves held more books, all shapes and sizes, bound in leather. Boxes and jars, labeled but too far away to read, were neatly stacked on the shelves amid other items of sorcery. A skull. Some feathers. An astrolabe. A crystal ball. And a host of other magical-looking paraphernalia she'd never seen or dreamed of.

A man sat at the head of the table, seven young men occupying the other chairs. The girl from the grove stood about a pace behind the old man's shoulder, the griffyn cub at her feet, lapping at a saucer of milk. She stood with her head bent slightly, eyes downcast, glancing up briefly to catch Vivian's gaze and then away.

"Satisfied?" the old man said.

"For now," she answered, taking his measure.

He was a tall, well-built man who held himself fully erect. No crippling of joints or spine, no thickening of the knuckles of his slender hands. A thin band of black metal circled his head. Long white hair cascaded smoothly over his shoulders. Clean-shaven, handsome face with expressive lips and a strong chin. Dark eyes, brooding and intense. He wore a simple black robe without any decoration or jewelry.

Leaning forward a little, fingertips resting on the table, he commanded, "Identify yourself."

"Release my companions."

"Not before you tell me who you are."

"Do I have assurance of their safety?"

"Would you trust me if I said it were so?" He sighed. "It seems we are at an impasse, as we both know my commands do not work on you. Very well, then. I will release the man. I regret that dragons are not allowed within the sanctum."

"And yet the dragon is with me."

"You presume! I can easily cast you out."

Vivian held her ground. "I think not. Your daughter has welcomed us into the castle. Do you not honor the invitation?"

The Master's dark eyes bent on the girl, who stood small and still behind his chair. "She, too, will pay for her presumption. The dragon may enter the castle. He will be housed and fed, but I will not allow him in my presence."

He meant it. Vivian sensed this. The girl caught her gaze and nodded slightly. Vivian didn't like it, but she had to take some action.

"Do we agree that he will not be harmed?"

"I promise that he will be held safe for you. Is it well?"

Vivian nodded. The Master responded with a small curving gesture.

A moment later, a door burst open and Zee strode in, sword drawn, his scarred face set in lines of battle. His eyes took in the room, the Master, the girl, whose face, Vivian couldn't help noticing, lit up at the sight of him like a morning sunrise.

Vivian caught his gaze and shook her head slightly.

His eyebrows went up, but he sheathed the sword. She smiled, hoping he would see her heart and understand, knowing he wasn't going to like anything that happened next. Then she turned back to the Master and took a step forward, Poe waddling right along beside her.

"I am the Dreamshifter, as I have told you. I am also dragon, yet another truth. And I am of the blood of the Sorcieri, direct descendant of the Sorceress Jehenna. In the name of the blood, I come to ask for your secrets, that the Dreamworlds might not die."

At the name of Jehenna, all seven of the young men turned their faces toward her in unison, dark eyes glittering. The girl looked up, her face full of alarm.

The old man's expression did not change, but currents of magic swirled around Vivian's feet. Tendrils explored her skin, trying to read her secrets. She strengthened her will and tried to shut them out, but even that gave him information. After a long moment, he leaned forward with his hands on his knees and said, "How does a woman come to have magic at all?"

Vivian blinked. "I'm sorry, what?"

Of all the things she had expected, coming to the place that had spawned a sorceress like Jehenna, this was not one of them.

"Sorcieri women have no magic. This is a law. Now here you are, barging into my castle, thrashing about, shedding magic that you obviously have no idea how to control, and you seem to think I shall reward you for this?"

"But Jehenna—"

"Precisely. Why are you here? What do you want?"

Too much was happening at once; she couldn't track it all. The itch in her brain distracted her, trying to draw her attention to a whole new level of experience she didn't know how to label or categorize or even understand.

Beyond getting here and dropping Jehenna's name, she'd never really had a plan. Intrigue wasn't a game she could play with any skill, so she went directly to the point.

"The Dreamworlds are dying."

"What does that matter to us? We have no use for them."

"Father," the girl said, her voice barely a whisper.

The old man made no sign that he had heard her.

Setting down the griffyn, she stepped around the table and knelt beside his chair. "Forgive me, but I must speak. The mirrors have gone dark. If it does not affect us, then why do we have the mirrors at all?"

Not even looking at her, as if she did not exist, the Master instead looked to his sons.

"Have you checked the mirrors? Is this true?"

All of the dark heads nodded as one, but only one of the boys spoke. He seemed to be the leader, his face more animated that the others, a keener interest in his eyes. "Three of the mirrors have gone dark, one of them the mirror of Jehenna. And the dreamflowers are dying."

"And again I say, what has any of this to do with us?"

Vivian caught a quick exchange of glances between the girl and her brother. His eyes widened, questioning, and then he turned to the Master and said, "There is a long tradition of minding the mirrors. We are the guardians—"

"To what purpose? To await, as the threadbare tales tell us, the coming of the Three in One?"

Again, Vivian caught what looked like subtle prompting from the girl before the young man spoke again. "And yet it appears that she stands before us now."

"This one? Pah. She is naught but a half-breed with a paltry power and no knowledge. We should throw her out. See if she can find a way off the island. That would be a true test."

The six silent brothers all rose to their feet and moved forward in eerie unison.

"No!" The girl grabbed her father's hands in both of hers and looked up into his face, pleading. "Please. You must listen—"

In answer, he backhanded her across the mouth, knocking her into a little heap. She crouched there, one hand pressed to a bleeding lip. The griffyn cub hissed once, then set about lapping at the blood with a pink tongue.

"Are we to become killers, then?" the son asked. He stood at his place behind the table. His voice shook a little, but he stared the old Master down. "Have we sunk to casting those who come to us, seeking, out into the dangers of the island? If you do not see fit to grant the request, might we wait at least until dawn to give them a chance of survival?"

"You try my patience," the Master said, a warning note in his voice. "But as my daughter has granted them welcome, and as you have spoken for them as well, I will heed your words. Take them to a room and let them rest. In the morning, I want them gone before I break my fast. Is this clear?"

The boy bent his head in submission. "Yes, my Master." He turned to his sister and ordered, "Take them, then."

She scrambled to her feet and bowed. "Come with me." The cub cradled in her arms, she turned, back straight, head tall, and led them from the room.

"You think Godzilla will be okay?"

Vivian stood looking through an open casement into a garden that wasn't really a garden. She could see a fountain and what appeared to be grass and flowers and trees. All illusion. But it wasn't the magic, or the dragon, that was really on her mind.

The sorcerer girl had seen to their needs. They'd had baths and eaten a simple meal. Vivian was now, after all this time, alone with the man who held her heart, who could make her knees weak with a single look.

The man who had always been off-limits for one reason or another.

"Dragons have magic, don't they?" He came and stood just behind her shoulder, not quite touching but close enough that she could feel the warmth of him, catch the good, honest smell of fresh sweat and the underlying scent that was purely Zee.

"They do, but he's just a baby."

Zee snorted. "Our young conductress will see to him, I think."

Again Vivian felt that little twist of jealousy. She turned to face him, half seated on the stone ledge, mostly to brace herself at the insane weakness that always grabbed her when he was so close. Her heart hammered and she found she couldn't meet his eyes.

"I wonder if she would have really told you her name?"

His hand cupped her chin and turned her face up so she could no longer avoid his eyes, the other hand tucking her hair back behind her ear. The simple touch finished her, heat following his fingers and lingering on her skin even when his hand had returned to his side. His eyes, that clear amber agate with the dark umber etching, looked into hers.

"Does it matter?" His voice had gone husky.

Vivian swallowed. "I think it does. It would be a demonstration of good faith." Or a confirmation of the way those dark eyes followed his every movement.

Zee's thumb traced the fine skin under her eye. Vivian tried to turn her face away, but he held her there, his eyes reading the emotions she tried desperately to keep hidden. Jehenna had tried to seduce him, she remembered. And Aidan had succeeded. Now this beautiful young girl, clearly dripping with both magic and desire, followed him with eyes that said he was the sun, the moon, the everything.

His hand fell away and made a small gesture of futility, even as his eyes dropped to the healing scar on her breast, the place where he had struck with the dragonstone and very nearly killed her.

Defensively, her own hand rose to cover it.

"It will always be there," he said. "No matter what I do, or you do, or how we try to pretend, what I have done will always be there between us."

Tears unshed shone in his eyes but didn't fall. He drew a quivering breath and began to turn away from her.

Vivian knew from the depth of her being that if she let this go now, it would be too late, that this was the last and only chance to heal, somehow, what had come between them.

"Zee," she said, letting all of the pleading and the heartache and the need and the fear come into her voice. "Please."

She took the hand that had dropped to his side and put it over her breast, the center of the palm directly over the scar. He tried to pull away, but she laid both hands flat over his and held him.

"You marked me, forever and always. I am yours, all that I am. If you'll have me."

His body jerked as though she'd slapped him. "If I'll have you? If? I've never wanted anybody else. Since I was fourteen, you've walked my dreams. And then there you were, flesh and blood..."

"And dragon." He had faltered, and she knew the sticking place. Her eyes held him in direct challenge.

"And dragon," he whispered.

"And when Aidan tricked you?"

He took a breath, set his jaw, stood up straighter, as if preparing for a firing squad. "When she came to me, it was as I first saw you, walking into the store. Her eyes were gray..."

"And she had no scales. All soft woman. What you wanted me to be."

"She was a dragon!" he cried out, pacing away from her across the room. "She, who didn't look it, was dragon full and through. You are Vivian. Dragon and all, ever and always, you are Vivian."

"The dragon isn't dead," she said, very softly. "Almost, Zee, but not quite."

"That doesn't change what I've done. Or what I am." His fists were clenched, the muscles in his arms knotted so tight, they stood out clearly defined.

"Not your fault," she whispered. When she reached up to touch his face, he flinched. She paused, reached out again, and this time he suffered her touch, quivering in the wake of the fingers that traced the line of his jaw, his chin, and then his lips. "They made you so, the forces that be. A cruel thing to draw us together in love. You the dragon slayer, me with the dragon blood in me. If I had power over fate..."

He grabbed her hand and pressed it to his lips. He was shaking now, breathing in great gasps. "Love, Vivian? Don't use that word lightly."

"Love," she murmured. Again she took his hand—such a beautiful hand, warrior and artist inherent in its strength and capacity for gentleness— and laid it over the scar, this time shifting it to cover her entire breast, tipping back her head to look up into his eyes. "It has always been love. Since the day I walked into that store..."

"My God, Vivian, you are everything. Heart and soul..." The words sounded torn from his chest. The hand over her breast trembled.

Vivian rose on her tiptoes, clasped both hands behind his neck, and pulled his head down toward hers, pressing her lips against his. Something broke in him then. He kissed her with the intensity of a dying man reaching for the last moment of comfort, his lips covering hers, then straying to her cheeks and eyelids, her forehead, and then lips again.

He was sobbing now, strong man that he was, his arms so tight around her, she could scarcely catch her breath, but she returned the kisses, surrendered herself to him absolutely and completely.

All memory of Jared was gone, all the betrayal and the jealousy and hurt and doubt washed away.

Zee's lips found their way to her throat, worked their way down toward her breast. Her body lifted toward him of its own accord, back arching, hips pressing upward and against his. She felt her nipples harden, the heat melt her from the core on out, every nerve, every sense open and aching to be closer to him.

"Please," she heard herself saying, "please oh please oh please oh please."

His fingers fumbled with the buttons on her shirt and then ripped it away, leaving her flesh free to press against his. He buried his face between her breasts for a long moment, his body shaking, and she knotted her fingers in his hair and held him close, feeling tears against her skin.

A long, quavering breath, and then his lips found their way, at last, to her waiting breast. She arched her back, breathing in the scent of him, letting go of everything but this moment. Dream memories of making love with Zee thronged around them for a moment, and then those, too, were gone and it was only the two of them. Here. In this moment, without past or future.

She needed his skin, was hungry for it, and pulled

away from him long enough to lift his T-shirt up over his head. The scars, the bruises caught her breath for just a moment, jarred her to the reality of who he was and what they were up against, but then his lips were on hers again and all of that slid away.

When at last her hands undid his jeans, he stopped her, both hands on hers, holding her away. His eyes looked directly into hers. "Are you sure?"

"It's you who should ask. I've got sorcery blood in me, too, Zee. I don't know what I am."

"Are you using magic on me now?"

"No."

"You are Vivian, whatever that means."

And then, "Please," she heard her own voice begging again. "Please oh please oh please oh please."

He freed her hands then so she could touch him, but only for a moment before he slid his own hands down over her hips and pulled her against him, lifting her in his arms so that her own hunger could match his.

"Bed," he said as she pressed against him, wanting him inside her more than she had wanted anything, ever, in the course of her existence. He carried her there, laid her down, and then knelt above her, his eyes on hers.

"My love," she said. "Oh, my love."

He didn't look away or close his eyes, and neither did she, so that as he entered her, the sensation swept away everything but his eyes and what she saw there. For a long, long time, he didn't move, just held her there, eyes and bodies locked together, until she thought she might scream with the need to move, to thrust, and only then did he begin to move inside her.

Slowly at first, bringing her up little by little toward the climax, eyes still locked, then faster, long, smooth strokes, each one striking a deeper pleasure than the last until she heard her voice break free of all control and cry out in a cresting wave of pleasure even as she felt his whole body contract, and his voice near her ear whispered her name, "Vivian."

They lay together for a long time, Zee still buried inside of her. She ran her hands over his back, stroked his hair, murmured her love to him. At long last, he rolled off of her and lay on his side, looking into her eyes. One hand tucked a lock of hair behind her ear.

"You sure there was no magic in that?"

"Only ours, pure Vivian and Zee."

"Beats sorcery." He kissed her, then kissed her again. "Before you even think to ask, this, with you, is beyond measure and beyond compare to anything I've had with anybody else."

"Even in dreams," she whispered.

"Even in dreams."

She was very drowsy, sated with love, his skin warm and alive beneath her fingers. "Don't ever leave me, Zee," she said, drifting.

In answer, he pulled her closer against him, and the last thing she knew before sleep claimed her was his strong hand stroking her hair.

Sixteen

Vivian slept as she had never slept before, deeply and without dreams, her small hand curled inside Zee's strong one. Bliss, she thought, as she began to surface to waking, and tried to wall off her mind to shut out both the morning light and the memory of what the coming daylight meant.

A pounding at the door shattered it all to fragments.

By the time she had her eyes fully open, Zee was on his feet, naked but with his sword in hand.

"What?" she croaked, groggily, sitting up and looking around the chamber in the dim light of early morning.

Again the knock came at the door, this time followed by a voice. "I'm coming in."

The door opened, and a slender shape slipped inside and pulled it closed again behind her. She held a silken cord in one hand, the end attached to a jeweled collar around the neck of the baby griffyn. The little creature was still thin, but some magic was at work, aiding in the healing.

"Oh, hell," Vivian said, looking from the Master's daughter to Zee's scarred and well-muscled body. The girl wore a long black dress that clung to every curve; her hair flowed silken over her shoulders to the small of her back. Her eyes were wide, her lips slightly parted, and she had never looked lovelier.

In the same instant, Vivian became conscious of her own sleep-tangled hair and nakedness, pulling a sheet up to her chest. The flicker of jealousy vanished when the girl's eyes went from Zee to Vivian and back again, registering the truth of the night and drooping a little.

"What do you want?" Zee asked, his voice a challenge. "If this is the eviction notice, you might let us get dressed"

"You need to come to the great hall at once."

Something about the tone of her voice pushed the fuzziness out of Vivian's head, made her look a little closer. No magic here, just years of working with people and reading between the lines.

"Has he asked for us?"

"Just come. Hurry."

"Why should we trust you?"

She turned back, already halfway out the door. "What can I say? We have no time to build trust."

"Give me your name," Vivian said.

The girl's face paled. A long moment she hesitated, then nodded. "That is fair. My name is Kalina. I give it freely and will not ask for yours." And then she slipped away, silent as a shadow.

"Treachery, you think?" Zee's eyes remained on the closed door, and he made no move to get dressed.

"Does it matter?"

He snorted. "Every one of them has more lies than an anthill has ants. Might not be her real name."

"At the least, I don't think she wants you dead, although I suspect she'd be happy to get me out of the way."

Vivian felt shy about being naked, all at once, but her clothes were across the room and she felt the sense of urgency. The vision of an unclad Zee with a sword stirred all sorts of other possibilities in her as well, and internally she cursed all of the Sorcieri into the depths of hell as she pushed back the covers and aimed for her clothes.

"Do we have to go?"

She felt his eyes on her, her skin glowing with the consciousness of his gaze, heat rising, but she pushed it back.

"I think so."

"So unjust," he said, still watching her. Her eyes met his, clung there, reading desire and love and so many things. He grinned, all at once, the grin that would always be lopsided now because of the scars on his face. His body had responded to hers, and she could barely drag her eyes away from the visible indication of his desire.

"Dear God," she said. "Please, for the love of all things holy, put some pants on. We really have to go."

"You are a cruel mistress, Dreamshifter."

"Don't make me throw cold water on you."

"You might have to." He sighed, put down the sword, and started pulling on his pants.

Vivian finished getting dressed, ran her fingers through her tangled hair as best she could, and splashed water on her face from the basin on a low dresser. She wanted a comb, clean clothes, a toothbrush. Maybe even makeup. None of which was immediately forthcoming.

And then Zee was behind her, his arms around her waist, his cheek pressing against her hair. It was beyond her strength to totally resist and she turned in his arms and wrapped her own around him, her hands settling on the muscles of his back, lips reaching up for a kiss which left her gasping.

"And the Between fell to the Nothing while the Dreamshifter and the Warrior lost themselves in love," she murmured, tracing his scarred cheek with a fingertip. "Let's go do our jobs, Zee."

"I have a bad feeling about this."

"You and me both."

Now that she was fully awake, awareness of the magic had returned. There was a disruption in the flow, a sense of urgency that had not been there last night. Something had changed.

"We need to hurry," she said. "You remember the way?"

"I think so."

She let him go first, even knowing that the sword would be no use against the Sorcieri, that they could turn his mind in upon itself in an endless loop if they so desired. But he was the Warrior, and this was the way of things. She followed, trying to open herself more to the magic so that she could see and understand enough to maybe have some control.

It was like trying to alter the course of a river or redirect rain. It flowed all around her; she could feel it, trace it, but her movement and her will had very little effect on what it decided to do.

Her mind fully on the magic, what waited in the great hall took her so by surprise that she stumbled over her own feet and would have fallen if Zee hadn't steadied her.

It was no longer empty and echoing. A silent throng waited in the shadows, unspeaking, scarcely moving, only the sound of collective breath marking them as alive. The Master sat once again on the wooden throne on the dais, Kalina kneeling beside him. In front of the throne stood a group of Giants. Five of them, four males, one female. Sandwiched between two of the Giants, back hunched, head bowed, was a man. His unwashed dark hair straggled down onto the collar of stained and ill-fitting clothes.

Vivian's brain flickered over him, briefly, wondering if he were hostage or companion and guessing the former.

And then moved on to the overwhelming reality of a group of Giants all in one place. The only Giant she'd been close to was Callyn. In a group like this, they were overwhelming, like carved statues come to life. Huge, dangerous, with a roughhewn magic of their own. Again she could sense it, but it was even farther beyond her understanding than what the Sorcieri had.

Still, the room was charged with tension.

Clearly, the Master had not expected them, and one unguarded flicker of his eyes let Vivian know that her presence here, now, was far from welcome. One of the Giants followed that gaze, turning first his head and then his ponderous body to size up the newcomers.

"You are the Dreamshifter." Where he had been standing to face the Master as an equal, he now dropped to one knee and bowed his head. The other Giants turned to face her and followed suit. The man remained where he was, facing the Master's throne.

Vivian's pulse sped with alarm. She felt Zee tense beside her and put her hand on his arm to warn him. A sword drawn here would be like a match to gasoline.

Her eyes met the Master's and she realized, with dismay, how she would need to play this. Ignoring the kneeling Giants, she let her voice ring out clearly across the hall.

"A courteous greeting at last. Quite different from what I was offered in this hall last night. Will you still cast us out to wander and die amid your enchantments at first morning light?"

She braced herself for retaliation, reaching out with all of her senses to monitor the flow of magic. It tightened, but nothing moved. The Master's face gave nothing away. He looked remote, untouchable, ancient beyond comprehension.

But the Giant, still on his knees, looked down on

her, his face grave. "Dreamshifter. We hoped to find you here. I am Kraal, emissary from her Highness, Alara, Queen of the Giants. We beg of you, stop the death of the Dreamworlds."

"I came here in search of knowledge to do that very thing, but the Master refuses to speak with me. Perhaps he will grant your request where he has denied mine." She pitched her voice to carry.

Kraal lumbered to his feet and turned to the throne. "She speaks truth?"

The Master shrugged. "As it appears you are here to take counsel with each other, perhaps you could take this conversation elsewhere."

Kraal did not acknowledge the rude dismissal, rising to his towering height and offering a courtly bow toward the throne. "Queen Alara has sent gifts to honor our contract with the Sorcieri."

He made a gesture with a hand that was bigger than Vivian's whole head, and one of the other Giants stepped toward the throne bearing a cloth-wrapped bundle about the size and shape of a small child.

"With your permission?" She set the thing down at the base of the steps and glanced up at the Master.

He nodded, still displaying no emotion other than boredom.

The Giant removed the swaddling cloths to reveal a faceted crystal fully four feet high. It was shaped like a flame and burned at its core with a scarlet glow that lit every facet and cast sparks of light like a fountain. It had magical properties, of that Vivian had no doubt. She felt a shift in the room at its revealing, heat, warmth, an amplification of her own power.

Her dragon blood stirred a little, restless, and the itch in her brain intensified. She wanted to put her hands on the stone.

"Cover it." The Master no longer reclined lazily in his chair. He sat fully erect, face drawn, lips compressed. A thin sheen of perspiration shone on his forehead, red like blood in the light of the stone.

The Giant complied at once, and the Master sagged back into the throne, breathing harshly. Kalina, who had been nearly invisible in the shadows behind the throne, emerged at his side with a flagon of liquid, which he took with shaking hands. Drinking seemed to recover him.

"Master, my apologies and those of the Queen. To our magic the crystal amplifies, strengthens—"

The sorcerer gestured for silence. "I am weary and will investigate its properties later. You have drawn me from my bed and I am an old man, as you may have forgotten. My people as well would like to be back in their beds." He gestured again, and the shadowed throng murmured an assent.

Kraal bowed. "So be it, then. One last thing, if you would indulge me. Queen Alara has also sent a gift for the Dreamshifter." He snapped his fingers. The man slumped beside the Giants jerked as though he'd been struck. Vivian had all but forgotten him, but now a dark foreboding made her suck in a breath.

"Turn and face your new mistress," Kraal ordered, his big hands enforcing his command. But the man bent his head and covered his face instead. The movement, the shape of the hands, was familiar.

Zee cursed under his breath.

"Don't be difficult," Kraal said, with a smack on the back that nearly sent the prisoner sprawling. The man's hands flung out for balance, revealing a face she knew, dreaming and waking, once full of entitlement and self-satisfaction. It had looked down on her, twisted with hate and lust. Somewhere in the distant past, it had been gentler, wearing an expression of what she'd taken for love.

Always it had been the sort of face that drew feminine eyes and held them. Now it was bruised and dirty. Blood smeared the cheekbones. And where the eyes should have been, there was blank green stone.

"Your Queen miscalculated," she said, even as her heart twisted with conflicting hate and pity. "What value could I hold for such a thing?"

Jared's chin lifted at the sound of her voice, his face swiveled toward her. One hand reached out in supplication. "Vivian. Help me."

She could neither move nor speak, for a moment, her heart warring in conflicting vengeance, pity, and guilt. And fear.

Jared had named her, openly, in a place where magic could use a name for all sorts of binding. Glancing at the Master, she saw him smile for the first time, and the smile was more dangerous than his frowns.

"Truly, this gift may be more to my benefit than to that of the Dreamshifter," he said.

Guided by some sense, maybe her breathing or a lock on the sound of her voice, Jared began to shuffle toward her, both hands outstretched. His right leg moved differently from his left, and a torn pant leg revealed that below the knee, the flesh was missing. The bones and tendons were encased in a clear resin that rippled as he moved, flexing, straightening; she could see the waves travel through it.

All the while, the face turned side to side, questing, the flat stone eyes in the living flesh making her own flesh shudder. Closer and closer. She could smell his unwashed flesh, the fear, the blood that stiffened his shirt and crusted his hair. If that hand touched her, it would surely brand some horror on her that she would carry to the grave. Poe hissed. His neck snaked out, his wings lifted, and he darted in to peck at Jared's feet, making the blind man stumble about in a grotesque dance.

"Shall I kill him?" Zee asked. "It would be a kindness."

Vivian turned to the Giant who had identified himself as Kraal. "What do you take me for, that you bring him to me tortured and mutilated? As if I would want a slave."

"The Giants see things differently, Dreamshifter. The Queen holds him at great value."

"I hold him at little value, but still he is a human being. Not to be owned by another or subjected to torture."

"He said he was bound to you by an oath of marriage."

She expelled her breath in a sharp hiss. "Marriage? You brought him here to me with this wild tale?"

"They were coming anyway." Jared's face had gone sullen. "Vivian, please. You're my only hope."

"Help me, Obi-Wan Kenobi," Zee muttered. "I left you safe in Surmise. Care to tell me how you turn up in the company of Giants? No? Give me one reason why I shouldn't kill you where you stand."

"He is a guest in my hall," the Master said. "There are laws governing such behaviors. Not that I object to his death. Or that of any of you. Just that I want you to step outside to die."

"He is under my bond," Kraal said. "You kill him, and I must kill you."

"Or die trying."

Vivian recognized Zee's tone, the way he seemed to have relaxed, the smile on his face. He must be itching for a battle he could actually fight, an opportunity to take action that wasn't hampered by magic. Killing Jared, helpless as he was, would offer no satisfaction. But a fight with a Giant was another thing.

"His death can wait." The authority in her own voice startled her, but she kept her face impassive. "You say

Alara values him, then?"

"She values the eyes she took from him. His presence here is a gesture of good faith. Tell her what you see, Jared."

Jared's battered face tightened in a grimace, as if he might resist, but he thought better of it. "A library, I think. Many books on wooden shelves. A polished table with a scroll half open. I cannot read the words; they are in a language unknown to me."

Kraal nodded. "The library. Is there anybody with her?"

"Not that I can see. She's looking at books now. I still do not recognize the language."

"Not much use, since he doesn't know how to tell us what he sees," the Master said, dismissively. "Although perhaps this—Dreamshifter—might find another use for him."

Kraal turned back to Vivian. "If we have misjudged and this man is of no value to you, how may we entice you to save our world and all the others?"

"I don't need an incentive. That's why I came. The Master has refused to help."

Kraal turned away from Vivian and approached the Master, the floor shaking with every step he took. "Would you so easily dismiss the long treaty between us, then?"

The master spread his hands. "There is little I can do."

"You lie. Always the Sorcieri have despised the rest of the worlds. Despite the fact that a power bent on destruction now is deep in the heart of the Forever. Do you think that even your kingdom will stand if the Forever is destroyed? You know what lies there and how it shapes us all. Aidan has returned there and I am certain she means nothing good."

"And how did Aidan reach the Forever? Only the

One can open the Gates," the Master said with a cruel little smile. "She who is Dreamshifter, dragon, and Sorcieri. Is that not true, Kraal, and what was once agreed upon and put into place by the Giants and the Sorcieri?"

"This is true," Kraal acknowledged.

The Master stroked one hand lazily across the scepter in his lap. "It was agreed that a Key would be provided to the One that only she could use to open the Gates. Is this not so?"

"It is so."

She heard no judgment in the words. Kraal's face was unreadable, the roughhewn, uneven planes disconcerting to her eyes, the slash of a mouth nothing more than a vehicle of speech. Like trying to decipher emotion from the Easter Island carvings.

"So, this one…" He gestured at Vivian, his tone dripping with condescension and sarcasm. "The Three in One, if you will, used the Key to open the gates, let Aidan and her dragons pass through, and then sealed them again?"

Vivian had no response. This was true and, put in that way, sounded like the stupidest thing ever.

The Master's voice rose and he leveled a long white finger at her. "You are a half-breed, a woman, and a fool. I tell you this much—Aidan has poisoned the dreamspheres. Water from the Pool of Life in the Forever might stop their destruction, but you have locked yourself out. You! And now you come sniveling here to me, expecting me to solve the problem you have created."

"There is a way." Kalina, still down on her knees, spoke the words.

"Silence!" The Master swung around toward her, magic gathering in his raised hands, ready to strike.

The brother stepped in between them. His face was pale, but his dark eyes glittered with an emotion that was anything but fear. "She speaks truth. There is a way."

A long moment they stood facing each other, magic against magic. Vivian tried to follow the flow, but something was wrong, a tangle she was unable to unweave. She was just on the brink of understanding when the Master released the threat and turned back toward her.

"Very well. My son is against me in this, and I will tell you this much and no more—Vivian."

Her name hung in the air, electric, dangerous. She chose not to answer, not to respond to his provocation. So, she looked him directly in the eye, unflinching. For all his derision of her powers, she had unmasked him last night, and they both knew it.

"There is a tale in the *History of the Sorcieri* which speaks of another way into the Forever. It is not based in fact but only on rumor. It has never been tested or tried, and even my grandfather did not know the origins of it. The tale says that she who is Three in One—Dreamshifter, dragon, and Sorcieri—may be given the power to enter the Forever by means of the Cave of Dreams."

"You know more than you're saying." Vivian was weary of sparring and intrigue. All she wanted was a direct answer.

"You cannot begin to scratch the surface of all that I know. Which includes this, and I will not say it again. The One who can complete the blood ritual to enter the Forever must be Dreamshifter, Sorcieri, and dragon. The dragon within you is as good as dead." The Master steepled his fingers together. "Now, Kraal of the Giants. Suppose you tell me this before you judge me in my own hall. Why have you really come? Why now? I know Alara and that she isn't acting out of concern for the worlds. What is happening to the world of the Giants?"

"Hunger. No safe foraging in other Dreamworlds, on which we heavily relied."

"And yet this is not all. Will you tell me? Any of

you?" All of the Giants remained stoic and silent.

"Very well," the Master said. "You. Human. Step forward."

Vivian recognized the Voice of Command, watched Jared's body jerk and then move him step by reluctant step, forward to the throne. "Now, why this excursion, and why is it important enough that they are dragging you along?"

"It's the dreamsphere," Jared said, the words sounding stretched and thin as though they were being vacuumed out of him. "There is a woman who holds the dreamsphere that contains the world of the Giants. Now she is gone."

"At last we come to a modicum of truth," the Master said. "You are here because the world of the Giants is subject to immediate obliteration."

He leaned forward in his throne, his face no longer detached and dismissive. "Do you know where she has gone?"

"Surmise," Kraal said. "I believe she has gone to Surmise."

Kalina's face went deadly pale, and she swayed a little on her knees. Zee reached out a hand to steady her, then snatched it back, shaking it as if he'd come in contact with something hot.

"Don't touch her," the Master said absently, his eyes looking in an entirely other direction. "So. The dreamsphere of the Giant world has gone to Surmise. And you came here?"

"A party also went to seek the woman."

"And if they find her?"

"She has been suffered to hold the sphere until now, as long as she stayed with us and cared for it. There is a group that believes the sphere will be harmed if taken with violence."

"But the Queen does not hold this belief."

"She does not."

A vision flashed into Vivian's mind of blood and slaughter in Surmise. Landon would never permit a group of Giants to come in and kill. He would fight. Maybe he'd win, but a band of determined Giants could wreak a lot of havoc before they could be stopped. They were so big, so implacable. This woman who held the sphere had to be Weston's sister. She'd left him that note that she'd gone to stay with the Giants, would have had to have a dream-sphere to get there.

"We hoped," Kraal said, "that you could look into your mirrors and tell us of Surmise."

The Master laughed, a sound without mirth. "My sons. Tell them of the mirrors," he said.

The seven brothers turned to face Kraal. Their faces were more like their sister's than their father's, beautiful but with a masculine strength. Long dark hair hung down onto their shoulders; their black eyes gleamed.

"The mirrors have gone dark," one of them said.

"All of the mirrors." Seven voices spoke at once.

Vivian shivered. In her peripheral vision, the forms of the young men wavered in and out of existence.

"What of Surmise?" It was her own voice, although she hadn't meant to speak.

Seven pairs of dark eyes turned to meet hers, glittering and shallow, with no more depth than Jared's green stones. "Surmise has also gone dark."

"This cannot be so," Kraal said. "Surely."

A whisper ran through the hall as of hushed voices in dismay. Cold crawled over Vivian's body, from her toes to the crown of her head. Poe had been huddled at her feet. Now, all at once, he waddled away. Past the kneeling girl, making a wide detour around the griffyn, who batted at him with a paw. He paused to extend his neck and peck at Jared. The blind man flinched and jerked away but said nothing, his head moving side to side, the blank stone eyes searching.

The penguin bypassed the Giants, waddling right up to the first of the seven young men standing in a row. And walked right through him.

Kraal broke a long silence that followed. "Nothing here is as it seems. I begin to see why you play games with us. You have locked yourselves away on this island for so long, you have died out, and you seek to keep knowledge of this weakness from the rest of us. How many are left? Speak truth."

"I need not answer any questions. This is my home. It is time for you to leave."

"Or you'll turn us into toads?" Vivian crossed to the bottom of the stairs leading up to the dais, Poe hopping along beside her. She put her foot on the first step. The magic pushed against her, warning her back.

"This is forbidden," the Master said. "What happens to you if you come farther is on your own head."

From here she could see a slight palsy of the hand resting on the arm of his throne, the tick in his jaw as he swallowed hard and then swallowed again.

She took another step. The magic felt almost like a solid wall now, pushing against her, trying to force her backward. She marshaled all of her will and shoved back. Her eyes met those of the girl, wide with surprise, and then Kalina nodded once, a tiny gesture that her father missed.

One more step and she was through the illusion.

A tired old man sat on a wooden chair. His clothes were threadbare, his hair thin, both hands spotted with age and trembling with weakness.

"You dare."

Nothing weak about his voice or the power he wielded, which snapped and cracked and swirled but couldn't touch her.

"You are a fraud."

Her voice amplified, expanded, without any more effort than the will that all should hear. So much magic to draw on. She had a brief impression that magic didn't like to lie around unused, but there was no time to think, and she went on.

"You said you have nothing to fear from what happens in the other worlds. Maybe that's true, but you are dying. You have two children left to carry on the entire legacy of the Sorcieri. And then what happens?"

"This matter is not your concern."

"It is my concern. It's everybody's concern." Vivian drew a breath and straightened her shoulders. "You're as bad as Aidan."

"You go too far!" The old man erupted from his seat, blue fire winding around outspread fingertips. His wispy hair stood out straight from his head, each strand ending in a spark. "How dare you compare me to that creature?"

A wind pushed against Vivian, so powerful she had to lean forward to stand against it, and still it thrust her back and away from him. A solid warmth behind her steadied her, gave her anchor.

She flung back at him, "Of the two of you, I prefer Aidan. What she does, she does on purpose. She's not a craven, cowering in a hidden corner, waiting for the world to end. You want us to believe you powerful and beyond the concerns of anything outside the Sorcieri. There are no Sorcieri, not anymore. You are a doddering old fool and your family line has run out."

The Giant named Kraal thudded into place at her side. "This is truth? All the throng but an illusion, your house fallen into decay?"

"Show him!" Vivian said. "Drop the threads and let your guests see what truly is."

For all his age, the Master was still stronger than she,

with powers at his disposal that she could not begin to imagine. Breath held, she waited for the lightning bolt that would kill her for her insolence, for crumbling the illusions behind which he hid both his pride and his shame.

Instead, the blue fires thinned, faded, and went out. The sparks died. And then the rest of the illusions began to fall away. No more voices or breathing as of a throng in the hall. Darkness. A smell of damp earth and old stone with the stink of decay.

"Light the torches," the Master said.

A flicker of honest yellow flame, and a low glimmer of light appeared next to the throne. Another, and another. Although most of the hall remained in darkness, around the throne light and shadow flickered and danced as the only son and heir to the Sorcieri legacy lit torches manually with a flint.

As the light brightened and grew, the disrepair of the room became evident. Walls and floor were nothing but cracked and pitted stone. Water dripped in the distance, and the air smelled as dank as a cellar. Light gleamed dull and heavy on patches of wetness. And still the youth lit torches, lining the path they had taken through the entrance hall, each one illuminating an echoing, empty space.

A chill wind blew from the open doorway, guttering the torches, raising goose bumps on Vivian's exposed skin. Poe puffed out his feathers. Even one of the Giants reached up and adjusted his cloak. Jared, in his rags, shivered miserably

On the steps, Kalina knelt where she had been placed, still obedient, with the griffyn cub cuddled in her lap. In the dim light, Vivian thought she saw a circle of luxurious, unfaded carpet under the slender knees, but when she looked again, it was gone. She also caught the barest hint of an unexpected stillness, like the calm at the center of a storm.

The old man sank down onto his throne, which was a throne yet, one of the few things in this place that had not been conjured by magic.

"This palace was built by the magic of thousands," he said, "or so my father told me. "By the time of my birth, there were barely four score of us remaining. Why the others died out, I do not know. That was a story never told, always unspoken among us. But even under the will and the word of a hundred, the castle was a glorious thing. A shared magic, built by combined and harmonious wills..."

"I know why," Kalina said, and there was nothing thin or stretched about her voice.

"Hush, child. When will you learn to be silent?"

"What will you do to me, old man?" She rose to her feet. "Will you strike me down in front of these? Or perhaps you will command my brother to do it?"

The youth, carrying a torch, could scarce hide the dismay in his face as he shook his head and retreated behind his father's throne.

Kalina laughed bitterly. "You wonder why the Master is afraid? I will tell you. His seed has run out. His consort fled from his foolishness and he has no chance to birth another. And the magic that might go to extending his own sorry life must be expended to maintain the illusions that there is a throng of Sorcieri gathered here, that I have many brothers, all of whom have magic. He cannot offer you refreshments or a dinner in the banquet hall because the expenditure of so much magic would kill him."

"What does it matter when no one is here to see?" Despite her own outrage, Vivian's heart twisted with pity. The Master appeared far older than when she had first seen him…was it only last night? As she reached out to sense the power that curled around him, she found it dimmed. He had drained himself to create the illusions. His silver hair was thin and wispy as dandelion fluff, the hands liver-spotted and thin, his whole body wracked with tremors.

"Pride," Kalina said. No respect or compassion in her tone; it was all purely contempt. "Perhaps he thought I did not see, girl-child that I am, what he was doing."

"You lie. Your magic was bound at birth."

"Magic-bound does not equal magic-blind."

The Master sagged in his great throne now like a rag doll with barely enough strength to keep himself upright. "It was done for the good of all," he croaked.

Kalina swept forward to stand before his throne, gesturing at the decayed hall. "Look around you, Father, and tell me that this is good."

"We did not know the women would stop bearing. Nor that the young would leave..."

"Barbarian!" The girl's voice cut through darkness and stone, a blade of truth and vengeance. "What did you expect? That women with their magic bound would become humble servitors, nothing more than receptacles for your seed? We have power still over our own bodies. The binding extends only into the outer world."

The old man gaped at his daughter, comprehension and horror at war in a face that had aged seemingly a hundred years in the last moments. "Surely..." he murmured. "Surely they did not..."

"What reason had they to live, to desire that their misery be visited on children to come? Magic-bound, forced to submit to men made their masters, all they could do was withhold childbearing."

"Your mother—"

Kalina laughed, a wild and bitter sound as far from mirth as darkness is from light. "Do not for a moment believe that my mother was weak. In the dark hours of the night, she whispered these things to me. Other sons were conceived, but she did not allow them to be born."

A spasm crossed the Master's face. One hand went to his heart. He bent forward a little, breathing harshly. Vivian took a step forward, thinking the old man suffering from a heart attack, but whatever ailed him passed almost at once. She felt the magic shift, flowing toward him rather than away. He lurched to his feet and spread his arms to gather it in, letting his head fall back.

Power swirled and shifted, gathering around the epicenter of the old Master. Vivian could barely stand, feeling the summons tugging at her, bone and skin and flesh. Her vision blurred, all colors and shapes running together.

When it passed, the Master was no longer old. Golden hair fell over his shoulders. His eyes were blue as the sea and as merciless. He leaned over his daughter, hands on her shoulders, and shook her.

"Where is your mother?"

"If she'd wanted you to know, she would have told you."

He slapped her. It was an open-handed slap to the cheek, hard enough to snap her head sideways, leaving a livid white blotch that rapidly turned dark red with the purple undertone that meant a bruise would follow. Tears stood out in her eyes but did not fall.

"You think you can force me with brute strength? Try again."

"No need." He was breathing hard. "There are other ways to compel you."

"You need that magic for other things."

Kraal intervened. "This is about a woman?"

The Master smiled. "Isn't everything? Either at the beginning or in the end. Now, my daughter, where is your mother?"

"Surmise."

His eyes narrowed. "Would you lie to me?"

"How can I lie? When you have laid the Voice of

Command on me, how can I resist?" Her eye was swelling shut but she didn't look remotely defeated. She glowed with a quiet triumph.

"Well," the Master said. "That's settled, then. Since you already know our secrets, let me invite you to a council of war. This evening, three hours hence. My so-very-obedient-daughter will show you all to rooms and fetch whatever you need by way of bathing or refreshments in the meantime."

Seventeen

Kalina led them not back to their room but out into the garden. The world outside had fallen into darkness, save for the lights in the sky. The girl glimmered faintly with a light that emanated from her skin, her hair. She held the griffyn in her arms, stroking the soft head.

"What do you want?" Vivian demanded.

"I wish to help you. You need to know he will do nothing, acknowledge no claim, unless you are truly the Three in One. Your inner dragon must be restored."

Vivian had never felt so helpless. She avoided looking at Zee, knowing that the girl's words would serve to resurrect all of the guilt she'd been working to allay.

"There must be something we can do," he said.

"There is always something," Kalina agreed. "In this case, much. If you are willing, of course."

"What are you suggesting?" Vivian explored the pattern of magic that wove around the girl, trying to identify the misgiving that rubbed at her like a pebble in a shoe.

"I can restore your inner dragon."

"I thought you said you have no power."

The girl shrugged a graceful white shoulder. "There are spells that require no special magic. My brother is willing to help." She paused long enough to let the words sink in, then added, "We also need the blood of a dragon."

Icy water could not have more effectively stolen Vivian's breath. Images flooded her memory. Jehenna. The dragon Mellisande long held in captivity, her blood used to extend the life of the Sorceress indefinitely.

"You mean to use Godzilla! I will not participate in blood magic to raise one dragon at the cost of another."

"And if all the worlds should fall as a result? All dead, for the sake of your fine sensibilities?"

Zee's warm hand settled on Vivian's shoulder. Instead of offering comfort, his nearness made a shiver run through her from head to toe. A poisonous truth unfurled within her breast. It wasn't concern for Godzilla or the living beings affected by dying worlds that filled her with this cold dismay. It was pure selfishness.

She didn't want to revive the dragon. Too much power, so difficult and dangerous to control. Power that might ruin this fragile understanding developing between her and Zee. She didn't want to see that loathing in his eyes again, the hardness of his face when he'd thrust the dragonstone into her breast. Selfish, beginning to end, more concerned about her own comfort than that of either Godzilla or the people of the dying worlds.

"What harm will be done to the dragon if we proceed? Speak the ritual," Zee said, his fingers tightening as though he could hear all the things she did not say.

"He will contribute blood, but no more than can easily be spared," Kalina answered.

Vivian reached out again to sense Kalina's aura and found herself once again shut out. Whatever was hidden behind that slick barrier was beyond her ability to decipher.

Zee placed his other hand on her other shoulder, turning her to face him. His gaze claimed hers, agate eyes dark. "You once told me this was bigger than our own small lives. Remember?"

She nodded, unwilling to speak the truth aloud. It lay on her shoulders to repair what had been done in so much as she was able.

He shifted his hand so that it covered the scar above her breast. "I would like to see the harm I did undone. Every time I look at you and see this, how can I help but remember it was my hand that killed a part of you?"

"A part neither of us wanted," she whispered. Her fingers curled into the fabric of his shirt and clung there, eyes lost in his.

No softness came into his face, no bending. He knew as well as she did what it meant to have the dragon between them, and he was not one to spout platitudes to ease or alter the truth.

Blood magic. She wanted nothing to do with it, but then she'd never wanted to be a Dreamshifter, or turn into a dragon, or have all of this responsibility. All she'd wanted to do was heal people. Instead, a trail of death and destruction stretched behind her, from the day her grandfather had died and named her Dreamshifter until now. And if she failed to act, if she denied this opportunity, then there would be even more destruction and death.

Trust or trust not. The girl had given them her name. It would have to be enough.

"What do I have to do?" she asked.

Zee's lips curved slightly in a smile that was anything but pleasure, his eyes dark.

"I will show you. We have little time, and we must not be seen." Kalina was all business now that the decision had been made. "Follow me."

She led them away from the castle, along the same winding path they had taken yesterday, back to the grove. Touching Zee's arm, she felt him taut as a bowstring, knew his hand was on the hilt of his sword.

When they reached the grove, the brother was

waiting for them. Kalina obviously expected him. She kissed him on the cheek in greeting.

"Leander—is everything ready?"

"All according to the book."

"I don't like this," Zee growled. "The more eyes to see, the more tongues to tell tales."

Vivian didn't like it, either. Something in the power dynamic between the two was other than it looked on the surface. This fed her uneasiness, but the choice had already been made and the time for turning back was long past.

"Let's get this over with," she said.

Leander bowed. "We will perform the ritual in the grove. Your dragon is waiting for you."

Only a few steps further and Vivian could sense Godzilla faintly. He was frightened and lonely.

"You've bound him!" Vivian said, turning on the two who followed behind. "There was no need for that!"

"It is for his own protection," Leander replied, smoothly. "If the Master found him roaming freely on the island, he would kill him. We have done him no harm."

Vivian, thinking again of Jehenna and Mellisande, quickened her steps. Godzilla stood at the center of a circle of lighted torches, the picture of misery. His feet were bound with silver chains that allowed him to move within a restricted area but blocked his magic. He gave a little bleat of greeting when he saw them, straining against the chains but unable to cross the distance. Zee went to him, and the creature pressed his head against the warrior's broad chest.

"Free him at once!" Vivian ordered. She knew full well how it felt to be bound with silver, to feel it damping all magic, constricting the ability to communicate.

"That may not be wise..."

"He's just a baby. He traveled with us, slept with us,

saved our lives. There's no call to chain him up like that. Unless you intend some harm to him."

"The ritual requires that we draw blood from the dragon, only a small amount. A cupful, perhaps two. You will drink it."

"You're forgetting something," Zee said. "The dragonstone wound. Let's say that drinking dragon blood restores and regenerates the dragon within. What then? We stand by and watch Vivian bleed to death?"

"I've forgotten nothing," Kalina said. "Do not make the mistake of thinking me a fool."

No, Vivian thought, watching. *Anything but a fool.* "You're hiding something," she said aloud.

Kalina's face remained remote, unmoved, its expression far too old for a girl of her apparent age. "I cannot clear your mind for you."

Zee bent to unchain the dragon's feet. Godzilla stretched, snorted smoke out through his nostrils, and leveled a golden-eyed glare at Kalina and Leander.

Filled with misgiving, Vivian ran again through all the options available and came to the same inevitable conclusion. There was no other way. Her only hope of stopping the deaths of the Dreamworlds meant finding a way into the Forever, and the only chance of that lay with the Sorcieri. The Master wasn't going to tell her anything unless she faced him whole as Dreamshifter, Sorcieri, and dragon.

Zee stood beside Godzilla, eyes moving from Kalina to her silent brother and back again. "What says the sorcerer?" he asked at last. "Can you speak?"

Leander's eyes gleamed in the torchlight. "It is as my sister says. We take blood from the dragon—given voluntarily as you require. Then a simple enchantment to reverse the effects of the dragonstone. Shall we proceed? Or will I have my sister conduct you back to your rooms?"

Vivian closed her eyes, trying to feel her way into whatever she was missing. All that her unschooled magic could decipher was smooth and slippery. No holds. No entrance to the minds of either of these two, who promised so much while revealing so little.

Turning her mind to Godzilla, she sent a message as strongly as she was able but feeling it faint and flickering even so.

Are you willing?

And to receive back, *It is a small thing.*

With a deep sigh of acceptance, at last she nodded. "I'm ready. Let's get this done."

Eighteen

It was all wrong. Zee knew this as deeply as he'd ever known anything, but he was unable to find any path that was right. He had no magic, no extra ability to sense things as it seemed Vivian did. But he knew people, and he didn't trust any of these Sorcieri with a hair of Vivian's head, let alone with her life.

His own guilt and reluctance didn't help anything.

What he wanted, in the moments when he was able to be honest with himself, was simple. An ordinary life. He wanted to go run A TO ZEE BOOKS and paint pictures and create sculptures. He wanted to make love to Vivian every night and wake up to her in the morning, to have children together. Their children, his and hers, not some hideous offspring like he had spawned on the dragon woman Aidan.

Which brought him back to the whole dilemma all over again. There was no normal life, either for himself or for Vivian. No matter how he might rebel against the twisted weavings of fate that had brought them here and set their paths together—dragon slayer and Dreamshifter—there was no going back. No waking up as if this were nothing more than some dark dream.

The part of him that was hardwired to the killing of dragons would always be stirred by Vivian's dragon nature. It had been an ease and a relief to him to have her inner dragon sleeping, and now not only were they were about to wake it, they were going to use blood magic in the company of people whose motives he didn't understand or trust.

Kalina and Leander were smooth as silk, and every word they said smacked of lies and deceit. He suspected they were engaging in the most insidious and effective of deceit—that which revealed a part of the truth while hiding what they didn't want known.

Every fiber of Zee's brain and body shouted out against this blood magic, even though he understood perfectly why they were here. He knew Vivian felt compelled to do this thing because there was no other thing to be done. Even so, it was all he could do to keep from dragging her away. Out of this grove, away from these people, and into a dangerous landscape that would swallow them alive in moments, he had no doubt, if the Master willed it.

"I don't like it," he said again, eyes locked on Vivian's.

"I know." Her voice told him everything. She saw the same things he did but had made up her mind to take the risk. There was nothing he could do but stand with her and do his damnedest to kill anybody who harmed her. If they zapped him with some sort of magic thunderbolt, at least he'd go out fighting.

Godzilla shifted uneasily, snorting smoke once again.

"The dragon should be bound," Kalina said. "He could kill us all."

"You're frightened of a baby dragon," Zee said, one hand resting on Godzilla's shoulder. The scales felt smooth and cold as ice beneath his palm, though each one reflected back a tiny image of the torches so that he gleamed like fire.

"Only a fool has no fear of dragons," she retorted.

"Even the great Sorcieri?" His blood stirred in the way it always had when a weaker person was bullied or threatened, even as he marveled that he felt protective of a dragon. "I won't have him harmed or forced. The binding was bad enough."

"He's willing to share his blood with me." Vivian's face was set in lines of stone. "I can't communicate well with him, but that much I can read." Her eyes asked something of him. It took a minute but he registered it at last and nodded slightly, despite a deepening foreboding.

A little of the strain went out of her. "Zee will draw the blood," she said.

"It's not customary—"

"None of this is customary," Zee said, cutting across Kalina's words. If they were going to do this, it needed to be done. Any delay could be merely a ruse to create time for the springing of a trap. "If we are going to go through with the blood magic, I will take the blood."

Something flickered in Kalina's dark eyes. Leander shrugged. "Give him the cup and the blade. Let it be done."

The girl bent her head in submission, though there was nothing submissive about the set of her shoulders or her chin. She reached into the leather pouch tied around her waist, producing first a silver cup and then a dagger carved from black stone.

Zee swallowed hard. He had seen a knife like this before, in Jehenna's hands. The blade had been hungry, had brought out all of his long-suppressed capacity for violence, and he had very nearly slit her throat with it. Things would be a whole lot better if he had followed that inclination.

He took the cup, careful to avoid Kalina's fingers.

It was a thing of wonder, and he couldn't help admiring it despite everything. Purest silver, untarnished, it shone as though with a light of its own. The sinuous body of a dragon was engraved along the rim, its wings forming the handle. It was heavy, solid, and masterfully crafted. Before taking any further action, he carried it to Vivian. "Tell me if it is enchanted."

"Is your trust so small?" Kalina demanded. Anger made her look taller, harder. A powerful woman, no matter what she tried to say or portray.

"My blood and body. My dragon," Vivian countered, taking the cup into her own hands. "It's clean, as far as I can tell. But I don't trust the knife."

Relief flooded Zee. If he must be the one to tap the dragon, at least let it be with an honest blade. But the reprieve did not last more than an instant. The two women stood, eyes locked, the lines of tension so taut, he could have cut them with his sword. It seemed to him that so much as the twitch of a finger or the blink of an eye would blow the whole room up like a powder keg. Leander stood off to the side, out of the line of fire, and that was when Zee saw the truth of it, eyes for magic or no. Kalina had power, if not of magic then of something else. She was the dominant of the two. Leander served her.

"I have compromised as far as I am able. Your dragon slayer may draw the blood," Kalina said at last. "This is fitting, in its way. But he must use the ceremonial knife."

Again Vivian's eyes found Zee's, and again they asked the question. She would never compel him to this, but what choice did they have in the end?

Still, remembering, he crossed the room and knelt at her feet, head bent. Keeping his voice formal, he said, "I offered you my protection, Dreamshifter, wherever that should take us, whatever it should cost. I tell you now I trust neither this blade nor my ability to control it once it is in my hands." He looked up at her, to let her see all that he could not say. "Last I held a blade that was not my own, I nearly killed you with it."

His hands were trembling, he realized. Never had he felt such fear, in all the years since he had first learned to channel the warrior spirit he'd been born with. It was not fear of his own death, which seemed a small thing in that moment. It was the realization of all the evil he could be made to do by forces outside himself.

If she'd gone soft then, if she had relented into Vivian instead of wearing the mask of Dreamshifter, if she'd stroked his cheek, or kissed his hands, he would have been undone. But her eyes remained golden and reserved, and instead, she was more fully something other than she had ever been, even when shifted into a dragon.

Dreamshifter, dragon, and Sorcieri, he remembered.

"The power of command is mine to use," she said. "If need be, I will stop you in your tracks. I promise you this."

Zee had heard her use the Voice, though never on him. It would have to be enough. He could not mention the dynamics of power he had seen between the two Sorcieri, would have to trust that she had seen it, too.

So, he got to his feet and took the blade Kalina held out to him. At the first touch, his bloodlust leaped in excitement. The black stone in his hand felt alive, thirsty. Dream after dream ran through his memory like water, dreams in which he had carried this blade. The blade cared not for right or wrong. It sought only the joy of the thrust, the hot salty gush of human blood, the black steam of the dragon.

Godzilla made a small bleating sound, more sheep than dragon, and shifted restlessly away.

Zee felt split into two different selves.

One wanted only to use the knife. A dragon was an abomination, a beast born to be slain. His practiced eyes glanced around the torchlit circle, taking in the small space, calculating the likelihood of intervention from, or injury to, the humans present. He sniffed the scent of dragon, hot rock tinged with brimstone, registering that his prey was young and frightened, not yet old enough to flame. An easy kill. One swift thrust, just there where the foreleg met the breast—

His other self held back the killing strike, disliking the way the knife tried to do the thinking for him. When he killed—if he killed—it would be by his own will. An open battle, not the slaughter of a cornered and frightened beast.

Wait. That wasn't right, either.

The dragon had a name and was not to be killed at all. And the woman standing beside the sorceress had a name as well, was important to him...

"Zee?" she asked, and at the sound of her voice, his head cleared, not all the way, but enough.

I'm okay, he meant to tell her, but his lips didn't move. He wanted to tell her that the woman, Kalina, shone like a red flame while the man nearly vanished into the shadow, but again there were no words.

He had a task to do, only a simple thing. Fill the silver cup with blood for Vivian to drink. The dragon—Godzilla—would allow this. He was not to slay the creature, no matter how hungry the blade in his hand. Didn't want to.

As he approached the dragon, he felt a change of sensation as drastic as stepping into a warm room from out of a subzero winter wind. He was still conscious of the enchanted dagger in his hand, but his head was clear. Dragon magic. This was why the Sorcieri wanted the dragon bound. Not because Godzilla might fight back, but because his magic could counteract their own.

Vivian spoke before he found the words.

"Fill the cup with the dragon's blood and bring it to me." It was the Voice of Command, and it struck him between the shoulder blades like the shock from a Taser. His body stiffened in response, his eyes locked on hers. Tears rolled down both cheeks but she was composed, her will like iron.

She had spared him the decision and the guilt, taking it upon herself. Maybe it was better this way, since he still didn't trust the black stone blade.

Godzilla shifted position and stretched out his long neck, providing easy access. His hands no longer his own, Zee held the cup in one and the dagger in the other. Standing well back to avoid splatter, he thrust upward through the soft underside of the neck, then withdrew the knife.

Black blood followed the blade, the first drops steaming on the grass. Zee thrust the cup underneath to catch the flow, shifting the grip to the handle as the metal heated instantly. It took only a moment to fill. The blood continued to gush and he wondered how to stop it but was still under compulsion and unable to speak or act until his task was complete.

Carefully, so as not to spill, he carried the brimming cup back to Vivian.

She took it from him, avoiding his eyes, flinching at the burn of the hot silver against her palms. But she lifted the cup and drank, though the blood was scalding and stank of sulphur.

Perhaps the first swallow burned, but as she drank, the gold in her eyes grew brighter, the scales on her shoulders darkened and spread up her neck and along the edge of her jaw.

One breath, no more, and then all of the color fled from her face, her mouth falling open in shock and surprise. The cup fell to the ground as her hand went to the place just above her breast where Zee had once nearly killed her with the dragonstone, and came away drenched in blood.

She staggered. Zee had his arms around her before either had time to draw another breath.

Kalina bent to retrieve the cup.

"Get away from her," Zee ordered.

The girl laughed. "Or you will do what? You have no strength of will to match magic. You don't want me to heal her?"

Despite the mocking tone, her face and that of Leander were deadly serious. Kalina held the cup below the wound in Vivian's breast. Zee swallowed hard, watching it fill with crimson liquid. So fast. Too fast. She was going to bleed to death while he stood by and did nothing.

Once the cup was full, Kalina thrust it at her brother. "Make the exchange."

He took the cup from her and crossed to Godzilla. Zee saw now that in the other hand, Leander held a hollow tube, carved of the same smooth black stone as the blade. It was widened at one end into a rough funnel shape. Godzilla shook his head and snorted, but the boy murmured something to him and the dragon settled, presenting the wound for inspection.

Leander carefully fitted the end of the tube into the wound, then began to pour Vivian's blood into the funnel.

"No," Vivian gasped. "Don't let them, Zee. Don't you see?"

He didn't. His brain felt slow and fuzzy. Both hands were pressed over her wound, trying to staunch the blood that continued to well out between his fingers, around his hands, down her shirt, and onto the floor.

"Hurry," Kalina said. "She's bleeding too fast."

They weren't trying to kill her, then. That was all he could think.

"Done." Leander poured the last few drops of Vivian's blood into the funnel.

Kalina raised both arms and began an incantation. It was almost music but not quite, rising and falling with quavers and ululations that raised the hair on the back of Zee's neck. As her voice rose to an intense pinnacle of sound, the frail body in his arms jerked violently and then went limp.

"Best step back," Leander said, behind him.

"Stay away from me."

The blood had stopped flowing, he noticed half a second later. He put his hand to her throat, his own heart pounding desperately as he sought a pulse. It was there, slow and strong. Her skin heated beneath his fingers, growing so hot he jerked away involuntarily. Scales emerged on all exposed skin. Her chin sharpened, her face shifting into a reptilian shape. Her eyes flickered open, looking into his as Vivian for only an instant before the pupil narrowed from a circle into a vertical slit at the center of a predator's golden gaze.

Having seen the transformation before, not knowing how conscious she would be of herself as Vivian at the first, Zee stepped back as Leander had advised. Something was different this time, but it took a moment for Zee to register the details. She had been a green dragon before. This time, her scales continued to brighten after the shift, as if heated by a fire so intense, their very color was supercharged to a brilliant red-gold that hurt his eyes.

The horned head snaked down at the end of the long, sinuous neck and came eye to eye with Kalina. Zee held his breath, knowing full well what a dragon could do and feeling it would be no great loss if the sorceress met her end between the sharp teeth. At the same time, Vivian would be sick with regret when she came to herself.

If.

A small puff of smoke set Kalina to coughing, and the glorious dragon spread her wings and lofted herself upward toward the stars.

A wet sound caught Zee's attention. Godzilla stood at the center of a growing puddle of steaming black blood. He had planted all four legs wide, as though to brace himself. His broken wing hung askew, his head hung low, misery and fear clearly apparent in both golden eyes.

Blood continued to flow from the wound Zee had made. Guilt stabbed him.

"How do we stop the blood?" he demanded, crossing to Godzilla, just outside the spreading black pool.

"It can't be stopped," Kalina said. There was something softer in her voice than he'd anticipated and he swung to look at her.

"Don't you see?" she asked him. "We made the exchange, first of blood and then the words were said..."

"You lied! You said—"

"I said we would restore the dragon to your lady and that she would be well. It was necessary."

Zee stared at Godzilla with sick horror. The little dragon's eyes were dazed. His sides wheezed in and out, retracting a little between the ribs.

"So, he's just to be left to die?"

"Given the opportunity, are you saying you would have chosen differently?"

Hatred for these people and their slippery ways warred with the sick pity and guilt. He was afraid of the answer to that question. "How long will it take him to die?"

She shrugged. "Dragons are strong. It could be days."

"Can you ease him?"

"There is no magic that will work on a dragon."

"Then what was that mumbo jumbo you just did?"

"The exchange? He participated freely. I'd thought we would have to bind him again, but she bled so rapidly, I was afraid there would not be time. He consented."

"And he wouldn't consent to an easing of the pain? Or some sort of healing?"

"There is no healing. Only another exchange. Do you have another dragon who would consent to the trade? It is sad, I admit. He was very brave. Now I must go help prepare for the council. Are you coming?"

Zee shook his head. He didn't want to spend another moment in her company. And since it was his hand that had brought this death to Godzilla, the least he could do would be to bear witness. "I'll stay here."

He waited until the other two were gone and it was just him and the little dragon.

"I'm sorry," he said. "I didn't know what they were going to do."

There was fear in the golden eyes; he could read it clearly now. The certainty of death, with no hope, no help, no comfort.

Godzilla shifted a little to one side, presenting the wound.

"I can't help you," Zee said, watching the blood continue to flow.

The dragon turned his head, a dull eye looking up into Zee's face, and then he understood.

"I owe you a favor." And the head turned away.

Zee drew his sword and placed the tip between the dragon's leg and his breast. His hands were slippery with sweat and he tightened them on the hilt. Godzilla stood steady, pressing toward him rather than away. Focusing his mind to guide his hands with the greatest skill he knew, Zee slid the blade into the resisting flesh, angling up to reach for the heart.

Godzilla sighed.

The braced legs loosened, collapsing outward.

Zee had just enough time to jerk his sword free and leap back before the dragon sank downward into the black pool of blood with a dull splash. His eyes were already dark. He looked smaller with the life gone out of him, pitiful and alone.

Zee dropped the sword, his eyes blurred by hot tears. Memory came to him then of Vivian on her knees in cold sand, tears cold on her cheeks, eyes bleak. "It's only a dragon," he had said to her. And she had answered, "But he was so young, Zee."

There followed on the screen of his memory all of the dragons he had killed in his lifetime, in his dreams and out of them, each of them rising up from a bloody death to take flight across a sky bright with stars. The curse of his birth struck him fully for the first time, that he should have been born to this fate. Each one of those deaths had seemed right and almost holy at the time.

Now he felt drenched in guilt and blood beyond the hope of cleansing. Moving away from the dragon but still inside the ring of torches, he sank down onto the grass to hold vigil for the first dragon to whom he had given a name.

How long he sat there he didn't know, looking up from his introspection only when he sensed movement. Vivian stood there, herself, more or less. Her hair glowed with an intense red that was not her normal color, her eyes a gold too bright for human. She looked from Godzilla to Zee, her eyes traveling with his to the sword that lay at his feet, still black with the dragon's blood.

A small strangled noise escaped her and one of her hands covered her mouth, even as her eyes met his. Too much for words between them yet again, and he looked away. How was he to explain?

But then, inexplicably, she was kneeling beside him,

her arms around him, her face buried in his chest.

"I didn't..." he began, and then broke off, not knowing what to say.

"Shhh, shhh, I know." She pressed her lips against his to silence him. "He asked you for the death. What else were you to do?"

Holding her always against his heart, he shifted her so that she sat on his outstretched legs. A long time they sat this way, arms wrapped around each other, silent, his face pressed against her shining hair.

"What now?" he asked, at last.

"We have a dinner to attend."

"I don't want to go." He tightened his arms around her. If he let her go now, if they left this place, she was going to slip away again.

"Neither do I." She leaned back and traced the scars on his cheek with her finger. "I'm so sorry, Zee, about, well, everything."

"Fate." He kissed her. "I've been sitting here mulling on our fate. It's a cruel path we've been given, the two of us."

"Would you change it, if you could?"

He glanced up at the dead dragon, and then back to Vivian. Her golden eyes still held that predatory gleam, the pupil not yet quite round. He traced a finger over the smooth skin of her jaw, still faintly marked with a pattern of scales. None of it mattered, not anymore. Her soul was still her own, and her heart. At the core, she was always Vivian.

"Not if it meant missing out on you." He kissed her then, lingering, aware that every kiss could be the last. Important to remember, then, the sound of her breath, the scent of her, woman laced with the lingering smell of hot stone, the soft fall of her hair over his hands.

Someday, he would paint her again, drawing on all

of these things. He hadn't had a chance to paint her from anything but dream, he realized suddenly. Since the day she'd walked into A TO ZEE as a flesh-and-blood woman, too much had happened too fast to allow for art. A loss, but again, one he would suffer willingly for the chance to stand beside her.

When she pulled away, her eyes, though still golden, had reverted to fully human, and the scales had faded. It would be easy to pretend, but he was done with all of that.

"If I were given the opportunity to choose," he said, "knowing all that I know now, I would still be here. Can you believe that?"

Her face went still and remote and he thought he'd said too much. But she laced her fingers into his hair and pulled his head down so she could kiss him. Then, not looking at him, her breath tremulous and warm against his cheek, she whispered, "Me too, God help me, if it wasn't for all those who died through my failures. What right have I..."

Her voice broke, and he gathered her in against his chest, feeling the rise and fall of her breast as she drew three deep, shuddering breaths. Not sobs, though. When she looked at him again, he saw what had been forged from all that she had passed through.

"My life is not my own," she said. "There may have been a time for me to walk away, but that is past. When the time comes—well, there may be no coming back to Vivian for me. Do you understand this?"

Looking into her face, he knew that it was true. Tracing the soft line of her lip with his thumb, he smiled a little, only to ease her, for his heart was full of nothing but shadows and heartache.

"You will always be Vivian, whether you come back to me or not. And I will guard you to my last breath, whether you be woman, dragon, sorcerer, or Dreamshifter, or all the things in one."

A soft cough drew his attention. Leander, standing in the shadows. "The council is about to begin. Will you come?"

Zee wanted to say no. To grab Vivian by the hand and take her away from all of this, but there was no place in all the worlds where they could escape from what they had become.

Nineteen

Leander led them back into the castle and through a maze of corridors. Vivian let him lead but could have found the meeting place on her own. Her dragon self, burning in her belly, supplied a whole new energy to her newly awakened awareness of magic. It was as though she had a living map in her head. She could visualize all of the rooms of the castle and how they fit together. She knew the books in the library and how to tell one person's spell-working from another's. Before she entered the council room, she could sense the magical ability of each person within, distinct as a signature. One soul burned especially bright, overpowering the others. A densely woven white light, so closely contained it seemed about to explode. The Master, she thought, as the door opened. Only the Master could have so much power.

But then she saw the truth. The room itself was unaltered by magic. Cracks spidered the stone walls and pitted the floor. All was cold, rough-edged stone, unsoftened by carpets or tapestries. Even the long table, running the length of the room, was bare stone, empty of all but goblets filled with water.

The Master sat at the head of the table, with Kalina standing just behind his left shoulder. On the table before him rested a seeing stone. Leander slipped into an empty chair to his right. The Giants and Jared filled seats down each side of the table. Two were yet empty, but Vivian chose to remain standing, Zee beside her.

As she entered the room the Master stopped speaking in mid-sentence. Every other head swung around, all eyes fixed on her. Even Jared's sightless gaze was trained in her direction. The awareness inside her registered a flare from each being capable of magic in the room. The Giants, their magic hard-edged and workmanlike. The Master, weaker than she would have thought. Nothing from Leander. But Kalina held an incandescent fire of power, closely compressed and hidden by a screening spell that mimicked the binding. Compared to her, the magic of all the others was nothing more than candle flame.

"As you see," Vivian said into the silence, "the dragon has been fully restored. Perhaps now we may speak of the way into the Forever."

The Master rose from his seat and came toward her, his fingers running across Leander's shoulders in a caress as he passed. *So weary*. The heavy use of magic in the last days had taken its toll. He shuffled. His shoulders were bent and fragile. Vivian's power was more than enough to match his.

The old man's eyes ran over the line of her jaw and down to the pattern of scales on her shoulders. She stood unflinching beneath the examination. When his eyes met hers, it was a direct assault, all the force of his will directing her to yield, to bow before him and acknowledge him as Master. If he had been kinder, she might have felt a hesitation, an inclination to humor him, but he was a harsh, selfish, unfeeling old man who had brought his demesne to the brink of extinction. To him she would never yield. So, she held his gaze, unblinking, matching him will for will, power for power.

In the end, his whole body jerked, as if in seizure.

His skin had grayed to the color of ashes and was wet with perspiration. “Anathema,” he whispered. “A woman’s power should be bound.”

Vivian kept her voice matter-of-fact, showing neither respect nor contempt. “I believe you have some information to share with us.”

She had broken him. He staggered and almost fell as he turned to shuffle back to his seat. Kalina, ever attentive, was there to catch him. As she took his arm to offer support, a tinge of color flowed back into his skin; his back straightened. Vivian felt the subtle shift in magic and marveled that the old man should be so blind as to miss completely what his daughter was capable of.

By the time Kalina pulled out the heavy oak chair for him, the Master had regained sufficient presence to speak with a quiet authority.

“You have asked me how to enter the Forever without the Key. Here is the tale as it was told to me by my father, and by his father before him. I call it a tale, because it may be no more than that. In living memory, there has been not one instance where this incantation has been attempted.” He closed his eyes and intoned:

“If she who is the Three In One—Dreamshifter, dragon, and of the sorcerer’s blood—shall come by night unto the cave that doth give birth to dreams, and if she shall there offer up the heart’s blood of a willing man, uttering the secret incantation, then she shall be given access thereunto.”

His eyes opened, trained squarely on Vivian, and the malevolence within him shone clear. He opened his hands and spread them wide, palms up. “Alas, I know not the incantation. Nor, to my knowledge, is it found in any of my books.”

“I know it,” Kalina said.

“Silence!” The old man lifted his hand and turned

as if to strike. Vivian braced herself to intervene but the Master stood frozen, his hand raised. The blow did not descend.

Kalina did not cower before him. Her chin was uptilted, eyes wide, and it was her magic that held him. "I am done with silence and pretense. These good Giants have traveled far. The Lady Vivian has sacrificed beyond measure to restore the dragon spirit that lies within her. We will treat them now with the respect they deserve."

"Leander." The old man rubbed the side of his face and turned to his son. "Subdue your sister."

The boy dropped his eyes, remaining in his chair.

"Don't look to him for help," Kalina said. "He has no magic."

"But—"

"He never has had magic. Not since he was a baby. I lent him mine all these years. He knows the truth of it. You were too blind."

"Yours was bound—"

She laughed. "You are not strong enough to bind what I have."

The old man rubbed his face again, as though the skin bothered him. The right side of his mouth had begun to droop, and the right eyelid hung half closed.

"All this time?" he asked, his words slurring slightly.

"I love my brother, so I let you believe. The time for childish games has passed. The destruction of the worlds must be stopped before we all die. You are too weak. My brother lacks any magic at all. I know the incantation; I know the spell."

Stroke, Vivian thought, looking at the way the old man's face drooped. His right hand wasn't working properly now. He tried to lift it in a questioning gesture but it fell back heavily on the table, a dead weight. His eyes followed it, confused. Vivian couldn't find it in her heart to feel any sympathy.

Kraal stood, turned to Kalina, and bowed deeply. "While we have been wasting our time here at the whim of a soft-headed old man, our world, along with the others, is in mortal danger. If we are to save anything, we must act swiftly. You say that you know the magic. Will you help us?"

A challenge crossed the room between the two, something that Vivian could not read.

"I know the magic," Kalina said.

"And will you perform the rite?"

"I will."

"What bond do you offer as good faith?"

"My magic and my life."

The exchange had a ritual flow to it, a sense that these were words passed down through generations. No matter how strong the magic coiled within her, Vivian was a stranger to the lore. Could not possibly know the history or the forms of ritual agreement or the shape of the rite Kraal and Kalina both seemed to understand.

And now both of them turned to her.

"And you—are you willing to act as the One, to perform the rite that will lead into the Forever?"

"Take care," Zee warned.

She heard him and understood that there was more there than she was being told. She also felt the darkness behind her open eyelids, knew that the death of every Dreamworld would take something more from the light until there was nothing left.

"I will," she said.

"What bond do you offer as good faith?"

"Me," Zee said before she could speak the words Kalina had spoken. "I am her bond."

A stark silence filled the spaces in the room. Kalina sucked in her breath. The Giants all sighed. And the old

Master began to laugh. He laughed until the tears rolled down his cheeks and he was gasping for air. He laughed until he could no longer catch his breath, and his face turned red then slowly purple as he wheezed and clutched at his throat. Leander rose to catch him as he collapsed sideways out of his chair and struck the floor.

Again, silence spread throughout the room.

"Dead," Leander said.

A stone fell from the ceiling and crashed down onto the table, cracking it in two.

"The castle was molded by his will," Kalina said, glancing up at the gaping hole above them. "I can hold it a little while, but not long. We must go at once."

"What about the body?" Vivian hesitated.

"There is no time for him." A sharp, rending noise reverberated through the room. Another rock fell. Kalina grabbed her elbow and urged her toward the door. "We must go."

Vivian braced her feet and held her ground. "He was your father."

Leander got to his feet. His face was streaked with tears. "The stones will bury him. It is as he would have wished."

The boy's grief eased her as Zee grabbed her free hand and pulled her toward the door. Poe was right at her heels. She caught a glimpse of Kalina stooping to pick up the griffyn cub just before a creak and a groan shivered from the soles of her feet to the crown of her head. A heavy wooden timber fell across her path, so close it skimmed the front of her shirt and scraped the skin from her hands.

One of the Giants picked her up like a child while another rushed to shift the fallen beam. All was a blur of crashes and falling objects, of trying to look back to see that Zee was safe, and Poe, to see another of the Giants carrying Jared.

It was dark in the corridor. Kalina called up a light, and Vivian, copying the shape of the magic, called up another. Through one corridor after another they ran, then outside and away from the disintegrating castle. But here, still, they were not safe. A geyser threw up mud and water fifty feet into the air. The earth rumbled and quaked.

"How do we get off the island?" Kraal asked.

"How did you get here?"

"A door. Between our world and this. It is closed now."

Again, the earth rumbled and trembled. Steam spouts emerged through cracks not far away. The whole thing was going to blow any minute.

Vivian slid down out of the Giant's arms, knowing what she needed to do next. Her eyes met Zee's and his lips twisted a little in a crooked smile.

"I'll hold your clothes," he said, and kissed her. "You are Vivian, always. No matter what."

Twenty

The shift was easy this time. Just a call to the dragon part of her, newly wakened and healed, and a letting-go of the control that kept her Vivian. Once in dragon form, everything became simpler, all geometric angles and planes. There was do and don't do, with no shades of guilt and anger and grief. She was hungry, and the first overwhelming rush of desire was for the hunt.

Her nostrils flared with the stink of smoke, brimstone, dust. Closer by was the smell of blood and fear. It wafted off the two-legged ones gathered together. They stood still, not fleeing, but were not defenseless. There were clubs and bright steel and those who would fight. A danger of magic from the smallest female, but not enough to bind.

One of the males stepped forward. He wore the bright sword but it remained sheathed. His hands were open. Danger flared in his eyes but he made no move to harm her or defend himself. He spoke one word.

"Vivian."

The word was like an arrow, a spike, straight to the heart. It held her in place, wings folded.

"Vivian," he said again. And then a third time, "Vivian."

Zee. Not the first time he had named her so when

she lost her human self in the wildness of the change. Memories of herself as also small and two-legged surfaced, along with the knowledge of the task ahead.

She bent her forelegs and knelt to him, stretching out her neck and resting her head on the ground. It was an act of trust. One of her memories was of mortal combat with this man and his hatred of dragons. He could slay her in an instant if he so desired.

Still, he did not draw the sword.

He turned and gestured to the others. "Hurry!"

"Will she carry us all?" one of the Giants asked.

Zee shook his head. "I doubt she'd make it off the ground. Is there another way off the island?"

"There's a boat," Leander said.

Zee nodded. "Kraal goes with us. Kalina and Jared. Leander?"

"The Giants are guests. I will go with them in the boat. I know these waters."

"Go, then." Kraal nodded his head toward the rest of his band, and Leander led them at a run toward the water. Zee helped Kalina, the griffyn cub in her arms, step up onto Vivian's neck, then Jared. Anger flared and a little puff of smoke escaped Vivian's nostrils as his uncertain footsteps made their way along her neck and onto her back.

"Easy," Zee said to her. "We will take care of him later."

The Giant came next. He was heavy, his footsteps crushing, but she was strong and could withstand his weight. Last of all, Zee, carrying Poe. Just in time. An explosion shook the earth. Off to the north of the island, a stream of molten stone spewed up. The last remnants of the castle crumbled and collapsed in on itself. The earth heaved and rocked. Vivian spread her wings and beat them, once, twice, three times before she was clear of the earth with her burden.

Below, Leander and the Giants raced destruction. The ground beneath their pounding feet heaved in waves like the sea. Leander lost his balance and fell. One of the Giants scooped him up. She could see the boat, not far now. But before they could reach it, the earth opened right before their feet.

"Back!" one of the Giants cried, retreating from the steaming crevice red with molten rock at the bottom. They raced along the side but it grew, cutting them off from their escape. One of the Giants fell, the earth giving way beneath his feet. He screamed as he fell, vanishing into the molten stone.

The Giant carrying Leander turned, pivoted, leaped wildly and cleared the fiery pit with only inches to spare. Another of the Giants followed successfully. The rest of them fell. Vivian was well above the chaos now, winging straight toward the open sea. Her last glimpse of the figures far below showed the survivors stepping into the boat.

An explosion half sound, half pressure hit her like an invisible giant bulldozer, driving her off course. Turning her head to look back over her shoulder, she saw the island erupt into a volcano. Feeling the passengers on her back sliding dangerously, she managed to correct her flight and tilt to the other side. The air continued turbulent and she did her best to ride out the rapid updrafts and drops. It wasn't going to be enough. She was flying without control. Worse, the air was filled with ash. It didn't trouble her to breathe it, but the humans would suffocate before long, if they didn't fall during one of the updrafts and die in the boiling water below.

Reaching deep into memory and what remained of Vivian, she encountered the other thing, the Awareness, full to the brim with magic. She could no longer ignore or deny it. Dragon magic and Sorcieri came together in a clear fusion of light. All at once, she could see the air currents, not only feel them. Tentatively, she pushed back at a wave heading toward her with her will. It slowed. She tried shaping it, smoothing it a little. When it hit, she was able to flow up over it and down again without being jolted and storm-tossed. She wielded this ability to smooth the air, pushing back the turbulence, creating a clear space through which they could travel.

Over and over again, she eased the air currents in the direction she wanted to travel. They were halfway across the lake that surrounded the island. Still a long way to go, and already she was tiring. Each beat of her wings, instead of feeling wild and free, required concentration and focus. Her muscles ached and the air felt thin. This confused her. She had not flown that far, and while the air currents made things more difficult, the magic smoothed them out.

That was it. The magic. Each use of that reservoir drained her strength as well, which set up a problem. If she used the magic, she was going to run out of energy to fly. And if she didn't, the wild currents in the air were going to crash them all into the water below. Even as she readied her will to smooth another air current, she heard a voice from behind.

"I'll manage the magic. You just fly."

The Sorcieri girl. Vivian could sense her magic, strong and bright. She waited, ready to take action if necessary, but the air wave smoothed before her and let her keep flying. A calm channel opened in front of her, farther than she could have managed in so short a time. It was also free of ash and debris. As she took advantage of the opening and increased her speed, a wind assisted her from behind.

She could fly faster now but was unable to chart her progress. The air directly around her was clear and calm, but outside the tunnel of safety, all she could see was gray. This made her uneasy. What would happen when they landed? The supply of magic was not infinite, and they were still close enough to the volcano to be suffocated by ash.

The world of the Sorcieri was neither Dreamworld nor Between, which left her a little confused as to where they were now. Her pendant had always told her the answer to this question, absent in the Dreamworld, present when Between. In dragon form, she couldn't look at it, couldn't check. What made the most sense was that the island and its weaving of magic barriers were something like Surmise, built out of the Between but separate. Which meant they were Between and she could open a Dreamworld.

If she dared.

They had barely survived the last encounter with a dying Dreamworld, and much of that had been luck. Chances of succeeding a second time were slim. As were chances of surviving on the ground below. Kalina was tiring. Strong as the girl was, there was only so much magic to be used before time to refill was necessary.

No safety anywhere. Only greater and lesser risks.

A fragment of dream came to her, memory from the long past when she had not understood what she dreamed. In the dream, there was a long, round tunnel, grayish white. At the end of it, a green door with a brass knob. She had been flying in the dream, with an odd sense of carrying weight that was not her own.

Faith. It was all she had left to her.

And so, calling on the Dreamshifter while still in dragon form, she focused on that green door, making it a reality. What lay behind it, she didn't know, and there was no time to wonder. Without a human voice to speak, she formed the word with her will and sent it out ahead of her.

"Open!"

She opened her dragon mouth and uttered a wordless cry, feeling the Awareness within join in the command. The green door slammed open, just in time for her to stretch out her neck curve her wings, and glide through.

Water as far as the eye could see. A stiff wind smelling of salt and seaweed blew directly against her and she curved her wings and altered her course to move with it rather than fight it. At first, her dragon blood surged at the scent of the sea and the wide sky. A desire to fly free and wild flowed through her, to shed the burdensome weight on her back. Friends, she reminded herself. But the longer she maintained the dragon shape, the harder it was to retain the memory of her human emotions.

Tacking back and forth across the wind like a sailboat, using it to enhance her speed and aid her flight, she swooped down lower for a closer look. The water rolled in even swells, the deep blue of open ocean. Dark shapes moved below the surface, but even her dragon vision couldn't get a clear lock on what they were. Too small for whales but big enough to be dangerous.

Her body was too heavy to allow her to ride the wind currents like an albatross, and her wings were tiring. She needed food to sustain the high-energy burn of carrying the additional weight on her back, a chance to recover from the magic she'd drained escaping from Sorcerer's Island. If she crash-landed into the water, she could float for awhile, but she'd never be able to launch back into the air.

Zee's voice called out to her, clear and beloved. "Are you able to open a door straight through into another Dreamworld?"

Maybe. Opening a door directly from one world into another would mean that they would have to be bumped right up against each other, side by side. There were likely parallel worlds in existence, but no guarantee that this was one of them. Any door she opened would most likely take them back into the Between, so dangerously unstable. But then, any Dreamworld, including this one, could be wiped out in an instant.

The thought of those worlds gone dark chilled even her dragon blood. She scanned the horizon for a blot of darkness eating away at water and sky. No sign of danger, but that meant nothing. Sinking ever lower as her tiring body lost altitude, she forced her thoughts away from the fear and toward a solution. If she could shape her will just right—that of dragon, Dreamshifter, and Sorcieri—maybe she could open a door directly into the Cave of Dreams.

She pictured the cave as it had been the first time she had seen it, with the living Guardian and the sound and color of the dreamspheres. She'd been so frightened then, by the vibration and the heat and the dragon. Now she would pay any price to restore the cave to what it had once been. Now the Guardian of the Cave was dead, murdered, the dreamspheres decaying back into raw dream matter and taking the Dreamworlds with them.

Aidan will pay for this.

Anger fueled her power and she used the surge to create a door. It formed unevenly at first, a wavering portal of light and dark completely unlike her usual green doors. Still, she flew toward it, all of her attention on shaping what needed to be, blotting out fear and the memory of her last experience with the raw dream matter.

Twenty-one

"Dragon down."

The report came through loud and clear, amplified into a buzz as every dragon received the message and sent it on. The tone was angry and edged with both fear and bloodlust. They were all hungry and water was in short supply. Three dragons dead in the last two days, and the rest weakening. The first two had been young and lacking their full strength. They succumbed early to the lack of water and food, lying down to rest and unable to rise again. The third, a cripple with a damaged wing, had simply dropped from the sky like a stone, exhausted.

"Volcano's soon to erupt," Teheren sent, but for Aidan alone. The big red-gold dragon flew in formation just on her right flank, in the tradition-honored position of first lieutenant. At all hours, in flight, waking and sleeping, he was there. Watching, waiting, offering up observations that always just escaped crossing the line into criticism or advice.

Now, Aidan ignored him, circling back to where a dragon crouched on the ground, sides heaving, neck extended, wings spread a little but not enough to take flight. It was an old male this time, his scales thickened and dulled with age. He hissed at her approach, shooting out a thin jet of fire.

This infuriated her, stirring her wild blood. She

wanted to swoop in from above and take his neck between her teeth. The crunch of scales and bone, the burst of hot blood, the taste of flesh. She, too, was hungry. With an effort of will, she restrained the desire and came to land in front of the fallen one, a safe distance from any more flames. Teheren touched down in perfect formation. No sense of fatigue from him, or anger, or hunger. No subtle undercurrents from him at all.

This was a concern, but not one she had time for, because she was picking up undercurrents in force from the rest of the flight. Discipline held for the moment, but barely. She felt them crowding the boundaries, all moving a little closer to the fallen dragon, who had already shifted in their minds to prey.

The old dragon lifted his head and stared them all down defiantly. "Have we fallen to this?"

Real speech, not just on the silent channels. She felt the echoes roll through the ravening throng behind her. They retreated, one infinitesimal step. Listening.

Teheren took this opportunity to cross the line from observation to advice. His voice came through on the private channel between them, loud and clear and without even the veneer of respect. *Great sky above. Pity you let him speak. Now there is trouble.*

Aidan remembered, all at once, that the red-gold had not eaten from any of the kills. Not once. Not a mouthful, not a bone. He had stood, always, silently watching. Too silent. She should be able to read him, but when she tried, there was nothing but a smooth, blank surface.

"Will you tear me apart before my death, as you did the others?" the old dragon asked, in the long-unused speech of the Forever. Unused but not forgotten. All of the dragons understood the words and reacted to them. "Have we fallen to such savagery?" He coughed, shooting a thin stream of flame. Not pure, Aidan noticed, but tinged with green and weak.

Not one of the dragons moved. They might have been statues, so still were they. Still angry, though. Still hungry. One wrong word and that hunger could turn into ugly revolt. If she killed the old one then, it would reassert her dominance, but his words would linger and fester, making her appear uncivilized and barbarian.

She hesitated.

"Go ahead," the old dragon said. "But know this before I die. My name is Olcifor and my mother was of the dragons of the Forever, so old am I. This land is not as she told it to me. All my life, I held out hope of meeting one of the true dragons, but it seems that they and the land are dead. Death is welcome, and I offer my flesh freely to all. I ask only for a clean death, worthy of a long life. Who will offer it to me?"

I will. Teheren sent the answer clear and triumphant , and then spoke it aloud, the words a little awkward from a voice long unused but all too comprehensible. "I will."

Rage ignited Aidan's blood, evaporating fear. How dare Teheren seize this opportunity, the one she needed to confirm herself as their just and decisive leader? Already, he stood in position. The dying dragon stretched out his neck, asking for the death blow. How did he know the ancient speech? Aidan herself did not know it. Her mother had been human and Dreamshifter; the dragon blood came from her father.

And so, she risked her one secret advantage and shifted into her human form. The softness of skin felt strange after the long stretch as dragon. Even stranger was the curve of her belly and the weight of the baby within. She should not be so far along with child and she was staggered by the reality. Her hips felt loose, her breasts heavy, the skin of her belly taut and ridged with red marks. She'd meant to make a decisive speech in the human tongue, but instead found herself staring down at the strangeness of her own body. The baby moved and kicked, a sensation so foreign, it nearly sent her into panic, as if the child were a parasite and not the much-desired warrior son.

In human form, she could not listen to the unspoken communications that surely ran through the channels. But every dragon in the flight had shifted its attention to her. Now it was her task to make sure they saw her as the leader and not as prey.

"The right and responsibility of the kill is mine," she said, moving into position next to Teheren. "But I grant this sacred task to my second-in-command." She bowed slightly to the old dragon. "May you find your place in the stars."

An ancient formula, taught to her by her mother before she died. The old one's response ought to be "Fly high; I go in peace." Instead, he shot a jet of flame at her. He was weak, but it was close enough to redden her now-vulnerable skin. "You blaspheme," he said. "A half-breed masquerading as dragon. I will not speak the last rites with you."

Teheren dealt the killing blow just a moment too late. The words were said and rang out loud across the ranks of the assembled dragons. Silence grew thick and heavy. The nearest ranks of dragons moved in, almost imperceptibly, drawn to the blood and the promise of meat. Unconsciously, Aidan's hands moved to cover the mound of baby.

"Hold ranks!" she commanded, pitching her voice to carry. "I am Aidan, daughter of Allel and the King of the Forever. I rule by right of blood and birth. Who among you dares to challenge my right—you who have been born in the shadows of the Between, who have no speech among you, no knowledge of anything other than blood and lust and flight?" She paused, watching them, gauging the response from visible cues and intuition.

So far, all held in position. There was tension, but the ranks held. Timing was everything and she didn't dare push the limits. Only a few seconds' pause, and then she turned to Teheren.

"Your kill, your right of command," she said, formally, handing over the responsibility of sharing out the meat. It would look like respect to the ignorant horde, she hoped, while relieving her of the difficulty of managing them while in human form.

Unless she had misjudged him, of course. He was no ignorant Between-born, and he could destroy her with a single blow of a heavy head swung on a long neck, a spike from a talon, or tear apart her flesh and swallow her in a single bite. She had given him an opportunity to gain status, though, and she doubted he would turn on her in this moment.

Teheren moved forward to stand between the dead and the press of hungry dragons. The sun struck fire from his burnished scales, making him look as though he was more flame than dragon.

In that moment she began, for the first time, to be truly afraid. When Teheren spoke again, her frail human flesh quivered before the impact of his voice, even as her soul raged against the way he kept twisting her plans.

"Dragons, hear me. You were born of the Between, it is true, and yet all dragons come from the Forever, and here we all return. We are no longer the feral Between-born, acting like the mindless beasts with which we have been surrounded. We must act accordingly. This dragon, Ulcifor, is older than any. He has come home to the land of his childhood, the land that belongs to all of us, and he has earned his rest. The flesh of dragons serves to nourish the earth; our blood makes the rivers flow. Look around you—you wonder at the devastation of the land, you ask yourselves if the legends were wrong and if we have come here only to die. I say to you—some of us shall surely die, but we will nourish the earth in death. If we consume the flesh of this noble dragon into our own flesh, we contribute to the decay of the land. I know you are hungry, as am I. But this, too, I know. If we carry his body to the place where the river once ran and leave him there to his rest, it will be the beginning of healing the land."

Aidan felt the tension ease little by little as Teheren spoke. He was insane. As hungry as the others were, they would surely break ranks and devour the fallen, allowing her to be again the bountiful leader providing for their needs. She would say something about how all were nourished by the one, that the health of dragons surely superseded any mumbo jumbo about the barren earth. Earth was earth. Life was life.

When he was done, he stood his ground, making it clear that he meant to defend the old dragon's body with his own. Good. Let there be more meat. Maybe a mouthful for all rather than only the select few. When the first of the dragons moved forward, she prepared herself, to speak if needed, to shift back to dragon if force became necessary.

And that was when the first of the pains struck her. Fierce and primal, it gripped her belly in a cramping vise that stole her breath and would have doubled her over if her will had been less strong. She endured, keeping to her feet, hoping that no sign of weakness had registered on her face. A vain hope. She could feel the cold sweat and the dragons would be able to scent her pain and the thundering of her blood.

Vision blurred, she watched the approach of the dragon vanguard, waited for them to tear into the kill. It would distract them. While they were gorging and Teheren was preventing chaos, she could slip away a little and recover. Surely she was seeing things wrong because of the pain.

She blinked and passed a clammy hand over her eyes.

The four dragons, two large females and two young males, took to the air in formation. Flying in low over the kill, with perfect precision they hooked their talons and lifted the dead weight up, winging a slow and heavy flight toward the dry riverbed. The rest of the dragons turned and followed on foot, raising a great, choking cloud of dust that blinded her, setting tears running down her cheeks.

No, no, no. This wasn't right. None of it was right.

Another pain took her, this time making her gasp and weakening her knees. No denying the source of the pain now and what it meant.

My son. It is too early.

She had seen dragons give birth to stillborns, tiny, perfectly formed creatures born too early. Some were far enough along to draw a few breaths and survive for an hour or two. But not this one within her, surely. It had only been a matter of days. Maybe it had to do with shifting from human to dragon and back again. The dragon's metabolism burned so much hotter and faster than the human, and the period of carrying the young was a matter of three months as opposed to nine.

If she shifted back to dragon it might stop the blinding pain, prevent the loss of the warrior child who had been so many long years in the making. Little by little, the contraction eased, and she was able to draw a full breath and think more clearly. She was surprised by a sudden longing for her mother. The calm advice, the gentle soothing hands. A thousand years gone, and still she remembered that touch. No human hands had touched her in all the years since, with the exception of the Warrior. His hands had been gentle enough, but then he had thought her someone else. When he realized who and what she was, he had spurned her.

The memory of the Warrior's rejection steeled her.

She would have her revenge on him, on the dragons who had made her mother outcast from the Forever, on all the worlds. By the time she was through, there would be nothing left. She prepared to shift to dragon, but another contraction swept over her. Fighting it, struggling for breath and for the energy it took to make the shift, she felt hands on her shoulders.

A shock ran through her at the human touch and she opened her eyes to see a man. His face was weathered, his golden eyes more dragon than human, the black pupils long horizontal slits.

"You mustn't shift now." His voice was deep and a little rusty from disuse. There was an odd accent to his speech, the vowels too short, the consonants overly pronounced, but she could understand him without difficulty.

"What business is it of yours?"

Her own words came out garbled, so close was she to the shift. She could feel the hard edges of her dragon consciousness, the armor of scales, the promise of flight, the safety of pure, brute strength.

Fingers dug into her shoulders, shaking her, distracting her. "You will kill the baby."

That stopped her. She wavered between the two states, listening, not fully able to come back to human or to continue into dragon. The pain began again, but it was a half pain. She was aware of it but could step outside and watch it with other eyes.

No words this time, she only looked her question at the man who would not let her go.

"Come back. You must go through the pain in order to deliver the baby. It is the way."

"It's too early," she said, feeling her body slipping back to its human half against her will. Those fingers, those eyes, disrupted her focus, as if the pain and fear were not enough.

The golden eyes shifted to her belly. “I think not.”

“As if you have knowledge!” She spat at him. “It’s been only days.”

“But you shifted to dragon, accelerating the growth. And then back again. Is it so?”

This time, she felt the contraction coming and fought against it, as if somehow she could stop her muscles from the rhythmic tightening. It was no good. And this time, it was worse. She staggered, and the man supported her, then lifted her from the ground and began to carry her.

She slapped at his chest, but the blows were weak and futile. By the time the contraction eased, she felt limp as a wilted plant, her entire body drenched in sweat.

“Put me down.” She wasn’t sure her knees would hold her, but if not, she would crawl. Away somewhere, behind a rock, hoping not to become prey.

“Shall I? And let them consume you and the child both? Here, you have at least a chance of safety.”

The air darkened and cooled as he stepped around a gnarled bush, which had a few dusty leaves still clinging to it, and ducked beneath a rock formation into a cave. Enough light filtered in for her to see that the floor was smooth dirt and had been swept. Her captor set her down with her back against the wall and stepped away, light and swift, before she could kick him.

“Who are you?” she demanded, staring up at him. He looked familiar, although she knew few human men. The Warrior looked much different, and the other one, the one she had spiked, was dead.

“You know me not?” He stood in the shadows. It was the rhythm of the speech, the accent, the eyes, that told her the truth.

“Teheren,” she said.

He offered a stiff half bow. “Flesh and bone.”

Why are you helping me? Before she could speak

the words, the pain came again, and after that, there was no speaking. They contractions were nearly constant, one on top of another with barely space to catch her breath. Panic beat at her, born of the thought that this would go on for days, weeks, years, that the child within would simply continue to grow until it consumed her flesh from within.

Time slipped and shifted. There was only the pain for very long stretches, and always the fear. Sometimes a face hung over her, and once she thought a hand smoothed hair back from her forehead. At one point, she roused enough to feel wetness between her legs, and looking down, she saw her thighs gleaming with blood. The dragons would smell it, would be upon her. Fear gripped her, but she was defenseless now, too weak to shift, too tired to run. Her eyes sought out Teheren, saw his nostrils flare, and braced herself for him to shift and attack. Instead, he crossed to the mouth of the cave, looking out.

"They are still busy at the riverbed. I suggested that they pile stones on the body. It is difficult for a dragon to move a stone. But they won't be long. This baby needs to come soon."

Her lips were dry and cracked. She licked them and managed one word. "Why?"

"Why am I helping you?"

She nodded.

"Too many dragons have died. I do what I can to save the few who remain."

So he was against her, then. Pain came again, this time in a mounting wave that felt like it would tear her insides out. She heard herself scream and was helpless to stop it. Something shifted inside under the power of that contraction. She bore down with all of her strength, and then there was a rush of fluid and a slippery body between her thighs.

Teheren was there, lifting the child, clearing his

mouth and nose. A slap to the bottoms of the feet, and a moment later, she heard the lusty cry of a newborn child.

"Let me hold him."

She stretched out her arms, then drew back at the sight of Teheren's face. He hesitated, then placed the baby on her chest. It was wet and slippery, smeared with blood and a thick, white substance. All legs and arms and fingers and toes present and accounted for. Scales patterned the neck and shoulders. Scars marred the right cheek, as if the child had been wounded in utero. The scars and the scales were strange but not surprising, given the way it had been conceived. But what was wrong with this baby was of such significance that Aidan could not grasp it all at once.

"No," she said aloud. "No, it can't be. There must be some mistake."

This baby had grown inside of her, had come forth through hours of wracking pain and fear. But it was not the warrior child she had planned for.

The baby was, undeniably, a girl.

Rage followed comprehension. Aidan had decreed that this child would be a boy. If this was not so, then it must be the fault of the child, who in some way must have set her will above Aidan's in order to be born female.

She pressed her hand over the baby's mouth and nose, blocking off air. A girl child was a dangerous thing, a rival, and of no use to her. The little one fought for life, kicking her feet, twisting her head side to side. Because she was so slippery, still coated with blood and body fluids, Aidan's hands kept slipping away, and the baby continued to cry.

"What are you doing?" Teheren wrenched the child away from her. "You must have a fever of the brain."

Aidan tried to snatch the baby back, but the pain began again, not quite so intense but enough to freeze her in place. She knew what this was, had seen it pushed out of dragons and other creatures following the emergence of a baby. A few minutes of intense cramping, pressure and pain in her torn birth canal, and the afterbirth slid out between her thighs, a gush of blood with it, filling the air with a tang of iron the other dragons would never fail to notice. Not now, not while they were so hungry.

The pain gone, she turned her attention back to Teheren. Still in human form, he stood at a safe distance, warming the baby against his bare chest.

"Too many have died," he said, repeating his earlier words.

Aidan began the shift to dragon. No reason now to retain the limiting human form. Saliva spurted into her mouth at the thought of the baby's hot blood and tender bones. She would eat the afterbirth as well. It was too small to be anything more than a teaser for a dragon, but it would be nourishing and full of blood.

"You forget your place, Teheren," she said, beginning the shift.

"And you are overlooking the obvious. Cannot a girl child also be a warrior?"

Halfway between dragon and human, Aidan heard the words and considered. Possibly he was right, but the dragon slayers had always been male, one to each generation for a thousand years. This child had thwarted a very long lifetime of careful planning. If she was quick about the change, she could kill Teheren in his human form. He had not even begun to shift. The other dragons would not resent the kill if he were human, and she needed the flesh to restore her strength.

Her body was already covered in scales and expanding. Just a matter of wings and tail and teeth and she'd be ready to attack.

Teheren set the baby down. It didn't cry, its clear gray eyes far too intelligent for a human of its age and size. The scars on its cheek made it look sinister and dangerous. Oh, the child must definitely die.

"You might consider taking your dragon form," Teheren said to the child as he began his own shift. "You are capable and it would be safer."

He transformed from human to dragon effortlessly, completing the process at the same time as Aidan. Oh, he was intolerable, and she would not back down now. She clapped her wings above her back and shot fire at him. He stood broadside, screening the baby with his bulk, and was far enough away that that the fire did little more than heat the scales on his shoulder to a red glow. It should have been a stronger flame, brighter, hotter. It should have reached farther. She hesitated, uncertain, frightened for the first time that Teheren would be the victor in a battle.

"Are you certain you wish to do this now, while you are weakened from childbirth?" He spoke aloud, in the dragon speech she did not know. The insolence of this fueled her rage. Jaws open, she rushed at him, coming in low and fast, ready to tear at the softness of his underbelly. Maybe to reach beneath him and snatch the child, if she could reach her.

Teheren blocked her effortlessly with his shoulder. The solid blow grated against her teeth, sent pain slashing through her jaw and into her own neck. A gash opened where she had struck him, black blood welling up and running down his foreleg, but there was no serious damage. No vital hurt. It wouldn't even be enough to slow him down.

Aidan retreated, ready for the counterattack. But the red-gold dragon did not move.

"I will defend myself and the little one," he said, still aloud. "But I will not willingly fight a weaker dragon. You might do well to pay attention to those."

Tuned to Teheren, she had missed the approach of

the others. Drawn by the smell of blood and the sound of battle, they congregated outside the mouth of the cave. Held off for a moment by the narrow entrance and the need to proceed one at a time, but not for long. They had been denied a meal when the old dragon was killed. The mood was not one that would be denied again.

"We will be stronger as a united front," Teheren suggested. "Shall we?"

It galled her that she could not respond to him in the ancient tongue, her dislike and annoyance growing into a festering hate. *It will take more than two of us to protect a bloodstained human child. I will not die in her defense.*

"No need, I think."

From under his belly emerged a black snout, and then a horned head, great golden eyes taking in every detail. The girl-child had shifted into a pure black dragon. Armored now with scales, able to run and fly, she would be not nearly so vulnerable. And the dragons were not yet hungry enough to kill and eat each other. A pure black dragon was special and rare. They had been willing to accept Aidan as Queen because of the color of her scales. And they would be hesitant to harm a young one of the royal color, no matter what.

You'll pay. Soon or late, you will pay for this.

Quick and light, the young dragon slithered out from beneath Teheren's belly. Before Aidan registered what it was doing, the afterbirth was in the creature's mouth, and then gone. With a cry of outrage, she swung her head, teeth bared, but the little one used her wings to get airborne and went over Teheren's back and into shelter behind him again.

"Together," Teheren said. "You and I walk out abreast. The child will follow."

Raging, Aidan subjected herself to this plan as the best she could hope for in the moment. She would not tolerate a rival. Neither this red-gold dragon with his delusions of grandeur or the small black that was born to be royalty. She, Aidan, would be the only leader. Until her plan was complete and there was no need for any leader anymore.

Twenty-two

"It's too dangerous," Landon said. His face was haggard with worry and lack of sleep. A smudge of dust ran across one cheek. His clothes were torn. He'd been working nonstop for two days and nights, side by side with the guards, making room for the flood of immigrants and doing the best he could to prevent war over scarce provisions.

Isobel handed him a glass of wine and a buttered roll. He smiled in thanks, his blue eyes warming to hers. She filled his plate, watching with a cold despair as he put half of what she'd served him back onto the platter.

"Not enough to go around," he said.

"You won't be able to continue if you don't take care of yourself." Already his clothes hung loose on a body that had always been lean. His hair was silvering rapidly and she didn't like the way his hand kept straying to his temple, as though his head ached.

"I won't be able to continue if something happens to you," he replied, touching her hair. "Tell me again why you think it necessary to undertake such a risk."

"All Dreamshifters must go to the Cave of Dreams as an initiation."

"And you think the child is a Dreamshifter."

They both watched the little girl, who sat cross-legged on the floor, tearing apart a piece of bread and feeding crumbs to the big black raven who stood solemnly in front of her, gently taking them from her hand, one at a time.

"How can I know for certain? But she wears the pendant and the raven has bonded to her. We are going to need a Dreamshifter if we are to have any hope of survival."

The words were as close as she could come to acknowledging her fear that something had already happened to Vivian. No way of knowing, other than a growing unease that had kept her awake at night to lie exhausted in her empty bed, staring up at the ceiling. She kept a light burning around the clock, fearful of the darkness. And now here was this self-possessed child, clearly transported from Wakeworld at the cost of a Dreamshifter's life.

"How can she possibly help? How old is she? Five?"

"My name is Lyssa, and I can hear you," the child said, looking up with eyes that were neither quite blue nor green and far too old for her face.

"I'm sorry," Isobel said. "It's just that we're frightened."

"What's a Dreamshifter?"

"Somebody who can open doors from one world into another."

"Like Weston. And Vivian." The child stood up and crossed the room, standing with one hand resting on Isobel's knee. It was so tiny, the fingernails perfect pink half moons. A scratch ran across the base of the index finger. Just a small thing, but Isobel was possessed of a desire to lift it to her lips and kiss it. She did no such thing, holding herself perfectly still and returning Lyssa's direct gaze.

"Yes, like that."

"I helped Weston with the door. He didn't like it, though. Because of Ella."

"And who is Ella?"

"An elephant. She was on the other side of the door when Weston opened it." The little girl's eyes brimmed suddenly with tears. "She's dead."

Isobel gazed helplessly at the tears spilling silently down the child's cheeks, knowing any gesture of comfort would be hopelessly inadequate.

"And Weston didn't like elephants?"

The curly head shook a vigorous no. "He was quite surprised to see her when he opened the door."

This served only to confirm what Isobel already believed. She ventured to put her hand on the child's hair and stroke it, as her gaze sought out Landon's.

"And the raven?" Isobel asked.

"Bob."

"Yes. Bob."

"He was Weston's."

"Dreamshifter or no," Landon said, in the voice that was more than just Landon, but also his I'm-in-charge-and-I've-made-a-decision voice, "you can't risk her by taking her out of Surmise now. You don't know that this cave even still exists."

"If it didn't, we wouldn't still be here," Isobel said. She was surprised to hear her own voice speaking in opposition to his. She had never disagreed with him before.

"I won't have it!" It was a sharp retort. Never had he spoken to her like that, and the tone cut her a little even as it made her realize how fragile he'd always thought her, how much he treated her with kid gloves. Probably afraid that any harshness at all would drive her back into madness.

Well, she wasn't mad now, nowhere near. She was right and he was wrong and he wasn't accustomed to listening to her. Still, she had to try. She opened her mouth but he cut across her words with his own.

"Look, Isobel, I'm sorry. I don't like to speak to you so. But I've got more than I can manage, dealing with the mess we're in here. I can't afford the distraction of worry if you venture out on some wild scheme to turn a child into a Dreamshifter. If we haven't got one, if something has happened to Vivian, all the gods forbid, then why risk the child now? Keep her safe. Comfort her. Take her to her initiation when it is safe to do so, for her and for you."

He pushed back his chair, wiping the back of his mouth with his hand. "We just had a pack of wolves come in. What am I to do with them? Nowhere to put them where they're not going to eat somebody or something. We're talking about building a separate structure." He bent and kissed her forehead and was gone.

In the echoing silence, Isobel felt small and deflated. He was right, of course. Trying to find the Cave of Dreams was a fool's errand. She was no Dreamshifter, had never been called to choose her dreamsphere, had no idea where or how to begin looking for the place.

"What's the Cave of Dreams?" Lyssa demanded.

"It's just a place. Go play with Bob for a bit, all right?"

"What kind of place?"

Isobel sighed. "I've never been there. But my father told me it is a cave, filled with light and color and sound. All of it comes from little round spheres that—"

"What's a sphere?"

"They look like marbles. You have marbles?"

Lyssa nodded. "I like the swirly blue and green ones best."

"Like that, but instead of the swirly color, they have tiny little pictures inside. Only, each picture is a real place, and the marble can take you there."

She closed her eyes and swallowed hard. So many spheres dead already, so many of those worlds lost.

"Like the dream doors," Lyssa said. "Can't a door take you to the cave?"

"I can't make a door," Isobel said. "It was just an idea, Lyssa. Like an imagining game. We can't really go there."

"I can make a door."

Isobel stroked the tumbled hair and then used a napkin to clean the tearstained cheeks. She needed to give this child a bath, find her a hairbrush, search out some clean clothes. "Doors are dangerous now. They could lead to the Nothing, understand? You and I will have to be resigned to waiting for Vivian to fix it. Okay?"

A knock at the door broke the moment.

The messenger was unfamiliar to her and looked edgy and ill at ease. He bowed briefly but then stood without speaking. Some of the immigrants had been brought into service without time for proper training, and Isobel guessed the boy was one of those.

"What is the message?" she asked, nudging him.

"It's for Prince Landon." The boy's eyes searched the room as if he expected to find Landon hiding behind one of the chairs or crawling out from beneath the table.

"He's not here. I can give him the message."

"She said it was for him alone."

"And I have the authority to act on his behalf." She stood and crossed to him, using her robes and her long dark hair and sparkling jewels to advantage. "Speak now."

The boy glanced wildly around the room. His eyes lit on the raven, and the bird croaked a warning. That did it.

"An old woman. Among those who came in yesterday. She's taken to bed and the Healer says she is dying. She showed me a magic ball and said it was very important and asked me to fetch—"

"Where is she?"

"In the South Tower, but—"

Isobel was already moving. "Thank you. Sit down, eat. You look half starved." She looked back at the child, hesitating, but she couldn't leave her here alone. She held out her hand. "Lyssa, come with me."

The little girl asked no questions, just took Isobel's hand with her small one.

"Bob, too?"

"Need you ask?"

The raven certainly wasn't waiting for an invitation, already perched on the child's thin shoulder. Most of the passageways in Castle Surmise were winding, slanted things, more like freeway on- and off-ramps than anything else Isobel could think of. People and creatures sat or lay in the halls, some wrapped in blankets, some covered in fur, some shivering in rags. The air was thick with the comingled scents of fur and unwashed bodies and food. Every face looked worried or angry. An undercurrent of energy vibrated through the castle, and she understood why Landon was working himself to death. Emotions could erupt into a full-scale blow-up of epic proportions. A small thing would do it. A slight. A slur. A perceived injustice. And if something bigger were to happen, like an interspecies altercation…

Even as she understood her husband's situation, her anger at being silenced like a child continued to burn. He hadn't really even listened to her. There was a truth about their relationship here that she did not want to consider, an imbalance. Was she really just a kept and pampered princess, beloved like a pet and of no more use, while he carried all the affairs of state? They had both been frightened that her mind would break again under pressure, but was the result worth it?

When they reached the South Tower, she focused her attention on her feet. This was no place for distraction; the only way up was a steep circular staircase, carved of stone and without handrails. Even a slight misstep could mean a ruinous tumble and almost certain death.

What had they been thinking to drag an old woman up here in the first place? No wonder she'd taken ill. Probably her heart had given out. Isobel had some concerns about her own. As for the little one, she scampered ahead, her short legs navigating the steps with ease, the raven flying above, the sound of his unseen wings unsettling in the near dark. All of Isobel's requests to go slowly and with care fell on deaf ears.

When they finally reached the top, Isobel had to stop to catch her breath. There were six chambers here, shaped like slices of a pie. All were full of frail or ailing humans in need of a bed. They found the old woman behind the third door. She was so thin and withered that she barely made a mound beneath the blanket. Long gray hair fanned out around her head. Her eyes were closed. A network of fine wrinkles covered her face and the hands on the coverlet were little more than blue-veined claws, both curled into fists.

Isobel had to look hard to see that the sheet over the concave breast rose and fell, so shallow was the woman's breath.

"I fear I have come too late," she whispered, touching the back of one of the hands. Icy cold it was, but the eyes snapped open, blue as a summer sky and unfaded by the years.

"Who are you?" The voice was stronger than it ought to have been, given the old woman's pallor, the faint blue tinge to her lips.

"Isobel. Consort of Prince Landon."

The blue eyes bored into her. "You are Wakeworld born, or I miss my guess."

"What has that to do with anything?"

"I have knowledge of a thing, a trifle to be coveted,

a plaything. Now, so late, I realize the importance of it. Especially now. It is important that I am careful who I speak to."

"You have a dreamsphere," Isobel said bluntly. "You showed it to the boy. Was that wise, do you think?"

"It was an act of desperation. The healers discounted me as a rambling old woman. The child was willing to listen."

The sound of wings made the old woman look up to where the raven had alighted on the edge of the single window casement. Her eyes widened, her lips parted, a faint flush came into her cheeks, and she tried to sit up.

"Easy," Isobel said, pressing her back.

The old woman coughed and subsided, but her eyes were still eager. "Who does the raven belong to?"

Bob fluttered down to Lyssa's shoulder. The child approached the bed, face grave. The old woman reached up to touch the raven's head and then curled her fingers around the leather thong that held the pendant.

"Let me see it," she said. Lyssa put the pendant in her hand. A long moment she held it, then let it fall and lay back on the pillow. Tears filled her eyes and flowed down her wrinkled cheeks.

"Where is Weston, then?" she asked. "How did he die?"

Lyssa climbed up onto the bed, flung her arms around the old woman's neck, laid her head on the thin breast, and sobbed as if her heart would break.

Isobel felt her own throat tighten, and the world blurred a little from tears gathering in her eyes. "He died saving the little one from what she calls the Nothing, if I understand correctly."

"He grew to be a good man, then. My father did not succeed in destroying him?" The old woman opened her eyes and looked up at Isobel, pleading for something.

"I did not know him," Isobel had to reply. "Only what Lyssa has told me. People were dying in Wakeworld, including her own father, and he brought her away to make her safe. Who was he to you?"

"My brother," she murmured. She drew a deep, quavering breath and stroked the little girl's tangled hair. "There, there, child. He lived a very long life. As have I. And since Weston made you his successor, I guess that what I carry falls to you."

"Oh, surely not," Isobel said. "She's so young."

"We haven't time for what would be nice or pleasant." She looked up at the bird and shook her head, her voice taking on a wondering tone. "Hard to believe you're still the same old pest of a raven. Going to outlive the both of us, looks like."

The raven *kronk*ed at her. She wiped away tears. "Well, then. I'd had a thought that maybe I need to wait around, lest I become Weston's heir when he died. I'm free, then, to pass on to whatever comes next. Sit up, Miss Lyssa. I can't feel my feet and my belly feels cold as ice. My life is running out, I think. We have very little time."

Lyssa pushed herself up to sitting, cross-legged. Her face was tearstained but the eyes were luminous and bright.

The old woman took the small paw in hers and pressed something into the palm. "There, now. Look, but not too deeply, and make no wish to go to the place you see."

She withdrew her hand, and on Lyssa's palm rested a clear crystal sphere. At its center shone a miniature walled city, radiant with the colors of gold and jewels. Only a glimpse, a cry of wonder from the child, and the old woman closed her fingers over the shining thing.

"The city within the sphere is real. And it is a thing of beauty, but the Giants live there and they would eat a little thing like you for lunch. If you gaze at the sphere, it will take you there. Put it away safe."

Lying back on the pillows, the old woman folded her hands over her breast and closed her eyes. "Now I think I'll get back to the dying."

"No," Lyssa whispered, a small hand touching the old woman's cheek.

"It is the way of things, child. Let it be."

A long silence followed, broken only by the sound of uneven breathing. And then the blue eyes flew open one last time. "Have you been to the Cave of Dreams?"

"Not yet," Isobel began, but a bout of coughing overtook the old woman and drowned out her words. And when the fit was over, there was no more breath.

Isobel smoothed a strand of hair back from the woman's forehead and folded the old hands more neatly.

"May you have rest," she murmured. "Lyssa, come, child."

Only then did she realize the little girl had slipped off the bed and was not immediately to be seen. It only took an instant to find her, sitting on the floor at the far side of the room, Bob perched atop her head. Set into the wall, where it had no business being at all, was a door. Isobel had seen doors into the Dreamworld before. Her father's had always been heavy oaken constructions, banded with steel and set into a framework of fitted stone. This was a child's door, so low that an adult would need to stoop to pass through it. And it looked like something out of a fairytale, rounded at the top, with cutout carvings of a moon and stars.

Isobel cleared her throat. "Come away, child. You have no idea what lies behind that door."

"It's the cave," Lyssa said. "I need to go."

"Too dangerous." Isobel ran her fingers over the door, then wondered how she had come close enough to touch.

Last she remembered, she'd been standing on the other side of the room. This frightened her. The curse Jehenna had bestowed on her by stealing the role of Dreamshifter meant that the only hope of sanity she possessed lay in staying away from the Between and the Dreamworlds.

"Make it go away." She spoke harshly, needing to enforce compliance.

But Lyssa had been called. There was something new in the child's eyes now, a glow of whatever lay beyond the door. "I have to go." She put her hand in Isobel's, looking up into her face. "You could come with me."

"I can't." She swallowed, feeling the draw of the Between as she always had, knowing what would happen should she follow. All of the years of shifting, sliding time and jarring angles of reality. The hospitals and the pills and the constant attempts to make it all stop with the help of a sharp blade.

And yet.

"Is the cave very big? And dark?" The child's face was pale and tight with worry.

Isobel dropped to her knees so as to be at eye level. "I've never been. Once it was full of light, but now, I think it may be very dark."

"I don't like the dark." The voice was very small now, and Isobel put her hands on both shoulders.

"So, don't go. Stay here with me."

Lyssa shook her head. "If I don't go, it will be all dark everywhere. And it's calling me."

Gods. Before Isobel could think of another thing to say, the little girl grasped the handle and pulled the door open. Isobel knelt on the threshold, staring at her destiny. In place of fear and paralysis, a wild thing fluttered in her chest, free and exuberant. A fragment of dream emerged from all of the other remnants, clear and shining. In the dream, she stooped and passed through this doorway and the feeling in the dream was triumph and love.

"Come on," Lyssa said, tugging at her hand.

And with a deep breath and a last long look at the safety of Surmise, Isobel ducked beneath the doorframe and entered.

Twenty-three

Zee was there, waiting, the instant Vivian shifted back to human skin. His hands gentled the transition, eased her vulnerability. She buried her face in his chest, her still-heightened senses taking in the smell of him, listening to the steady rhythm of his heart.

"I've got your clothes." Zee's arms tightened around her, his cheek pressed against the top of her head, and he made no move to release her.

Nakedness was not a concept understood by her dragon nature, and it took a few more breaths before the self-consciousness kicked in, heightened by the knowledge that beyond the protective bulwark that was Zee, a small company was watching and waiting. As she began to pull out of Zee's arms so she could dress, he whispered, "You should know that your mother is here."

"My what?" She peered around his shoulder. Poe and the griffyn were engaged in a stare-down, mediated by Kalina, who kept a tight hold on the leash. Kraal kept one hand on Jared's shoulder, as if expecting the blind man to bolt at any moment. And Isobel stood quietly waiting, holding the hand of a wide-eyed child.

"Maybe you should close that door," she said. "You never know what might come through."

"Mother? What in all the worlds? Wait, just a

second." Vivian scrambled into her clothes, secured the dream door with a thought, and went to give her mother a hug. Isobel's body felt thin and frail, the bones too close to the skin. There were new lines in her face and her dark hair had given way to gray. But her eyes were clear and her lips set in lines of determination.

"Did something happen to Surmise? Is Landon…" Vivian broke off, unwilling to say the words.

"Surmise is fine—for the moment. Crammed to bursting with refugees from the other worlds. Landon is busy."

"Then what on earth are you doing here?"

"I brought Lyssa," Isobel said, as if this was an answer.

Vivian's eyes went to the child, who stared up at her out of eyes of an extraordinary shade of blue-green, clear as a mountain lake, and demanded, "Are you going to stop the Nothing?"

A familiar raven clung to the little girl's shoulder, hoary with age. With a cold dread, Vivian saw the pendant hanging from a leather thong. She looked from the child to Isobel. "Where's Weston?"

The little girl's eyes welled up with tears. Isobel didn't answer.

There was a tightness in Vivian's chest that made it difficult to breathe. *Oh, Weston, oh, my dear.* She'd made the wrong choice then, taking him back. Now he was trapped in a half-life with her grandfather and all of the other dead Dreamshifters, waiting for her to free them.

"He died saving Lyssa," Isobel said. "She's important."

Of course she's important. Every child is important. Vivian bit her tongue on the words, taking another good look at the child, who was surprisingly calm given how strange this must all be for her. And those eyes, the way the raven had adopted her…

"I didn't know what to do with her," Isobel went on. "So, I brought her here. I never expected to be lucky enough to find you. Now you can teach her."

Somewhere, somehow, Weston had found another Dreamshifter. Vivian's heart leaped at the thought that she was not the last, and then the reality hit her. Only a child. Another life become her responsibility.

"You have to go back," she said. "The cave isn't safe now. Last time we were here, all of our worst nightmare fears came alive." She shivered at the memory.

Isobel shook her head, a stubborn set to her jaw. "This is where she's supposed to be. There's a reason."

Vivian took both of Isobel's hands and looked into her eyes. "I know you meant well. It means a lot that you brought her. But it's going to take blood magic to get through into the Forever. I don't know if any of us are going to survive that, or what waits for us beyond if we do. You're right about Lyssa. If something happens to me, you'll still have a Dreamshifter. But we have to keep her safe."

"She can make doors," Isobel persisted. "She can help you."

"She's a *child*. You don't know what that means. You never did. Do her parents even know you've brought her here?" The rush of bitterness surprised her and she regretted it at once. Not fair. Her lack of a childhood was not her mother's fault. She was about to apologize when Lyssa tugged at her hand.

"Is that a Giant?"

"Yep. His name is Kraal."

"The Nothing got Daddy," Lyssa said, matter-of-factly. "I have a marble with a Giant in it. The old lady in Surmise gave it to me."

"It's a dreamsphere," Isobel said.

"With Giants in it?" Kraal thundered. "That dream-sphere belongs to me. Let me see!" His footsteps shook the earth as he strode over, hands outstretched.

Lyssa screamed and wrapped her arms around Isobel's hips, hiding her face. "Don't let him get me!"

"Kraal's not going to hurt you, honey," Vivian said with a warning frown at the Giant. "He just wants to see."

The little girl tightened her hold, shaking her head. "Grace said the Giants were mean and not to show it to anybody."

"Wise woman," Jared muttered.

"The sphere belongs to my people," Kraal said. "What idiot put it in the hands of a child? Give it to me."

"Don't you dare touch her." Isobel knelt and wrapped both arms around Lyssa, staring defiantly up at the Giant who loomed over both of them.

"Kraal," Vivian ordered. "Stand back. You're scaring her."

Kraal hesitated. Zee's hand went to his sword.

"Just use the Voice," Kalina said. "The longer we stand here, the more likely it is that one of us will stir up the dream matter. Make her give it to you."

But the child had obviously been through a great deal already. Vivian remembered the very first dream-sphere she'd had in her own possession, and how hard it had been to give it back to her grandfather. Surely, there was no need to use force. Sinking down on her knees, she looked directly into Lyssa's eyes.

"Since I'm the Dreamshifter, I think maybe Grace wouldn't mind if you show the dreamsphere to me."

"Grace is dead."

Another grief. Weston had come so close to finding his sister again after all these years. Vivian closed her eyes and took a slow breath. Grief upon grief. What could she say?

She had underestimated the child, though, who reached out for the pendant she wore around her neck and examined it, gravely. "I dreamed about you and the pendant. You're supposed to stop the Nothing before it kills more people. Will it help you to have the dreamsphere?"

"Yes, I think so."

"You can keep it for me if you want. Maybe then the Nothing won't get it."

Lyssa dug into the pocket of her jeans and produced a small round sphere, which she held out to Vivian on the palm of her hand. Kraal took a step forward. Vivian reached out, but before she could touch it, she felt a sharp spasm of warning that nearly made her cry out. Lyssa screamed. Jared fell to the ground and curled up into a ball, both hands pressed over his eyes. "Dark, dark, it's all gone dark," he moaned.

"I killed it," Lyssa wailed. The dreamsphere was now only a small heap of black dust on her palm.

A heartbeat later, she began to scream. "Get it off me! Get it off!" She whipped her hand back and forth through the air, flinging bits of dream sand to the ground, where they began to eat away at grass and dirt, turning it into empty space, into Nothing. A flower vanished. A grasshopper, as a black nothingness opened up at Lyssa's feet.

Again she screamed. "It's going to get me."

Vivian's blood ran cold in horror but she couldn't think of anything to do. Then Zee's sword flashed silver in the sunlight, followed by a wide spray of blood. What remained of Lyssa's hand fell to the ground at his feet, the palm and fingertips eaten half away. Blood spurted from her wrist, turning the earth to crimson. Zee caught her up in his free arm and dragged her back and away from the growing patch of darkness.

"What have you done?" Isobel cried.

Vivian clamped her hands around the child's mutilated arm, squeezing hard to compress the radial artery. "We need a tourniquet."

"No point if that darkness keeps on coming." Zee shifted the little girl in his arms. Her eyes began to glaze over with shock, the screams fading to heartbreaking whimpers. Black nothingness ate away at the earth not far from their feet, spreading like wildfire in the grass. Zee kept walking backward, Vivian moving with him, hands still clamped around Lyssa's wrist.

"Into the cave." Kalina dragged Jared in that direction. He moved like a zombie, stiff and awkward, still with his hands pressed to his eyes and muttering incoherently about darkness. "Quickly," she cried, "before we're cut off."

There was only a small spit of green left between them and the cave. If the Nothing claimed that before they crossed, then it was all over and they had failed.

"She's right. We have to run for it."

"Move now." Zee ran for it, the little girl pressed against his breast.

"I don't understand," Isobel said, her voice blurred and bewildered. Vivian grabbed her hand and dragged her into the cave. Everybody present and accounted for, but now they had the dream matter to deal with. At the entrance, there wasn't much of the stuff, but inside….

"Hold up a minute," she called to Zee, running to catch up. Lyssa moaned and stirred, a sound that went straight to Vivian's heart.

"Sleep," she commanded, using the Voice, and the little girl sighed and snuggled up against Zee, her face peaceful, chest rising and falling in easy breaths. Calling her Sorcieri light, Vivian swiftly examined the wound. It was a clean cut right through the wrist joint, the bones of the forearm intact. The immediate problem was the bleeding. Closing her eyes, she settled into the place where the magic waited. *Just another door, really, or a series of doors. If she could just weave them closed so no more blood could get out.*

When she opened her eyes, Zee was staring at her with an odd expression on his face.

"What?"

He didn't answer, and she looked down at Lyssa to check her work. The bleeding had stopped. What had been a jagged, bloody stump was covered with a weaving of color and texture that shifted in and out of focus.

"Like the door you closed in the Between," Zee said. "Will it harm her?"

"I don't think so. We'll worry about it later. We need to keep moving." She turned to the group huddled around her, their faces all pale and eerie in the dim light. "The cave is full of dream matter," she said, keeping her voice matter-of-fact and as calm as possible. "It can be triggered by your fears and hates, as it was for Lyssa."

"But she wasn't even in the cave," Isobel said.

"The dreamsphere died in her hand, reverting to dream matter." Even as the words left her mouth, it truly sank in that the world of the Giants was gone. Kraal's face was etched with lines of grief. Jared moved like a zombie. She had no comfort to offer either of them, and went on with her little speech. "Lyssa most feared the Nothing and so has brought it here. What you fear, what you hate, can come alive in this place. So, choose something good to think about. Focus on one simple, beautiful, wonderful thing. And if an ugliness arises near you, do not engage. Don't try to harm it; you will only make it grow. Keep moving. Kalina and I will do our best to shield you. All right?"

"The Nothing is coming," Kalina said. "I can feel it."

"What is that stink?" Isobel asked, covering her nose

and mouth with her hands.

"Dead dragon, mostly. There may be other things. Kalina—you're the one who knows the ritual. Would you lead?"

The girl nodded. A golden ball of light appeared in her hand, shedding a warm glow over the smooth stone walls and the polished floor. The roof of the cave remained obscured by darkness. Anything might lurk there.

Vivian brought her thoughts back, seeking the one good image she had urged upon the others. This turned out to be a slippery problem, her thoughts skimming in and out of all of the complicated relationships and places of her life, all with some darkness attached. And then her eyes fell on Poe.

The little penguin bobbed along just in front of her, behind Kraal and Jared. He had been her steadfast companion since she had become a Dreamshifter, and often her guide. She kept her mind focused on him with love. In her peripheral vision, more penguins appeared on either side of her. All of them built like Poe, not quite the right size or shape for any Wakeworld penguin breed, with bright yellow breasts and even a crimson patch on the chest marking the spot where Poe had once been pierced with a sword.

Other figures filled the cave, pacing silently along beside them. Callyn walked beside Kraal. Another Vivian walked beside Zee, golden eyes and scales, and her heart overflowed with love for him. Kalina produced no specter, walking steadily ahead and lighting up the dark.

Jared was another story. Thronging around him so thickly, they tripped him up at times, were manifestations of himself. All were deformed. Blind Jareds with blank eye sockets, legless torsos dragging themselves along with their hands. Twisted, ugly, muttering things.

Vivian began to build up in her mind all of the things she most wanted to preserve. Flowers and grass sprang up around her feet. Birds flew overhead. But blood ran red through the grass. Blades appeared in the air, razors and knives and shards of broken glass. Vivian knew only too well who was manifesting these horrors. Isobel wept silently, tears pouring down her cheeks.

"Think of something else," Vivian pleaded. "Landon. Some good and beautiful thing."

"All I can see is darkness and blood."

"You can change that." Grabbing her mother's free hand, she towed her on, keeping her own mind empty of blades and blood and even of the good things, just breathing. Breathe in, breathe out, put one foot in front of the other. Keep moving.

The narrow walls widened and they entered the large chamber at the heart of the cave. Here the decaying corpse of the Guardian was draped over a heap of dream matter that half filled the chamber. If any dreamspheres were left alive, buried beneath the dark sand, not one was visible. Vivian faltered at the full extent of the deaths represented here. So much lost that could never be replaced.

Kalina led them around the dead Guardian to the far side of the chamber, not stopping until she stood about a foot from the wall. Then she turned and thrust the griffyn cub at Isobel.

"Here—keep him for me."

Then she turned back to the wall, raised both of her white arms, and began an invocation. An aura of lurid red light formed around her. Her voice deepened, strengthened, taking on a tone and texture as it filled the cave, echoing off of floors and ceilings. Flames wreathed her body but did not consume her. With a command in an unknown tongue, she touched her hands to the wall, and the stone itself began to burn.

Amid the flames, an arched doorway took shape, glowing crimson like molten lava. A gesture of Kalina's hand, and the melted stone flowed away, revealing a small alcove. Within stood an altar, translucent as colored glass and the color of blood.

Flesh and bone responded to that stone in a pulsing vibration that made the world spin. The wound in Vivian's breast throbbed brutally with every beat of her heart. She could scarcely catch her breath. Her vision darkened. She closed her eyes, but even behind her eyelids, she could see the shape of that altar. It was hungry, and she knew what it was hungry for.

"Bloodstone," Zee whispered.

Kalina, robed in flame, turned to face them. In a voice so charged with power that the words themselves took on weight and shape, she commanded, "Petitioner, present your request."

Vivian stepped forward. No time for last words with Zee, or to soothe her mother, or tend Lyssa's wound. No room for second guesses. Only one way forward now, one last hope, dark as that way might be. Black dream dust rose in flurries with each step, glittering red in the light of Kalina's flames. She felt her eyes changing as the inner dragon woke and stretched. As she passed through the arch from the cave to the alcove, she felt a shift that nearly dropped her to her knees.

The three powers at her center sustained her, and when she spoke into the waiting silence, it was with the voice of dragon, Sorcieri, and Dreamshifter as one.

"I request passage into the Forever."

"For yourself alone?"

"For myself and my companions."

"A sacrifice is required."

She had tried to tell herself that only an offering would be required. A few drops of blood, no more. But this bloodstone altar demanded all or nothing. Sacrifice, in the fullest sense of the word. Swaying a little, holding herself upright by sheer force of will, she said, "I am willing."

"Blood must be spilled, flesh of your flesh and yet not your own."

"No," she whispered, the full realization sweeping over her at last. All of the veiled hints, the old Master's laughter. The meaning of Kalina's cryptic words.

Zee stepped up beside her, still holding Lyssa in his arms. "I am the bond and I freely give my life."

Blood of her blood, flesh of her flesh. Vivian's heart lurched and then went on beating around a pain that far surpassed any wound her body might be asked to bear.

"Accepted," Kalina said. "The altar awaits."

Zee turned to Kraal and shifted Lyssa into his arms. "Take the child. Be gentle with her." The Giant nodded, cradled the little girl in one arm, then bowed, touching two fingers to his forehead. Isobel's eyes were wide with horror.

"What's happening?" Jared stretched out his arms, waving his hands through the air as though he could see with his fingertips. "Somebody tell me."

Zee unsheathed his sword and held it out to Vivian.

"No, Zee. I won't do it."

He smiled a little. "You must," he said. When she shook her head and put her hands behind her back, he laid it at her feet.

Zee stripped off his shirt and lay down on the altar, hands folded over his breast as though he were already dead. Vivian backed away, stumbling over a stone and nearly falling. Kraal's strong hand steadied her and she leaned against his rock-solid support, her knees shaking so hard, they would barely hold her.

"Are you all insane? How can you even ask such a thing of me?"

"It is the only way into the Forever," Kalina said.

Vivian had eyes only for Zee. "You really think I

would do this? Spill your lifeblood with my own hands?"

"I die, one way or another. Kill me now, and you have a chance to save the others." Zee lowered his voice to a caress. "You are the only one who can save them. And what's left of the Dreamworlds and the Between."

"I hate the Between! I wish I had never been asked to walk there. Good riddance."

"And Wakeworld?"

He had her there, and he knew it. So many lives at stake. The nurses she had worked with at the hospital. Brett Flynne. The postman and her hairdresser and the little old lady who lived in the apartment next to hers in Krebston. Kraal and Lyssa. Jared. Even Kalina, though Vivian's rage burned against the Sorcieri enchantress.

"I can't," she said again. "If it must be done, if it must be Zee…" Her voice broke as the beloved name passed her lips. "Somebody else will have to do it."

"The petitioner must spill the blood," Kalina intoned.

"I am willing to be the sacrifice." Kraal's deep voice filled the cavern. "Would that ease the task?"

A wild, guilty hope welled up in Vivian's breast. Killing Kraal—killing anybody—would be the hardest thing she could ever be asked to do. But if it meant sparing Zee, then she could do it. Would do it. Especially with all of the lives at stake.

"Blood of her blood, flesh of her flesh," Kalina responded. "There is no substitute."

"Vivian," Zee said. "Come here." His voice drew her, trembling, to stand beside him at the altar. He cupped her chin in his hands, caressing her cheeks with his thumbs, wiping away tears. "My love," he whispered. "It must be done. Let me help you. Bring the sword."

Gathering some comfort from his calm, at last she turned back to do as he bid her. It was heavier than she expected, and even two-handed, she had to work hard to raise it up off the cave floor.

Zee put his hands over hers and brought the tip up to rest on the altar. Then he rolled onto his side, facing her, so that the tip of the sword lined up with the notch at the base of his throat.

“Get your weight behind it and hold it steady,” he said. “We’ll do it together, on the count of three.”

“Wait,” she said. “Please. Just one more minute.” She wanted a clear memory of his face to carry with her, but tears blinded her, blurring him in and out of focus.

Footsteps shuffled up behind her, somebody standing so close she could feel body heat, could smell sweat and blood.

“Vivian,” Jared said.

For God’s sake. Not now. She ignored him, blinking to clear her vision. She gripped the hilt harder, trying to steady her shaking hands. She closed her eyes, trying to imagine what it must feel like to hold it as he did, as if it were just an extension of his body.

“Vivian, listen.” Jared touched her shoulder.

“Get the hell away from me.” She shrugged him off, just a small gesture but it moved her hands enough to nick Zee’s skin with the tip of the sword. Horrified, she watched as the first drop formed, grew into a crimson teardrop, and fell. It seemed to take forever to fall, but the instant it touched the bloodstone, the altar came fully alive.

A glow ignited at its center and the stone itself began to pulse in concert with the beating of her heart. Reflexively, she pulled the sword back, recoiling from ravenous bloodlust of the stone. The blade slid off the altar.

Somewhere behind her, Isobel screamed, followed by a shout from Kraal. “It’s coming! Do it now!”

Vivian glanced over her shoulder. Saw the jagged

edge of black emerge through the tunnel to begin eating away at the cavern floor.

"Get the sword ready," Zee ordered. "Now or never."

Her eyes cleared. Her hands steadied. Tightening her hands around the hilt, she heaved its weight back up and onto the altar.

"I love you," she whispered. She wanted to look away, anything other than watching the light go out of his eyes. But she needed to see. The blow must be quick and accurate, like a surgical incision. He must not suffer.

"Three," he said, his eyes holding hers.

"Two."

"One."

Bracing her weight against the sword hilt, tightening her grip, she lunged forward, driving the tip of the sword toward Zee's exposed throat.

At the same instant, Jared flung himself facedown onto the altar between the sword and Zee.

The blade struck bone with a scraping, grinding sensation, then slipped forward between the ribs. Jared's mouth opened in a soundless *Oh*. His body stiffened. And then, improbably, he smiled.

The Nothing was coming. She could feel it. Summoning all of the reserves of her will, she tried to withdraw the sword. It was stuck, embedded almost to the hilt. Zee made no sound. Maybe she'd pierced two hearts in one blow. Maybe she was going to have to try again. She felt sick and numb with shock and horror.

Bracing both feet and using her body weight, she pulled with all of her strength. She staggered backward and nearly fell as the blade came free. Blood gushed down onto the altar. Light flared up, so bright it nearly blinded her. A deep, cosmic pulsing sucked the strength from her body, feeding off the magic of Dreamshifter, Sorcieri, and dragon, amplifying it until the whole chamber seemed to be one giant beating heart.

With a sound of rending stone, a door opened on the far side of the altar. Kraal herded Isobel and Poe through the opening. Vivian was too spent to move. Her knees buckled, dropping her to the floor of the cave.

She could see the Nothing only inches away. Time for one more deep breath, and then it would all be over. She found that she was grateful. But before the dark could take her, strong arms scooped her up and carried her through the door.

Twenty-four

"Put me down," Vivian said, struggling in the arms that held her. Instead of letting her go, the embrace tightened and warm lips pressed against hers. There was only one person who could kiss her like that.

She broke away, looking up into a pair of clear agate eyes. "How?" she managed before he was kissing her again. This time, she did not resist, giving her whole self to that kiss, arms locked around his neck, tears pouring down her cheeks. Maybe this was a crazy, messed-up dream, but if so, she wasn't going to miss out on the opportunity.

"You need to close that door before the Nothing comes through."

Kalina's voice, ordinary now. Zee broke the kiss, then touched his lips to hers once more, gentle and lingering, before he set her on her feet, supporting her in the circle of his arm. She looked around, dazed, trying to catch up to what she saw.

Kraal still carried Lyssa, the raven riding on his head. Isobel held the griffyn. Poe, all of his feathers ruffled, had set himself as guardian in front of the open door. Almost absently, with half of her attention, Vivian willed the door closed.

She laid one hand on Zee's throat, smooth and whole except for the place where she'd nicked him. Ran her hands over his bare chest.

"I thought I'd killed you. And then I thought I'd have to kill you again."

"Seems like one victim was enough."

"I don't understand," she said, thinking of Jared. He'd saved Zee, saved them all. It wasn't what she'd ever expected from him.

"He offered himself," Kalina said. She looked ethereal and thin, as if light could shine through her. "A willing sacrifice."

"But—there was all that talk about the right sacrifice. You said—"

"Blood of your blood, flesh of your flesh."

"Yes, that. It hardly describes Jared."

Kalina shrugged her slim shoulders. "Does it matter? The sacrifice was accepted. The door was opened."

Zee cupped her chin to look into her eyes. "And the two shall be one flesh. In the Biblical sense, I'd guess."

"Because I'd slept with him?"

"That."

"Or, maybe, you were blood of his blood and heart of his heart," Kalina said. "Whatever the reason, we owe him a debt."

"But—Jared." Vivian recalled all of his many sins, realizing as she did that most of them had taken place in the Dreamworld. Still. It was going to take a lot of time to get her mind and heart lined up on the subject of Jared. She pushed the problem away for later and looked around the place the bloodstone altar had brought them, and all hope vanished.

"This can't be the Forever," she said. They stood on a wide, dusty plain devoid of anything green. Not even sagebrush or tumbleweed broke the expanse of dirt. Skeletons of trees stood here and there, the bark worn away so that nothing remained but bare, worm-eaten wood, carved by wind. It looked more like the place where her grandfather and the other Dreamshifters were trapped between life and death. The Forever made the badlands look like a paradise.

"Perhaps the spell was miscast," Kraal said.

"Or the wrong blood spilled with the wrong intent," Kalina retorted. "If Vivian had been quicker—"

"I would not be here," Zee finished, silencing them all.

Vivian shifted to what she knew by habit, her eyes running over her companions to check for injuries. Zee's arm looked bad. The edges of the wound had turned an angry red. Isobel had aged visibly, her hair more gray than black, fine lines spider-webbing her cheeks. Lyssa lay unmoving in Kraal's arms. The little girl's forehead was cool to her touch but not cold or clammy. Neither fever nor shock. Her breathing was even and she appeared to sleep.

"What do we do now?" Isobel asked.

"There's a riverbed to the east. I suggest we follow that." Kraal shifted the sleeping child to his shoulder and pointed.

Vivian could just make out a darker line cutting across the plain. No gleam of water, though. No movement at all.

"Or we could fly," Kalina suggested. "This is the home of the dragons, after all."

Vivian shook her head. "The minute I shift, they'll know we're here. I'd rather go to them than have them come to us. If we are in the right place and there are any dragons to be found."

"They are here." Zee had turned toward the North. He sniffed the air, tipped back his head, and stared up into the empty sky. "They have been here, and they are traveling in that direction."

"I think we should cross to the riverbed and follow it along," Vivian said.

Kraal shook his head. "Lost time for no good purpose. There is no water in it. If the dragons are north, I say we travel north and be done."

"I can't say why the river matters, but it does." That dark gash drew her, for good or ill.

"I've seen an ancient map," Kalina said. "The river ends in a waterfall, directly into the Pool of Life. And built on its shores is the City of Dragons."

"Then that's the way we travel." Zee drew his sword from the sheath and cleaned it in the sand. Vivian shuddered at the dark blood that marked it. Too many had died. And the longer they lingered here, the more deaths were occurring.

"How far do you think?"

"No more than a day's good hiking. If the sun is to be trusted here, it is early morning. By dinner."

"I have water enough to carry us through a day," Kraal said. "A little travel bread. That is all."

"Enough to get us there, then, if we conserve," Zee said, and Vivian just nodded. Whether there was water and food enough meant nothing. They must make the attempt. There was no going back.

A morning of steady walking brought them to the empty riverbed, where a dead dragon stretched out in a shallow pool of liquid.

"Just like a dragon to defile the only available water," Kraal muttered.

"Blood and body fluids, not water," Zee said, sniffing. "It hasn't been dead long."

Vivian bent to investigate. The creature's scales were thick and dulled by age, its body marked with old scars, teeth worn and broken. Something had ripped out its throat. Its position was formal, laid out neatly with wings folded. No dying dragon would assume that position on its own.

"Maybe some infighting," Zee said.

"Looks like. If we're lucky enough, maybe one of them will kill Aidan."

"Aidan is mine," Zee growled. One look at his face and she chose not to argue.

All afternoon, they followed the riverbed, dry and cracked by the heat of the sun. Old dragon bones littered the banks at intervals, most of them scattered and separate from each other. Late in the day, they reached a wide, deep place so full of bones, they must have dammed the flow of water.

Zee stood at the edge of the boneyard with a look of wonder. "This matches the tale the hermit told me of the war that broke out over Aidan's mother. Dragons slaughtering dragons."

"And many of the dragons left the Forever at that time rather than give service to a king who would order the killing of his own," Kalina added. "I've read the tales. But to see this…"

Vivian and Zee exchanged a long look. No need for words; she knew he saw what she did. Faced with evidence of a dragon war on such an enormous scale, their small band looked pitiful. And they were very near their destination.

Dust stained the western sky. Not far. Even in her human form, Vivian could sense the dragons, the thought channels like radio static she was unable to tune into.

Isobel sank down onto a dragon skeleton, her hands pressed over her ears, rocking back and forth.

"What is it?" Vivian knelt with her.

"The voices are back."

"What are they saying?"

"I don't know. I can't tell. There are so many…"

"Easy," Vivian soothed. "It's the dragons. You're not losing your mind. I hear it, too."

"Why can't we see them, then?"

"According to the maps, there should be a cliff ahead," Kalina said. "A sharp drop where there once was a waterfall. At the bottom, the City of Dragons stands all around the edge of the Pool of the Forever. They used to bathe in it. Doubt there's much bathing going on now."

"What if there's no water left in the Pool of Life?"

"We should have a strategy." Kraal set Lyssa down in a cradle made by a curve of dragon ribs and stretched his arms. "I can't fight while carrying the little one."

Bob perched on the skull and *kronk*ed once before starting to preen his feathers.

"I can carry her. Make me good for something." Isobel went to sit beside the child, smoothing her forehead. "Are you sure she's okay? She's not wakened since…since…"

"I put her to sleep," Vivian said. "But I suppose she'll need to wake now. She needs to eat and drink and be able to use her own legs." She looked at Kalina. "Can you do something about the pain? I don't know how."

Kalina nodded, and Vivian followed the flow of her magic, partly to learn, partly to guard against any more betrayal.

"You're checking up on me."

"I don't trust you."

"I would never hurt a child!"

Vivian didn't answer. Everything seemed okay with the spell, and she called the little girl's name. "Lyssa, time to wake up."

The blue-green eyes flew open and the little girl woke up screaming. "The Nothing is coming. Run!"

Isobel tried to draw the little girl into her arms but she pulled away, kicking and hitting like a cornered animal.

"The Nothing isn't here," Vivian said. "Not yet. We're in the Forever."

A quavering breath and a trembling lip as those big eyes welled up with tears. "My hand…"

"Does it hurt, sweetheart?"

Lyssa shook her head. Her good hand explored the stump, running over and over the strange, light-filled weaving. "No fingers," she said. And then, unexpectedly, "When can I see the dragons?"

"Soon enough. Here, now, you should have a drink."

Lyssa accepted the waterskin from Kraal after a brief hesitation and took a good long drink before pouring some out into the concave hollow of an old bone.

Vivian stopped her. "We can't play with it, Lyssa. There isn't enough."

"Bob needs water," the little girl insisted. "And your penguin and the kitty."

The entire animal contingent had gathered around the child, a little wary of each other but drawn like flies to honey. Bob and Poe stood on one side of the bone, warily watching the griffyn, which was crouched low, tail lashing.

"Hold on to the leash," Vivian warned Isobel, who held the other end. "It's just a cub, but it's hungry."

Poe hissed, snaking out his neck, and the cub retreated into Isobel's lap.

"Do we have a strategy for this battle? What's the prime objective?" Kraal retrieved the waterskin, took a swallow, and handed it around. "One drink for everybody, I think. Then that's gone."

Zee took his turn last. Instead of drinking, he handed the nearly empty skin to Lyssa. "Drink up, kiddo."

Even for this small gesture, he used his left hand, the right pressed stiffly against his side. There were lines of pain on his face, the skin around his eyes pinched. Vivian dipped into the magic, moving around the edges of the wound, exploring the inflammation and growing infection.

"Vivian? What do you want to do?"

The voices seemed far away and unimportant as she examined the struggle between healthy cells and contagion, the brutal rift in the structure of muscle and skin. She could feel the dying cells and the damaged ones fighting to repair and rebuild. Cells as a community, where one lost affected all of the others. Warrior cells and healing cells and the invading bacteria. And she could see that the bacterial colony was going to win.

Her clinical brain kicked in with words like cellulitis, gangrene, amputation. This was Zee, the Warrior. He needed his arm if they were to fight with dragons. He needed his arm afterward if they survived. And so, she used the magic to intervene, blowing up bacteria like tiny little bombs, accelerating the reproduction of new and healthy cells and the speed with which debris could be carried away.

When it was done, she found herself drifting through a space that she didn't know, dark and quiet. She felt emptied and tired but peaceful. Lights and shadows, shapes and the negative space between shapes, all like a movie she could watch without feeling the need to intervene.

A bright flare of energy disrupted the serenity and Kalina's voice burned into her. "What are you doing? Come back here now."

She fought against the command, but it pulled her against her will into a place of invasive light and heat and decay. Blinking, she began to register objects and put names to them. Sun. Dust. Bones.

Zee. Flexing his right arm and running his left hand over a wide, jagged scar. But it was a scar, not an open wound. He turned to her with a touch of wonder. She didn't like that expression.

"Functional?" It was hard to access words, so she used only the one.

"Seems to be."

His expression shifted to one she knew and recognized, the one that meant he was about to kiss her. Except for damned Kalina, who got in the way.

"If you two are quite done wasting time, can we talk about that strategy now?"

Strategy. What did she know of strategy? She had no idea of how many dragons they were facing on what type of terrain. Had Aidan joined forces with the dragons of the Forever? No matter what tactics they took, the chances of winning against an entire contingent of dragons were pitifully small.

She tried to think of her companions in terms of resources and liabilities instead of people she loved and wanted to protect. Kalina had powerful magic. Kraal, a Giant's strength and a thirst for retribution born from the destruction of his home world. Zee, so lethal with a sword, born to be warrior and dragon slayer.

But looking at the boneyard stretched out for miles, she doubted that it would be enough.

"We need to get to the Pool of Life, steal some of the water from it, and get away. How we're going to do that, I hadn't thought."

"I'll kill Aidan with my bare hands as a beginning," Kraal growled.

Kalina's magic surged, blue lightning flickering from her eyes and fingers. "She's mine!"

"I owe her several deaths," Zee said. He paused. "What about the child?"

"Lyssa?"

"No. Aidan's unborn." He didn't say the words Vivian knew were in his mind.

"Any spawn of hers will be vermin," Kraal said.

"Kill it along with her."

Kalina was more perceptive. Her eyes went from Vivian to Zee and back again. "You two know something. Why is this a question?"

"Killing Aidan or her child won't stop the Nothing," Vivian began. Zee laid a restraining hand on her arm.

"Because the child is mine," he said.

Silence followed, the little group staring at him in disbelief. Vivian alone knew what this admission cost him, and laced her fingers with his in solidarity and support.

"Killing Aidan won't stop the Nothing." She moved to the center of the group, turning in a circle to make eye contact with each one. "If killing her will facilitate the objective of carrying the water of life to the Cave of Dreams, then we need to consider killing her. We all want her to die a thousand fiery deaths, but if doing so distracts us or keeps us from what we need to do, then we let her live once again. Understood?"

A deep silence followed, which she chose to take as acquiescence. "Strategy needs to revolve around how we get away with water from the sacred Pool."

"If there's any water in it," Kalina said, with a meaningful look at the cracked and pitted riverbed.

"If it does not exist, we fail, and all of this was for nothing."

"We must assume it exists." Zee's eyes glowed with the fire of the hunt. "As for strategy—either we fight our way through or we use trickery."

Vivian knew full well what his preference would be. Zee would confront all of the dragons in the world without fear and die with a heart full of the joy of battle.

Kraal, although his eyes also shone with battle lust, spoke on the conservative side. "They will outnumber us greatly. We are a lethal company, but even so, we cannot win through if they all stand against us."

"Maybe a mixed tactic, then," Zee said. "Some of us do battle, creating a distraction, while somebody makes a break for the Pool."

"Not me," Kalina said. "I can fight. You need my magic."

"We also need Vivian as a dragon, I think... It may have to be you, Kalina."

"Lyssa and I will get the water," Isobel said. Her voice was tentative but determined.

"It's not safe."

Isobel smiled. "It's a little late to be worrying about safety. Let me be useful for once."

This was hard to argue with. If they failed now, everybody was going to die. Still. Vivian swallowed hard, looking at her mother, at the little girl, already damaged. Somehow, it was the missing hand that cemented for her the finality of where they were.

"Basic strategy, all down through time," Zee said.

Vivian had to try. "But if the dragons find them, they're dinner."

"Isobel's right. They're dinner hiding behind a rock."

"We could leave them here."

"And if you don't come back? No water, no food. Nowhere else to go."

"It's the only thing that might work," Zee said.

"You didn't bring us here," Isobel said. "Not me. Not Lyssa or Zee or any of these others. You're not responsible for a single life. Fate brought us. Every one of us. For a reason."

"We're wasting time," Kalina said. "Every minute we stand here talking, another world dies."

"Zee?" Vivian said. "What do we do now?"

Zee would have given a great deal for a pair of binoculars. The little group had made its way to the top of a towering cliff that must once have been a thundering waterfall. Sheltering behind a boulder, he peered down at the landscape below and tried to picture a strategy that ended with access to the Pool of Life and the survival of everybody in their little company.

Try as he might, he couldn't see it.

The City of Dragons was laid out in a grid that stretched for miles. What dragons needed with houses, he didn't know, but there were thousands of them, separated by wide streets and spacious outdoor bathing areas. All of the basins were full of dust, except for the one that mattered.

At the base of the dry falls lay a round, steep-walled chasm, just large enough for one full-grown dragon to bathe. It was almost empty, but there was a golden shimmer at the bottom that promised a hope of success.

Just beyond the Pool stretched a wide, sweeping curve of land paved with flat stones, large enough for a host of dragons. At the center was a massive protrusion of stone cut with steps. On the top hunkered a platform made of what appeared to be solid gold. It was carved all around the edge with images of dragons, their eyes set with stones that flashed blue, red, and yellow in the sunlight.

How many dragons were down there? Had Aidan and the dragons of the Between wiped out the dragons of the Forever? Or was there a host beyond counting, hidden from his sight? He could smell them, sense them. But nothing moved below and he couldn't begin to guess at their numbers. Not that it really mattered whether there were a hundred or thousands.

He stiffened as a black dragon emerged from around the corner of a building. He knew her, recognized the shape of her and the way her scales seemed to absorb the light rather than reflecting it back. As he watched, she slithered up the steps to the golden platform, stood there for a long moment with her nostrils raised, scenting the air.

"She knows we're here," Vivian said. Her eyes had shifted to dragon, golden, the pupils horizontal. It made her look dangerous and wild. "Get ready. The others will all pick up on her warning."

"Shit."

But instead of raising an alarm, the dragon shifted into a slender, dark-haired woman.

"What's she doing?"

"I don't know. I can't read her when she's human. But then, neither can the others."

Another dragon moved into the square.

Kraal crouched beside Zee. "There is no strategy to encompass this. Too many of them, too few of us. Picked off one at a time over a matter of days, that we could do. But to take them all at once? This cannot be done."

"We don't need to kill them," Vivian reminded him. "Just to get to the water."

"And back again. How do you propose getting to the Pool without being seen?" Zee asked. "Magic?"

Vivian shook her head. "Dragons sense magic. Even if they don't see through it, they'll be drawn to it."

"The rest of us serve as a distraction," Kraal said. "Bait."

"A suicide mission, then?"

The Giant's voice and face were granite. "We are expendable. We must distract them long enough for Isobel to reach the Pool and fill the waterskin. This is all that matters."

"What about after the Pool? It counts for nothing if they don't get back to the Cave of Dreams."

Isobel seemed not to even hear. She sat on a stone, her hands over her ears, trying to shut out the dragon voices in her head. But Lyssa, cross-legged in the dirt with the griffyn in her lap, was all attention. "If I get the water and take it to the cave, that stops the Nothing?"

Kalina, kneeling beside the child, rubbed the cub's ears. "Of course. You get the water and pour it out at the entrance of the cave. Make sure some of it gets onto the dream matter and the decay stops."

Vivian gave Kalina a warning look. "Don't lie to her. She at least deserves the truth. We think it will stop the Nothing. We hope so. Nobody knows for sure."

"If it doesn't work, the Nothing gets me." The little girl's eyes were wide, her face serious.

"If it doesn't work, the Nothing gets everybody," Kalina added. "Since we're being honest."

Lyssa's lip trembled but she held her head high and returned Vivian's gaze. "I'll go. Isobel will be with me."

"After they get the water, how will they get back to the cave?" Kraal asked.

"That part's easy." Lyssa plumped down on the ground and closed her eyes. A door opened in the air beside her. It looked like something straight out of a fairytale picture book, complete with twining vines decked out with small purple flowers.

Vivian cracked it open and peered through. No fairytale princesses behind that door. She slammed it shut and leaned all of her weight against it. Trying to keep her voice casual, she said, "Lyssa, could you lock that up tight?"

The door vanished and she took a deep breath.

"What is it?" Zee asked.

"Definitely the cave," Vivian said. "Or what's left of it. Look, Lyssa. When you open the door, you might want to just pour the water through and not go all the way in. You hear me?"

"I'll be careful."

"Gods," Zee murmured. "How old did she say she is?" He shook his head and turned to the rest of them. "All right, then. Here's the plan, such as it is. Isobel, Lyssa—you need to be quick. Kraal, I'm thinking you and I launch an attack on the side farthest from the Pool. Vivian, are you going in as a dragon?"

She nodded. "The minute I shift, they'll be aware of me. I'll get some of them into the air." Poe pressed up against her leg and she knelt to smooth his feathers. "You should go with Lyssa."

Poe fixed her with his inscrutable penguin stare, then pressed his head against her for an instant before waddling over to the little girl. He hissed at the griffyn cub and it growled in response. Lyssa tapped it on the back of the head. "Behave."

Zee turned to Kalina. "Can you provide some sort of shielding for the little one and Isobel? Because if they are seen…"

"I can make them invisible, I think."

"What does that mean, that you think?" Vivian demanded. "Tell us what you know."

"I mean that we're dealing with dragons. They have magic. I can make an illusion, but they'll sense it. And if they are focused enough, they will be able to unravel it."

Kraal nodded, grim as death. "So, they must not have a chance to focus. Shield the little one and Isobel until they are close to the Pool but far enough still not to stir interest. Then I will engage the dragons from the earth, Vivian from the sky. Kalina shifts her shield to Zee until he's close enough to Aidan. He kills her. There will be a moment of confusion then—dragons can all hear each other's thoughts, yes?"

Vivian nodded. "If—when—Zee kills Aidan, every one of them will know. I would expect them to turn all of their attention to her death and her killer for a moment. But not long. Dragons follow a leader but they are also independent. They won't just fall apart, and they'll be outraged."

Zee wanted to paint her again, with that expression of obstinate courage. But he was destined to die holding a sword, not a paintbrush or a chisel. He would content himself with knowing she was engraved on his heart and soul.

"Long enough," Kraal said. He turned his gaze on Isobel and Lyssa. "You two must wait in hiding until you see Aidan fall. Then run as fast as you can for the Pool, fill your vessel, and make the door to the Cave. Understood?"

"I understand." Isobel's hand rested on the little girl's tumbled curls. Lyssa just nodded. Bob perched on her shoulder. Poe stood protectively at her side and she held the cub in her arms. She was so tiny, so young for so much responsibility. And so much danger. Even if she won through, she would always be maimed physically, psychologically. Zee tried to smile for her, but his lips refused to cooperate.

"The griffyn stays behind," Kraal said.

"No." All of the women spoke at once.

Kraal raised his hands in a gesture of frustration. "Talk to them, Zee. It's cute and all, but this is war. The birds are bad enough, but at least they take care of themselves."

"Her name is Grace, after the lady with the Dreamsphere," Lyssa said, her small jaw jutting stubbornly. "And she stays with me."

Zee looked down at the child clinging to the cub as if it were a living teddy bear, and shook his head. "I'm not taking anything away from her."

His fingers itched for the sword, for the chance to release his grief and rage in battle. He was about to reach for Vivian, to give her one last kiss and try to find a way to say good-bye, when a sharp hiss from Kalina drew him back to the view point.

"You need to see this."

Zee peered down between the rocks. A man stood on the dragon throne next to Aidan. He had a knife and they appeared to be arguing. Hope and regret warred in his heart. The need to kill Aidan with his own hands was overpowering but dead was dead.

Other dragons emerged from the streets in response to some signal invisible to him.

"The alarm," Isobel said. She looked as though she were sleepwalking, all of her attention focused on something Zee could neither see nor here. "They know about us."

"We go now," he said. "Hurry!"

And so, there was no time in the end to tell Vivian all that he wanted to say. Not even for a kiss. One last look between them, and then she was shifting and he felt the magic shield form around him. Without a backward glance, he took to the cliff, letting himself down, handhold and foothold, while dragon wings beat the air above him and Kraal jarred the earth as he ran down the hillside toward the plain with an ear-shattering battle cry.

Twenty-five

Aidan jolted wide awake from deep sleep, all senses on full alert. Sunlight poured into the sleeping chamber, which meant she had been asleep for only a few hours. Nothing moved around her. Her sharp ears picked out only the sound of the unceasing wind. She saw only the walls and ceiling of golden stone. Nothing moved. She smelled only dragons and the hot, dry earth.

Letting her mind run through the dragons' thoughts, she found the same mild disturbance that had been going on for days. Most of them slept, dreaming of food and of the golden river. There were eddies and swirls of discontent, a lot of hunger, but no outright danger. Finding themselves in the City of Dragons, a place of legend none of them had ever thought to see, had gone a long way toward calming their rebellion.

Whatever had wakened her was not a current threat; maybe some intimation of the future. Because the peace wouldn't last. Their hunger would continue to escalate, their anger would return. She would be unable to hold them, and she couldn't kill them, at least not all at once. If she picked off one or two, the rest would turn on her, if Teheren didn't do it first.

She needed to set them against each other. So far, Teheren had foiled all of her experiments in that direction, calming altercations, quieting rebellions. He needed to die, and soon, but he was stronger than she, and he never seemed to sleep. Even now, he was awake. She could sense him, even though he sent nothing out over the channels. A quiet, brooding presence, watching over the fitful dreams of her offspring sleeping in his chamber under his protection.

For a brief flicker, she thought she sensed another mind, familiar, but not one of the dragons in her flight. On her feet, she lifted her head and scented the air but came up empty. Whatever she thought she'd sensed had dissipated. Still, sleep was out of the question and she did not lie back down.

Legends had never spoken of dragons owning human slaves, but she thought they must have. Hands had built the spacious rooms with their wide doorways, high ceilings, and glassless windows. Hands must also have hauled in the loads of luxurious sleeping gravel. The city itself was empty, not a dragon to be found. No bones here, either. The bone fields they'd flown over would account for most of that but not all. Something had gone wrong with the dragons of the Forever.

Which only made her task easier. Killing all of the dragons she'd brought with her would be challenge enough. The regret that she could not avenge herself on the Old Ones, though, that rankled. Most of her long life, she had dreamed of the moment when she would confront and kill the King of the Dragons. And now, it seemed, there was no King. Unless the dragons had moved on deeper into the land. But if so, why? Following food, perhaps? Seeking water?

She dragged her heavy body out of the sleeping chamber, through the sunning room, and out into the wide street, all the while tuned to the channels, listening for danger. The streets were empty, all of the dragons resting after the long journey. Nothing to impede her progress to the massive throne at the head of the mud pit.

Based on her mother's stories, she knew this had once been a pool of sparkling water, filled by a waterfall fed by the golden river. How the gold was transformed into water was part of the mythology of the place. Now the cliffs were dry and barren. Not so much as a trickle passed over them to fall into the Pool beneath.

In one version of her plans, she had reigned here as Queen over a few worthy dragons, her vengeance completed. But this—the endless nothingness, the pointlessness of a place called the Forever that was nothing but a barren land—this pleased her more. All that remained was to end the rest of the dragons.

Something tweaked at her senses, something out of place. Intruders. And she was pretty sure she knew which intruders. Before her thoughts could betray her over the network, Aidan shifted into human form. While she was human, there was less chance that any of the others would tune in to her thoughts. They'd get static, of course, and if any of them took the time and trouble to tune in deeply, they would hear her. But they would have no cause to do so, all sound asleep in their comfortable new lodgings.

She would not raise the alarm. Let the stupid worms sleep until the dragon slayer was upon them. He'd rejected her, refused her offer of alliance. But now he had arrived to unwittingly do her work for her, and this was good.

"I fail to find the humor."

Aidan startled, looking about wildly for the speaker. Teheren, damn his soul to endless torment, hiding in the shadows somewhere behind the throne. How a dragon of his size and coloring could conceal himself so well in broad daylight was a mystery. But he'd spoken in the Old Tongue, which meant he must be in dragon form. She heard the warning go out, the other dragons stirring and waking.

She was about to shift back herself when he materialized in front of the throne in his human form, a dragonstone blade in hand.

"That's not your throne."

Aidan kept her eyes on his, peripheral vision tuned to the blade. Death was all well and good, but it was too soon. She wasn't ready. Leaning back, crossing one naked thigh over the other, she let her eyelashes droop over her eyes and gave him a slow, seductive smile. "Care to join me?"

"You want them dead. All of them. Why?"

"You're no fun." She thrust her bottom lip out in a pout and leaned forward, reaching out to touch his face.

He slapped her hand away with a force that stung and reminded her of the weakness inherent in this form. Enough of games. With a feral snarl, she began to shift, but he pressed the flat of the blade against her thigh. "Shift one more cell and I will cut you."

Aidan's breath froze in her throat and she held perfectly still. Death by dragonstone was agonizing and slow, and the slightest movement could mean a cut to her skin. In human form, perhaps it would do no harm, but the tiniest cut was death to a dragon.

Down below, the others were gathering. He was an upstart; she was the Queen. If she was patient and careful, she could use them against Teheren.

The news that she was captive in her human form spread rapidly alongside the warning of intruders. They gathered in a wide half-circle around the throne. Teheren turned to face them, speaking aloud in the Ancient Tongue.

"Treachery! Intruders are in the land. Your Queen has chosen not to alert you, though she knew. I hazard a guess that she knows also who is coming."

Aidan laughed, scornfully. "You are all so pitiful.

Yes, follow the great Teheren. He will be your savior, as he has been of the dragons in this land before you. Look around. Where are they? Ah, yes. Lying in the great bone-yard outside the city. Why? Because he is such a great and noble leader. He dares to use dragonstone against one of his own kind. Yes, I'm certain he will lead you well in a battle against the Warrior and his company."

The murmuring spread through the ranks like wildfire. One of the older dragons sent a direct question over the channels.

"He came with us into the Forever. How can you say he led the dragons to slaughter?"

The truth was a gamble, but she had nothing left. "No. He did not enter with us. Did any of you see him in the Between? No, you did not. He joined us in the night and made pretense he was one of ours."

She let this register, trying to look both brave and pitiful.

"This much is true," Teheren said, at length. "I am the last of the dragons of the Forever. My people died of famine and thirst. You see what has become of the land."

"Or the land is cursed," Aidan said. "Cursed because he has murdered his own people with the dragonstone. It is Teheren's crimes against dragonkind that have turned the promised land into a desert. Kill him and the land will become fertile again. The river of gold will flow, and the Pool of the Forever will become life-giving once again."

She felt their blood surge at her words, and yet they hesitated, reluctant to move against one who had served as leader and guide.

"Oh, my foolish ones," she intoned, infusing her voice with deep sorrow. "Allow him to kill me with the dragonstone blade, and who will be next? Perhaps he is the one who has invited the intruders into the land through some secret way we do not know. My life is a small thing, but you are the future. All that is left of dragonkind in all the worlds. Do not allow this deceiver to destroy you."

The ploy was working. A bold young dragon emerged through the ranks, snorting flame and ready for battle. Another joined him. Teheren released the dragonstone and shifted into his dragon form. He was larger than the others, the sun blinding on his red-gold scales as he cried out, "I will defend myself if I must, and yet I say to you that she lies. You would be better to turn your attention to the threat that is coming—"

His voice was cut off as the two dragons attacked, one on each flank. Aidan bent to pick up the fallen knife, taking care to keep the blade well away from her own skin. She watched the battle, suppressing a fierce desire to shift and join in. Teheren was a match for the two. He was mostly taking evasive maneuvers, holding fast to his philosophy that no more dragons should die.

Aidan hoped he would survive. She wanted the pleasure of killing him herself. The last of the Old Ones. Not the King, her father. It was too late to exact that vengeance. But a descendant. One fully deserving of her long-simmering hate. And so, she sat on the throne in her frail human body, watching the battle, listening to the thoughts of the dragons, and waiting for the Warrior to come to her.

The shift felt different this time, all of Vivian's human emotions and the Sorcieri magic staying with her. It was too much at first to contain it all and she began by circling high above the battlefield, getting acclimatized to so much sensory input. The dragon city was laid out in perfect geometry. Rectangular sleeping buildings, widely spaced to make room for dragons to move between them, the basins that had once been for bathing, the throne and the square wide enough for a thousand dragons. Her sharp eyes picked out Kraal, surging forward to his certain death with five dragons turning to confront him at once.

Knowing her mind was open now on the dragon channels, she did not look for Zee, or for Lyssa and Isobel, not wanting to give them away. Instead, she kept her gaze on Aidan and the three dragons fighting in front of the throne, tuning in to the frequencies. *Look up,* she broadcast with all of her strength. *Come and get me.*

The entire flight lifted their heads to search her out. One by one, dragons launched into the air. A dangerous thing, she realized too late. Distraction, yes, but aloft, they could see what should be hidden. Kalina's magic surged, potent and demanding, and at the right angle, she was an easily visible target.

Vivian altered her course to move away, sending out taunts as she flew, keeping her mind on her own flight and the challenge issued. The first of the dragons was already upon her and she turned to meet the onslaught, drawing on her magic to guard her flanks. Images flashed into her like stills. Three dragons coming in from the west. Two more from the east. A gray dragon altering his course and circling back to the ridge where Kalina stood chanting.

Vivian feinted to avoid contact with the dragon that had charged her, moving to intersect the gray dragon before he noticed Kalina down below. But the oncoming dragon swerved in the air and set a new collision course. Another closed in on her left flank. Kalina would have to fend for herself.

Isobel crouched behind the rock as Zee had directed, clutching her head with both hands and trying not to scream with the pain. She knew Lyssa was beside her, and that she should be guarding and comforting the child, but it was all she could do to stay in place and hold on to a few shreds of sanity.

This many dragons up close was overwhelming. They were so—alive. More so than humans. Larger than life, crystal clear, as if they had an extra dimension. Their scales, in all the colors of the rainbow, reflected the sunlight in a blinding glare.

But it was the voices that were destroying her.

Her mind was fully human, and the hundreds of dragon voices all coming at her at once, were pain beyond her endurance. In Wakeworld, where she should have been beyond the hearing, the constant noise had reduced her to insanity. At best, she'd heard static. At worst, there had been a battering of sound so intense, it made her try to end her life. Often, she'd felt close to making out individual words, had tried to write down messages, but had succeeded only in jotting down garbled nonsense.

Now, with the dragons so close, the impact of their communications took on a new dimension. All of it was agony, but she couldn't let it destroy her. Not now. She had a job to do. Breathing hard, she forced herself to lower her hands, to open her eyes, to watch what was going on around her so she would know when to act. It wouldn't be long. She could hold out for a little bit. Squinting against a light that threatened to burn her retinas, even though she knew in reality it was a dull day, she looked for the other players in this living chess game.

Vivian had taken to the sky. Kraal was at the center of a group of dragons, swinging his club, smacking noses. They would take him in a minute. Zee was invisible, hopefully close to his target by now. And Kalina—

Her heart stopped.

The Sorcieri girl stood at the top of the cliff, partially screened by the stones. Her eyes were closed, her hands held out in front of her, palms up, a faint blue light flickering from finger to finger. And behind her stood a dragon. It was small for a dragon, gray, the color of the stone, and it moved with the stealth of a hunter. It must have flown up onto the ledge and landed at a distance, creeping up behind its prey.

To shout a warning would have been to betray their own position. And so she put her hands over Lyssa's eyes so that the child might be spared this one pain, and watched in silent horror as the wide jaws opened, exposing rows of razor-sharp teeth. Quick as a snake it struck, the head darting forward on the long neck, the jaws clamping down. Kalina's head and upper body vanished. Her hips and legs stood for an impossible instant, then collapsed to the ground, only to vanish a moment later into the dragon's jaws.

The screening veil dropped and Zee became visible in the middle of the dragon throng. He was too far from the throne and Aidan. Too many dragons in the way. Vivian would be unable to help. Kalina was dead.

The distance to the Pool seemed impossibly far and was terribly exposed. But there was nothing for it. Now or never. She took Lyssa's hand and tried to smile. "Let's go."

"Zee said to wait—"

"The plan just changed."

Lyssa shook her head, small jaw set in stubborn defiance. "But Zee said—"

"Lyssa. Kalina can't hide him now. Or us." Isobel eyed the child. She could be carried, but if she screamed or fought, it would draw attention at once. It was Vivian's odd penguin that decided the thing.

Poe nudged Lyssa, then took off toward the Pool. Bob lifted into the air and followed. The child looked up at Isobel for one long moment with those eyes that did not belong in a child's face, and nodded. Then, the cub still in her arms, she took off at a run, without waiting for the lecture on keeping low and trying to hide.

Isobel followed, crouched, moving more slowly. Her joints ached, her back throbbed. Her gown was in the way and she gathered it up with one hand to free her feet. Ahead of her, Poe skirted the edge of the plain, avoiding the dragons by a margin that was far too narrow for Isobel's taste. They seemed not to notice, their attention held elsewhere. Dragon voices hammered at her, against a background of static.

A deep, powerful voice with a ring of authority.

And then, female, cold and high.

The rest was a muddle of fear and anger and confusion.

Isobel ran with all her strength, even after her legs turned to jelly and wanted to collapse, when every breath burned like dragon fire. The penguin kept pace with her, his wings outstretched for balance.

Lyssa skidded to a stop at the edge of the Pool, hesitating for the first time. The raven, fluttering down at her feet, bobbed his head, walking back and forth on the edge. Isobel skidded to a stop beside her. What had looked like water at the bottom of the Pool was an illusion, a sheet of shining stone. At the very center lay a small puddle of foul-smelling mud.

Her heart sank and dark spots swam before her eyes. This was it, then. The last hope dashed. Even if it had been water at the bottom, there was no way of reaching it. The sides were slick and steep, too high to climb and damp and coated with moss. The bottom of the basin was stone. Jumping was out of the question; it was too far. Bones would be shattered on the bare stone.

"How do we get down?" Lyssa asked, her unearthly eyes reflecting the sky.

Isobel's heart was doing its best to beat its way out of her chest. The voices hammered at her, the pain increasing as the volume of the voices rose. There was no hope, but since she was still alive, she would continue to try.

A wide crack ran down one side of the basin. Maybe just wide enough.

"Come here, Lyssa." Taking the child in her arms, she braced her back on one side of the crack, pressing with her feet on the other, and lowered herself, little by little, down toward the bottom.

The dragons had seen them.

They lumbered toward the Pool on land or swooped down from the sky. She kept on moving down, ignoring the stabbing pain in her knees, her aching thighs and back. She let the voices flow through her instead of trying to shut them out, turned herself into a lightning rod for their energy.

For the first time in her life, she felt like a perfectly tuned instrument, vibrating to the perfect chord. In that moment, the voices separated into words and thoughts, all clear and comprehensible. Isobel's heart, head, and body sang with wild exultation. She was, for once, exactly where she was meant to be.

Depositing the child safely at the bottom, she turned to see Poe sliding wildly down the crack, flapping his wings as if he could fly. She caught him before he hit the bottom and set him gently down beside Lyssa.

"Take care of her." She turned to Lyssa. "If there is water to be found, get it. Be quick."

And then she turned and began working her way back up to the surface. She had a thing or two to say to the dragons.

Zee was only halfway across the plain when the cover spell lifted. It had dimmed the world, as if all of his senses were muffled by a veil. Colors were grayed, sounds seemed farther away, smells less intense. Climbing down the cliff had been difficult because the hand- and footholds hadn't felt solid. He'd tumbled the last ten feet, jarring his shoulder. It was all right though, his whole arm working better than it had in days because of Vivian's healing.

He both heard and felt her launch into the air but stayed focused on slipping between the dragons to get to Aidan's throne. And then the colors were suddenly bright, the hot stone smell of dragons sharp in his nostrils, the sounds of dragon battle overhead loud. He knew he had been exposed, that he was a visible target.

It was too soon. His stomach twisted at the thought of Lyssa and Isobel out on that plain, unveiled and surrounded by dragons, but he steeled himself. So far, the dragons hadn't noticed that he was right beneath their feet, and he tried to keep it that way.

He kept moving, darting from one dragon to the next, using their massive legs for cover like tree trunks. A dangerous prospect, given that every leg ended in poisoned talons. Just one nick from one of those claws and he'd be burning up in a matter of hours. One burst of flame would incinerate him, close as he was. One pair of jaws could tear him apart. At the moment, their attention was divided between the air battle still going on before the throne, Vivian in the air above them, and Kraal's mad, suicidal assault.

It couldn't last. Zee felt the moment when the first dragon became aware of him. She was blue-green, medium-sized, lowering her head to rub against some itch on her right front knee. For the space of a heartbeat, he saw himself reflected in her great golden eye, saw the pupil constrict as she recognized him. And then he was moving, away from her, toward his goal.

Aidan's death was in his hands.

He was driven. No matter that he had been seen. They were all going to die, Vivian included, and the one thing that would give that meaning was Aidan's death. No time to falter, no room for hesitation or his chance was lost.

His momentum, his rage, his pain, all fueled him. Heads turned to follow him and he braced for attack. Instead, they drew back, away from his pounding feet and his bright sword. Just before him lay a clear space in front of the throne. Up until then, he had used the bodies of the dragons themselves as cover, but once he reached it, he would be fully exposed, open to attack. No other way to reach the throne, though, so he kept running.

Wind from the dragon battle over his head stirred up a dust storm, blurring his vision. He squinted against it and kept moving. In his peripheral vision he saw large bodies closing in.

He had time. Dragons were fast in the air, quick to strike, but slow-moving on the ground. He had reached the stairs to the throne. They were wide and steep, but adrenaline seemed to give his feet wings. Up the steps, onto the level, the sword already moving for the killing blow. If she was pregnant still, the blood of the child would be on his head. There was no room for regret. Hell was a price he was willing to pay.

Aidan's face was turned upward, laughing aloud at something in the sky. Without a pause to draw a breath, to secure his aim, or have a second thought, with all of his weight and strength behind it, he drove for the space just below her rib cage. Felt the sword enter flesh and let his momentum drive it deep, twisting as it went.

Her body stiffened. Blood gushed from her mouth and down over her white chin. Her eyes, dark with pain, focused in on his. And she smiled. She held out her right hand, clenched around the haft of a wicked blade, as red as her own heart's blood.

Dragonstone.

"It's yours. Use it well," she said. Her eyes rolled up

in her head. Her hand went limp. The knife clattered to the stone at his feet.

Zee felt no satisfaction, only a vague relief that her belly was flat and not swelling with a growing child. Perhaps she had lied about that, along with everything else. But the way she smiled as she died, as if she had triumphed mightily, worried him. A trap. She'd wanted him to have the knife. Which meant he should leave it. It would help him kill dragons, but it wasn't enough to save him and the others. Twice in his life, he'd touched dragonstone; both times had been disastrous . First Vivian, then Godzilla. This time, he'd stick to the sword.

But as he turned to descend from the throne, a scream reached his ears, high and piercing, from over by the Pool. Isobel and Lyssa. That errand could not be allowed to fail. Before he could run to their rescue, a shadow fell over him, the wind of giant wings nearly knocking him off his feet as the great red-gold dragon alighted on the throne. There was no time for a sword battle, not if he had any hope of getting to Lyssa in time.

Zee picked up the knife. It felt alive in his hand, with its own malevolent will. Only evil could come from using this blade, but failure would be a greater evil. Their whole passage here had been bought by darkness and blood. It was too late now to quibble about tools forged for dark purposes.

Once accepted, the blade ceased to feel foreign. It molded itself to his grip, made itself part of his body and blood of his blood. As if it had nerves connected to his. It shared his hate for dragons, his thirst for dragon blood, fed his need for revenge. He could feel the exact location of the needle-sharp tip, the razor edge of the blade. It was hungry. His arm drew back in a smooth contraction of muscle and sinew, ready to throw, knowing there would be no missing the mark with this weapon. It would fly like a heat-seeking missile, directly for the dragon's heart.

Before the knife left his hand, another form stepped between him and his mark. A young dragon, smaller even than Godzilla had been, with great golden eyes and scales so mirror-bright, they reflected the sky despite being black as night. Not a threat, this one. The eyes were curious, not hostile.

If he released the blade, it would kill the young one, not the monster behind it.

His inborn hatred for all things dragon warred with his need to protect the young and helpless. Memory of the trust in Godzilla's eyes just before the killing blow speared him. Something about the small dragon made him think, too, of Vivian.

"I've no quarrel with you. Get out of the way," he shouted.

The red-gold seemed to have the same idea. Bending his neck, he nudged the small one aside with his great head, gently enough not to do harm but firmly. It was a gesture so human, it shook Zee again, drew him away from the melding with the dragonstone. His eyes went to it; he felt it working on his will, guiding his hand, his muscles quivering with the effort of holding it back.

All of the years of hate warred with a new awareness. Vivian was a dragon and he loved her. Godzilla had saved his life, had died to save Vivian's. The hate that ran through his veins was bred there by design. That was what decided him. He was master of his own fate, not a tool to be manipulated. He would not, at the least, be used by the dragonstone.

It clung to his fingers as if it were a part of him, resisting separation. He could feel it ache, needing blood. With a desperate gesture, he flung it backward at Aidan's lifeless body. Then, with only a blade, he faced the big dragon, ready for a fight to the death.

Sword ready, he stood at a half crouch, in a defensive posture, ready to fight his last battle. But the big dragon did not attack. It stood just out of reach of his sword, eyeing him with caution and an echo of the young one's curiosity.

A voice rumbled out of him, deep and powerful, echoing up into the sky. Words, Zee knew, though in a language he could not understand. The dragons above replied and shifted into a circling flight path. Vivian was still up there, still flying. Hurt maybe, from the way she flew, but not crashing.

The dragon's scales rippled and stretched, his flesh stretching, bunching, constricting. And then in its place stood a man. Tall, broad of shoulder, gold of hair and blue of eye. "Hail, dragon slayer. Must we do battle?" he said, his speech colored by an unfamiliar accent.

Zee's fingers tightened around the sword hilt. Dragons were liars. Hesitation meant death. But he couldn't kill a man in cold blood.

"Call off the other dragons," he said. "Then maybe we can talk."

"I can't do that. The penalty for desecration of the Pool of Life is certain death."

Zee glanced across the battlefield. All of the dragons had turned to the Pool. *Lyssa.* They lined the edge, standing in ranks.

"She's just a little kid," he said. "And she's not desecrating anything."

"Only dragons of pure blood can touch the water. None has been worthy in thrice three hundred years." He eyed Zee. "Why did you not use the dragonstone?"

"Aidan wanted me to use it. Tell me why she wanted you dead."

"She sought to destroy all things."

Zee absorbed this. "She's done a damned good job of

that. She poisoned the dreamspheres—we've come for the water of the Pool of Life to reverse her curse."

"You might have asked," the dragon man said.

Zee snorted. "Right. Just waltz into a bunch of dragons controlled by Aidan and ask. You're a funny guy."

No smile met his words. "I am Teheren, last of the old dragons. My word is my bond. Is this also true for you, Warrior?"

Sobering, Zee nodded. "My word is my bond, Teheren of the dragons." And then, formally, he went down on one knee. "I ask for one thing—that the child may take water from the Pool to the Cave of Dreams in hope of saving what remains yet of all the worlds. My life is forfeit."

"And your companions?"

He very nearly choked on the words he must say, but they must stay the course. "All of our lives for the life of the child and a draught of water from the Pool."

Teheren's eyes were deep, more dragon than human. "I see truth in you, Warrior. But there is no water in the Pool. I am the last of the Old Ones. We have died, one by one, and the land has died with us."

This truth struck home. All Zee need do was look around at the desolation and the gathering of dragons which seemed suddenly small, seen through Teheren's eyes. "All of these, then, came with Aidan?"

Teheren nodded. "Yes. And they, too, will die. There is no sustenance for them."

A sudden suspicion narrowed Zee's eyes. "So, if all of your people are dead—how are you still alive?"

A look of sadness so deep it was beyond comprehension passed over the handsome face. "I was king here, once. I bathed often in the Pool. It takes a long, long time to die for one who has bathed in the Pool. The dragonstone blade might have been a favor."

Zee fought against his choking despair. "There must be some way," he said. "It cannot truly be the end of all things, even the Forever." He turned his eyes up to the sky where the dragon that was Vivian still flew, far above. She was no longer circling but on a course toward the Pool.

Zee began to run, Teheren falling into step beside him. The baby dragon wasn't far behind. Maybe Teheren sent messages over the channels, maybe the dragons feared his sword, but they made a path for him. He arrived at the brink of the pool just in time to see Vivian fold her wings and dive. A moment of confusion, and then he could see Lyssa, mud-covered but alive, standing between the dragon legs.

No great explosion of magic, no fireworks to herald Kalina's death, but Vivian felt the shock of it clear to her core. The instant of distraction cost her a long gash along her side and very nearly a broken wing. A blast of her own magic repelled the attack but left her weakened. All she could do now was fight her own battle, to kill or be killed.

She was weakening. Another dragon, a large green male, winged toward her, and she knew this one would be too many. And then Lyssa and Isobel were seen by the pool. A clamor of outrage rose from the host of dragons. A voice of great authority commanded, *Cease fighting. Wait and watch.* The green dragon, jaws wide open and about to strike Vivian's neck, rolled in midair, folding his wings and dropping like a stone to avoid collision.

On guard, not trusting this cease-fire, she took in the scene below. Aidan dead on the throne. Zee talking to a tall man whose red-gold hair blazed in the evening light. A stampede of dragons rushing toward the Pool.

At the bottom of the basin, Lyssa scrabbled in the mud with her one good hand. The griffyn cub dug away beside her. Poe stood beside her, overseeing things, the raven right beside him. And above her, balanced on the edge of the Pool, Isobel stood between the oncoming dragons and the little girl, her arms held out as if her frail body could be an effective barrier.

Vivian tried to fly faster, to stop the tragedy about to play out below, but she wasn't going to make it. Isobel was brave, but this was a stupid, pointless waste. They would hesitate to go down into the Pool of Life, water or no water. She could have bought herself some time staying there with Lyssa.

Then Isobel's voice came into her mind, clear and sharp as a blade, cutting through all of the clamoring voices.

What is so sacred about mud?

The dragon stampede came to a standstill, holding back a respectful distance from the edge of the basin. Isobel confused them. She smelled human but had spoken as a dragon.

The water will flow again, one said in response, but his voice was uncertain.

It will, indeed, Isobel sent back. *Because of what the child is doing. She is here to help you. Only a stupid dragon would eat her.*

Miracle of miracles, they were listening. But their rage and hunger were great.

Vivian circled the Pool once and then came in for a landing. She thought Lyssa might be afraid of her in her dragon form, but the little girl just shouted up at her, "You have to dig."

Oh, child. It's over. Make a door. Get away. Maybe you can survive for a little, moving from dream world to dream world.

Of course Lyssa couldn't hear the dragon speech. But the other dragons could.

She must not be allowed to make a door.

Water or no, a human has dared to enter the Sacred Pool.

Stop her.

The anger rose to a crescendo, and Vivian readied herself for the last battle. She would die defending the child. Reaching for the Dreamshifter part of herself, she began to build a door. It shimmered into the air just above the pool, her usual green door with the brass handle.

"No." Lyssa turned to face her, hands on hips, eyes flashing. The child appeared more angry than afraid. "I won't go. You have to clear away the mud. I dreamed it."

Vivian knew better than to argue with a dream. Using her clawed front feet, she began to paw at the mud. It was warm and stank of decaying flesh. Of blood. Of corruption and darkness and long-festering hate. Below it, though, was something else, a promise of clarity and purity and hope. A little clear water welled up and she dug faster.

A fountain of water erupted from its prison, dancing up into the air in a sparkling jet that caught the sun's rays and trapped them in rainbow droplets.

Dragon voices subsided in awe. Looking up, she saw Zee and the strange man standing beside Isobel, looking down. There were tears on the man's face. "So many years," he said in a broken voice. "What are you that you can do this thing?"

"Dreamshifter, dragon, and Sorcieri," she replied, letting her voice ring out so all of the dragons could hear. "I am the Three in One. I ask permission to take a cup of water to cleanse the Cave of Dreams, so that the remaining Dreamworlds might be saved."

Already the water in the basin had risen to cover her feet, pure and sparkling. Poe dove and surfaced. The white of his feathers seemed whiter, almost blinding. An eternal penguin, she thought, on a bubble of laughter, and then realized that she herself was standing in the pool, that

Lyssa and the dragon cub were there with her. She had no desire to live forever and no idea what effect the water would have on a human and a griffyn.

She needed to remind Lyssa to fill the waterskin, to open the door and go. For that, she needed words. Just as she made the shift into her fragile human skin, the earth shook beneath her feet. A deep rumbling noise vibrated through her. And a rush of molten gold topped the riverbed at the top of the cliff and began to fall. As if frozen in time, she stared up at what was coming. Even from a distance, the heat felt like a furnace blast against her naked skin. No human could survive immersion in that. There wasn't time to shift back to dragon.

"Lyssa!" she screamed. "Go, now!"

The oncoming wave hit her with the force of a battering ram, sweeping her off her feet, pounding her mercilessly. *Cold water. Not gold.* She called on the magic to form a shield around herself and then reached out for the others. No trace of Lyssa or the griffyn, no matter how hard she searched. Poe she found and shielded. And then, still unable to find Lyssa, she shifted, easily, back into dragon form.

The water was a wonder, invigorating and wild. It made her conscious of every scale. The sensation of life was almost more than she could contain, infusing every part of her with energy and vitality, healing the wounds from battle. Laughter and great joy bubbled up, and for a moment, she almost forgot—her many dead, the ravages of the Nothing, Lyssa at the mercy of the roiling waters.

Clearing her head, she resumed the search for the little girl. A door stood open at the center of the Pool, not her green door but one of Lyssa's making. Water poured through it and into the Cave of Dreams. Looking through the open doorway, she saw the flood, thick at first with sludge and debris, begin little by little to clear.

Lyssa was inside the Cave, perched at the top of the highest mound of dream matter, beside the dead guardian. She held the griffyn in her arms. The water lapped at her toes. Vivian half waded, half swam over and felt the child climb onto her back. Through the door and out into the pool she carried the child. Then, lifting her wings, she rode the air up and onto the plain. Dragons stepped back to make room.

Teheren, last of the Old Ones, stepped forward to meet her.

Vivian set Lyssa gently on the ground and shifted into human. So easy now. Once it had been a wracking change, often against her will. Now it was as easy as breathing. Lyssa flung herself at Zee, who caught her up in one arm but still held his sword ready.

Vivian did not kneel before Teheren. King he might be, ancient beyond belief, but she was the Three in One and would not grant him greater rank.

"You have taken what is not yours," he said, gesturing at the water still flowing into the Cave of Dreams.

"I have taken nothing. I freed what was locked away, awakened what was sleeping. Will you punish me for this?"

"This is not mine to say. The laws are older than I," he said formally. Turning to the dragons spread out before him, he spoke in the Ancient Tongue. "What shall we do with the interlopers, my people? Do we follow the laws? Offer them mercy? Or punishment?"

Through all the channels ran a litany of hunger and a long, simmering anger. But the Warrior's sword was bright and sharp, and the Three In One had restored the water. *What know we of laws? We are a free people.*

Vivian spoke in the same language, wondering as she did so how she had come to know it. "You have killed my companions, and yet I am willing to forgive. We have given you back your land. Will you not let us go now in peace?"

It was true. She felt the earth warming into life beneath her feet. In the distance, the golden river flowed, its banks already green with the return of grass. Overhead, the sky cleared to cerulean blue with a few fluffy white clouds. Something moved in the distance. Improbable, but her senses told her it was a deer.

Another thread rose through the dragon channels, this one of a silent wonder and a growing exultation. This was more like the land Aidan had promised them. They would bathe in molten gold, feast on fat deer. And the intruders had wrought this by some magic. One and all, they bent their knees in submission.

Teheren kept his feet and held her gaze. "You speak the Ancient Tongue."

"I guess?"

He was a beautiful man but lacked a sense of humor. His face remained serious, his eyes intent. "These are wild and untaught. They know nothing of order or of laws, but they have spoken and the law would agree. The pool is not out of bounds to any of the ancient blood. If you speak the tongue, you must run deep. And if the little one is under your protection, then she, too, is permitted." He frowned down at Poe, still playing in the water. "I know nothing of flightless waterfowl."

The basin was now full of diamond-bright water. Zee, looking at it, shielded his eyes, but to Vivian, it was life. If one bathed in the water every day, there would be no need for food or other sustenance.

"Will you stay?" Teheren pulled her attention back. He had shifted into regular speech, and his eyes and words were for her.

"What?"

"Stay here. Help me teach them. It will take a very

long time to civilize them." He was very bright, more than human. To stay in this place, with access to the water of life, to rest, to fly the skies as a dragon…

She looked up at Zee, scarred and weary, holding the child protectively, his eyes full of loss and love. Her heart turned over in her breast. There was nothing that she wanted in all the worlds more than to be in his arms, but she couldn't go to him, not yet.

"Unfortunately, I'm sort of busy. Not done saving the worlds and all." Just a small gesture with her right hand and the door into the Cave closed and vanished. "The Pool is yours, and the responsibility for the dragons of the Between."

Improbably, Teheren bowed his proud head in acknowledgement. "There is one thing more." He turned and beckoned, and the baby dragon dogging his heels came forward, wide golden eyes curious and solemn. "The choice is yours," he said, and the little creature swung her head around to look at him with a flicker of fear. There was something different about her. Something familiar.

She pressed close against Teheren, eyeing Vivian and Zee. The raven had been circling, but now it fluttered down to the ground in front of the baby dragon, staring in turn out of coal-black eyes. Poe came out of the pool, shook himself, and took up his watch-penguin pose beside the raven.

A rippling of scales, a changing of skin, and where there had been a dragon, a baby girl sat on the grass. Her eyes were gray. Scars marred her right cheek. A faint pattern of scales lingered on her collarbones and shoulders. She didn't cry or fuss, just sat quietly with eyes that held too much intelligence for a child so young.

Zee's breath caught in his throat; his face went pale.

"Aidan's child," Teheren said unnecessarily. His voice was sad but edged with the clear thought processes of a dragon. “Aidan expected a Warrior Son who would help her destroy all dragonkind. When the baby was born a girl, she tried to kill it. I intervened. I still know not whether I did right or wrong in this.”

A chill ran through Vivian, head to toe. What might such a child turn out to be?

But.

“The child is also Zee’s,” she said. “And her birth is not her doing.”

Teheren looked to Zee. “I would not ask you to commit the act, but I will give you the choice whether she should live or die.”

Vivian saw horror in Zee’s eyes but also love and wonder. He swallowed. “Vivian is right. The child did not choose her mother.” After a difficult moment, he added, “Or her father, for that matter. She deserves a chance.”

“So be it.” The dragon king inclined his head to Zee in a gesture of respect. “I advise that you leave her here with me. There is no knowing what she may become. It would be easier to manage her here.”

“What’s the baby’s name?” Lyssa asked, squirming out of Zee’s arms. “Why is she naked? Can I give her a bottle?”

“She is nameless and so shall remain,” Teheren answered. As if the decision was a foregone conclusion. “A name would only grant her greater power.”

Lyssa plumped down on the ground and pulled the baby onto her lap. Still unsmiling, the little one leaned back against warm flesh with a little sigh. Poe stalked over, inspected both children with his inscrutable gaze, and then took up a flank position. The raven hopped over to the other side.

“She’s family,” Vivian said, her eyes on Zee. “Family sticks together, no matter what.”

“You’re sure?” Zee asked.

She smiled backing answer, then walked over to pick up the baby. The child stiffened. The scars pulled up the right side of her lip into a macabre grin. But Vivian sensed no well of magic, no darkness, and after a minute, with a little sigh, the baby softened and leaned her forehead against Vivian's shoulder. One hand stole up and closed around a lock of hair.

"This is a mistake," Teheren said. "Maybe—"

"I have claimed her," Zee said, and Vivian recognized that undercurrent of danger. She braced herself for a battle.

Teheren must have heard it, too. He sighed. "I fear you will regret this choice. She is safer here, and the world is safer with her here."

"I doubt she was born to be locked away," Vivian said. "We need a blanket. And she looks hungry."

Zee nodded. "Let's go home."

First, Vivian made a door into Surmise for Isobel. The instant it opened, Landon charged through. His face was haggard, his eyes wild, a drawn sword in his hand.

"Landon," Isobel cried.

A sunrise dawned on his face as he caught her in his arms, burying his face in her hair. His shoulders shook, and his voice was broken when he said, "I thought I'd lost you."

"I'm sorry, but I had to go." She freed herself from his embrace, gently but firmly, and tilted her head to look up into his face. Vivian had never seen her mother's gaze so clear and direct. "I'm not a child. You take risks, I take risks. That's how it works."

Landon wiped his eyes. "I was trying to protect you."

She shook her head. "You can't always shelter me. I've realized I can't stay cooped up and safe until I die."

"You've changed," he said, tracing a bruise that marked her cheekbone.

"I grew up. About time, don't you think?"

Lips curving into a smile, Landon took her hand in his and kissed it. "It looks good on you. I'm sorry. I didn't mean—"

Isobel stopped him with a kiss.

Vivian dashed tears from her cheeks, her heart full to bursting with emotions she didn't fully understand. The baby started to cry, and Isobel broke off the kiss and turned to them. "I know you can't stay," she said, "but you'll be back."

There was a note in her voice that rang like prophecy. "Of course." Vivian caught her mother in a hug. "We'll be in and out all the time, I imagine."

Lyssa tugged on Isobel's hand. "Me, too?"

Isobel laughed and bent to scoop the little girl up into her arms. "Of course you, too. Give me a hug." Lyssa flung her arms around her neck and smacked her on the cheek. "And Bob?"

"Like you could go anywhere without him. And Gracie too, if you like."

Lyssa looked down at the griffyn cub. "Gracie should stay with you," she said in a small but determined voice. "Because I've got Bob and the baby and Poe to take care of."

"It's going to get awfully big," Isobel said, looking alarmed.

"All the more reason it should stay here," Vivian said. "I'm afraid we'd run into some trouble managing it in Krebston. As if a dragonshifter baby won't be trouble enough."

The griffyn meowed and rubbed against Isobel's leg, purring like a motorboat. Isobel glanced at Landon, who shrugged. "Your decision."

"All right, then; Gracie stays with me."

That settled, there was another round of hugs and

then Vivian opened a door into Wakeworld. She peered through with a shiver of fear, not knowing what they would find on the other side. But there was A TO ZEE BOOKS, looking as it had the last time they'd left it. There was the chair where she had left Weston. Tears blurred her eyes and Zee put a hand on her shoulder.

"He brought us Lyssa."

"So he did."

Lyssa spun around in a circle, taking in the books, the sculptures. "Am I going to live here?"

Zee and Vivian exchanged a look. He nodded.

"Some of the time," Vivian said. "And some of the time in Dreamworld. Or Between. If you want to."

"And the baby?"

"You. The baby and Poe and Bob. And me and Zee." Her eyes sought his, asking permission after the fact.

"Always and forever," he said. "Dreaming and waking. If you'll have me."

"Always and forever," she repeated.

Twenty-six

There was no need for bloodstone to buy passage from the Ferryman this time, or to travel his fearsome river at all. Calling on her magic, digging deep, Vivian made a door directly into the unworld where the dead Dreamshifters were trapped. As if they had known she was coming, they waited on the dusty plain.

Her grandfather stepped forward. "I had faith that you would remember us."

"It was not a question of memory, but a near thing all the same." She kissed his cheek, but her eyes were all for the bearded man in the old flannel shirt who stood off to the side, grinning.

"You sure you're not a sorceress?" Weston asked.

"Turns out you were right about that after all." She couldn't stop smiling. "You look good, considering."

"What were you expecting?"

"I wasn't sure. Considering the Nothing, and what it does—"

"You found Lyssa." He was smiling now, too. "She's all right?"

Vivian nodded. He didn't ever need to know about the missing hand. "Fine. Your raven has adopted her. She and my mother are currently busy creating new worlds out of raw dream matter."

Weston laughed, a foreign sound in that place. "That should be interesting. There may be a heavy elephant population in the new world order."

There was so much she wanted to tell him. About Grace and the baby and Aidan's death. But the crowd of Dreamshifters were gathering close, drawn by what she carried. Weston's smile faded.

"It's time, Vivian. Some of these have waited years for their release."

"I know, but—"

"This is no life, Vivian. Let us go."

Her grandfather moved to stand beside Weston, nodding his agreement. Vivian drew her sleeve across her eyes.

"Good-bye, you two."

"We'll be seeing you soon enough," her grandfather said. "Make it count."

Blinking back tears, she tried to smile for them. "Go in peace," she said, and emptied the precious fluid in the waterskin onto the dry dust at her feet. A great sigh rose up from the Dreamshifters. The light dimmed from half light into dark. A sound of running water began, growing deeper and closer. A spark of light appeared in the distance, burning ever brighter as it came closer, and she recognized the raft of the Ferryman. When he drew up close, he raised the lantern that he might see her face, his dark eyes gleaming beneath his hood.

"This is not a part of my journey. Why do you call me from my work?" But he did not sound angry.

"Will you carry these across, Charon? They have waited long."

"I will carry them for naught but the asking. You are certain you will not stay with me awhile?"

"Not now. There is much work to do."

"You have done well." He bowed to her and turned

to the silent congregation. "Come aboard. Let me take you home."

Silently, one by one, they stepped aboard the ferry. Last of all went her grandfather, and then Weston. Both smiled for her, though neither spoke a word. Charon poled them all away, leaving her alone in the dark, with the river running past her feet.

A long time she lingered, mesmerized by the flowing water. No work to do here. No suffering, only the murmuring water and the peaceful dark. But there were Dreamworlds to be rebuilt. Children to be raised and taught the secrets of the Between. And a man whose love shone bright even into the land of the dead. She was smiling as she made a door and stepped through it and into his waiting arms.

"Brett Flynne was here while you were out," he said before he kissed her.

"And what does Flynne want now?"

"Some strange creature down on Finger Beach. Attacked a tourist."

"Can it wait?"

"I don't think so." He kissed her again, his hands caressing her back, sliding up beneath her shirt. "Well, maybe just a little."

"Please, Zee," she whispered.

And he picked her up and carried her off to bed.

THE END

About the Author

Kerry Schafer writes fantasy with its teeth sunk into reality, mystery that delves into the paranormal, and women's fiction that embraces the dark and twisty realms of humanity. She is the author of *The Books of the Between*, the *Dream Wars* novellas, and a brand new paranormal mystery series with Diversion Books called *Dead Before Dying*. Kerry lives with her Viking in Colville, Washington.

Visit her online:

http://kerryschafer.com
http://facebook.com/kerryschaferbooks